Founder
of
Rome

A tale of the Ancient Republic

Ken Farmer

Other books by Ken Farmer
Outlander of Rome
Scrivener of Rome
Defender of Rome
Artisan of Rome
Wanderer of Rome

https://theromanrepublicblog.wordpress.com

Publishing eHistory
First 4/16/15
Second 11/6/15
Third 03/23/16
Fourth 08/24/17

Dead Tree Publishing History
First 2/20/18

Dedicated to my wife
for all the long work of editing.

Forward

This is a work of historical fiction set in the years before 244 A.U.C*, or 509 B.C.E, when the city of Rome supposedly converted from a monarchy to a republic. It is the misfortune of historians that the Gauls destroyed virtually all of the written records of Rome in their sacking of the city about 387 B.C.E. The major characters, places and actions have at least some possibility of having existed, however, the early history of Rome was written by historians long after the events and it is almost certain that much of what is 'known,' never existed and never happened. Even the accepted history of the conversion of the city of Rome from a monarchy to a republic is suspect. Little factual information remains to tell the actual tale. To the novelist, this is, in a way, a good thing since the broad story of history acts as an outline and can be filled with people and actions without worry of contradictions of actual events.

It also means that even an extensive research into the actual life and times of people who existed almost twenty five hundred years ago can come up with very little, and most of that is written by historians many centuries later. Lucius Tarquinius Superbus, Sextus Tarquinius, Lucius Junius Brutus and Lucretia Collatinus seemed to have lived as actual persons, but many, if not most of the tales about them are probably - well, historical fiction. So, the reader is warned that this novel is for entertainment, not history assignments.

On a minor note, the Brutus of this story, set in the later Monarchy, is not the man in the tales centering on the murder, in the Forum, of Julius Caesar. That Brutus, so popular in stories, movies and mini-series, lived almost half a thousand years later than the time of this story.

Some of the assumptions: Coinage for example. The use of stamped metal for exchange was invented in China, India and Ancient Greece (and probably elsewhere) around (very roughly) 700 B.C.E. There is little or no evidence about the use or production of flattened metal coinage in Rome in the time of the Monarchies, but it difficult to imagine a city of that size, and the associated communities, existing and prospering solely by barter. Just the act of purchasing the evening meal would take an inordinate amount of time, trying to trade this for that, with the long and inevitable give and take of primitive merchants and their customers. The assumption is made that, at the least, coins were brought in from the Greek mainland and used, even if Rome itself did not produce them. In addition, the

Etruscans must have used something of the like, since, at the time of this story, they were a very powerful and extended people, touching Rome on every side. Coinage from them would have been even more prevalent than from Ancient Greece, although there is no way of knowing - we have even less knowledge about the Etruscan people than about the early Romans.

Nonetheless, the broad outline of Rome, starting as a village on the banks of the Tiber, growing first into a cluster of villages, then a city with a king, forcibly converting into a republic, and finally descending into a state of empire is a story supported by history. This is a tale of that city that spans only a part of a man's lifetime, and, unlike most writings about that ancient city, is set long - many hundreds of years long - before that favorite trio of novelists, Julius Caesar, Mark Anthony and Cleopatra.

I use a lot of old Latin terms in the story, mainly for seasoning. Many are so similar to English that they need no translation, but in the event that the word is completely different, I give the meaning somewhere around the use of the word. I apologize if I stick in a word that remains unexplained. In addition, some words are used that are neither good English nor Latin, like gladsome, plainsome, repairment and wharfside, and again are inserted for flavor.

A note for those that might have received their knowledge of Rome from the various documentary channels. The title Tribune can be misconstrued easily, since the characters with that rank are plentiful in fiction and shallow infotainment programs. There were actually two separate positions that the term covered - they were Tribuni Militum and Tribuni Plebis. In English, the translation is Military Tribune and Tribune of the Common People, respectively. Unfortunately, most usage of the rank, today, gives only the first part of the title(s). To put it into modern context, a person might be introduced as Dr. Halfner, and without further information there would be no way to know if that individual was a professor of history or a doctor of medicine - two entirely different vocations. In this story, the rank is always that of a military officer, the other coming only decades after. (At least according to some very uncertain historical records.)

The military title for Tribune covers a high - very high - rank in the Roman army from the earliest days of the city. Today, the position would be roughly akin to a one-star general - in charge of a division of many men, but who would be under the command of a higher general who commands the entire army.

The Tribune of the Plebs, or common people, had nothing to do with the military. Rather, it was a high rank within the government of Rome and was not created until about 494 B.C.E, or several years after the Republic had been founded. A man of that rank could would be somewhat like the Governor of a state, in the USA, lower than the President, but still of a very high political position.

*A.U.C. Ab urbe conduit. A Latin phrase meaning "from the founding of the city of Rome." The year 1, representing the year that the city was founded corresponds to the current dating system of 753 B.C.E. Note, however, that this is a mythological date and Rome did not suddenly spring into existence in one year. Rather, it grew from a primitive village, or villages, and gradually became a city around the 7th and 8th centuries B.C.E. Note, also, that the term A.U.C. was not used by historians until almost the time of the Roman Republic changing into the Roman Empire. It certainly wasn't used by the people. The citizens of that ancient city actually used many different calendars over the years of its existence.

Book 1

The Waif

Flight

Marka could not see the sun from the bottom of a forest of dense needle trees, but he knew that afternoon would be turning into night in a short while. It was time he was getting back to the village. His hunt had been fairly successful - he had taken no large game, since the large ruminants were in the lowlands at this time of year, but his bag had three white hares, a marmot, and a badger. All in all, it was food for his family and good furs for trading for himself. By now, he had enough pelts from an early winter of hunting to trade for a real set of arrow points like the pair that he was hoarding in his quiver. With a sheaf of shafts pointed with the hard and black metal, a hunter could take game all year long. The metal points made an arrow much lighter than one with flint tips, which allowed it to be longer - and much more deadly. With a quiver of those, he could start taking bear and the large cats, the fur of which brought a premium in the trading posts of the lowlands.

As he walked around the mountain, he paid no attention to the usual paths that the village hunters used - he would walk them if they would carry his feet toward his destination, but otherwise, he would just strike off into the forest in a direct line for his goal. His ability to determine a proper direction was something that he took for granted - any young man growing up in the wilderness had the same skill in some measure, or his life would tend to be short. The son of the village chief was one of those without much sense of way - cold and wet, he would often stumble into his family's hut the next morning, after spending a most uncomfortable - and hungry - night in the forest.

It was almost dark by the time he crossed over the log bridge of the little stream, and suddenly he could smell the smoke from the village as the womenfolk made the evening meals. Only, it didn't smell like cook-fire smoke. It had the acrid smell of the refuse pit that lay away from the village. Suddenly, the worry that a hut had caught fire sprang to his mind. It had happened before - he had seen it almost every year since he was a small boy.

Hurrying now, he strode with long steps down the well-known path. He had seen about three handfuls of summers in his life and was now a handsome if still winsome young male. It would be at least three more summers before he would be filled out to his final frame, but, already fathers were visiting their hut to present daughters and their dowries for consideration. That he would be a catch for a girl was a given - already he was known as an expert hunter, even among the men of the village whom would seldom admit that there were any better than themselves. Often, in the last two years he was invited to a group hunt, but in the main he preferred to stalk alone. He didn't make verbal comment on his views, of course, but to his opinion, many of the men of the village were no better than clumsy sloths, stumbling around the brush and making enough noise to scare off even the auroch, which feared almost nothing.

His fair hair was kept short - long, it could not only get caught in a bowstring, but it hung on briars and twigs as he stalked. A pair of years ago, he failed to bring down the largest stag that he had ever seen because his locks became entangled in a dead branchlet that snapped and spooked the game. Now it was as short as he could cut it, or more often, sheared by his older sister, bribed with a piece of honeycomb from one of many hives in his knowledge.

His barely noticeable and immature beard he pulled out as it appeared for the same reason - at least, that is what he told himself. Most of the men of the village were almost bearlike in their appearance - some with dark hair covering most of their body and with thick beards to match. His skin, by contrast, was fair and almost hairless - at least so far. His hair, while not of the golden tint of the far northern peoples, was a light shade of brown. Many were the jests about where his mother might have spread her legs to receive such fair seed.

As he walked out of the wood into the clearing of the village, he stopped, frozen in horror - but only for a heartbeat before his natural reaction of a threatened animal caused him to bolt back into the trees. Still disbelieving, he skirted the treeline with stealth, stopping to view the burned huts whenever an opening gave a line of sight. In the gathering gloom, it was obviously not a fire that was caused by a careless cook. Most of the huts were just charred coals, but several were still collapsing in flames. He could see nobody at all in what had been a bustling village and by the time he had made a full circle of the village clearing, he was sure that there were none left in the village.

He was wrong about that. By now, it was full dark, with just a sliver of moon showing a glint on the very light powder of snow in a few places. Slowly, and as a fox sniffing for a possible trap, he walked toward the cluster of burned and burning huts. Suddenly, he stopped, frozen in place again. On the ground in front of him was a person and, with a few heartbeats of inspection, he knew that it was a body. But of who, he could not determine without rolling the unfortunate over to see the face. Looking down the line of huts in the light of the residual fires, he could see more shapes on the ground, and as he walked, he could tell that they were probably males. Now, closer to the light of the fires, he could see that many had received horrible wounds - the black puddles on the ground telling the tale of just how grievous the killing stroke had been. In fact, some were missing limbs and not a few had been separated from their heads.

With fear mounting in his heart - and his bow strung and a shaft at the ready - he approached the position of the village that had held his home, and that of his father, mother and two sisters. As he slowly walked up to it, he was dreading what he would see. It had completely burned down, with just hot coals showing and, he realized with relief, that there was nothing inside the ring of embers that in any way resembled a person.

The relief was short-lived. If they were not inside, then where were they? He continued his search of the village proper, recognizing here and there a figure that had not been mutilated to the point of being unidentifiable. Tabu, the priest, had an arm missing and a gash that almost severed his neck. Jons, their old widower neighbor, was just a pool of blood. Next to him was the man's father, old and blind...

Suddenly, he realized that all of the bodies were those of men. Where were the women and children? He knew, but as yet, his mind refused to admit the thought. Obviously, the village had been raided by brigands - probably from the northern mountains. Now, Marka was feeling the rising wrath that is the worst of all furies - knowing that an ultimate villainy has been done by evil persons against his own kind and that he was completely helpless to either rescue the situation or to avenge it. As he stood there sobbing, he knew that even if he were to discover the identity of the evil men who had done this thing, there was nothing that he, as a boy of about fifteen years, could do about it. He had no sword skills, nor even blade knowledge beyond carving with his little iron knife. Even had one of the nebulous gods, that the village shaman mumbled to over his holy fire, condescended to show him the way, he would need far more than the assistance of a deity to fight a band of murderous raiders.

He walked back to the edge of the wood so as to be out of any light, should the bandits return. There he sat down to ponder in the midst of his sorrow. He was still refusing to think about the fact that his mother and sisters were probably now roped together and being pulling across the hills toward some unknown destination. It was in his mind, and he could glimpse it, but he would not bring it to the forefront of his thoughts.

Summer had gone - the season between it and winter was well along. He would have to find a place to hole up - not only to hide but to keep from freezing to death at night. Food he had, for now, with the meat from the rabbits in his bag. All he would need was water, but the little carrying gourd at his belt would be entirely insufficient for that. Walking back to the line of huts, he picked up a smoldering stick, then waved it until it was properly alight. He began to look among the embers of his hut, and his neighbors, until he came upon an undamaged water jar, of the type that women carry to the little watercourse and back. It was dirty and covered with black soot, but he could clean that later. On the morrow, he would come back and examine the village in the light of the sun.

Carrying the smoldering firebrand, he headed up a path, climbing even higher into the hills. He had used this trail since he was old enough to enter the forest alone and needed no light to keep his feet on the path. Eventually, long after the sliver of moon had set, he came to a rocky cliff and stopped beside a dark shadow. Without a sound, he approached the entrance to the cave, his delicate sense of smell trying to detect anything out of the ordinary. Slowly, he pulled the dead brush away - a covering that hid the opening and had been placed there by himself. Finally, with a dab of grass, he waved the firebrand alight again and carefully entered the cave, eyes straining to see ahead.

He had used this cave in a rainstorm just a handful of days ago, and there had been no ursa in residence then, and almost certainly wouldn't be now, but a bear is not an animal that a person disturbed and lived to tell of the encounter.

The cave was empty, so he set his weapons down, and the jug, and lay back on the grass that he had put here for a bed during the summer. This was his personal hideout, his secret fortress that even his two closest friends knew not about. In it were a few items that were important to a boy - his old bronze knife, used before he traded for the black metal one, and a small pile of flint that he had collected when taken along on a gathering trip by the men of the village. There was no food - that would just have drawn vermin and animals to the cave, no matter how well concealed.

Now that he was safe, he allowed himself some more sorrow, but still tried not to think of where his mother and sisters might be. As he kindled a tiny fire from the smoldering firebrand, he thought of the others in the village, most of whom he had known all his short life.

Old Terpa - he had a myriad of stories for when he was a bowman in the army of... of... well, in the army of some despot of some city somewhere, until a spear through a knee ended his career. As Marka grew older, his tendency to believe everything in the stories of the old man lessened considerably, but there was no doubt that the oldster knew the bow and he had taught the village boys his skills.

A hare was crackling and hissing over the fire as he continued to think of his past. Youngsters in any remote village learned to make bows and arrows at an early age, but the ability to craft such does not make one an archer. Eventually, most would return to their slings. Those weapons were more fun, easier to carry, and were far easier to learn. Stones could be picked up anywhere, and once slung, could be forgotten. Arrows, on the other hand, were laborious to make, and every practice shoot had to be followed by a session of trying to find them all.

Marka, however, took the bow as his own. After fashioning the little sapling weapon of a small boy, under the instruction of old Terpa, he learned how to make the real weapon of an archer. In his family hut, above his pallet, were... had been several staves of wood, carefully selected and hung to season properly. With his father's borrowed knife, and later with the one that he had traded for - using the furs gathered with the previous bow - he would spend evenings around the fire carefully carving the piece of wood into his next hunting weapon.

Every day, Terpa would inspect it, giving advice and insight to the young bowyer. As he grew, and his strength waxed, another bow would be made to take advantage of the growing sinews in his arms and back. He learned that some woods made an excellent weapon - at first - but the strength would wane in a short time. Others would last, but had little spring when released. What was needed was a sprig of a sapling from a yew, or a nut tree, or a white bark - clear with no knots or imperfections. All the woods had their strengths and weaknesses, and the master bowyer had to know how to work with them.

Arrows were the other item, the production of which that filled many a cold and snowy or rainy evening. He carved each one as perfectly as could be made, fletched them with feathers of water fowl and animal glue and pointed them with the chipped barbs of flint. After he had shown a seriousness in the art, Terpa gave him two pieces of the hard black metal - small triangular thin wedges that turned a serious weapon into a deadly one. He dreamed of the day when all his arrows would be tipped with the sharp points.

Even at his young age, he was... had been considered by the men of the village as a deadly marksman, just waiting for his full strength to wax and a bow to match it. A year ago, he had accompanied several of the men to the lowlands on a trading mission, taking a full load of pure white pelts of the white snow hare, on his back. With those, he came back with a beautiful knife, of the black metal known as 'iron,' the blade as long as his hand and capable of taking an edge sharp enough to shave the few hairs from his body. The tang had been bare, but in a few nights of careful work, was soon covered with an attractive set of grips, carved from the horn of a stag.

Aye. He owed old Terpa a lot and repaid him with haunches of meat from his hunting. And there was Yeera, the hunter, who knew everything about tracking animals. Marka would spend hours listening to him speak on animal lore and watching as he pointed to this and that as they walked through the woods...

He finally fell asleep, more from exhaustion of the soul, than need for sleep. But his primitive internal timekeeper automatically woke him before sunup. He looked out at the stars to determine how long it would be until dawn, then took only his knife and bow - and the piece of rabbit that he had saved to break his fast - and rapidly retraced his steps of the night before.

He arrived at the burned village before daybreak and found a spot where he could view the clearing and the main path leading away from it. The fires were out, with just a little smoke rising here and there, but there was still no movement to be seen. Not that he expected any - he doubted that the bandits would return when there was little left to loot, but his inborn sense of wariness ruled. He would wait and see.

At half light, he moved out of his vantage point and scouted around the perimeter of the village. It did not take long for him to find the point of entry and exit of the raiders. He had no need to recall the teachings of old Yeera, the hunter, to follow the trampled path of the invaders. No surprise, it led toward the cold lands, following a course between the towns of the lowlands, toward the sunset, and the almost impassible mountains over which the sun rose. All morning he followed the trail, until he stopped, hearing voices ahead. Instantly, he disappeared into the brush that was fortunately far more dense than in his usual hunting fields of the upper mountains.

Bow in hand, and arrow on the string, he crept slowly forward until he could see a small party of men. He knew that this was no band of raiders, or even a hunting party - all of the men were jabbering to each other as they slowly moved along, gathering the firewood for their huts. Rather than continuing, he sat down against a tree and tried to think through his sorrow.

If he were to continue and even were he to find the evil men who had destroyed his family and village, what could an ungrown boy do? Even with his skills as a bowman, all he could accomplish was to feather a few bandits before they cut him down. Despite his deep sadness, he had no desire to depart the world as yet.

And another, more likely outcome was to fall into the clutches of men who would see him as a youngster to be seized as labor for their village. Finally, with the realization of the finality of his only choice, he rose and began to move back the way he had come. By evening he was back at the now barely smoldering village, standing in a copse looking over the area of ashes and...

Movement. But, it was just animals - wild dogs - that had come to feast on the broken bodies of the village men who had died in its defense.

In the half light, he moved out of his vantage point and scouted around the area for... he didn't expect to find anyone, and if he had asked himself what he was looking for, he couldn't have answered. But no one easily walks away from their entire life without looking back - even one that was as short as his. Other than the mutilated bodies of the older village men and a few younger ones apparently killed in the fighting - now even more ghastly to the eye than before - there was little that was left. The bandits would have taken anything of value and certainly anything made of metal. He found another intact water jug and an old hide scraper - it had a metal blade, but had been trodden into the ashes and apparently missed by the looters. There were pieces of unburned fabric - actual cloth bought from the traders in the lowlands and he collected all that he could find. On a bush at the edge of the clearing was a blanket spread over bushes for drying - apparently overlooked also. Shortly, he stood and just looked for a few moments, then turned and walked into the forest.

Lair

The first real snow was falling but by now he had the cave as comfortable as he could make it. In the back was a large stack of kindling and some dry grass, along with an iron spike and flint as a fire starter. The pieces and parts of fabric and the whole blanket gave him a warm bed on cold nights, although deep into the cave the temperature was greatly moderated. His lair was snug, no matter how hard the snow demons howled outside.

He wove a cover for the entrance out of sticks and vines. Not to keep out people - it wouldn't - but to prevent animals from scavenging his larder, consisting of hanging haunches of mostly rabbit. In the entrance, the cold was a natural refrigeration - at least for the winter. There, he could store many days worth of food, against the times of rain or heavy snow that would prevent him from hunting.

He had all winter to plan out his future. Almost grown, he wasn't as likely to be seized as a source of free labor as would be done for a fledgling boy, but still, there was always the chance of a villager deciding that he was young enough to enslave. In the past, he had visited a few of the nearer villages, on trading trips with the men, but knew no one in any of them enough to trust to ask for sanctuary.

So, he would stay by himself, hunting the winter, and when the green returned to the grasses, he would move down into the lowlands with a bundle of furs for trading. It would be the first time that he would have done that on his own, but now he had no choice.

On the crystal clear days between snows, he could see to the horizon and the smoke from the scattered villages on the lower reaches of the mountain range. He hunted, skinned the game, and tied the pelts high in the trees below the cave. Storing his furs in his lair would have given greater security for his stash, but green hides in an enclosed location gave off a stench that even his uncivilized nose could not abide.

Game was plentiful, and, since he would be able to take far more furs in the winter than one young man could carry off the mountain, he concentrated on taking the white rabbit that was greatly valued by the lowlanders. Only cat pelts and that of the ursa brought a higher value, and neither were to be found at this altitude - the big cats never left the woods, and the bear was in his sleep for the winter. He also searched for the best staves that could be found, to be carved into future bows, and had a bundle stacked next to his bedding. They would take at least a year to season properly and their carving would be a task for the long nights of the next winter.

He moved around warily during the day, not only because of the game that he hunted but because he did not want to be seen by any hunters that might be passing through. Only twice the entire winter, and that far down into the forest, did he see parties of men on the hunt. He just froze in place both times and let them pass. The long nights needed to be filled with something besides sleeping, and since bow making was out of the question, he made the only other thing that he had any use for - arrows. However, since the time was great, and especially during the many days-long storms, it must be said that the number of shafts that piled up in a corner of the cave might have equipped a small army.

His recently cut staves were far too green to be made into bows - his stash of seasoned wood was ash at the place of his family's hut - but he continued to fill the long nights with thoughts on his craft. The wood from the white bark nut tree was sturdy and held whatever form it was given as it dried. A bow made of it would send an arrow across the mountain tops, except that a man would have to have the strength of the male ursa to draw it. The weaver tree was what supplied the wood for most of the bows that had been made by the men in his village. It was straight grained and gave a good release to the shaft, and could be drawn into almost a half circle without breaking. Its drawback was that it too easily took a set over time, even if the bowman was careful to string it in reverse when not in use.

He had attempted to join thin staves of both woods to make a bow that might have the characteristics of them together, but the strength of his hide glue was wholly insufficient to the task. His buildings fell apart as they were being drawn the first time.

Of course, if he could find a tree with the goodness of both the weaver tree and the nut tree, he could make a bow superior to any he had seen. But, he also knew that if such a tree existed, then it would have been discovered long before his appearance in the world.

He had little else to do besides the arrow making and the daily maintenance required for living. In an extended open area under the tall trees, he set a butt, made of packed moss and needles from the trees, held together with strips of inferior hides. On reasonably climate days, he would practice his marksmanship until his fingertips called a halt for the day. With the luxury of a huge surplus of shafts, far more than his needs, he had no reason to spend his time scouring the ground for a lost arrow.

While laying beside his little fire at night, his thoughts would roam to little Pita. The daughter of one of the hunters in the village was a season or so younger than Marka. When he was an unfledged youngster, she was both an object of derision and a thorn in his side. Like all immature boys, he had had no real idea of just why the gods created little women. That his mother used to be such a creature never crossed his mind until he had seen enough summers for his pouchstones to begin to drop, and even then, it was slightly incredible. Girls certainly could not hunt and besides, their incessant need to talk would never have allowed them to get within even sight range of an animal, let alone close enough to strike. Little Pita could not even draw the boy's bow that Marka had first constructed. He knew - one day he had let her attempt to nock an arrow and shoot. She had struggled to pull the string, failing to draw even halfway, but still managed enough bend in the wood for the twanging bowstring to bite her wrist. It was with a boy's satisfying feeling of contempt and superiority that he watched her running for home, in tears and wailing her hurt.

Fortunately, as he grew old enough actually to hunt away from the village, that problem resolved itself. The girl would never walk out of sight of the village trying to follow him - not into a forest full of frightening unknowns. Still, as time went by and his man-parts began to develop, he began to have indeterminate feelings about the young woman - and others. He knew fully well how the cycle of life was started - no child in a village of one-roomed huts could fail to notice the nightly mating of the parents, but it had not yet occurred to him that the action between the sexes would apply to himself and a female.

That changed one day on his return from a hunt when he had reached the little stream on the outskirts of their village. The warm season was not the time for hunting for trade - animal fur was thin and wretched after the spring shedding. Other than the pleasure of the hunt, the only reason for the foray was for meat, and as usual, he was returning with as much as he could carry. At the place of the kill, there had been no water, and as a result, he was even more covered with blood and offal than usual and was looking forward to the cleansing water of the stream - and the coolness after the humid forest.

Unusually, for this time of midday, the deep rock pool was occupied - someone was bathing and in a few heartbeats he could see that it was Pita. She was sitting in the water, near the far bank and singing softly to herself, as women do when not occupied with a chore that requires concentration. She only noticed him as he stopped on the large rock that was used by the boys to launch themselves far into the pool. She was ungarbed, of course - the idea of wearing garments while bathing would be developed by other peoples an inconceivable number of seasons in the future. He was wearing only a simple wrap around his midriff - not for modesty, which was a concept totally unknown to the people of his village, but to keep his delicate man-parts from being attacked by the brush and foliage during the hunt. He lay the carcass on the rock, then pulled the tucked end of his wrap loose and let it fall from around his body. Holding it, he jumped from the rock.

He was comfortable in the water and could paddle through the deeps without fear of sinking. As he touched the bottom of the deep pool, he began to scrub himself of the animal remains with his loincloth - the action cleaning both his body and the cloth. Finally, as his breath ran out, he surfaced and began to swim backward slowly, kicking with his feet and still enjoying the coolness.

"The mighty hunter returns. Your hunt was with success."

It wasn't a question, and he looked over at the girl before replying. He stopped and began to tread water until he realized that his feet could touch bottom. "Aye. It is not difficult to hunt in the hot season with the leaves offering concealment from all directions."

She was smiling. With her torso above water, her developing paps were visible and... For the first time, he noticed that the bothersome child that he had always called "little Pita" - usually with derision - wasn't a flat chested girl-boy any longer. It had been several years since the lessons from the older boys had taught him how to gain pleasure by stroking his member, but only in the last season or so had the connection between his urges and females began to resolve itself. It wasn't that the concept was kept a mystery from the village children - far from it - but that Marka was so engrossed with his impending adulthood and his freedom to roam the forests on the hunt, that little time was left in the day to associate with females.

Now, the girl stood and waded over to a projecting rock to sit down, leaving just her legs dangling in the water. Not only were her little mammaries in full view, but now also the mysterious cleft that the village boys made jest over. All, of course, claimed intimate familiarity with the female organ, but few - if any - actually had experience with such. Daughters were of little more importance to the men of the village than anywhere else in the world. Most would be traded for young women in other settlements to bring in new blood and never seen again - but still, fathers tended to look in askance at any dalliance with their young females that was not countenanced by both families.

He waded towards her, his body rising from the water as the rocky bottom shelved toward the shore. Suddenly, she put her hand over her mouth to try to stifle a laugh. Then, she said, looking down, "So, you no longer think of me as a child."

He stopped, confused, then realized that his now visible svans was erect in full glory and pointing toward the goal that it wanted. Embarrassment was an emotion that had little use in their primitive lives, but with some confusion at his feelings, he fumbled with his wet loincloth and managed to wrap it around his midsection. "The water is cold," he muttered. "And I am weary from the hunt."

Still smiling, she said, "That is interesting. I was told that cold water was the cure for such a condition. And that weariness inhibited such displays." Now he knew for sure that she was no longer a child, subject to his teasings and contempt. In fact, she had the mastery of this conversation, and he was the butt of the jape. Had it been the season before, he would have cursed her and stomped off to the village with his game, but now, the attraction of a naked female was sufficient to override any male pride. She patted the rock. "I am jesting with you. Sit here beside me and warm yourself."

As he sat down, she continued. "I was not jesting with you about your success. My father says that you have the gift of the hunting goddess." She looked down at the bulge that still showed under his waist cloth. "Know you that my father is to offer me as your mate?" At Marka's wide-eyed look of surprise, she continued, "He will tender the dower-offer before the full moon."

Marka was now speechless. Nothing had been said to him, but of course, that was the norm. Matings were made between families and without any consultation with the two young people involved.

She laughed quietly again. "Calm yourself. The stalking of a woman is no more dangerous than the taking of a stag in the forest." She put her hand on his chest and ran her fingers up and down between his useless male nipples. That touch did little to subside the bulge under his waist cloth. "I would have you lay me on that moss and spread my knees apart to let you test the hunting fields that will be yours, but my father would be most wrothful should your seed find a fertile field before we are joined by the shaman." She raised herself slightly with open palms on the flat rock, moving close enough that their upper legs touched. "But, should you want, just after the time of my woman's moon, you may try the path in safety."

Marka had not the slightest idea of what she was saying, other than the veiled offer to let him join with her after some nebulous happening. The intimate functions of the female were a subject that would never touch his thoughts, even if he had the knowledge to wonder about them. He knew full well what to do with his svans and a willing woman - the act had been described and bragged about by his boyhood friends at every gathering - and seen almost nightly when his parents lay down for their rest. The actual act, however...

The union before the shaman had never taken place. Only a moonday before the ceremony, the raiders came.

Now, even without the offer of the use of her femaleness, he would have welcomed her into his lair for a person with which to converse. Any person would be accepted, in fact - even his village nemesis, Turba, who never passed an opportunity to import the fact that his father was the head of the village.

He had no education - in fact, the idea of writing and reading little marks on reed-paper had never even presented itself to him. The only writing he had ever seen were the marks over the merchant stalls in what had passed for a trading city, during his only visit. He never connected them with the idea that information could be presented other than by mouth. Even the old priest in his village made his obeisances by rote, passed down from his father, and his father's father.

Like any primitive, Marka believed in gods, demons, and spirits, but gave them little thought. Early on, he discovered that his prayers to various deities brought no result, and decided that, either he did not know the proper forms, or that they had little interest in a small boy. Since then, he had returned the lack of interest and ignored them. Of course, he hid his disdain from the village leaders, and definitely from the shaman, who would have boxed his ears for the blasphemy.

Pythes

Finally, the snow began to melt, and the warmth of the days commenced its return.   He began to make ready for his foray into a city, far down in the lowlands.   By now, his green hides had mellowed, and he selected only the best - those of thick fir and pure whiteness - and rolled them into a ball, securing them with strips of the fabric torn from his bedding.   Even with only his bow, a quiver of his best arrows, knife, water gourd, and a small pouch of jerked meat, the roll of hides was almost more than he could carry.   But, he decided, a too-heavy load could always be made lighter, whereas anything left behind would probably be gone forever.

A bright and sunny morning arrived, showing the new grass beginning to appear on the wet ground.   He put on his single garment that he wore in the summer - a short pullover of soft cloth with holes for arms and neck and which fell halfway to his knees.   Had he not been wearing the garment under his furs on that evil day at the end of the last summer, it would have been looted with all else in his village. His winter furs would be far too hot to wear from now on, especially down in the lowlands, and he rolled them into a tight ball, wedging them between two rocks at the back of the cave.   Then, securing his fortress with the cover made of woven sticks and pulling thick brush over that, he started off down the mountain.   He had no idea if he would ever return but, at least, he knew that there was one place in the world that he could call his own.

Never using a path, he moved down the mountain, stopping only to rest and shoot small game to eke out his meager supply of provisions.   In the evening, well away from any trails, he would roast the meat that he would eat, then partially dry the rest over the small fire for the morrow.   Then he would kick the fire out, bury it under the dirt and move away to find a place to sleep for the night.   For his caution, he saw no one for the first several days.

The terrain began to change, from the thickly wooded forests of needle trees in the mountains to the woods of broad-leaved trees of the lowlands.   He had never been this way, and in actuality, had little idea where he was.   He only knew that the vast sea was somewhere toward the setting sun and along the coasts were great cities.   Of course, all that he thought he knew might have just been tales of the older men around the village fires.   However, he had seen at least one city and had visited it once with the men.

Finally, one evening he came to one of the very wide trails that lowland folk called a 'road.'   This, he was fairly certain, would take him to some village, or city, eventually, but he still was wary of just walking along the road, a young boy with valuable furs on his back. A bow was not a good weapon for defending one's self. It could not be carried strung, since the constant bending would mar the strength of the pull in a short time, and, unstrung, it was less dangerous than a big stick. His knife, while of fair quality, was small and no match for a sword, even if he were skilled in blade play. It was best to stick with the road, close enough to follow its winding path, but out of sight of anyone using it.

That evening he stopped, decided to make do with the few pieces of jerky in his pouch and not build a fire. The wind, it was true, was blowing toward him from the road, but the brush was sparse and would probably allow his little fire to be seen as a sparkle through the foliage. As the night was warm, he ate the dry meat and settled back for his rest.

It was almost entirely dark when he heard voices toward the road and noises that suggested the making of camp. Shortly, he was sure of it as a fire suddenly sprang into view through the brush. And what a fire. From his vantage point, it would seem that the party on the road must be massive to require such an inferno for their cooking. He would learn, eventually, that all lowlanders built big fires and sat well back, whereas villagers in the mountains made theirs only as big as needed and sat next to them.

No matter, the road was many strides away, and there was no reason for anyone to enter the brush that hid his night encampment. He decided against moving on, knowing that the lands would get more crowded as he got closer to the coast and he might as well start getting used to that, now. He lay back down to rest until sleep would come.

He was still listening to the clamor of the road party when he suddenly smelled... he didn't know, but it was wonderful. For all of the winter and up to now in the time before summer, he had eaten well, but it was always roast hare, or rodent, or fowl. Roast to break his fast, for the noon meal and in the evening. Roast upon roast. He had only been in his cave-fortress a few days when he began to lust for his mother's soup, or stew, or porridge, bubbling in the iron pot over the fire. In fact, in the craving of his hunger, he made another visit to the village to scour it again for any cooking pot he could find. Without success - the bandits had taken anything of value, including all of the metal pots of the village women. Even the clay vessels that might have worked over a fire were broken. The water jugs that he had found before were all that remained of any use, and he knew that they were too thin to be used over a fire.

Unable to resist, he got up and began to move slowly toward the road, making sure to keep any dense foliage between him and the fire. He hadn't gone far when a nagging in his mind made him return to gather up his weapons. If he had to run, he might abandon the furs, but not his bow and knife - that would be the end, he was sure.

Finding a leafy shrub next to the road he crawled up and moved until he got a view of the fire by looking under the brush. It was a large blaze, but there were only four men that could be seen around it. He could see a handful of beasts tethered in the treeline and many bundles stacked up beside them, but for now, his eyes went back to the kettle hanging over the flames. That was obviously where the delicious aroma was coming from, but even in his craving, he gave no thought to announcing his presence and begging for a share of the pot.

Still, he wasn't sleepy and viewing the party of men by the road gave him something to pass the time. Their speaking was strange - he could understand many of the words, but the meaning did not register. Had he any knowledge of the peninsula of Latium, he would have known that the common language was from the Etruscan peoples. Even his village had spoken a dialect of it, taken along by the people as they had moved into the mountains in the unknown past, and brought in even now, by young girls, swapped between villages to bring in new blood in the form of wives.

One of the parties was apparently a... a... He did not understand the sight that he was watching. It was as if the man were a boy under the wrath of displeasure of his elders. He deferred to the others, did most of the work and sat alone to eat. The other three jested and talked to one another as equals, although it was obvious that the older man was the leader. As the night passed, the food was eaten and they threw more wood on the fire. That was strange. The only reason for a big blaze at night would be to keep the wolves...

"Snap." He froze as his ears strained to hear. To one side he could hear brush being moved slowly and the faint crackle of leaves as a foot or hoof was pressed down on them. Moving his head, so slowly as to take many heartbeats to see to his side, he stared through the brush for whatever animal was creeping up to the road. In the dark and brush he could not make it out but, whatever it was, it was large.

He very slowly rolled on his side to allow his bow to slip off his shoulder. Then, reaching into his pouch for his bowstring, and cursing to himself when it came out knotted, he began to unravel it, slipping one loop over a nock on the end of the wood. Stringing a bow while lying down was not easy and managing the effort quietly, even less so. Still, by bracing the nocked end between both feet, he succeeded in bending the wood enough to loop the other end. Quickly, he drew out an arrow, nocked it on the string and rose to his knees. At least now, he wasn't completely helpless against the... Looking again, he still didn't know.

Suddenly, he got the answer. Very quietly, but also very plainly, he heard a male voice speak in just more than a whisper. A man! And more than one. He debated what to do - stay or run? If he could find an open place, he would be a match for two or three foes. But in this brush... As old Terpa had said more than once, "An archer on a hill is a king. In close combat, he is a dead man." Immediately, he decided that he would wait and stay hidden. The night was dark, and a man would almost have to step on him to be discovered. If he were seen, he would run. It was unlikely that anyone could follow far - and would probably hesitate if the first follower received an arrow out of the dark.

The question remained of who they were and what they were after. Anyone sneaking up after dark had to have no good purpose in mind, and then he reminded himself that he had done the same thing and without any malice to the watched party. Looking over the brush, he could see the four, still sitting around the fire, apparently without fatigue from their day's journey, since they seemed to be in no hurry to sleep.

Then, from the direction of his little camp, came more footsteps. This man, like the others, came to the edge of the brush, but in his case, close enough for Marka to see, outlined against the starry sky no more than two body lengths away. There were more murmurs, then quiet. For a considerable time, the night was silent, except for the low murmurs of the men around the fire. Then, he heard quite plainly, "Now is the time. They be fire blind. Kill not the slave." A pause, then a grunt and he heard the brush being pushed aside, without worry of quiet.

In amazement, he saw three men striding quickly across the road toward the fire. All were holding blades of some kind. Suddenly he knew - these were bandits, stalking the night ways to find the prey that they would kill and loot. The memories of his slaughtered village were still green, even half a season later, and any thought of that evil day would cause his gorge to rise in fury. Many were the times he wished that he had the ear of some god, somewhere, to supplicate for even a hint of where the cursed fiends had come from - and gone.

Suddenly, one of the men around the fire spotted their onrushing doom and shouted, causing all three to leap to their feet. But for that shout, all would have been dead within heartbeats. Surprised, they managed to fend off the first blows, although the man who had shouted received a stroke on his body. The older man only had a long staff, but he managed to stop the descending blade before it split his body in twain.

In the madness of the thought, that these might have been among those that raped his village, and if even not, were brothers in kind to those murderers, Marka stood up, pulled the already nocked arrow to full stretch and released. At that range - barely more than the leap of an escaping stag - the flint tip of the arrow passed halfway through the body of the man who had gotten first blood. In his fury, Marka made no mark that this was the first man he had ever killed.

The other two bandits, in their concentration of the fight, made no notice until their comrade fell to the ground, the feathers of the shaft clearly visible in the bright firelight. The man who had swung on the old leader turned around to see this new threat that had suddenly surprised them in the night. Marka had no idea if he could be seen, in the dark and across the road, but it made no difference as he planted the next arrow in the man's chest. This bandit did not die peacefully, but with a scream and a long cry of agony that made his remaining comrade look in fear, then bolt off into the forest on the far side of the road. For a heartbeat, Marka had him sighted over the shaft of another arrow but held the shot as being too uncertain and too approximate to the other men. It made no difference - for a considerable time, the thrashing of the man in the forest could be heard as he blundered through the trees in his escape.

Marka just stood there for a moment, with an almost orgasmic feeling that he had received a small portion of the revenge that he had craved all winter. Around the fire, two of the men were ministering to their comrade, laying on the ground and unmoving. In a few heartbeats, they stood, shaking their heads at each other, then turned to face the direction from which their salvation had come.

"Come, friend," called the older man. "Enter the light and allow us to convey our gratitude." Several of the words were meaningless to Marka, but he recognized the call as an offer of friendship. With an arrow still nocked, he stepped out of the brush and walked toward the fire.

He had made it about halfway when the other man suddenly said, "By the gods, Pythes! It is a stripling!"

"Hold your tongue, Valens," barked the old man. "Speak not down to the man who has saved you from Hades this night." He held up his hand and said, "Welcome, young lad. We must give our gratitude for a most timely deliverance." He waited, then continued. "Might we know the name of our sudden friend out of the night?"

The boy stopped a few paces from the fire, and replied, "Marka. From a village in the mountains."

"Welcome, Marcus, from the mountains. I am Pythes, of the city of Rome, and this is my man Valens." He looked down at the prone figure and continued, "And that be Arga, my drover. He has joined his ancestors." He looked at the other two bodies on the ground. "But for his shout and your shafts, we would be with him." The conversation did not go quite as smoothly as that, as both had trouble with each other's accents. They had mostly the same words, but the sounds of many were different. Nonetheless, no friendship based on combat was ever much impeded by lack of words.

Marka unstrung his bow as the two men carried their comrade off the road and over to the tethered asses. The man, Valens, searched for a moment in the bundles, then pulled out a blanket with which he covered the body. At the fire, Pythes waved, then waited until the young man had sat down, cross-legged. The night was fairly warm, so the need for the fire, once the meal was cooked, was only for light and pleasure. However, Marka realized that had it not been for the high flames, he probably would have been unable to hit the two bandits in the dark.

He looked across at his host. Pythes was an older man, not frail, but he had to have seen at least thrice the number of summers as had himself. He was dressed in a fabric garment that was sleeveless, belted and reached to his knees. He would come to know of this as a tunic, worn by all of the lowland people during the warmer part of the year. It wasn't much different than the one that the young man wore, with the exception of being far less ragged. But, where Marka went with bare feet in mild seasons, the man had some type of foot covering that had straps crisscrossed halfway up his calves. His hair was gray, as was his short beard. Except for the fact that his clothing was of a far higher quality, he could have passed for any of the older men of the village.

His man, Valens was younger and much taller and just wore a cloth wrapped around his waist, although he must have had a belt to hold the scabbard and sword that was laying beside the fire, during his traveling.

"How happened you to be standing over there, ready for combat, young man?"

Marka was beginning to relax, or at least to dull the knife edge of the fear of unknown persons. It had been far too long since he had talked to anyone and he found that he missed that.

"I was encamped - over there," he pointed. "I smelled your cook pot, and crawled close to see."

"Ah." Pythes smiled and asked, "Have you eaten this eve time?"

"Only a palm of jerked meat."

Pythes turned and shouted, "Cleo! Is there any stew left in the pot?"

The man jumped up and replied, "Nay, Master. It was finished."

"Make a goodly bowl for our young friend." The slave began to scurry around as Pythes turned back to Marka. "You travel far from the mountains, young man."

"Aye," replied the boy. "I have pelts to trade... somewhere."

The talk went on, and the old man gradually drew the story out of the boy. He had even greater success when the youngster was handed a steaming bowl of some delicious ragout. It was the best food that the boy had tasted since his mother... all winter. The older man convinced Marka to join their encampment for the night - the young boy intrigued him and wished to know more of his past.

The boy brought his few items from his little camp - the ball of furs and the bundle of staves - and made his bed under a canopy tree, many strides from the fire circle.

Morning time brought all awake at first light. First was the ritual of laying their comrade to rest. The ground was hard and stony, and there were no earth tools in the baggage of the traders, so the unfortunate man was laid out behind the first line of trees, and his body covered with stones. Back at his village, the priest would have jabbered and shaken his bones over the grave, to plead with the spirits of his ancestors to accept the unfortunate into their fold. In the case of the drover, Pythes merely sprinkled a few drops of wine over the stones and made a short proclamation to some god in the sky.

Back in the camp, the wild dogs were already sniffing at the outskirts of the little clearing, waiting for their chance at the two other bodies on the ground. Valens pointed to the closest. "By right of law, theirs is yours." Confused, Marka looked back and forth between the older man and the bodies. "Their equipment. Anyone who kills a bandit is given anything they possess."

Suddenly understanding, he walked over to the closest man and looked him up and down. With Valens helping, they stripped both bodies of everything. Marka had no use for their garments and indicated that his helper could have them. But the sword of one - actually, a long knife - made his eyes sparkle. He had no training on blades, but a weapon like this would have made him wealthy in his village. All that he took was the blades - two short swords and a pair of daggers - from both bandits, knowing that he could trade them even more easily than furs.

Pythes walked up to them. "Marcus, lad. I would that you join my caravan. I well know this trade route, and we can repay part of our debt to you and assist in your trading. Your furs can ride on one of the pack-asses and leave your back and legs unwearied."

Then, Valens walked up and handed him a pouch. "This was around the big fellow's neck. Look, inside, lad. The gods may have favored you this day."

Pulling the drawstrings open, he poured the contents into a hand - pieces of metal of irregular shape, but flattened and stamped with various images. Most were kuprum, it appeared, but there were three disks of a silvery color. Puzzled, he held one up and watched it glint in the early morning light. "Argentum," said Pythes. Realizing that a boy from the mountains probably had knowledge of items made of copper, but almost certainly never seen actual silver, he explained, "That is a Greek drachma. Valuable. Just one of those of that weight is worth your entire roll of furs."

Marka had traded all his life. Only once in an actual city, but many times between boys in his village. That was the way that a person garnered new things and ridded himself of unwanted or too numerous items. Value for value, and that depending only on the desire of the receiver. But, the idea of trading goods for pieces of metal was entirely foreign to him. Metal was valuable when it was in a knife, or a scraper, or even a pretty bauble around the neck of a woman, but he couldn't quite make the connection between the raw material and the finished goods. Yet.

But he would learn. Realizing that he had not replied to his host, he said, "I will go with you. I would learn more about the lowlands."

With that, they rousted the asses, slung the burdens across their backs and set off down the road.

The Trader's Route

Marka thought that the road leading from the camp was a major route leading to the cities of the lowlands. That was based on all the trails and pathways that he had used and seen in his life. The few people they passed seemed to be migrating crowds, but by midday, they came to another roadway that made the last seem to be a mere trail. Suddenly, they almost were never out of view of other travelers that now seemed to be swarming mobs. Pythes assured him that the road was almost empty compared to what he would see in an actual city.

Marka was fascinated by the sights on the road. In the mountains, all that was to be seen, he had seen. The village seldom changed, nor did the people in it other than all growing older over time. Occasionally a young unmated woman would leave to be replaced by another from afar, traded as wives to bring new blood to the villages. And the mountains never changed - all that he would see in his hunting forays was what he had seen all his young life.

But here, on a road of the lowlands, every hill, every turn might bring a new sight, something to astonish or delight. As to now, they had only passed through a few small villages and the city of their next trading stop was just ahead - Valbora, it was named. At the trading stalls in the several villages that they had passed through, the older man had told him to keep his furs bundled, that he would get a much better trade in a larger city. He took the advice. Much had been learned from his new friend, and his man, as they talked and walked down the road.

By the standards of the roads leading up and down the coastal cities, this one was sparsely traveled, but to Marka, it was crowded with humanity. Just the first day, he had seen enough people to fill his village many times - from ragged individuals like himself, traders with lines of burden beasts... 'asses' ...and strange looking... 'oxen,' and on occasion, a platform on which some richly robed individual sat, carried by as many as two handfuls of men, in front and back.

"Etruscan nobles," said Pythes, then had to explain both words. The boy just stood and watched a carrying chair disappear into the distance. In the last few days, he had seen many such sights - displays that he had no experience to understand. He had no idea why a man would have himself carried down the road when his legs would move him much faster, nor why, in such warm weather, the same man would wrap himself in garments that looked as thick as the furs that his people had worn in the cold season.

In the first larger town that they passed through, Pythes told Valens and Cleo to stop at the outskirts and feed the asses. Then he and Marka entered the gate and, after asking a citizen, were steered to a brick building in the city center. Inside, Pythes spoke to a scribe - although the designation had no meaning to the boy. "We would speak to the magistrate." In a few moments, a robed individual appeared, wearing a brassard proclaimed his status as the city official.

"May I be of service, Sos?"

"Aye. We would report on an attack by bandits last eve. Three in total, two were killed and a man of my party." He added, "On the road to Parmia, almost to the Little Rock Wash." The report went on, with the magistrate asking questions and dictating to his scribe. As they left, Pythes said to the boy, "Other than an occasional drunken soldier, brigands are not common on the road. If they are caught, they are hung head downward on the city walls - not a death that you would want to experience. But, as traders, it is in our measure to report all incidences so the authorities can determine if a band has moved into the trading routes." He pointed. "Here we be."

Marka looked at the little stall, in front of which they had stopped. It had a table and benches and a fat merchant waiting at the doorway. As they sat, he came over with a smile and said, "What might be the pleasure of you good men?"

"Two bowls, merchant. Small ones. We still have far to go today." As the man disappeared through the curtain, he continued his instruction. "Now, if we were heading northwards, toward the Eturian highlands and beyond, we would join an armed caravan. In those lands, between cities, the bandits are fierce and numerous. In numbers there is safety, and the different merchants in the train contribute to hiring an escort of soldiers. Ahh, here is the good man."

The merchant set two bowls on the table, then filled them with the purple liquid. Marka had tasted spiritous drink before, in the fermented juices of berries and small fruits that the villagers made for feast days, but the taste of wine was new to him. Pythes watched him for a few swallows, then satisfied that his younger cohort was not repelled by the drink, put his bowl down. "Marcus. You have said that you have no village to which you might return and a lad with your fiber has no need to bury himself in the mountains." There was no reply, so he continued. "I would not be dissatisfied if you were to accompany me on my travels, and then back to Rome where I have a household and shop. I can use a young man with spirit. You would learn a trade and have a place to call home."

The boy wondered again at the bending of his name by the older man. Apparently, the ear of the older man heard the name of Marka as it would be pronounced in his city. Not that he cared - names had little meaning for him other than a label for a person. But the offer was something to be considered. He was still very young and knew that he had much to learn in what was a hostile world. When he had gathered a few more summers and could stand in the presence of others as a full man, he could decide on his destiny. But for now, the offer was attractive, especially for a boy who could be taken for forced labor as being unattached and underaged by anyone he came across. Finally, he answered, "You are kind. I will avail myself of your generosity until I can make my own way."

Pythes gathered up his bowl, finished it, then said, "Excellent, my lad. Finish your wine. We have far to go before darkfall."

For several days, they walked the road, stopping in villages and transacting a little on occasion. Both Pythes and his man, Valens, passed the time by tutoring their apprentice in the ways of the lowlands. He learned new words, the way to speak to a friend, a superior, an official, and such. Also taught was the concept of weighted metal pieces as a convenient way to carry value from place to place. And, tales of their pasts. Pythes had once been a sailor, a soldier, and several other trades. He was too old, now, for combat, but Valens had come from a battle several summers before. "Our city of Rome has no army. When danger arises, the men gather in formations under the command of the King, then return to their farms and shops when the strife is ended."

They came to the large city of Nepa, where, with Pythe's assistance, Marka sold his furs - and the lesser blades from the bandits - at a price far above what he would have received had he attempted the transaction himself. With more copper pieces in his purse, he asked about the purchase of arrow points. Pythes escorted him to the section of the city where the smiths did business. There, he purchased the triangular shapes, made of the hard and dark metal - iron, he remembered. Again, he was assisted in the purchase by his mentor and received an entire bag of the points, and at a price far less than he would have paid by himself. Smiling at the boy's gladness in his purchase, Pythes then took him to a weaver-merchant, and for a snippet of copper, purchased him two tunics, of coarsely woven cloth, but neat and clean.

Then it was to the leather-merchant for a pair of sandaliae. The soles of Marka's feet were as hard as iron and he had never worn footwear other than boots for snow, but he allowed Valens to tutor him on the method of lacing the straps around his ankles and calves. It took a day or so before he stopped noticing his strange appendage additions, but eventually they disappeared from his consciousness.

He had no idea where he was or where he had been. In truth, if he had decided to return to the mountains, he would have had little idea of which way to walk. In actual fact, their trading route was a long, flattened circle - first northward through the inland towns and communities, then back down the coast toward their home city. Marka soon realized that the trade goods on the backs of the asses were only a modicum of the business of his new friend. Most transactions involved items that would be delivered by boat to the city of Pythes - Rome. And again, as happened many times during the trip, the unheard-of concept had to be explained to the boy. In this case, firstly that there were huge bodies of water in the world, and that men used them for travel and trade - in floating huts of some kind.

Most nights were spent alongside the road, a cook-fire and blanket costing nothing, whereas a bed in a taburna and stables for their asses cost dearly in either trade goods or coppers. The nights being longer than the need for sleep, Marka would sit and listen to the tales of his two mentors and carve on sticks to half days into arrows - only, these arrows were to be with iron tips, not the heavy and cumbersomely chipped flint pieces.

"You are obviously more than a novice bowyer, Marcus. I am guessing that you made your bow, yourself?" At the lad's nod, Pythes continued, "That would not be an unsuitable trade for a man. Weapons makers are respected and sometimes grow wealthy." The idea didn't resonate with the boy. He had never even considered what a merchant was, or that a maker of anything would do it as a way to feed himself. In his village, anything one had was made by the person wanting such, or traded for from a fellow villager. The concept of a man specializing in the production or vending of a particular item, over and over, had not taken root in his mind yet.

In any city large enough to have smiths, he would pass through the area looking at the various items being offered for vending. The swords, spears, knives, helmets, and suchlike were interesting, but even though he had a fair blade, taken as a prize from the bandit, he had no idea of how to use it and even less of how he might learn. But, he had eyes for the bows and shafts that were displayed in a shop here and there - far fewer, it was certain, than the other weapons, but in any smithy area he would see at least a few. But, in the large city of Rusellae, on the coast, he saw something that drew his interest - nay, his excitement. It was a bow, of course, but a strange one. Instead of the gentle and continuous arc of a normal weapon, this bow was made with just sharp curves at the ends.

The shopkeeper saw the young man staring at the strange device hanging from the roof sticks, then smiled, noticing the bow, reverse strung and carried across the lad's body, asked, "Are you an archer, boy?"

"Aye..." he answered, then remembering his tutoring, added the honorific, "Sos." He pointed at the strange weapon and asked, "Might I ask about that one? I have never seen such a bow, if that is what it is."

"You ARE an archer, lad. My patrons look at it and think it is a string spinner, for starting a fire." He took it down and handed it to the boy. "This is a bow from a Hesos, or Hyscos outrider - whatever the cursed people were called. I am told that they conquered the blacklands around the Nilos river, many years ago. A place called Egipa or something like that. String it and try the pull."

Marka looked over the strange implement, then said, "It IS strung, Sos, but..."

"Nay, lad. It is as yours is now - strung backwards so as to not destroy the pull in storage."

That made no sense, If it were strung the other way, the curves would be toward the target, not away. Smiling again, the bow merchant took it, clamped one end between his closed legs and, with considerable force, slipped the loose end of the bowstring over the nock on the end. Then he handed it back to the boy. "Now try the pull, lad."

Marka looked at the strange bow - now even stranger with it forced into an unnatural shape with the nocked bowstring. But when he held it straight-armed out and tried a pull, he suddenly realized what he was holding. This bow had thrice - nay, many times the power of the one carried on his body. In fact, he could barely pull it to full bend. An arrow - especially an iron tipped one - would bury itself to the fletchings in a stag at almost any distance that it could be hit. It would probably go all the way through the body of a man at any normal range.

After a few test pulls, and looking down imaginary arrows, he relaxed his sinews and then just examined the wonderful weapon. What made it so powerful? The merchant, knowing what the boy was puzzling about, answered that question. "Look closely at the edge of the curves on the end. See that white material? That is horn of some kind for stiffness, buried between two layers of bow wood. Notice that it is wrapped at each end with some kind of wire - electrum, I would guess, for strength. Some I have seen have many layers of different material, one upon another."

As he examined the structure that the merchant was pointing out, Marka asked, "Did you make this bow, Sos?"

"Nay, lad. I am a merchant of weapons, not a bowsmith. But, I can tell you that no bowyer in my knowledge has ever managed to copy these barbarian instruments. And they have tried, but their efforts splinter as if made of dried reeds." He shook his head. "Nay, these come from soldiers who have picked them up as loot from foreign battles and were down on their luck. I have seen fewer than a handful in my life. And they are dear - this one will bring six oxen or two hundred modius of grain."

Marka shook his head. The price was inconceivable - had he hunted furs for the length of his grandsire's life, he would not have enough to purchase it. Inspecting every inch of the weapon, and then again, he eventually reluctantly handed it back to the merchant, who unstrung it and put it back on its hanger. "My thanks for your kind instruction, Sos. I would buy your wares if I were able."

That night, sitting by the fire, he held an arrow shaft, but only whittled on it in absentmindedness. His thoughts were on that hanging weapon and the power that it represented. Who were the people that had mastered such a craft, and why had they not conquered the world by now? Why would a soldier that had found such a treasure trade it for a mere bagful of metal lumps. Of course, he knew the answer - accomplished bowmen were far less numerous than spear-carrying soldiers. To be effective with the missile weapon took a lifetime - even if it was a short and young lifetime - of practice.

He inspected the images of the weapon in his mind, over and over. He realized that his futile attempts to join different woods together was the key to the weapon he had seen. How did the maker get the end curves to... well, curve, without being pulled by a string? What kept the layers of wood and... horn, the merchant had said ...together? The binder made from boiled hide that he used for fletching would have nowhere near the strength - he had proved that many times.

"You are deep in your thoughts tonight," commented Valens.

With a start, he broke off his musing about the magical weapon he had seen and entered the conversations of the two older men. Before they could inquire about his concentration, he said, "The road is crowded in these parts. As you said, we will be in your city on the morrow?"

"Aye, and it will be good to walk through my own doorway and sleep on my own pallet," returned Pythes.

"I hope that old Darius has not given away the market in our absence," japed Valens.

Since he would probably make their city his, Marka asked, "Might I ask about your city? Is it different than those we have visited?"

Pythes smiled and drained his cup, then held it out to the man, Cleo, to fill again. "Aye, those were mere assemblages of rabble, compared to Rome. The city of seven hills is beautiful, with wide colonnades and buildings of stone, not logs and thatch.   The Temple of Jupiter is the greatest shrine to a god anywhere. You will see it gleaming on the hill of Capitoline.   And the Palace of the King is beyond compare - I am told that it is filled with riches that would make Croesus envious."

Much of that made no sense to Marka, but he asked, "This King is your leader?"

Pythes smiled inwardly at the unworldliness of the boy to not have knowledge of a monarchy.   "Aye. He is King Servius Tullius. The sixth in his line since Rome was founded by Romulus long ago." Pythes looked around as though fearful of wandering ears, although they were alone on the side of the road. "Worse men have taken the Kingship before - and I am not just speaking of Rome.   He is a goodly and fair leader." He thought for a moment. "He has been on the Throne for four and forty years, if my memory is good.   Rare for any Kingship. That alone will tell you that his satisfaction by the people is good."

Morning time found them on the road early, with only the cold ends of the meats from the night before to break their fast.   Pythes had said that their destination was only a half-day's march and he was anxious to reach it.   There were a considerable number of travelers on the road, most carrying burdens - apparently farm-stuff being taken for vending, he assumed.   On occasion, they would now pass a hut, usually on a high knoll, or other location where the road could be seen with advantage.   Always, on a platform was a soldier, or two, holding a long spear - far longer than the flint-tipped hunting shafts that had been common in his village.   The sight of the outposts gave some substance to the richness of the putative city ahead, to be able to have men do nothing with their time but act as guards for a road.

The closer they got, the more crowded the road became until it was a solid stream of people, asses, oxcarts, and other conveyances - almost all heading toward the city. Finally, they crested a hill and before him was their destination. He just stared at the vision that seemed to stretch to the horizon. Up to the time of his encounter with Pythes, he had seen a few villages and a small town, that, in his ignorance, he had thought to be a major city. The real first city that he had seen on the road seemed to him to contain most of the people on earth. Then each one after that continued to astound him with sights and sounds that he had never imagined, let alone seen. But this...

The City

They stopped for a while, enjoying the expression on the face of the boy as he looked at the sight that he could not even have imagined in his wildest dreams. Then, moving down the hill, they came to a large river. "The Tiber," said Valens. Spanning it was a bridge, wide and tall - tall enough to let the many boats that could be seen, both under way and tied up, to pass under it. He had little time to speculate as they crossed in the crowds, but he wondered how such a massive structure could be made by men. Then the sights and visions as pointed out by his elders came too fast to assimilate. Indeed, it was many days before he even began to grasp the magnitude of the city.

Firstly, they passed an enormous, flat field, with some kind of wooden structures surrounding a road with no end and shaped like a flattened circle. "That is the Circus Maximus," said Pythes. "You will visit it often if you reside here for any length of time. The ceremonies of the temples are held here. And races on the holidays. Even mock battles of warriors, to please the crowds."

Pointing, Marka asked about the structures. "Those are the tiers for the citizens to sit during the performances. That stone edifice across the way is where the King will watch and reward the victors."

This day, the Circus was empty, but next to it was a feature of the city that was anything but. A huge area of corrals with animals - asses, oxen, swine, fowls and many animals that were new to him - was elbow to elbow with people. In addition, there were stalls and kiosks selling everything imaginable that could be consumed - baskets of grain, breads, cheeses, haunches of meat, and boxes of fish. Tubs held nuts and fruit - most of which were unfamiliar to him. In addition, there were huge structures made of stone, with columns supporting the overhead that was many times the height of a man from the ground. These were various temples to the gods, the particular names of which failed to register on Marka's overloaded senses.

They passed a large flat area - exceedingly crowded with the citizenry - that he was told to be the Forum of Rome. This one was even larger than the one dedicated to husbandry. He only had time to take glances at the various sights, but again, the size and opulence of the buildings now in view from the huge square was overwhelming. Pythes pointed to a magnificent edifice on a hill. "That is the temple of Jupiter. You will not find a greater tribute to any god anywhere in the world." As they passed it, he was awed by the garments of the men standing on massive stone blocks and apparently exhorting the passersby... for something. In their headdresses and robes they were barely recognizable as human beings. Seeing his stare, his mentor said, "Priests. Canvasing for offerings."

The people awed him. Not only the numbers, but their modes of dress. Some men and women - obviously the wealthy - had habiliments of all colors. That was something that he had began to see on the roads that he had trekked with Pythes, but never in such a panoply of display. His life, until now, had been in shades of green and brown, with the blue overhead of the sky. And the white of snow in the winter. Except for the occasional bird, bright colors were not in his experience. In his village, the garb was as it was. If not furs, then an off-white cloth that was traded for in the lowlands. In fact, the age of the garment could be estimated by the amount that it had faded to gray over time.

Suddenly, he goggled at the women standing in front of a large temple, fronted with massive columns. For a young man from a primitive village, nudity was a fact of life. His village had always bathed communally in the stream, and during the hot nights of the summer, few people wore anything during sleep. But, these women were different in their... nakedness. Women without garments he had seen many times - his mother doing the laundry in the stream, his sisters and her female friends bathing in the same water, but this was different - totally different. These had a strange effect on the young man, for a reason that he could not...

The temple with the women disappeared behind them, and more massive structures appeared in his sight. He could only wonder at the construction of... everything. There were gigantic blocks with a far larger than man-sized image, in stone, at the top, buildings that would encompass his entire village, and the several temples were taller than the needle trees of his mountain. All of the men in his village could not have shifted some of the blocks and stones that composed the lot.

Eventually, they came to an area of the city that seemed to be dedicated to shops and storefronts. Down a long avenue, filled with stalls and merchant fronts, they stopped at a wooden gate - the entryway through a low stone wall into a compound of significant size. It was far less opulent than some of the houses that they had passed on their walk through the city, but again, it wasn't a ramshackle homestead, either. Marka now knew that Pythes was a merchant of some wealth, although the concept was still green with him. As Valens opened the gate, the merchant said, "Marcus, if you would help Cleo bed down the asses, I will roust the household staff for some good repast when you are through."

The compound was apparently composed of a courtyard and a large, single floor dwelling.   At least, that is what it looked like until Marka followed the train of animals around the side.   In the back were several smaller buildings and one open-sided structure that he would learn was the stable.   Under the straw roofing, the man stopped and began to remove the various loads from the backs of the animals. Marka walked up and asked, "What can I do, Cleo?   I know little of beasts of burden."

The man bobbed his head and replied, "I can manage, Master. You need not sully your hands with the work."

Puzzled, Marka asked, "Why do you call me 'Master'?   I have no standing in this house, or any other."

Perplexed himself, the man replied, "I am a slave.   You are a free man.   How else would you be called?"

Marka knew of the concept of forced labor.   Any young man was subject to it in any village he had ever visited, including his own. The youngster was required to do what his father commanded, or the Headman, or even just a passerby male.   The consequences of a refusal could be both instant and painful as most boys found out at sometime in their young lives.   And, it was not unheard of a young boy, orphaned or a runaway, to be snared by the men of a village and put to menial labor.   But, eventually, the young man would grow into his size, and the subjection to servile commands would cease.

But the idea of a grown man being...   he didn't know the words to describe the attribute of slavery, even had he known of its existence.   He couldn't even struggle with the concept, since he had no idea that it existed.   "My name is Marka, or Marcus if you wish to follow the naming of Pythes."

Cleo looked in the direction of the house, then up and down the open area.   Then, "Nay, Master.   I could be triced up and lashed were I to use your name."   Again, the young man was at a loss for understanding, but did not press the issue.   He would ask Valens about the status of the helper.   For now, he just began to unload the train, watching and following what the slave man did.   Once the packs were unloaded, he turned to go, then realized that he had no idea how to enter the house - at least from the back.   He walked back the way he had come, then stood looking at the front of the building.   Aside from the small magistrate's building that they had entered to report the bandits, and the odd taburna along the way, he had never entered a manmade structure that wasn't a hut. And never one as large as this. And certainly not one with an actual door.

He stepped up and pulled on the rope that allowed the door to swing outward. Again, the concept of a solid barrier, rather than a movable straw or hide cover over the entrance to a hut, was new. Inside, he didn't know what he was expecting, but... what greeted his eyes wasn't it. A large room - far larger than even the meeting hut in his village - was full, top to bottom with... Boxes, barrels, piles of items, unknown parcels hanging from the ceiling, and on the walls. What...?

"Ah. You be the new ward that the Master spoke of." Marka looked around a pile of leather to see a large oldster walking toward him. "Greetings, young Sos. I am Darius, the shopkeeper. Why be you wandering through the stores instead of waiting at the table?"

"Aye... Sos. I am Marka... Marcus. I was unsure where to go... Sos."

The man smiled and waved him to follow. "Come. I will show you to the common room." Marka followed through yet another wooden door, then down a hallway. It was just a tunnel to him - the word hallway would have had no meaning had he heard it. At the end was a large room, square and very... again he didn't know the words. It was decorated with a piece of thick cloth on the floor, and from the walls hung other... pieces of cloth. He looked with no understanding at the several flat-topped pillars with the image of a man or a... a... There were several decapitated heads, apparently carved from stone and... At the sight of a strange half man, half bird image, he just stared. Art in any form was a luxury not to be found in a mountain village, other than a carved piece of bone or a decoration painted on a woman's cooking vessel.

"Ah, Marcus. Come." Pythes waved him to the center of the room to a table with short legs, then bade him to recline on a mat. "You have met Darius, my storekeeper." The older man just gave a smile and a slight bow and returned back the way they had come. "Yon round woman is Clerma, my cocua. She is the best cook on this street, as you will find out." The woman just smiled and waddled out of the room.

Already, viands and dishes of food were on the low table, as were jugs that Marka now knew to hold the drink that all Romans imbibe - wine. Pythes waved his hand at the table and said, "Recline and eat. You will find this repast to be considerable superior to the fare that Cleo fed to us on the road." Markus came from a people who usually had the same thing for every meal - meat and bread. Despite the disparagement of his slave's food, the boy had found it both tasty and filling. This repast would be no different.

Even the position of eating was strange.   In his village - and on the road with the traders - the men sat cross-legged before the fire and gnawed their meatbones and bread.   Here, he was apparently expected to recline before a low table for his repast.   He watched as Pythes settled on a mat and against a large bundle of... cloth?   A pillow, he would come to name it as the days went by but, for now, he emulated his elder and reposed on a mat across the table, supporting himself on an elbow.

Marka looked for Valens to appear, but it seemed that this repast was just for himself and his host.   The meal was simple, but filling, even though he had little idea of what most of the plates contained.   No matter, a gourmet he wasn't - the fact that his belly was filling was sufficient.

As the fat cocua cleared the plates and platters from the table, Pythes leaned back in his cushions and said, "Let us speak of your future, if you will."   Marka just nodded.   "I have need of a young man with spirit, as you certainly have demonstrated." He waved his hand. "Fear not - I have no wish to turn you into a merchant traveler.   My thoughts are that you should look to your obvious talents and enter the realm of bowsmithery."

Marka knew what the term meant, from all the weapons merchants that he had both seen and spoken to on the journey.   But, what...

"The usual progress for a boy to enter a trade is to become apprenticed to a master..."   Pythes stopped, realizing that the young man knew nothing of the learning paths of a city-boy.   He started again.   "In Rome...   In any city, a master of a trade will take on a young man to both assist in his work and to teach another who will someday assume the business.   It might be, and usually is his son, but many childless tradesmen will take on a loose young man.   Do you understand?"

Marka nodded.   It was the same in his village.   A boy learned from his father, or from the other men.   How else would it be?

"Like your life in the mountains, here a man must work or starve and such a trade would not only allow you to eat, but prosper." He settled back on his mat.   "You are somewhat too old to start out as a new apprentice, but I would say against that in any case.   The unfortunate fact is that for the first years of a young man bound to a tradesman, he is considered to be almost free labor, and many times is taught very little so that he cannot leave and begin anew.   You are far beyond being a beginner in bow making, and need not waste your young life whittling arrows for another."

The man leaned forward. "Here is my offer. You may reside in my household and eat at my table. I will have Valens give you a small space in the back for your craft, and to sleep. In return, you will assist me in my occupation when needed." He paused, the said, "And fear not, you will have much time for your trade-learning."

Marka was taken aback at his host's tender - an offering that was far beyond what he had expected. He knew now that he had no desire to return to the mountains - the sights and visions that he had seen of the world had pushed his boundaries far beyond their limits of only a season ago. And he would see more - not bury himself in a never-changing wilderness and years of nothing but hunting to live.

He had little knowledge of the verbal intercourse between civilized men, but he attempted to express his thoughts. "I... I am most gladdened with your offer, Sos, but I see little chance of giving back any..."

Pythes leaned forward, interrupting the confused thoughts of the boy. "You saved my life, Marcus. And that of Valens and without need or cause of profit. The binding is indeed lopsided, but it is for me to wonder how to bring value to the friendship, not you." He waved the reply down. "I have no son. My good woman was taken by the spotted pox years ago and our only daughter barely a season later. You will forgive me if I pretend that you are the young son I never had."

Marka just stared for a few heartbeats. Even had it not been a most generous offer, his only other recourse was to set off on his own. He now knew that his metal lumps could be traded for food, and he had enough to last for a long time. Still, for him to attempt to begin a new life on his own, here, would be like a young man of the city setting off to live in the wilderness. Neither would probably survive in the new environment for more than a few sunrises and probably come to an end in a far shorter time.

"Aye... Sos. I will avail myself of your generous offer and stop here to begin my life."

The rest of the day, he followed Pythes around as the man inspected the household that he had been absent from since the start of the greening time. Inside the compound were several buildings of which the house was the largest by far, but for the reason that the entire front section was given over to storage of merchandise. In the back, as he had seen, were several buildings of various sizes, although all were far smaller than the house proper. The latrine he was soon shown, after expressing a desire to relieve himself and knowing that it would be an affront to do so in the courtyard.   There were the stables and several windowless structures backed up to the wall.   "Those hold bulk items..." Again Pythes had to back up and simplify the meaning of an unknown word.   "I am not a street merchant.   Rather, I deal in large quantities that I vend to men who sell out of their kiosks or stores.   Those buildings usually hold quantities of an item, or items. Or wares that are noisome because of their makeup, or age.   For instance, you will know of the stench of green hides..."   A nod from the boy.   "Should I receive a quantity of pelts, fresh from the killing fields, they will be stored in there, rather than the store at the front, where even a cesspit slave would choke and heave at the smell."

At that, Marka stopped, looking at the back of the house where Cleo was working on something.   "Sos.   I do not understand the... the..."   He could barely find words to even ask the question.   "Why cannot your man Cleo speak to me as a man?"

Pythes just stopped and stood, marveling in the innocence of the boy who was ignorant of the concept of bonded service.   Carefully, he began the explanation of slavery.   "Cleo is a slave.   That is, he is bound to me the same way as...   well, as those asses.   I purchased him for his labor."

Marka just stood mute for a moment, understanding the words but not the concept as yet.   "He...   He has no choice?"

"Nay.   Should he refuse or try to run, he can be punished - even severely."   Seeing that the boy was having trouble with the idea, he put his hand on his shoulder and said, "Let the concept lay, Marcus. It will reveal itself in time.   And ease your heart - yon Cleo has a better life than he would have had grubbing shellfish on the shore.   He is well kept and sleeps in the dry - something that many free persons cannot take for granted."   Waving his hand toward the house, he said, "Follow me.   We will inspect your new quarters."

Inside - through another wooden door again - and just down a short tunnel that was called a 'hallway,' they came to a small room. Small it was to Pythes, but to Marka, it was as large as the average hut in his old village.   It was bare of all but a raised platform that was covered with a...   a thick cushion of some kind.   An opening in the wall let in light but was covered by a very thin piece of cloth - far thinner than any he had ever seen.   The older man pointed, "You will want to keep that gauze over the window this time of year.   Our nighttimes can be less than comfortable during the seasons when the wind is from the swamps - the water flies will almost drain you of blood in season.   I will have Dedi bring blankets and linen before the night." Marka assumed that the name referred to yet another servant in the household.

Waving his arm, he continued, "This will be your quarters, to live in as you wish. As you see, all that is here is a bed, but if you wish other items of furniture then you only need to ask Darius." Marka had no idea what was meant by 'furniture', but he just held his questions. With a smile, Pythes said, "Alas, the household has no young woman to be your bedwarmer, but a youngster such as you will have no problem finding one to share your mat."

That night, he just lay awake and stared into the dark. All of his life, until the marauders had destroyed his village was... well, fairly placid, with any excitement usually being that of the hunt. Now, every day - nay, every part of every day brought new sights and meanings that were immediately replaced by others without the leisure to understand what they were about. He was not unhappy with his new life - he was enjoying it, especially after a season of talking to himself in front of a tiny fire in a cave every night, but, he wished events would pause to allow him to at least understand part of their meaning.

He understood the occupation of his host. Pythes traded items for items, just as had been done between boys and boys, and men and men, in his village. Only the scale was different. And, on occasion, instead of kind, he would give or take the metal lumps in the transaction. Marka knew the concept of trading value for value, and was beginning to understand the idea of the metal representing the value on one side of the bargain, and that a small nugget of argentium could stand in for a large pile of hides. It was only a short jump from that knowledge to realize that the small bag of lumps in his pouch represented a large quantity of food - far more than he could carry at one time. The concept was glorious once he had understood it. Instead of journeying with a burden of goods, the small poke would allow a man to travel far and fast, purchasing food and shelter without the cumbersome method of trading at every need.

The city, itself, had come as a shock, even though he had been gradually accumulated to ever-growing sizes of human habitation ever since he had left the mountains. But, Rome was nothing that a young man from the mountains could begin to grasp in any short interval of time. Most of the questions that he had were beyond his ability to ask - the necessary words not even in his vocabulary - even such basic wonderments, such as, how did all the people in the city find food to eat? He knew that the number of citizens just on the single street of this household would have quickly stripped all the game in a day's walk around his village.   And that number was not even a drop in a jar of water to the population of the city.

His previous disinterest in the spirits and gods that were the subjects of incantations and offerings by the people of the village was another area that was making a seasonal change in his mind.   He had never seen any evidence of their being, other than the supposedly sacred bones and sticks of the shaman, but here, the few temples that he had passed were larger than the entire area of his village and magnificent beyond understanding.   And that was just the view of the structures themselves.   Apparently, the gods of this city were powerful beyond belief.   The habiliments of the... the... what was the word he had been given... priests.   Aye.   The richness of the garments on only a single one would have traded for a season's worth of salt and provisions in the trading city down the slope from his village.   Of course, here, everybody wore far more garments than was normal for his people during the cold season.   Even Cleo, the slave...

He began again with the troubling thought of a person being owned by another.   Could anyone...   How did one become a slave?   What authority chose between freedom and bondedness?   Could he, himself, be chosen to become the property of another?   He knew that should it happen, only actual bonds would keep him in thrall.   On the first dark night, he would vanish into the closest woods and dare a city-man to try to bring him back.

With such thoughts, the mental exhaustion finally took command, and he slept.

Rome

The following days were filled with even more learning - and excitement. Despite the careful pronunciation of his name that Marka used to his host, Pythes' ear apparently heard what it wanted to hear. No matter - it was of little interest to himself what he was called, so, he would become Marcus.

Despite his nagging worry that some unknown official would suddenly select him for serfdom, he enjoyed himself as he began to assimilate into the city. First, came the introduction to the purpose of the house. Pythes was a merchant and one who thought of nothing else but trade, and the value of an item if moved from one place to another. The first morning, as his host and Darius were discussing... merchant talk, Marcus assumed, he wandered around the vast rooms in the front of the house that served as a warehouse - another word he had just learned. Certain items he could recognize or, at least, have an idea of what they were used for, such as bales of cloth, strips and hides of leather, iron tools of for some unknown purpose and so forth.

Much was incomprehensible to him. In a lean-to against the main house were jugs - sealed and stacked in piles three high. He first supposed that it was the wine that all lowland citizens loved, but one jar had a loose stopper which allowed him to open and dip a finger through the hole. It came out covered with an... oil of some kind, like the liquid fats that the women of his village had boiled out of animal carcasses.

Back inside, he wandered down the narrow aisles looking at this and that. It was obvious that city-folk required much more to maintain their lives than the simple people of the mountains. There, a man needed a hut, knife, and hunting weapon and, in winter, a warm animal skin and boots to wear were necessary, but little else. Of course, his woman needed cooking pots and such, but few families had more than they could carry on their backs - a necessity when the village was moved, which happened on occasion.

He was examining a strange looking tool when Darius walked up and said, "A good morning to you, young Marcus. Pythes says that you will be assisting the house in work for a while."

"Aye, Sos," he replied. "With whatever I can do, but I am unsure of what that might be."

Darius was a large man, overly broad and barely able to maneuver down the narrow aisles of merchandise, But, as Marcus would find, he was always jovial with an outlook that always seemed to be at ease with the life that the gods had given him. "Bosh. Pythes has told me of your brave actions of that night when the marauders struck. Young men with far less iron in their spirit have done well in Rome." He waved. "Come. We have a delivery to make and your young sinews will be useful." Looking at the boy's waist, he asked, "Where is your blade?"

"Sos?"

"You have a pugio, do you not?" At the boy's nod, he continued, "A man does not go out unarmed. There is little worry about man slayers in the city, but thieves are everywhere and to appear without a weapon is to announce to all that this is a lamb to be sheared."

"Sos. I have no skill in the use of a blade, other than for cutting."

Darius just smiled and said, "No matter. We will find an education for you in time, but just the carriage of steel will give pause to a cutpurse. He will have no knowledge of your lack of bladeplay skill."

After procuring the small dagger that had been taken from the nighttime marauders, he followed the big man to the back yard where Cleo already had a two-wheeled wagon hitched to one of the big beasts that city-folk called an ox. It was led to the side of the house, and all three carried armloads of plain white cloth to the wagon. Then, with Cleo leading the beast, they started off down the crowded street.

Again, Marcus was thrilled to walk the city streets. He had still not passed beyond the wonderment of so many people in such crowds. As they walked, Darius would point and explain this vendor, or that kiosk. Once, waving, he shouted, "Yo, Porcia. How be the day?" To Marcus he said, "She is a baker that you must befriend. Her bread is as light as the clouds. Widowed, in the war with the city of Gabii." The woman, portly and white with flour dust, waved back. Darius pointed to the young boy and said, loudly, "This be Marcus, new in our household." Now she smiled and nodded, obviously too busy to chatter with passersby.

"Might I ask, Sos, where is the area of the weapons merchants?"

Darius looked at him for a moment, then replied, "Aye. Pythes said you were a budding bowsmith. But relax and enjoy yourself for the day. The house of Pythes does not work its members to exhaustion. You will have much time to explore the city, but he wishes for you to have an understanding before you strike out on your own."

Marcus conceded that it was good advice. After all, he could not walk through the city with a nocked arrow at the ready, and his skills with any blade were limited to cutting meat or whittling bow-stuff. He just walked beside the cart and looked at the sights, asking Darius as they passed this temple and that colonnade.

"...Aye, the Temple of Venus." The building was massive, even for a Roman, and glittered with white marble in the sunlight. "For a small coin, you may have one of the temple virgins for an evening." At the boy's stare, he chuckled and said, "But for a much smaller fee you may have just as much fun with a taburna maid."

"...That is the street of the Argentariae. Money lenders and changers." He wagged his head. "Do not, if you value your freedom, set foot on that street for the purpose of borrowing."

"...Ah, here we are. The shop of Claidus, the dyer." Marcus had no idea what that occupation was but helped Cleo unload the wagon, stacking the bales inside the stall of the merchant.

For the next weeks, he saw more of the city, as merchandise was moved to and from the household. Most that came in was unloaded from boats at the docks, apparently the result of Pythes' dealings during the last trading mission. His first visit to the port was another unbelievable experience to a boy who had never seen a body of water larger than the small stream by his village, until his journey to Rome.

The boats and ships seemed to be magical, sitting as they were on the water and without sinking of their weight. He immediately recognized the method of propulsion of the smaller craft, being rowed or poled through the water, but the larger vessels with the tall poles and flapping cloth were, as yet, utterly beyond comprehension to him. Then, according to Darius, who was pointing out this and that as they walked to their destination, he was informed that the really large ships were downriver at the actual seaside port. He could not imagine anything larger than what he was looking at - at least nothing that could move at a man's command.

He began to get a feel for the city, more from tutoring by Darius, than any discoveries on his own. He knew where the major sections lay, even if he had not been to most of them, and which were inadvisable to enter without accompaniment. Each section was called a quarter, but that made little sense. He now knew that a quarter was a forth part of a whole, but there were far more than just four sections of the city. "Ah, it is tradition," said Darius, to his inquiry. "When Rome was new, it was indeed divided into four separate sections, but as the city grew and more were adjoined, the description was kept."

His first foray by himself was to the Forum - a huge square block of the city that held more than a mountain boy could see and understand in an entire season. Since even younger women could be seen throughout the area, it was obviously a safe place for the citizenry, and made doubly so by the frequent patrols of Vigiles - officers of the law - here and there.

Fascinated, he wandered slowly among the vendors. Everywhere were kiosks where one could sit and eat - or drink. Men hawked tunics, sandals, nostrums, and items for which Marcus had no name - or even an understanding of what they were for. One area had white togaed oldsters standing on platforms, giving and taking responses from their listeners. The time that he had accompanied Valens through the area, the men had been given the name of sophists - a word that had made no sense at the time, even with an explanation. Even now, he understood only the words of the converse - the meanings still far beyond his comprehension.

More interesting were the weapons merchants. Many were the dealers in blades, or spears, or armor - even slings, but the few bows that he saw were far inferior to even his efforts of years back. Apparently, bowmanship was not considered a high art by the citizens of Rome. But, the shafts were superior to his in fletching, if not straightness. He bought a single one.

Strolling back to the household, and still examining the multitude of shops and merchandise counters along the way, he suddenly became aware of a delicious smell... Stopping, he realized that he was standing before the pistora of... of... what was the name that Darius gave the widow? Porcia, the widow baker. Aye, that was the name. He stepped up to the counter of the bakery and waited to be noticed. Finally, the woman partially turned from her poundings of a wad of dough and saw the lad.

"Ah. What might you want, stripling?" She pointed to the clay oven at the back of the room. "Smelled my wares, did you?"

"Aye... Domina."

In astonishment, she stared for a moment, then laughed. "By the gods! I have been ennobled to the highborn." She leaned over the table and said with a mock expression of grimness. "You jape with me, lad?"

Marcus shook his head. "Nay, Dom... My apologies if I have offended, but I have newly come to the city and do not yet know the forms..."

She pointed. "Aye. You are the stripling that I have seen with Darius and Valens. My name is Porcia to all and one and not even a

Domina in my dreams." He nodded. "And you wish to taste my wares?" At his nod again, she turned and picked up a piece of steaming hot... bread? ...from the top of the oven. "Try this and see if you approve."

Now he shook his head. "My thanks, good... Porcia, but nay. I cannot take your wares without remittance."

Astonished, she straightened and just stared at the boy for a moment. "By Ceres and his eternal cook fire! A youngster with both politeness and scruples? Jupiter himself must be watching from high Olympus!" She held it out again. "Come, boy. It is in form to taste the food of a merchant before committing the purchase."

He took the slice from the woman and began to sample it. Still warm, it was like no bread he had ever tasted. Far better than the loaves of the household cook, Clerma, and certainly vastly superior to the hard cakes that had been made in his village from grain bought in the downlands. All too soon it was gone and he looked back to the woman. "It is delicious. I have never tasted the like." He looked around her to the stove, then continued, "Might I ask as to the price of a whole piece?"

She smiled at her admirer. "Mean you a bun, like that..." she pointed to a shelf with small breads. "...Or an entire loaf, like those warming over the oven."

"The big one."

"Aye. Do you trade with kind, or with metal?" In answer, he reached into an inner pocket and brought out a small copper flat piece. Eyes widened, she exclaimed, "You must be the son of a noble, boy. That would keep a full family for a week."

"I have nothing smaller, Dom... Porcia. But I can bring some kuprum snippets from my household that would..."

"Nay, boy. That will do. You may purchase two and twenty loaves with that. Enough for a month of good eating - and more."

Marcus was doubtful. "Will your wares keep for that long without hosting the green growth?"

She laughed again. "I meant not that you should take a cart full of bread today. The piece will buy you those loaves at any time. You need only stop by and take another. We will both keep the accounting of your remuneration." He nodded and handed her the copper piece, then she said, "I have new bread that will be ready in a short while. May you wait for the freshness?" He nodded again, and eventually, she opened the door of the oven, and with a long wooden paddle, extracted several loaves from the inside. Taking a small basket, she placed a loaf in it, then covered the steaming bread with a piece of white cloth. "It will remain hot longer as you travel back home, boy. But, mind you bring back my hamper and cloth when you return."

Very shortly, he was hurrying down the street, but instead of entering the house, he steered his way around the side to the back yard. Cleo was pounding on some item of harness when Marcus strode up and said, "Let that lay awhile. Come." He led the slave to the small bench that he used in the stable for his woodwork, then uncovered the basket. The bread was still steaming slightly, and he immediately sliced it into generous pieces with his pugio. Handing one to the surprised slave, he said, "Enjoy it. It is good."

Both sat and began the delicious meal, then suddenly Cleo jumped up and disappeared around the corner of the stall. In a few moments, he was back with a jug and a cup. Pouring the wine into the single vessel, then handing it to Marcus, he said, "This will take away the dryness of the bread." Both used the same cup as they enjoyed the repast, then Cleo said, hesitantly, "Might I ask a question of the Master?"

"Do not call me Master. I am not your bond holder. My name is Marcus, as I have said." He swallowed and continued, "What is the question?"

"You are from the mountains." It was a statement, not a question. Of course, Cleo would have heard many of the conversations between Marcus and the other men during the trading walk. He nodded. "Your people keep no slaves?"

Marcus shook his head. "Nay. I knew not even of such matters before I came to the lowlands." Another bite and, "No man would stand for such bondment. He would run in the first night, and any who hindered him would die."

The slave nodded. "Tell me of your people, if you will." For the first time, Marcus gave the full tale of the horrible night that he returned from the hunting. And of his sojourn in the mountain cave, and decision to seek his life in the downlands.

Cleo listened intently, even forgetting to eat the delicious bread at times. Finally, he said, "Your tale is even of more sorrow than mine. My mater still lives and I see her at some feast times. But yours are gone..." He stopped, realizing that the thought of where the women of the young man's family might be was far worse than the memory of the night of woe. "You would avenge their fate were you able." It wasn't a question.

"Aye. I would kill those men like lice in a winter blanket. But, I have no idea of either their tribe or where such might be found."

Between them, they had finished about half the loaf when Cleo stood up and said, "My thanks for the repast... Marcus. I sorrow for your loss, but I am glad to meet such as you. I have had no person treat my presence as you and I give my gratitude. But now, I must get to my work lest Valens come and find me larking." Marcus just nodded and wrapped up the remaining bread in the basket of Porcia, then headed to his room.

As Darius had said, there was much time to himself as the days went by. He spent much of his spare time whittling bows and arrows. The shopkeeper was impressed with his efforts and suggested that he sell them in the forum. "That will begin to establish you as a bowsmith. In time, you could have your own manufactory and a respected house, yourself."

Noncommittally, Marcus just nodded, then, after some thought, replied, "I have much to learn. My fletchings are frail. Should the hunter find himself in rain without cover, he would find that a quiver of my shafts would be just wood and feathers." At a question, he answered. "I have not managed to prevent the water from loosening the feathers, although a coat of wax helps." He had examined the arrow that had been purchased from the forum merchant to try to ascertain what binder had been used to hold the feather spine to the wood. And without success.

The next day, in the store, Darius handed him a dark block of what looked like hard wax. "Try this in your feather work. This is the glue of oxen hooves. Put it in a bowl of hot water until it melts. It will float and you may dab it at will. When you are finished, just let the water cool and the glue will store itself again."

Most of his woodworking was done in the stable. The building, open on three sides, had plenty of light and shade from the sun. And the spoil from his carvings had no need to be cleaned up. It was here that he still explored the bond condition of the single slave in the household.

Despite his fears, Cleo felt a friendship growing between them, if that word could be used between master and slave. He was treated well in the house of Pythes, but still, there was no gainsaying the gulf between owner and owned. Except with the new young man that had appeared on the trading road...

With none of the pre-concepts of city life, Marcus had always taken the objects in the world as what they were - not as what custom decreed. Animals were prey for skins or meat, as in the hare, or could be dangerous predators, like the huge ursus. The idea that some could be revered, or even worshiped, as he had seen of bulls at a temple in the city, was... was...   He had no word for ridiculous, but he well knew the concept.

And people were people. Some were good, or bad, friendly or hostile. But it was what they were, not what some vague custom decreed. To him, Cleo was a person that was somehow obligated to work without giving his sanction. The abstract idea of the stigma of being a bound person meant nothing - or would mean nothing if he had any small concept of the word.

Marcus called the man - only a handful of years older - by his name, and treated him as an equal, insisting that his name be used in return. It was a while before Cleo could bring himself to use it with comfort, and even then only after many glances to make sure that they were alone, but eventually, he became comfortable in the presence of the likable young man.   In return, he helped his new friend understand some of the customs of the city.

Marcus had noticed that the citizenry were constantly opportuning this god or that spirit. Cleo explained. "All citizens are concerned with the notice of the gods.   Some will not even make water without craving attendance from some spirit or other. Others give obeisance only on the high days."

"So the belief is general among citizens."

Cleo nodded. "Aye. At least outwardly. It would be... risky to declare disbelief in the gods.   The temple priests are powerful."

"And you?"

A half season before, Cleo would have never responded as he did, but now he said, "I have little knowledge of gods, existing or no." He looked around to make sure that they were alone in the back yard, then continued, "But, I have fair evidence that they have no interest in myself."   From the tone, Marcus knew that there was more to it than just disinterest, but he decided to leave the subject alone for now.

From Cleo he began to make sense of the social structure of the city.   At the very top, of course, was the King and his family. Below him - just barely - were the houses and families of the nobility, of a group known as the 'Patrician' class.   Of course, even the Patricians were graded in rank, from those that advised the royalty, to mere nobles of no particular distinction other than wealth and family line.   From that exalted class and downward was the vast bulk of the city - the commoners, or 'Plebeians.'   Marcus came to realize that even Pythes, a man whom he considered wealthy beyond belief, was a mere pleb in this city.   And not even wealthy, as compared to the real riches in the houses of the Capitoline quarter.

And of course, below even the poorest pleb, were the slaves.

The glue that Darius had given him had worked.   In fact, it was marvelous.   His exercise of his bowskills was of necessity short ranged, limited as it was by the length of the way from the front wall to the storage building in the back, along the side of the big house, but now his practice arrows could be used over and over, without need of constant refeathering.   Even a shaft that penetrated past the fetching was usually still intact when drawn through the straw butt.

Still, many a night he lay on his mat, looking into the dark, thinking of that wondrous bow that he had seen on his travel to the city.   On the walls of the stable was a drawing from memory of that weapon that he had seen at the merchant stall on the trading walk. Much thought, over and over went into the idea of how such a weapon might be made.   He well knew the different attributes of wood when bent.   Some tree wood made excellent and powerful bows - for a short time, after which the continual bending became part of the form.   The staves from which his bows were made had that defect, only partially compensated by reverse stringing the weapon during the times of non-use.

Other woods were very difficult to bend when cured but always sprang back to their original form.   If he could find a tree that combined the two properties, he would be well on his way.   But, in his memory he could see the form of that almost mythical bow - it was not only curved the wrong way but bent as much as the outside of a wheel. How did they make the bend?   And make it stay in that form?

In any case, he would soon need to journey to the forest again. His small stock of staves that he had brought from the mountains was exhausted.   He had a double handful of unstrung bows leaning against the wall of his room.   With the addition of strings, they would be usable.   But, the binder that Darius had given him was an exciting addition to his work that he was very eager to test.   It could be the missing item that allowed him actually to make a weapon that might approach the fineness of that wondrous bow that he had seen in the shop.

With such musings, he would soon be asleep.

Book 2

The Youth

Reality

Marcus was adjusting to his new life as a citizen - a life that was busy and different at every wakening. Some days he would give assistance to Pythes, either helping Valens or Darius with obtaining new merchandise, unloading and stacking it in the storerooms or the opposite - loading an ass-cart with particulars and delivering them to all parts of the city. As a side effect, he was learning to number - an absolute requirement for anyone selling or purchasing anything in any quantity that would overmatch the fingers of both hands.

On the days that he was not needed, he would put on his rough garb, along with his latest bow creation, and begin the hunt through the dense forests surrounding the city beyond the grain fields. The meat merchants of Rome would pay well, and in copper pieces, for game freshly killed and delivered. Not only did the hunts add to the coin in his purse, but the openness of the outback was a welcome change from the sometimes overbearing closeness of city life.

The first major incident of his beginning life in the city was purely an accident, caused by his very minimal education in reading. The art of deciphering written marks was presented to him slowly, and mostly by either Valens or Darius pointing out this sign, or that scribble, then announcing the individual words one at a time. Marcus was gradually building up his vocabulary in this irregular way, and he had a long road ahead, but at least he could decipher some of the signposts.

On a day of a successful hunt, he decided to purchase something that he had promised himself since his city hunting had started. The carcass went to a vendor near the forum - one who had offered him good metal for a fresh side of meat. The animal brought five coppers and Marcus already had a use for the money.

The young man needed little to live - his daily needs were supplied by the house of Pythes in return for his labor. Unlike the other youngsters of the city, for whom a bit of metal would not last past the first sweetmeat or wine vendor, Marcus's stash of coin under a floorboard in his small room continued to grow. Rather than spend his metal, he usually traded the results of his hunts for the few things he desired. Now he wanted a pair of boots. Sandals might be the normal footwear for the Roman citizen, but for a hunter in the thick lowlands, bare feet and legs were a target for nettles, thorns, and the myriad of blood sucking insects that would feast on him while he waited in his stalking stance, unable to move to either scratch or swat.

It was after the time of the noon meal before he had re-entered the city, exchanging greetings with the guards at the gate, then delivered the meat to the vendor. Then, with the coppers safely in his hidden poke, he started back for the household for a meal and a turn in the baths. In the mountains, he had cleansed himself on occasion, as did all the other villagers, by splashing in the small stream beside the huts. Had he known, the act of water bathing was inherited from the Etruscan peoples from which his people were derived. The custom, while not followed to the extent of those city people, was still sufficiently inherent in the villagers to give pause to appearing before his fellows with an odorous body. In the winter, of course, few people would subject themselves to the freezing water, but the men, before an active hunt, would cleanse themselves thoroughly, even if it had to be done with a rag from a cooking pot. An animal could detect the scent of a human no matter how well scrubbed, but a hunter with an air of redolence from sweat and dirt would stampede the prey before it was even seen. Of course, this reason was far more compelling to Marcus than the social aspects - an attitude that was no different for young boys throughout all time.

Romans were different. Here, baths were common and continually taken. In fact, a person would be quickly ostracized from his fellows for not bathing sufficiently often. Indeed, it was not unheard of - although Marcus had not seen it happen - for the magistrates to cite a person for appearing in the Forum or another public place in a state of uncleanness. He had cleansed himself of blood and offal from the hunt in a convenient stream, but still, he carefully maneuvered through the crowds with haste, so as not to offend some cultured nose that might be passed.

On the way, he traveled through the Capitoline section of the city. Having passed that way many times on his delivery treks, he knew this area fairly well. The area of name was a hill, actually, and on one side was a large cliff of sheer rock, and with what looked like a temple on the flat top - the Tepian... No, the Tarpeian Rock, as he remembered. This day, he was surprised to encounter crowds of people milling around at the base of the formation - or, rather, in the flat area of the Forum set away from the cliff. On the top, he could see a crowd of persons, dressed in the finery of either nobility or magistrates - or maybe priests. He assumed that this day must be one of the many that Romans dedicated to this god or that and that a ceremony to that deity was in progress.

The crowd was festive, with vendors pushing carts filled with viands, and wine and water carriers walking here and there to sell a cup on a hot day. Whole families were in evidence, with some having their own feasts, obviously brought with them. Having little use for the ceremony, and with no understanding of the deities of the city, he quickly moved his way through the mob.

Suddenly he noticed that the crowd had become silent, almost as a single person. Assuming that some holy ritual was coming to a climax, he stopped, worried that his apparent disinterest by continuing to walk might be offensive to the people. Looking up, he saw nothing of any difference, except that the men on the cliff top were standing to face the crowd. Even with the quiet of the crowd, there was little chance of any harangue being heard at that distance, so the...

Suddenly, he realized that a struggling man was being manhandled to the cliff face, then to Marcus' total stupefaction, was hurtled over the edge onto the rocks below. The crowd shouted in a deafening roar.

Eyes wide, but unable to see the now broken body behind the crowd, no doubt sprawled in broken death on the rocks below, he looked back up to see another man falling to his death. Three more times it happened, with the mob of citizens giving their loud approval each time. Finally, one of the overdressed men stood on the edge and apparently waved a blessing or other gesture to the crowd and after receiving the loud applause of the mob followed the others out of sight over the top of the cliff. Still stunned, Marcus finally began to move again, this time taking as direct as course a possible to the household.

The house was empty, except for Darius in the storefront, bickering with several merchants, so he continued down the hall, unnoticed. In the atrium, he saw Didi dusting the various items around the room. He gave no idea of stopping with her. A young man did not ask questions of life from an old housekeeper. After a long stent in the warm bath, he dressed in his best tunic, then sought out Clerma in her cook-den. She gave him a platter of cheese, with slices of bread and meats and answered his question with, "Nay, young Marcus. Masters Pythes and Valens are to the docks for some matter. They gave notice of their return by the evening meal."

Marcus thanked her, then decided to continue to the Viminalis quarter of the city to find the address of the boot-maker that the baker, Porcius, had supplied. Unlike the Palatium quarter, given over to prosperous merchants and shipowners, this one was dedicated to workers and manufactories. Anything that a city could provide in the form of a grown, raised or manufactured item could be found here.

Now, Marcus used his minimal knowledge of the written word. He could certainly recognize most of the markings of the trades - at least, he could pick out the words that indicated a baker, or a cobbler, or even a medicus, even if he might not quite construe the symbol groups around it. As he approached the area of his quest, he began to examine the signs and banners. Of course, most merchants could be recognized by the symbol of their trade, usually hanging under or before the sun roof in front of the shop. Charcoal vendors, fish mongers, and tailors were easy to spot, but what did the hanging ball with the stripes mean? And the shop with a wooden pig hanging from the post? He could see no evidence of any pork haunches within.

He passed the Crier of the quarter, standing on his tall wooden block and reading the news of the day, along with offers from merchants and the occasional decree of an award for this runaway slave, or that stolen ass. But finally, he saw a shop front that seemed to match the description that had been given to him. At the entrance, he looked into the dark recesses of the open doorway, his sun-blind eyes seeing nothing but darkness. "Hello, within?" he called.

He heard movement but saw nothing until an elderly woman suddenly appeared. "Fie, youngster! She has no use for unannounced suitors appearing without conversance."

Confused, Marcus just stared for a moment, then said, "Pardon, Matrona." He stumbled for words. "I... I have no understanding of your meaning. I was..."

Suddenly, a girl appeared behind the woman. His eyes were still adjusting to the seeming darkness of the room, but he could tell that the neat white stola was covering an attractive young woman. "Who is it, Mother?"

Turning, the woman said, "Another of your suitors, come to supplicate without sanction."

At that, Marcus was indignant. He had not heard the word that was used to describe a young man wishing to court a girl but had no problem in understanding the meaning. "Nay, Matrona! I have no need... have not come to..." Again the words for his situation were not yet in his knowledge, but he manly struggled to state his position. "I beg your pardon if my intrusion is unseemingly, but I was told that this house is that of Jakob the boot-maker, on the street of the Swans."

"Nay, youngster." The old woman had retreated from her indignant attitude somewhat but was still wary. "You have the wrong house on the wrong street. So, be off with you."

The girl stepped forward. "Wait, Mother. Let us not condemn an honest mistake." Looking at Marcus, she said, "I am Sabina, and this is my mother, Decima, wife of Nikias." She waited a moment, then asked, "And you might be..."

Marcus was of age to appreciate women, and normally, he would be like the boys of the city - prowling and looking for any opportunity to engage with the opposite sex. But, in the mountains, he had had little opportunity, other than his very short arrangement with Pita, and that was never consummated. Since coming down to the lowlands, his daily life had been filled with an eternal feast of new sights and experiences - many almost unbelievable to a waif from a small village - that covered his hunger for female companionship. The household of Pythes had no young girls - indeed, the only two women in residence were the cook and housemaid, neither of which would cause arousal in a young man. He had certainly seen desirable young women on the street and in the forums, but only in passing. This was the first time since he had left the village, that a female of his age had even spoken to him.

Hesitantly, he replied. "I am Marcus, of the house of Pythes in the Palatium quarter." The young girl was still smiling, so he continued. "I have not long been in the city, having come only last season. Again, may I give pardon for my mistaken entry into your household and I will take my leave."

The girl looked at the older woman and said, "Mother. This seems to be an unusually polite young man. I doubt that my womanhood is in danger from Marcus." To the lad, she said, "I would also apologize for our rude behavior on your entrance, but we are only two women in this house and have no man for our protection." She waved. "Please, let us introduce ourselves over a cup of wine."

"Nay, Femina. I would be finding my..."

Now, she actually put her hand on his arm. "Please. I seldom get a chance to talk to anyone of my age. Indulge me for this. Our wine is good, I assure you." To the woman, she said, "Mother, would you please serve us at the window mat." Before he realized what was happening, he had followed her into the house to the small room just inside the door. By now his eyes had adjusted, and his sight was sufficient to see a small dwelling, but one that was neat and clean. Through another opening, he could see... piles of cloth, maybe.

The girl waved for him to recline on the mat next to the opening - a window with a covering of thin white cloth that let in light, but not insects. In a few heartbeats, the older woman had set two cups and a clay jar on the low table, then turned and left. The girl smiled and said, "You must forgive my mother, Marcus. She is over protective of me and considers all young men to be potential ravishers." She poured his cup half full, then her own.

Trying to put himself at ease in a totally unexpected situation, Marcus knew he needed to respond to her opening comments - comments that were obviously intended to allow him to relax. "Aye," he replied. "My mother would break a jar over the head of a boy that tried to... to become over-familiar with my elder sister. And again, I am sorry to have assaulted your house in my ignorance."

"You were looking for Jacob? To purchase his wares?" At his nod, she continued. "He is on the street of the Swan."

Puzzled, he asked, "And this is not? The sign of direction at the Crier's circle had the word."

She laughed. It was like the tinkle of water from a fountain, rather than any derision of his blunder. "Nay. This is the street of the Poet." A pause, then, "But the mistake is understandable - the words are the same but for one character."

Chagrined, he replied. "Ah. I have little learning in the matter of the marks. My people had no understanding of the writing of words."

He instantly knew that he had surprised her. Wide-eyed, she asked with a definite air of incredulity. "None? They had no... But you can read - you just said that of the signpost."

He shook his head. "I am learning the markings, and I can construe the words with which I am familiar, but I cannot read." He hesitated, then asked, "Can you?"

Sobered, she nodded. "My father was a tutor..." Seeing the puzzlement come over his face, she continued, "A man who teaches students to read. He was a scribe, firstly, in the office of the Quaestor, then a Rhetor in the Forum. Finally, he had a scriptorium of his own until he died of the apoplexy three years ago. But he taught me well, even though a reading skill is given to few females in this city." Both tasted their cups - filled with a very good wine, he noticed, finally. "My Mother and I keep ourselves with our seamstress work and with the rent from my father's scriptorium. We do not live in excess, but we do not starve."

Actually, Marcus was only listening with half an ear. He was suddenly aware of being in the presence of a lovely young woman and the feeling was... almost overwhelming. His past experiences with young females were mostly confined to trying to avoid them or at the least, drive them off. But none of the girls of his village, until the encounter with Pita at the stream, had given him this feeling of... of...

"You are of the house of Pythes, as you mentioned." He nodded. "That is the house of a wealthy merchant. But, you said that you have only come to the city in the last year." It was a question, plain and simple.

He nodded. "The tale is long..."

Time passed. Far more than he realized as she drew out the history of his life. By now he was somewhat at ease, basking in the presence of a young female - hoping that she would not suddenly rise and call an end to the innocent tryst. In turn, she gave a few details of her young life, although it was filled with far less adventure than his.

The mother was in the other room - he could see her, on occasion, through the open doorway, usually carrying this or that length of cloth. With the closeness of the small house, he knew that she was a party to all that they were discussing. Finally, they looked up as the old woman brought a plate of cheese and bread, and another small jug of wine.

"All this talk and without food is not good for the liver," she said.

As she left again, Sabina watched her go, with some surprise showing on her face. She leaned over and quietly murmured, "You must have impressed her, Marcus. I have never seen her give a good word to any man of less than her age, and certainly has never offered them a repast." She grinned. "More likely would be for her to throw the slops in their direction."

By now the natural stirrings of a young man were coming to the fore in Marcus. He had never had a feeling for a female like this before, and it was confusing him greatly. As they ate, he desperately tried to concoct a plan to extend the visit or, at least, find a reason to return. Biding his time, he braced himself then began, "Do you follow in your pater's footsteps? To, teach the art of the written marks, I mean?" Before she could answer, he hurried on. "I am desiring to learn and have coin to pay. Or, if not you, do you know of another who could be engaged to assist me?"

Sabina was young, but no warded female. She knew full well what were the thoughts and desires of young men, and Marcus was no different than any in that respect - at least, she hoped so. But, unlike all the neighborhood boys, he was the only one that did not express them in either words or less than subtle actions. She wasn't sure if it was politeness or ingrained shyness that kept him from moving closer and testing the strength of her defenses, but she had an intuitive liking for the boy of her age. She was sure that, even in the unlikely event of them being alone, he would not take any advantage. More importantly, her mother obviously thought so, displaying her approval with the unexpected largess of food for a stranger.

She smiled and replied, "I can help you with that, but you need not pay me. I would welcome the distraction from the boredom of this house."

"Boredom?"

She realized that he could have no concept of female life in the streets of the Viminalis quarter. From his tale, she knew that the girls in his past could have come and gone at will. All the men of his village would unite in the protection of an unattached female and woe to the young man who forced unwelcome attentions upon her. Here, it was different. A single girl would be cornered by street toughs before she even got to the well, and at the least, stripped and fondled, if not worse. The few times that she left the house were in the company of elders on the way to a feast, or the temple or suchlike. So for her, the offer of a polite young man to visit on occasion was as a present from Olympus.

"I wish to do more than just make and mend garments in my life. Assisting you would be a welcome change." She looked up at the covered window. "But for now, I fear that I have caused you to miss your meeting with Jacob."

Following her glance, he was surprised to see the dimness of the light. He had been talking and enjoying the company for the entire half day. It was almost dark. Quickly, he rose and said, "I had no intention of marking your entire day. I must be off. My principle will be wondering about my absence."

She also rose and put her hand on his arm. "I am indeed serious about assisting with your need to learn. Please come back at your leisure."

Unbelieving of his good luck, or maybe the blessing of some god that he had pleased, or whatever had led him to this house by mistake, he stopped in the doorway to the cloth room. He said to the old woman, "My thanks, Matrona, for the generous repast for a blundering stranger." Turning to the girl, he said, "And to you for a most enjoyable afternoon. I will visit again when I can plan to spend time on word learning." With that, he half bowed and walked into the street.

The sun was already down, as he strolled along, letting his feet direct him to his destination. He was ecstatic over the prospect of seeing the lovely young girl again, and already planning his days ahead to make time for... He turned at the sound of a footfall behind him. The movement was fortunate since the stick or club only glanced off the side of his head and impacted on his shoulder - otherwise, it might have split his skull. Still the blow was sharp enough to knock him to his knees, but he immediately sprang up to defend himself, knowing that an animal which cannot rise can easily have its throat slit.

His hand fell to his belt for his pugio, or rather, where it should have been had he not forgotten to bring it. He had no time to curse himself for a fool before he was overwhelmed by the mob. Fortunately, the thugs now only used their hands and fists and were apparently not trying to kill him. But in heartbeats, blows to the face and body had knocked him to his stomach. Still conscious, he heard them giving advice to each other.

"Quickly. Quickly, before the watch turns the post corner." "This is a swell - look at those sandals." "And the tunic. Hurry!" In only a short time, he was laying naked in the street, shorn of everything he had carried, including his garb. How long he lay there, he had no idea. He didn't think that he had passed out, but he couldn't be sure. But, finally, he gathered the strength to rise and stumble through the dark - falling twice - to eventually reach the gate of the Pythes compound.

The front door was barred from within, as was done every evening, so he stumbled around the side to the kitchen door. There, Clerma looked up from her day's end of work, then suddenly shouted at the top of her lungs, "Pythes! Valens!" Dropping her load of rags, she moved to the boy and guided him to a stool. "Sit you here before you fall down." She immediately dipped a rag in the water barrel and carefully began to wipe the blood from his now swelling eye.

Valens was first to appear, stopping in the doorway with a curse, then called something down the hall. Then, Pythes arrived, dressed in nothing but a ragged pullover - apparently he had been in the bath when called. Soon, with the arrival of Didi, the maid, and Darius, the entire household was standing in the crowded cookery while the two women tried to clean the boy's wounds.

Pythes was distressed but Valens was shaking with rage. "By the stinking piss of Jupiter's whore! Who did this to you, boy?"

Marcus tried to answer through fat lips, but was quieted by Clerma. "He can give you his tale when he is not offering to the blood demons." She pointed and said, "Come. Carry him to his mat so we can bind his wounds."

"Aye. Aye, of course." Pythes was frantic in his worry. "Darius, you lift his legs and you, Valens his shoulders."

In a short while they were in his bare room and Didi began to bath the blood and dirt from his body while Clerma wrapped clean strips of cloth around the wounds. The cook was now issuing orders as though she were mistress of the house. "Valens. Bring the good wine. It will help him sleep. Darius, have you still a supply of henbane in store?"

Both men disappeared, glad to be able to do something but stand and watch the women. Pythes asked quietly, "See you anything that is... is..."

Clerma shook her head. "I feel no broken bones, and his teeth are intact. His eye is bloody, but it still sees." She looked up and nodded. "He is young. His body will mend back to what it was."

"This is my fault. I made oath that he would learn the manly weapons and I have been too busy to fulfill it."

Valens had entered with the wine - enough, in fact, to inebriate an entire barracks of soldiers. "Nay. We are all at fault. His outgoing trust in the street cozened me also into thinking that he needed no protection." He was still red-faced and ready to lay low the perpetrators of this outrage. "But, be sure of this. When he is able, I will rectify that shortcoming. I swear by Jupiter that it will be done."

When Darius arrived with the anaesthesinum powder, she mixed a pinch into a cup of wine and, holding the boy's head up, urged him to drink. The drug hit him like the clubs of the street toughs. Very shortly, he fell into a blessed sleep.

Adjustment

"Excuse me, Master. I would find Marcus of the house of Pythes. The storekeeper said he would be in the back of the house."

Marcus was sitting in the sun, in the backyard hard by the stables, watching Cleo moving stacks of hides into one of the outbuildings. It had been several days since the attack - he was by no means healed, but in the last two days, he was able to stand up and move about somewhat. The medicus that had been engaged by Pythes encouraged the action. "Movement of the sinews and ligaments will promote their healing," he had said. To Pythes, he had added, "But within reason. He should not put a strain on the wounds until the Kalends of the month, at least. And feed him flat breads and cheese without garnishes."

He needed to get away from the care of both Clerma and Didi. He appreciated their efforts and concern, but there are times that a man finds his fill of female smothering. In the backyard, he would sit and casually whittle on his wood - not with any desire to produce, but to keep his hands busy. He knew he would heal, and just needed to let enough time pass, but his heart gnawed at the fear that the girl, Sabina, would think that he had merely toyed with her that day, and had left with no intention to return. In fact, on the yesterday, he had Cleo call in a local urchin and had given the boy a copper snippet to deliver a missive to that household. It had to be verbal, since his pitiful understanding of words certainly did not stretch to the act of writing on a tablet or papyrus, and he hoped that the boy had delivered the message accurately. Or that he had even bothered to deliver it at all.

The newcomer was carrying a pair of baskets, covered with white cloths. He was either a bound servant or a slave, but that was of no accord. To the man, he said, "I am Marcus."

"Ah. Then, I have these for you." He set them down as Cleo came over to see what was happening. "Porcia sends the bread and her wishes for your swift recovery and hopes that the time will not be overly long." Marcus could tell that he was reciting verbatim, some message. "The tree fruit is from Legos, the fructus vendor, the sweetmeats from Olan, who sends his regards." More thought, then, "Ah. The figs and dates are honey coated and the wife of Luciens warns you against your tendency to gobble them. She also bade me to tell you to drink wine fortified with the kernels of barley, as it thickens the blood. That is all."

Marcus stood, carefully, so as not to stretch any muscles wrongfully, then said, "Stop a moment." He hobbled over to his small bench under the stable roof and pulled a copper from the small stash that he kept for payment on occasion, for various items or services. Tossing it to the young man, he said, "My thanks to you for your message and for bringing the baskets. And you will please deliver my gratitude to all involved in these presents."

"Aye, Sos. I will do it." With that, the young man bowed and hurried out of the back yard.

"Well, Cleo. Let us see what might be in the baskets. Bring them to my bench."

Both sat and enjoyed the repast from the street vendors. By now, both were friends - not close in the terms of manhood gatherings - that wasn't possible given the underling state of Cleo, but both could talk as equals - in private - and confided in each other as young men do everywhere.

In the aftermath of the assault, Marcus had totally forgotten the events of the morning of that painful day, but suddenly, it came back to him with clarity. After describing the events to Cleo, he asked for the meaning. As a born Roman, the slave was well aware of what Marcus was describing.

Handing a filled cup to his friend, Cleo said, "To your question of the cliff itself, I have no idea of the calling, nor its name of Tarpeian. I do know that the temples on the top are shrines to the Sabines, but not who they were. I can remember my mother telling me stories of a beautiful priestess and golden bracelets and such, but the tales did not stick in my memory." Tearing the bread apart, and handing half to Marcus, he continued. "It is now used as a place of execution, but not for ordinary crimes. My wonder is the number of men you saw thrown down to the rocks below. Five it was?" At his friends nod, he said. "To be hurled from the rock is a mark of disgrace and is usually only done to traitors, or murderers and suchlike. I have never heard of so many being executed at once. Most criminals are either crucified or strangled in the circus."

After they had enjoyed the repast, and Cleo had moved back to his labors, Marcus just sat and thought about... anything. He wondered if he could ever become an actual citizen of this city, in the sense of belonging. Or, did one have to grow up in the complicated maze of civilization to understand it.

As the medicus had predicted, a month of days saw his body mostly mended and the pains gone. All of the men warned him, time and again, not to walk the streets at night, at least while alone. Marcus had no issue with that advice - he now well knew the folly of an unarmed man out of his domain. Still, he had no intention of hiding within the household and soon he was moving about again - during the day. Of course, one of the first places his feet led him to was the household of Sabina and her mother.

First a stop at the weapons merchant's stall, Aetius, just to speak to a friend and to see if anything new in missile weapons had appeared in his shop. Then up the street of food vendors to speak to, and thank the various acquaintances and friends who had sent good wishes and hopes during his long absence. That took far longer than he had wanted, each asking about the assault and the extent of his injuries, but finally, he could point his feet to the house that he had thought about endlessly during the long month. Now, he carried his short sword and pugio, and unlike the last time he had set foot in this quarter, his attention was on his surroundings and not roaming with thoughts of women and suchlike.

His fears of the effect of his absence were not realized, and he was told, with relief, that his message had indeed been delivered. Over another meal, this time augmented with viands that he had brought, the tale was told. He had to comfort the girl - another new challenge for him - as she assumed the guilt for his attack by keeping him far into the evening. The meeting was very pleasant and, after much hesitation, he asked if she might accompany him to find the kiosk of Jacob, the bootmaker.

Interestingly, the mother had apparently decided that the young man wasn't an immediate threat to her daughter's virtue, and made no protest, except for the demand to return promptly. "...and do not stray from the path to the street of the Swan and back." Since it was in the middle of the day with citizens and magistrates walking the streets, there was little danger from more street toughs - only the occasional cutpurse. The young couple drew glances from passersby as they walked - his neat and clean tunic and her blindingly white stola gave notice that these were not a pair of waifs from the alleyways. Marcus was reveling in the presence of the girl and marked very little on the way - in fact, had she not been guiding their feet, he might have walked to the Tiber without knowing.

"You have almost performed another of the labors of Hercules." At his blank look, she said, "Never mind. If we begin your learning, you will know what I have said. But, what I meant, is that you are the first young man that my mother would let sit in my presence - her allowing you to escort myself without accompaniment is beyond believing."

He thought about that for a moment. "Are all of the young men of this city... untrustworthy around a girl?"

"I doubt that the trait is confined to the boys of Rome," she said with a tone of drollness. "You are different only because you have it under control."

Not entirely sure what "it" was, he made no comment. In a short while they were at the shop of Jacob and were talking to the taciturn man about bootwear. It took little time before the measurements were taken of his feet and legs and a price agreed on, and he was told to return on Nones of the month. The transaction was concluded far too quickly. Marcus certainly didn't want the day to end so soon, and thought of inviting Sabina to visit the baker widow for fresh bread, but remembered that the mother had been most insistent that they not stray from the direct path to the bookmaker and back. Still, she had not specified the pace that they must return.

The girl, also, had no urge to hurry back. In fact, unknown to him, this was the first excursion that she had ever had that was not in a group of oldsters - all ready to admonish a young woman who let her eyes roam to unseemly sights. Being able to walk the street freely, looking and doing as she wished was as at treat from the gods. She was even more unhurried than her female-struck companion.

They walked slowly and casually, often stopping to look at this headscarf, and that tunic - anything that was displayed along the long street of vendors and shops. Marcus could not have listed just what they had examined, his entire store of thought being on stretching the time of the journey as long as possible. As a ploy to ever further extend the outing, he would point to a sign and attempt to read it aloud. Then, both would stop as Sabina coached him through the words of which he did not yet have knowledge. Finally, he realized that they needed to return - engaging the wrath of the mother with extreme tardiness would not ease his future ability to befriend the young woman.

Fortunately, when they finally returned, the mother had nothing to say, beyond a greeting and an askance of their journey. For the rest of the day, both sat in the front room and wrote and erased on the learning slate, both enjoying each other's company, especially when their hands touched on the board.

Encounter

Marcus could have been one of the stone statues that were standing all over the city of Rome.   For a time long enough for the few rays of sunlight, reaching through the forest canopy, to move the distance of his foot, he had only allowed his eyes to move.   The young hunter from the mountains would have never recognized himself as the man stalking in the low-land forests of the plains.   Rather than the ragged and faded gray pullover of that youngster, with holes for his head and arms, and a wide loincloth for protection of his lower body, he now had a proper tunic, with sleeves for protection against insects and thorns.   Below it was a long skirt, divided into two tubes for the same defense to his legs.   The fabric was a shade of green, but not for the purpose of prinking before his fellows - although the garment was handsome enough - but to blend in with the foliage of the forest.   Topping it was a wool cap, pulled low to protect his head and ears.   On his feet were tall leather boots, replacing the city-sandals that had been wholly insufficient for standing in the vermin-infested undergrowth.

He had quickly learned that hunting in the lowlands was far easier than the timbered lands in which he had stalked game in the mountains.   There, the trees were tall and the underbrush scarce and required any stalking of game to be done with extreme stealth.   But down here, far from the city walls, the trees were short, and the undergrowth was very dense.   If one chose to hunt after a rain, allowing the detritus on the ground to be wetted to silence, a hunter could almost creep close enough to his quarry to strike with a blade.

For a considerable time, he had been watching one of the four-footed ruminates - this one a hind, rather than a stag - slowly graze through the underbrush.   A few more strides and the animal would be within clear reach of his bow.   The ease of stalking in such dense foliage was offset by the same greenery limiting the sight range to any prey, but usually, the shaft was released over such short distances, that a kill was almost always the result.   And it was this time, as well.

As the animal's head dropped to the ground, and behind the low bush, he lifted, drew and released.   The iron-tipped arrow made a clean kill, with only a few leaps by the unfortunate animal before it fell, quivering in its death throes.   Marcus had come to the forest to search for bow and arrow wood, as he had done many times in the year since his coming to the household of Pythes.   Each time, he found the plentiful animals to be too easy to take for the opportunity to be passed.   The meat jobbers of the city paid well, and in good copper pieces, for fresh game, and an animal of this size would bring good rewards.

Using his long leather rope, he hung the animal from its hind legs, then slit it open to drain.   For the interval, he continued to scout around for saplings of any possible use.   Unfortunately, he had yet to discover - on any of his short trips into the forest - any new woods satisfactory for bow staves.   Arrow wood was plentiful, but he seldom made those shafts to sell - the giving-price was not worth the effort.

He had made friends with several of the weapons merchants who had taken a liking to the young boy.   His enthusiasm for the bow and his skill in both using and making the weapons was discussed with good-natured laughter by the vendors of the area.   And his apparent honesty and refusal to accept gifts without payment made him welcome in the shops of the weapons peddlers.   During the visit, he would be shown any new bow that might have been obtained since his last appearance.

It was not only the weapons vendors with which he was on good terms.   Darius - and Valens - were astounded time and again, as they made their way to or from the shop with a cart load of merchandise, to see this cloth merchant and that cobbler wave or shout a greeting to the boy as they passed.   And the baker widow, Porcia, would turn away from a customer to greet the young man as he approached.

One morning as they were pulling the cart, old Legos, the Greek fruit peddler, tossed a ripe apple to Marcus as they passed, with the words, "Yo, Marcus. My woman is mending well, now and would speak to you at your leisure."   Marcus nodded and waved back.

Looking back, Darius exclaimed, "By the gods, boy! Pythes was worried about a waif such as yourself wandering the streets of Rome without course.   Little did he know that he was befriending the future King of the alleys."   Marcus just smiled, but the older man knew that the boy never took without payment, so it was obvious that he had performed some service for the old peddler.   Pretending gruffness, he continued, "Yon Greek would not throw a rotten plum to me without his palm being crossed, and you he feeds like a stray dog."

Marcus had learned from Porcia, that the wife of the peddler was bedridden with the flux, and was needing solid food instead of the produce of her mate's baskets, which would just aggravate her situation.   He had been struck with the concept of debt and payment, learned at the start of his friendship with the widow baker.   The idea that one could store up trade with an honest person, taking only what was needed at the moment and drawing on his previous payment over time - it was a revelation as great as the sight of the city had been. Taking a haunch of meat from a kill, and a half loaf of bread, he had approached the fruit vendor with the proposal of a trade. As a result, besides a new friend on the street, whenever he passed that way, he was assured of a treat from the best wares of the old peddler.

"Care you for this apple, Sos? I need not it all after Clerma's morning feast."

"Nay, boy. It is yours. Besides, I am as full as you at this moment. Save it for later."

The work for the day being to deliver, rather than receive merchandise, he asked to take his leave of the empty cart after it was unloaded. Darius nodded and said, "Shoo, boy. I can deliver it to Cleo without your help. You are yearning to visit the bow vendors, I'll be bound."

"My thanks, Sos. I will return later."

At the kiosk of a weapons merchant, Aetius by name, he was greeted and waved to enter. "Come, Marcus. I have something that will interest you." All of the merchants knew that he was looking for a curved bow like he had seen on his first journey to the city. All knew of what he was speaking, but few had ever actually seen one, and fewer gave him much chance ever finding such. "Unless you travel to the highlands of the barbarians, yourself," said Aetius. "And I would not recommend that unless you are at the head of a Legion."

In the back of the shop, he lifted a... a... it was actually one of the curved bows! But in defective condition. It was obvious that any attempt to draw, or even string this weapon would cause immediate failure of the wood. "A traveling mercenary had this in his pack. I saw it and recognized it as a sample of what you are seeking." Marcus took the pieces and examined them with excitement, as Aetius continued, "He claimed that he was to deliver it to a bowsmith in Antium to have it mended, but it was just a ploy. I am not an artisan of the craft, but even I know that the smiths of Apollo himself would be required to repair this bow." Smiling, he continued, "His thirst was greater than his desire to bargain and I obtained it for a copper snippet."

Not taking his eyes from the pieces, Marcus said, "My thanks, Sos. I will make good your payment and more. This will allow me to work with more than just my memory."

"Nay, Marcus. Just bring me your next building, and we will include this in the bargain." Thanking his friend profusely, Marcus almost ran back to the household, just acknowledging the calls and greetings of the street with a return wave.

That was a half season ago. Since then he had carefully dismantled the bow, layer by layer, inspecting the pieces over and over, and then again. He was a long way from duplicating the weapon, but even so, his current efforts made his boyhood efforts seem to be mere bent sticks. Today, he was using his latest creation - testing it actually - made of two dissimilar woods, glued together while being pressed under a man-weight of stone. His first efforts at that type of bow were powerful, but not long lasting. The violent spring on release would cause the two thin staves to separate eventually, usually splintering in the process. A period of thought and work came up with the solution of a double handful of wraps of thin hemp cord, dipped in the ox glue, then immediately wound around the bow ends while still hot.

His bow today was the latest in his creations. It was durable, without a doubt. He had used it on his last two hunts, and with many practice sessions on the compound range. So far, his young eyes could see no evidence of failure.

And it was powerful. The shaft had buried itself to the fletchings. Still, it wasn't the equivalent of the bow that he had seen on his first journey. The skill to make one like it was still in his future, hopefully.

The morning growing long, he returned to the hanging animal and hoisted it across his shoulders, first coiling the valuable rope and hitching it on his belt. This carcass would go to a vendor near the forum - one who had offered him extra coin for a fresh side of meat...

He froze, looking and listening, then dropped the carcass and whipped his bow off his shoulders and quickly strung it. An arrow nocked, he raised the weapon in the direction that the animal was approaching. As the sounds grew louder, he began to draw tension, waiting for the appearance of what had to be a large ruminant on the move. Hopefully, it would be a stag-sized animal worth many coppers in the meat markets. It would mean a quick trip into the city to dispose of his earlier kill while the latest beast was draining, then back to claim the meat before the forest creatures found it.

He saw the brown of the beast through the brush, pulled a full stretch and lowered his aim to make sure the shaft would hit the vital area. Then...

He lowered the bow and released the tension. It was a horse. And one with a blanket and rope, but no rider. Standing there, he watched the beast lope past him, then disappear into the brush in the opposite direction. He knew nothing about the animals that were used by soldiers, having seen them on occasion, and only at a distance, but he knew that they were expensive to both procure and maintain.

He unnocked the bow, then began to move in the direction that the horse had appeared. His assumption was that some rider had fallen off and would probably appear running and breathless as he chased his mount. For a woodsman such as Marcus, following the deep impressions of the hoofs was as simple as a city man finding his way across the Forum. For a considerable distance - almost halfway back to the city, in fact - he followed the tracks until he found the unfortunate.

Laying on the ground was a young man, apparently the about the same age as himself, but there the similarities stopped. The tunic on the man was gold laced and of a far higher quality than the neat and clean, but plain garment, that Marcus usually wore. He was unmistakably of the Patrician class - a part of the city that was a blank slate to the young hunter. However, it was obvious that bones broke just as easily on the rich as the poor, with the leg of the prone man bent at an unnatural angle. It took a few moments for the man to notice Marcus as he came up, but finally, his eyes focused, and he groaned, then said "By Jupiter. I am dreaming. What chance of another being in these woods?"

"Much chance, Sos. I am here often. But, only on my own two feet which I count as far more steady than your ride." As he spoke, he dropped to his knees to examine the bare leg that emerged from the short tunic. Broken bones and wounds were not strangenesses to his village folk, no more that they were to any other peoples in the world. And while he had no fine knowledge of the repair of the human body - he was no shaman apprentice - he certainly knew about blood stanching and bone straightening. Besides, it would be obvious to anyone that the leg was cleanly broken. "Might I offer assistance?"

"I would be most appreciative, Sos. I would ask you to carry word to the city that I might be retrieved from here." The words came with some pain and much body water issuing from his face and skin. "Although, I fear that you might not find this spot again." He tried to look around through the dense foliage, then continued, "There is little here to use as marks for finding this place."

"There is little chance of that, Sos. The city is indeed confusing to me, but I can find my way through any outland. Hold while I find some sticks to restrict your leg movement." He rose and scouted around for two straight limbs of the proper length, then trimmed them for use with his pugio. Back at the broken man, he kneeled, then said, "I will bind your leg with these sticks, Sos, and some rope. I fear that it will feel less than goodsome when I move it."

The man just nodded, the drew in his breath as Marcus carefully and slowly pulled the broken limb to some measure of straightness. Laying the sticks on either side, he cut several lengths off the rope hanging at his belt, then began to bind the leg between the wood. As he tied, the unfortunate asked, "Might I ask the name of my savior?"

"Aye. I am Marcus, residing in the house of Pythes in the Palatium."

"My greetings to you, good Marcus. For myself, I am Lucius of the house of Junius. You may have heard of my family."

Marcus shook his head. "Nay, but let that not surprise you. I am newly come to the city and have little knowledge of it as yet."

"Ah. I had a notion of your foreignness. Your accent is not heavy, but neither is it of the Palatium." He paused, then continued, "I meant no denigration by the statement."

Marcus just turned and smiled, still tying the short ropes. "The tale of my coming to Rome is far too long to suit these surroundings, but I will say, that I have plans to make the city my home." Finishing, he stood up and let his internal sense determine the direction to the road. Unlike city-bred folk, he could almost always point absolute directions - from the time of day, the position of the sun through the trees, the slope of the ground and... he was unaware of how he did it and had never given it a thought. It was just a sense of the wilderness people had that atrophied in those that walked the cobblestones.

He pointed. "The road is in that direction. I will go for assistance." Pulling the water flask from his belt, he set it beside the prone man. "I do not know if I will have to journey to the city, or find men on the road, but I will be back. Take no worry from that."

"I am grateful, Marcus. And this will not be forgotten."

The road was not far, and while it wasn't the Via that connected the cities up and down the coast, it was still fairly well traveled. He watched the different travelers - mostly traders - pass until he saw three men coming toward the city and pulling a cart - mostly empty. It was obviously a father and sons - one being a graybeard and the other pair, not young, but in the prime of life. Marcus waited until they pulled up to him then stepped out with his hand up. "Pardon my forwardness, my good men. Might I engage your services? For the succor of an injured man. He cannot walk and will require a traverse into the city." He held out a hand that had a palm of copper pieces - six in all and the entire contents of his traveling purse.

The men stopped, wary but not too concerned about the hail from a single young man on the road. The older man looked at the metal pieces in surprise. "Indeed, youngster, you are the savior of an otherwise unproductive journey. Lead us to this unfortunate." Telling the younger man to stay with the cart, he and the other followed Marcus into the underbrush. As they walked, the old man asked, "This unlucky person - he is your friend? Or maybe your sire?"

"Nay. I was on the hunt and came across him, lying with an impaired leg." He pointed. "Just over that rise."

Shortly, they had come to the place where the man was lying. It only took one look by the elder before he said, "You were not misspeaking when you described his need of carriage. That is a broken bone in his leg, and no mistake." In a lowered voice, he added, "And he is not a woodman, fallen from a tree. Look at his tunic and sandals."

Marcus had already determined that the injured man was of the nobility, but that status had little value in the forest. Stooping, he said to the prone man, "We have a cart to take you to the city, but we will have to carry you to the road. And it is not likely to be a pleasant journey."

The man - Lucius - nodded, and said, "Aye. But my fate is sealed if I just lie here until the leg heals. And I am grateful for your efforts - be assured you will be rewarded." He lay his head back and said, "I am ready."

Marcus said, "If you," pointing to the younger man, "will take him under the arms, and you, Sos, support his middle, I will carry his legs." The process was excruciating to the young man, but he only gritted his teeth as the body water issued in streams from his forehead. Immediately, they began to move back toward the road. Other than some involuntary groans, the trip was made without incident and mercifully was not long. There were some blankets in a pile - obviously, for cover during nighttime stops on the journey. Marcus folded two of them to make a soft support for his injured leg to lay on. Then he asked, "What part of the city holds the place of your house?"

The pain of the portage now subsiding, the young man replied, "The house of Titus Junius, in the Capitoline." That meant nothing to Marcus, but it obviously did to the other men. As they stepped off, guiding the two asses pulling the cart, the older man said to Marcus, "This is a noble indeed. The house of Junius is high in the stature of the city rulers." Marcus had not heard the family name, nor would it have meant anything to him if he had. The Capitoline quarter was just an area for him to pass through on route to somewhere else, and if he noticed the ornate and massive houses, they had made no impression on him.

Trusting that the older man knew the way, he just followed the cart as they first entered the city, then threaded their way through the crowds of first the Caelius quarter, then the Palatium and finally the wider and less crowded streets of the noble areas. Pulling up to a enormous brick structure that sat on the very edge of the street, Marcus stepped up to the door and rapped the swinging knocker several times.

The servant that opened the door was not impressed by the visitor. "What want you with the household, boy? We do not trade with mendicants that knock on the..."

That was as far as he got when the injured man lifted himself above the side wall of the cart and called - and not with patience. "Cerberus take you to Hades, Nonus! Call for the servants to carry me! And the Domina."

Wide-eyed now, the man looked at the man in the cart, then stammered, "Master? Master! You are with injury? I..." With that he disappeared, shouting, but was back in mere heartbeats with a handful of servants, who carefully lifted the man from the cart and carried him inside.

As the door shut, Marcus handed the older man the promised coins and said, "My thanks, Sos. Your assistance was most timely." The man gave a nod and a wave of his hand, then the cart was turned and trundled back up the street. Since the day was well along, he decided not to resume the hunt. Besides, the carcass that he had left on the ground was no doubt a feast of the woods creatures by now. The idea of visiting the weapons merchants was attractive. After that, he would...

He turned as the door opened and a servant ran out and down the street with only a glance at Marcus. As he watched in mild surprise, a voice from the door said, "You. Young man. Come." Turning again, he saw the original servant gesturing for him to the doorway. "The Domina calls. Come to attend."

Through the doorway, Marcus immediately received an education in relative prosperity. To himself, Pythes was one of the wealthiest men in the world. His household was far beyond anything that the young man had even dreamed of in his days before coming to the city. But, it took only a glance inside the massive house to realize that, aye, while his mentor might be wealthy, he was as a beggar on the streets in comparison to... to whoever belonged to this household.

The ceiling was high. Higher than the entire house of Pythes. Even taller than the temple that he had glanced into on one feast day. On the floor was thick fabric that he now knew to be a rug, but this one, instead of just being a comfort to the feet, was woven with an intricate pattern of color. On the walls were other hanging fabrics - again not the white of the natural fiber, but somehow colored in brilliant shades. Dyeing was not completely beyond his experience - some of the village men had soaked their hunting garments in a pot in which the galls of the nut tree had been boiled, to give a shade that allowed them to more closely blend into the forest foliage. The idea of coloring such massive amounts of fabric in such brilliance - he had not even the knowledge to wonder how it was done.

Tall stone pillars supported the ceiling while much smaller and shorter ones held the usual statuary that Marcus saw everywhere in the city. Meaningless at the time of his coming to Rome, he now knew that any sculpture inside a private home was probably a likeness of a departed relative. Added to the room were tables and mats and strange structures that seemed to be a cross between a chair and a bed, and...

"What is your name, young man?"

A woman had suddenly appeared in his vision in the dim room. Not a woman such as was in the house of Pythes. This one was... was... There was no doubt that this was an actual Domina, in the real sense of the word. Everything from her hairstyle to the folded robes - a stola, he remembered - said that this was a wealthy woman. Of course, in this house, he hadn't expected to encounter a street trollop. He bowed, then said, "I am called Marcus, Domina. Of the house of Pythes in the Palatium quarter."

She was no doubt the mother of the injured man - her age of middle years and just her presence made that an almost given. "Where are your men, young Marcus?"

"My men, Domina?"

"Those that assisted you in bringing my son to the house."

"Ah. They were not with me, Domina. They were a troop that I found on the road and willing to hire their cart for his carriage. I have paid them, and they have gone. I know not their names." A pause, then, "If you wish to talk to them, I may be able to catch the cart before they are away completely."

There was a silence, then she replied, "You hired a cart to convey my son from his place of injury." It was a statement - not a question.

"Aye, Domina. His horse was last seen far away and I could never have carried the ma... your son to the city without further injury. We are fortunate that the men with the cart were immediately at hand."

"Fortunate indeed," she murmured, obviously with her mind on something. The door to the street opened and the servant that had run out of it earlier entered behind two others. From his own experience, he could recognize a medicus and his apprentice. "Ah, thank you for coming with haste, Eroclese. Come, Lucius is in his cubiculum." Turning back, she waved her hand to Marcus and said, "Please relax until I have spoken with the medicus." Across the room she called, "Bring drink and repast for our guest."

Before he could protest, she had turned and gone, following the medical man into the gloom. But, he was hungry, as a young man usually is, and sat at a table as wine and platters of meat and foods were brought. As he ate, he looked around the large atrium. The inspection was without envy, Marcus having no sense of the necessity of the accruement of unneeded property - at least, that aspect of city-life had not settled on him as yet. Still, he could be impressed by even the garb of the servants, which matched the overall magnificence of the house. He wondered if the under folk were actual slaves, like Cleo, or hired persons like Darius. Visually, there was no indication, all in the house being dressed in finery better than a prosperous freeman on the streets of trade.

Finished, he just sat and waited, watching a servant, usually a female, hurry from the back of the household and down the dim hallway into which the principals had gone. He had decided that the day was wasted and that he would just walk home from here, after... after whatever happened. Suddenly, he saw the mother walking unhurriedly across the room. He stood and waited as she approached and stopped in front of him.

"Marcus, you said?" He nodded and she continued. "Our family does not forget those that have done us a good turn. Lucius would gladly give his gratitude, but he is resting with the suppurative of the medicus and will not wake until the morrow."

"His leg will mend, Domina?"

"Aye. It is straightened and captured between bars and will become whole in time." She paused, the continued, "You mentioned the rendering to the cartage men. I would repay that and reward your actions."

"Your pardon, Domina, but that is not a necessity.   The attendment of a man in need is a given among my people."   Or, at least, it had been, he told himself.

"Nonsense.   Friends are scarce enough at any time and I would not let one who has befriended my son to just walk away, unappreciated.   Please give me your place of domicile."   Turning, she called to a servant, "Lars.   Bring a purse."   Back to Marcus, she nodded as he recited the address of the house of Pythes.   "My son will express his own attitude when he is able, but for now I would make good your expenditures on the cart usage."   As he opened his mouth to protest, she said, "Nay, we pay our debts, even if unable to match the service that was rendered."   She opened the leather poke that the servant had given her, looked for a moment, then handed it to Marcus. "This is not payment for your good service, but just a gesture to make your purse whole again."

He saw no way to refuse the quittance, so he just bowed and said, "My gratitude, Domina and my hopes for the goodness of mending for your son.   And now I must be on my way.   My principal will be wondering about my long absence."   With that, they exchanged farewells, and he headed back to the household.

After the evening meal, he examined the purse he had been given and was stunned by the contents.   Frugal he was, storing his slowly accumulating coins for the future, but the contents that he poured into his hand were worth many times the hidden poke under the floor.   There was a handful of silver coins - large and heavy - and each worth an entire double handful of copper pieces. With them, he saw what he thought was a copper piece, shiny and gleaming.   On inspection, his eyes widened as he realized that it was an aurum coin - the first he had ever seen.   That alone was worth a hundred large coppers and more.   What was the word he learned from Darius...   A 'centum,' he finally remembered.   A hundred was the highest that he could enumerate as of now, but it expressed only a part of the worth of the gold piece.   This coin with the image of some man was worth more than his entire life's collection of metal pieces.   And all the furs of his youth.

That night he lay on his mat, enjoying the cool breeze that wafted through the cloth of the window - a breeze and a coolness that was unseasonable for this time of year.   His thoughts ran to the past - from the escape of the destruction of the village, the only male to have done so to his knowledge, to the encounter with Pythes in such a way as to take favor from the meeting.   And now a new life that would not have even been in his imagination had he stayed in the mountains.

Idly, he thought about the concept of his fortune being directed from somewhere. Did the gods actually exist that pointed his feet in a favorable direction? He had no indication of such guidance - none at all - but the list of events in his still young life seemed to be more than just happenstance.

With such thoughts, sleep finally came.

Education

He was expecting the assault, but the arm that suddenly wrapped around his neck was still constriction enough to cut off most of his air.   Desperately, he pushed upward with a hand, while moving his head as far back and to the side as possible.   The angle released much of the pressure from his windpipe and with a sudden push upward with all his strength, he managed to force the elbow of the assailant up and over his head.   His dominant hand pulled his weapon from his belt, then, instantly dropping to a crouch and spinning on his heels, he drove the end into the belly of his attacker.   A sudden "oofff" from the man gave proof that he had connected.

"A creditable effort. But, remember to arch your back and push with your feet and legs. An assailant that is worrying about stumbling to his backside will pay less attention to his grip on your neck." Marcus took off the cloth blinder that had prevented his knowing from which direction the attack would come.   He looked at his fellow student - his assailant - and received a nod that gave notice that the belly that had taken the 'thrust' was in good order. The long green fruit that he had used as a 'weapon' was now useless, either as a play-pugio or for a garnish for the midday meal. He tossed it into the grass away from the sand pit of the training area.

The words from the Hastilairius, Dursus, were almost effusive praise compared to the usual obscene reprimand for actions that did not come up to his expectations.   Since there was little for the reservists to do for their half-pay, most enhanced their income by instructing the sons of both nobles and well-to-do in the martial arts. In the training unit of Dursus were three other boys, in ages from fourteen years to about twenty.   As all young men of any land, most lusted and dreamed of becoming the next conquering hero of the ages - except Marcus. He saw no use in trying to slaughter other men and chancing the very real possibility of being killed himself and to no purpose. Sometimes fighting was necessary, as on the road when the party of Pythes had been attacked, but his natural sense gave no reason for the wars of cities.   Still, Marcus knew the value of being able to defend oneself, even in a city that considered itself to be civilized and well ordered.

Some moon cycles before - months, the Romans called them - he had returned from a trip with Valens and found a man waiting in the atrium with Pythes.   The stranger was middle aged and most definitely not a merchant.   Immediately, his mentor pointed to the lad and said, "This is Marcus, of our telling.   He has no small skill with the bow, but little with his other weapons." To the lad, he said, waving his hand to the man, "This be Dursus, Hastiliarius to the army of the King, now on reserve status." Knowing that the young man would have no idea of the title, he added, "He trains the farmers and shopkeepers to wield their blades without slicing off the feet of their comrade - or their own."

Marcus bowed, and replied, "My greetings to you, Sos."

Looking somewhat askance at the boy, the soldier said, "A polite lad, to be sure. I have misgivings as to his manliness for blade work."

Valens spoke up, with some fervor. "Nay. Be not deceived by his age. He has already killed two bandits and saved our lives in the process."

The soldier looked at Pythes and received a nod, then back at the boy for another evaluation. "By Mars. That is a different tale. Possibly he could be taught the manly skills." A pause then, "Very well. I will attempt the transformation - at least to the point that we will know if he should stand in confrontation or run to hide in the cookery with the maids."

For the last several months, on every third day, he walked to the eastern gate, then into the stockade nestled against the wall. The guard well knew him by now, and just nodded his greeting. This was the permanent training encampment of the city - one of them, at least. As of now, it was almost deserted, no wars having been fought for years and apparently none being plotted at the moment. Only a double handful of reservists were living in the wooden barracks - one of which was the Hastiliarius, Dursus.

"That will end the instruction for the day. My belly is complaining about the space between my backbone and my omphalos button." The four young men came to attention and saluted the soldier, then turned and walked toward the barracks to change into their street tunics.

"We would visit the baths, Marcus. Do you follow?" This from Isagoras, the closest he had come to making any male friends of his age, other than Cleo, the slave. The young man, or rather, his family was from Ionia, an island in some far off part of the still unseen central sea. As the tale was told to Marcus over time, the family had left before one of the perpetual wars of that region and had settled in Rome many years ago. His pater was a well-to-do jobber of grain and had residence not far from that of Pythes. The other young man - an older boy, in fact - was named Margo and was the son of a wharf official.

By now, Marcus had become used to the perpetual desire for cleanliness of his adopted city, and now enjoyed the ritual of bathing. He nodded his acceptance as he removed his now soiled training tunic for his clean street garb. "And you, Caius?"

Naturally, Caius, of the house of Florus, declined the invitation. Collecting his pair of armed servants that accompanied him to and from the barracks, he waved his refusal, as usual, and left. His was a family of the Capitoline, with their own baths and bathing slaves and as such, he had little interest in socializing with inferiors. In fact, Marcus was at somewhat of a loss as to his presence on the training field. To begin with, he was an unenthusiastic bladesman, giving only enough effort not to be continually cursed by Dursus. And as a member of a rich and noble household, he was accompanied at all times by armed protectors and guards. There was little chance of his needing to take iron to defend himself. However, according to Isagoras, the minimal training was obligatory to his class, less for the ability to claim warrior skills than the very real need to be able to pull his blade in formal salutes without slicing off a limb - either his or his fellows. Shortly, Caius and his party had departed.

With his belt wrapped and tied, and the pugio and short sword stuck in the loop, he looked up as the Hastilarius entered. "Sos," he began, "We would go to the baths. Might you care to accompany us?"

The older man threw his soiled tunic to the floor and reached for another, hanging from the wooden wall. After a pause, he replied, "Aye. I would not look askance at a session in the waters. We can purchase some viands on the way." He looked at the other two young men and continued, "I have some words to give to you, and the baths will be a good forum for it." Marcus had stuffed his exercise clothes into the carrying bag, and the three young men followed the soldier out of the barracks and through the gate of the encampment.

The Apollinian Waters was a bath for prosperous citizens, both freemen and freeborn and was very popular, Marcus was told, with the soldiers from the training fields, probably because of its proximity to the barracks. It was one of Marcus's favorite destinations, especially after a session of hunting or swinging a wooden sword in the heat of the day. The house of Pythes had a bath, but it was just a stone pool large enough to sit in - convenient but of no comparison to the pools at the huge thermae. The distance was not far from the east gate of the city, and the path took them past several vendors of food, from which they bought meat and cheese to eat as they walked.

Finally, after reaching the thermae and paying the entry fee to the door-slave, they were soon disrobing in the apodyterium, placing their garments on shelves around the room. A small coin to the watch-servant gave them the ease that their possessions would be watched over during their stay.

First the purgo-slave dumped a large pot of warm water over the visitors, then as they stood, feet spread and arms out, slaves with strigilea moved the blunt and curved blades up and down the arms, legs and torso - to remove any dirt and body effluents from the skin. Following another pot of water as a rinse, the four moved into the terrace of the tepidarium. As they passed the arch leading to the smaller women's area, the younger lad, Myros, pointed and giggled. The thermae served both men and women, and while the two genders did not mix in the same waters, the two areas were not particularly private from one another. All three comrades looked in appreciation at the sight of several younger women taking their leisure in the waters. And of course, the looks were accompanied by the usual comments given by young men the world over whenever such displays of female flesh are encountered.

Marcus didn't hesitate at the edge of the lukewarm pool - the tepidarium. He jumped as far out as his legs would take him, then began to swim across the bottom for as long as his breath would allow. He was comfortable in the water, having sported in the deep pool by his village from the time he could walk. For a while, the young men splashed in the water, jesting and chasing, while the old soldier just relaxed in the pool, lightly bobbing up and down on his bent knees. Then, as the play began to subside, he called to his flock of young play-soldiers, "Isagoras. Marcus and Myros. Attend me." The young men immediately moved to take a position in front of the officer, his back now resting in a corner of the pool.

He waited as they arranged themselves in a naked formation of youngsters, then began, "We are not now on the training field, and what I have to say is for your usage. You have no requirement to listen nor to take my advice. I give it to you to use at your will."

The boys looked at each other, mildly surprised. To date, the soldier had mainly just given instructions and commands - usually in a loud voice and accompanied with various curses and references to the private organs of this or that god. Here he was more as a scribe giving lessons to pupils. It was an interesting change, at least. Isagoras replied, "We would be fools indeed not to hear the words of a man who has seen much more of the world than all of us if we were one."

The soldier nodded, and continued, "There is... talk. Among the Hastilarae." Marcus could see him trying to formulate his message

- an unfamiliar task for a gruff soldier, indeed. "It is like the calm and heavy air of a day of dark clouds. Nothing can be seen or heard, but you will sense that a storm is about to be unleashed by the gods." More thought, then, "Rome is under those clouds and the air is still and full of the potential for the god-strokes of lightning and thunder." Since it was a beautiful day, with white clouds in a blue sky, the boys had no problems with understanding that the soldier was making a reference to a coming event, and not to the wrath of the gods.

He continued. "Do not ask me what the storm will be. I have no idea, nor do my fellows. And, for my meaning, it is not important. In any case, it will involve the armies of this city and others, and that is where you will be affected. You three are at my command of teaching because of the standing of your principals - Caius I leave out since his status in the city will carry him elsewhere, no matter the cause." He leaned forward, then said, "Here is the nugget of my meaning. Should the army be reassembled - and it will be sometime again, no matter what the reason, whether for this one or another - you will be inducted into it as new Miles - basic soldiers - as will all the younger men of the city. As such, you will be a part of a formation that will hack and spear as a unit, with no cause for your prowess with weapons. It is time for the caldarium." Pointing, he led them to the far side of the pool, where they climbed out and then jumped into the heated pool. The stinging hot water was not a place conducive to continuing the conversation, which lapsed until even the sun-browned and swarthy skin of the old soldier was pink and steaming.

From there, they launched themselves into the frigidarium, the cold water of which caused them to breath in short bursts until the shock had worn off. It took only a short time before they were comfortable and again lined up in front of the old soldier. The water, bone-chillingly cold at first, was only seemingly so and in reaction to the steaming pool from which they had come. In actuality, the water was only of the normal temperature of the spring from which it was piped.

Dursus continued his lecture. "Were I you, young and in possession of coin for the proper equipment, I would enroll in the reserves as Immuniae. Now." He waited for a moment, then continued, "As an Immunis, and enrolled before a war, you would be spared the rigors of life as a common soldier, and I can attest that the status of such blade-fodder is not one to be sought after."

"We would be in the army as soldiers, even now?" asked Marcus.

"Aye, but with only a duty day on the kalends of the month, with a formal assembly in the spring and durnal aequinoctiae. If the army were assembled, you would be assigned duties as specialists to a Commander, maybe even to a Praefectus or Legatius. Most importantly, you would be eating in the senior cookeries and sleeping in tented quarters and not slogging in the mud with the common soldiers. If giving good service, you may even be promoted to sub-officer."

The young men thought about the new ideas for a while, as the soldier waited for the offer to resolve itself in their minds. Then, "To qualify for Immunis will require a charge of accreditation from two senior Hastiliarae. I will, of course, sponsor you, and one of my comrades will serve as the other warrantor." He waved his hand, then prepared to exit the pool. "Do not decide in haste. Think on it and if you wish to request the position, inform me at any time." With that, the group moved to the laconium, where they were dried by slaves with towels, then to the apodyterium to retrieve their garments and weapons.

Clean and relaxed, he set his feet on the street to the household. The quarter of the Palatium was well patrolled and free from crime during the day, with the exception of the very occasional cutpurse. Still, Marcus took a young man's pride in the fact that he walked the streets as an armed citizen, his blade at his side no longer just for show. A seasoned swordsman he wasn't - far from it - but, his skill, after months of tutoring by the old Hastiliarius, was far more than sufficient to handle any street toughs that might try him.

Reaching the house, he entered the front door to ask Darius if he was needed for any work. There was none, both Pythes and Valens having just returned from some purpose at the docks, so he gathered up the two bows that he had finished for vending. Aetius, the weapons merchant, was always glad to speak with Marcus, recognizing the budding and talented bowsmith in the youngster. Even now, he considered the young man's bows to be superior to any that could be purchased in the city.

Marcus had donned his best tunic and sandals, and had given his farewells for the day to Pythes, when Darius rushed into the atrium, breathless and excited. Both men looked in surprise at seeing their fat friend move faster than they had ever seen, but before Pythes could ask, the storekeeper blurted out, "Master! In the courtyard! There is a noble from the House of Junius! He asks for Marcus!"

Utterly surprised, Pythes looked at the young man and exclaimed, "How would you be in the attention of one of the first ranks of the city?"

Marcus had not told the tale of the broken man in the woods, and now was not the time to start such a long story, so he merely said, "I was of some assistance to the man while on a hunt a month or so past."

Hurrying through the house to the front storerooms, then to the porch, they exited the door to see a carrying chair sitting on its resting posts, with a handful of slaves standing quietly.   On the chair itself, was the young man that he recognized as the unfortunate from the encounter in the woods.   Seeing the men appear in the doorway, the occupant rose carefully and stood to wait as Marcus, uncertainly, walked up to him.

With a smile, the young man said, "Ave, good Marcus. We are well met again." With that, he reached to take both of the young man's arms in the usual Roman greeting between males.

Smiling himself, Marcus replied, "Greetings, Sos. I am gratified to see that your leg did indeed heal."

"Ah, not as yet. It is only in the last few days that I can actually stand and walk a short distance.   But, the medicus gives me hope of recovery by the second Ides." He looked over Marcus's shoulder at the three men of the household.   "These are of members of your family, maybe?"

Marcus turned toward the house, then gestured toward the noble lad.   "Might I present Lucius, of the house of Junius?"   Then, "Sos, this is Pythes, of this merchant-house, and this Valens and Darius, his men."

Lucius replied, "My greetings, and thanks for harboring a man such as Marcus. But for him, my family would be seeking a mask-maker for a pedestal."   All three men bowed, as he continued, "If I might impinge upon your favor, to borrow Marcus for the afternoon?"

Pythes spoke up with a smile, "Of course, Sos. He has no pressing duties this day."

To Marcus, he said, "If you would favor me with your presence at my household. I would welcome the chance to both express my gratitude and learn more of my rescuer.   Oft-times, friendships spring from sudden encounters."

"Aye... Sos. Certainly."   Marcus was astounded as were the men of the household but willing to see where the proposed friendship might lead.

Lucius turned and sat down heavily in the chair. He laughed and said, "I would walk with you, but I fear that our journey would lead into the night before arriving." To his steward, he nodded and an order was given. The slaves lifted the chair and started through the gate and down the street, Marcus walking beside.

Lucius looked at him for a moment, then said, "Your pardon, Marcus, but your features do not follow the master of the house. It gives credence to your statement that your genesis was not in that household."

Marcus laughed. "Aye, Sos. I come from far away in the mountains. My association with the good man Pythes is a tale of some length."

"I would hear it, but in private and in a place of more comfort. I have no understanding why most elders insist on the use of a lectica for traveling. I fear that the status one derives from the use is far outweighed by the discomfort to one's hind quarters." The talk went on until they stopped in front of the huge brick house that Marcus had seen on that fateful day. Dismounting, Lucius walked slowly to the door, which was opened by the steward. There he stopped, and waved Marcus to enter, firstly, then followed.

As they walked into the vast atrium, he saw the young man's mother approaching - not at a frantic pace, but still, faster than he had seen most upper born walk. As she walked up to both with a smile, she held out her hands to take his arms - the first time he had seen a woman use the greeting. "Good Marcus. Welcome to our house. We would have had you come before, but Lucius insisted that we wait until he could give the invitation himself."

Marcus gave a bow with a smile of his own. "The honor is mine, Domina. And I am astounded to be received." Over her shoulder, he noticed another woman - a young girl, actually, approaching.

Turning, the Domina said, "This is Iulliana. My daughter."

Marcus bowed to the young woman, who said, "My thanks to you also, Marcus, for the good turn you did for my brother. By chance, are you an equestrian?"

Marcus had no idea what she was asking, but he was sure that he was not a... whatever she said. "No, Femina," he replied.

With a frown, she said. "That is unfortunate. My brother could certainly use a tutor in the art of riding a horse." The sudden grin gave the notice of her jape, and all laughed at the jest.

The Domina gestured and said, "Please recline with us. And do not fear, we women will not stay to intrude the conversation between two young men." Servants had already placed cups on the round mensa, and Marcus kneeled to lay back on a mat beside the table. After the first cups, the women excused themselves and departed, leaving only Lucius and Marcus reclining on their mats.

Marcus learned something of the noble house. The Dominus, by the name of Titus, and the elder brother of Lucius - Titus the younger - were currently on a tour of the family's widely flung properties. The girl, Iulliana, was sixteen, and the only other child in the family. The house of Junius was one of the wealthiest and most influential families in the city, equaled by only a handful of others. Both the Dominus and his elder son were high in the court of the King and had several official titles that issued from the Throne. Lucius, himself, was destined for the same, once he had placed a few more seasons behind himself. The Domina was the center of the powerful women of the city, although some of the words and descriptions of her activities were beyond both the vocabulary and understanding of Marcus.

For his part, Lucius listened in fascination to the tale of his guest, from the early times in the village to the present. At the mention of the suggestion of the old Hastiliarius, that he and his friends should enroll as Immuniae, his eyes moved away as he evidently began to ponder something. Marcus stopped his speaking, noticing the sudden shift of attention, then said, "Pardon, Sos. Have I said something that is... troublesome?"

Starting, Lucius looked back and said. "Nay. Just a thought that came to me as you spoke. Your Hastilarius is wise. You would indeed be inducted into the army when any reason exists for it to be reassembled. And to be a common foot-soldier is not a life that any intelligent man would aspire to, especially if one found himself in the front rank of a battle. The idea of becoming an Immunis, especially between times of war, is an excellent suggestion. You would have seniority, and a choice of position." He thought for a moment, then, "But, perhaps I have another..." He stopped, looking past Marcus, then said, "Ah, Mother. Please join us. I was about to suggest a plan of action to my friend."

The Domina reclined on a mat, then waited for a cup to be placed before her, and filled, then smiled and said, "I fear the troubles that two young men might be planning."

"Nay, no trouble at all - at least, not now. But, mark what I was about to tell Marcus." He looked across the table and continued, "It was two years ago that I surrendered my boy-amulet for the man-toga, and soon I will be starting my military service by being inducted as Tribune. As such I am accorded a batman with the rank of Adiutor. He would travel with me as my companion, sharing tent and table in a far more comfortable position than even an Immunis attached to the Legator." He drank from his cup, then continued. "What think you of the idea?"

Marcus just stared over his cup for a moment. Was this offer just a happenstance, or, were the gods, once again, pointing his feet to even yet more adventures? "Sos. I am indeed honored by your trust, but surely you have... friends, acquaintances, others that you would want for such a companion. You know nothing of me or my quality."

The Domina spoke up, and both young men waited for her words. "My son is impulsive, as are all young men, but he has wisdom that I trust. Indeed, he has friends - good ones and loyal - but they are friends of the son of Titus Junius, whereas you are becoming the friend of Lucius." She held up her hand to stop his protest. "You assisted my injured son, unknowing who or what he was, and with no thought of reward. Your own purse was used to hire the cart and you would have left without asking even for remuneration, much less for a well-deserved reward. Such quality is scarce indeed, in noble or in common families."

She let the words lay for thought before she continued. "You would find the association with our family to be beneficial, I would hope. Our house has always been strong because any who become a part of it, be it a woman come to wife, or a male-child born to it, are never allowed to think they are superior to others merely because of our name." She smiled, then continued, "I still blush to remember the young and haughty girl who came to this house as the wife of the elder Titus, and being told, in no uncertain manner by the Grand Domina, to report to the cocua in the kitchen to learn how a cookery works. Then, a few days later, pointed to the laundry for the same reason. And then with the bed maids to clean and arrange." She glanced at Lucius. "And the sons did not escape the education. Lucius, and his brother, both, made chores in the stables, the cellars, and assisted the woodsmith in repairs on the roof, coming down in the evening looking like wraiths from the black pits. We are strong because we are willing to work for and defend our station, not because of any belief in favor from the gods that has somehow made us superior to others and immune to manual labor. You would find us a substantial rock on which to anchor your new association with Rome."

Lucius spoke. "You need not decide now, of course. I will not enter the induction for three months. But... Think on it. I would be..."

He stopped as the door knocker sounded through the room, then some murmurs came from the hallway, followed by three men - two young and one somewhat older - entering almost faster than the steward could precede them. Stopping at the entrance to the atrium, the servant announced in a loud voice, "Masters Tricipitinus, Publicola, and Collatinus!"

One of them called, "Ah, still on your backside, I see."

All three stopped and bowed to the Domina, who rose and stood for a moment before saying in a droll voice, "Was it not you, Publicola, who wagered with Lucius about the quickness of your mounts?"

Sheepfaced, the young man nodded, and replied, "Aye, Domina. But I did not know that he would attempt to test the course alone."

Marcus had risen as the visitors entered the atrium. These were obviously close friends of the young Dominus, and come to see of his healing.

The Domina pointed and said, "This is Marcus, of the house of Pythes, in the Palatium quarter. He is the man who came upon Lucius in the woods, and arranged for his carriage back to the city."

The three looked him up and down, instinctively knowing that he was not of the noble classes, despite his neat and clean appearance. However, since the house of Junius had apparently given him the auspices of acceptance, they could do no less. All three nodded in a slight bow to the young man.

"I have asked to engage Marcus as my Adiutor when I am called to service," said Lucius.

Marcus knew their names from the introduction of the steward but had no idea of which belonged to which, with the exception of the one called Publicola. One of the others said, "Ah." Looking at Marcus, he asked, "Have you accepted?"

Before he could answer, Lucius broke in with, "Nay. I have just given the invitation. Give him some time to think on the offer."

Realizing that he was far out of place with the addition of the visitors, he said, "Your pardon, Sos, and my thanks for your gracious invitation to the hospitality of your home..." Turning to the woman, he bowed. "And for yours also, Domina. But it is time for my return to my house and work. I will most definitely give thought to your most generous offer, Sos."

Lucius slowly stood up, testing his balance then bowing himself. "The honor of the house is yours, Marcus, and it is for us to feel gratitude. I will talk with you again. So, farewell and may the gods go with you."

"Nonus!" This was the Domina. "Show our guest to the door."

Martial Places

Generations of historians, in a future inconceivable remote, would speculate on how a small cluster of hamlets grew into the greatest power in that part of the world. Even the populace in the time of the monarchy could not have said, other than quoting myths and stories of the past. The tale of the founding of Rome on the banks of the Tiber, by the brothers Romulus and Remus, after being abandoned in infancy and given succor by a she-wolf, is a construct of a far later age, when Roman scholars were attempting to give the then-Republic a past enshrined in both glamor and legitimacy.

The actual reason is a mixture of happenstance and self-preservation. The cluster of hamlets had the advantage of location - the land was rich, well watered and suited for husbandry of grain and animals. Hills allowed for a measure of fortification against raids from outside. And indeed, the cluster was surrounded by the early civilization of the Etruscans, barbarians, and bands of men for whom banditry and looting were the way of life. As the habitations grew into villages, then into an extended town, the citizens realized that they had to band together to survive. Thus, the concept of the citizen army arose - the citizens willingly leaving their fields and farms to form into military units to meet the current threat, then disbanding after the skirmish to return to their homes.

Even now, as Marcus girded for his military service, the idea of a professional standing army was far into the future of Rome, when both the size and wealth of the domain allowed for such an expense. As a monarchy, the city only maintained a bare minimum of professional soldiers - training officers and certain veterans and specialists. Later historians also counted self-preservation as another reason for the lack of a permanent military - more times than can be counted, and all over the world, ambitious officers and unhappy soldiers sometimes decided to change their lot, and the ruling entity, with force.

Marcus had given his acceptance to Lucius Junius of the offer to be the young noble's batman, and had accoutered himself appropriately. Standard uniforms, or even military garb that was fairly similar, were a feature of Roman armies that would not appear for a century or more. Still, certain conventions had arisen just from practical reasons. Leather armor, for those who could afford to purchase such, was of a close sameness, being just a shell that covered the torso. Helmets were of all types - Etruscan, Greek, Phoenician and some that defied any knowledge of ancestry - although the convention for all was colored horsehair plumes to indicate specialties, or ranks of officers. The head cover of Marcus, for instance, had a fore and aft brush that was white, indicating a staff officer, or aide.

The idea of a man who wasn't expected to match metal with a foe, having to wear a hot and heavy animal hide was ridiculous to Marcus, but he knew that the opinions of a young man were expected to remain unheard by the upper ranks. Nonetheless, he prepared himself properly for the instance of combat. With the assistance of Aetius, the weapons merchant, he searched for a decent sword among the streets of the smiths. Unlike many of the young men taken as aides by senior officers, he looked for quality rather than appearance. Indeed, some of the gilded and over-bejeweled arms that he saw at the side of his comrades, he doubted would survive the gutting of a stag for meat, far less in actual combat with a real foe. He had purchased a plain short sword - a gladius, the army called it - that was missing the hilt - the metal tang sticking out and unwrapped. But, the blade was old and of Spartan steel, proofed with massive blows against hard wood and rock to demonstrate the absence of internal flaws. For a craftsman such as he, the missing hilt was easily replaced. By the end of the next day, the sword sported a handsome handle of leather wrapped around the tang and perfectly fit to his hand. The blade itself was polished to a high shine with oil and sand, under a leather wrap, then carefully stroked to a sharp, but not fine edge - a result of advice from the old Hastilarius.

Important to himself, the weapon, held in a plain leather scabbard, received the approval of the Hastiliarius, Dursus. This blessing meant far more to Marcus than any accolades that might come from his fellow aides. And the old soldier gave him many practical pointers in his preparation for service, including what to wear, to take, and to leave behind. "You will find, young Marcus, that items you may consider essential for comfort will be quickly discarded on the long march. A lightly accoutered soldier is far more content than one trying to carry his household on his back. Be sure of it." At the advice of Dursus, he made a list of practical items to take, besides what he wore. An old tunic for training, along with some sturdy but less than noble sandals. A clean and neat tunic for nightly wear - "Don't wear your good habiliments on the training field - they will be rags in short order" - a spare cloak, another water flask, but flattened and empty at the moment, and several cloths for washing.

Under the leather, and also for times when the armor was not to be worn, he had a tunic, thickly woven for protection from chafing. Finally, attached to the armor at the shoulders was a woolen pallium -

a cloak - that trailed down his backside - to him, it was another effete garment with no actual use. The time would come when he was grateful for the hindering drape when he discovered that it made a welcome blanket for cold nights in the field.

As the diurnal equinox approached, Marcus dressed in his martial best, along with a water skin and his loculus, the leather satchel for personal items. Other than a spare tunic and cloak, he had little to carry, but still, Clerma and Didi insisted on packing the bag to its capacity with cheeses, dried meats and other staples that would travel well. Since he was, or would be part of the headquarters, he had no need to carry his share of a tent, a digging tool or eating gear. The farewells were tearful from the women, despite his amused insistence that he was off to a training camp, not to war. The men, for their part, gave him sincere parting words that made Marcus realize that, indeed, he was part of the family.

With one last wave, he walked through the gate toward the household of Junius. There, he was welcomed by the Domina and offered wine while waiting for Lucius. In a while, his new superior walked into the atrium, accompanied by a man that had to be the Dominus Titus - the first time that Marcus had seen the patron of the house. Spotting the young man waiting in the atrium, the father walked up to him and stopped, looking up and down. Apparently, he approved of what he saw. "So... You are the man who gave service to my son at need. I have heard much of your character, and I wished to see if the vision of my eyes matched the tales of my ears."

The tone was jesting, but it was good-natured, the man having a contented expression on his face. "Marcus, it is?" At the young man's nod, he continued. "Then, good Marcus. I charge you to keep my son from damage in his usual sportive antics. Remind him, on occasion, that he is now a man with a responsibility to both Rome and the family."

Marcus had no idea how to respond to that, other than with a respectful, "Aye, Dominus."

He stood by as the family gave their farewells, both the Domina and his sister failing to hold their eye water. Marcus was well accoutered, with spotless garb and leather torso armor and sandals that shown with polish, but Lucius was resplendent in his habiliments - an entire village could have been fed for a season on the cost of his uniform and accouterments. Finally, with the family and the servants standing at the door - Marcus was astounded at the population of the house and the number of menials that were apparently required - both set their feet on the long walk to the training field on the far side of the city.

"One would think that we had been condemned to a mission of sacrifice," said Lucius, as soon as they were out of hearing of the house. "My apologies for the lamentations the women. Usually, they are in control of themselves."

"Nay, Sos. I experienced the same as I gave my farewells. Indeed, I was fearful that the day would be gone before I could make my departure."

As they walked, Lucius looked with approval at the garb of his aide. "A blade, dagger, bow and double quiver - do you plan to make war so soon, and as an army of one?" He was jesting of course, and Marcus just grinned. But he did give the impression of a well-endowed young man - Lucius knew that the young man was far from a destitute waif, but the fineness of his habiliments was... unexpected. It had been unexpected by Marcus, as well.

He had given his leave of the Sabina and her mother on the last eve, wearing his full military vestiture. It would have been less than natural had he not taken enjoyment from displaying his new status to the women of the house. In fact, the display was on the insistence of Sabina, the evening before, having asked him to wear it when he returned. Before he left, he was shown the reason.

Marcus had removed all but his tunic, for comfort, after the admiring inspection by the women. Her mother took the cloak, saying, "Let me look at your robe for loose threads, or suchlike, Marcus." He gave it no thought, turning to Sabina and following her into the little street side room.

For the afternoon, while the mother was busy with her weaving, or other cloth work, both sat and talked. The girl leaned against him as she polished and over-polished his torso leather across her lap, and then the brass fittings on his beiteus - the military belt to hold his pugio and waterbag and such - until they shone as if made of gold. He was very aware of her presence - her stola was wrapped with less stringency than usual, gaping open somewhat on occasion as she leaned this way and that. The upper parts of her mounds and the valley between them were very evident to his eyes, looking down past her face into the neck opening. He was thankful for the thickness of the military tunic which allowed him to hide his involuntary response to the vision of paradise.

The truth be known, the girl was fully cognizant of what she was doing and what was being affected. It was her present to a man about to leave for a military mission - a vision, as it were, to speed his return.

Eventually, the day was over, but the last surprise was not yet given. The girl gave unnecessary help as he girded his uniform and he was surprised when she folded his gray woolen cloak and set it on the table. Wondering at the broad smile on her face, he saw her mother enter with a fold of thick red cloth in her hands.

"This is our present for your new position of authority, Marcus," said Sabina. He watched in disbelief as the older woman held up and shook out a pallium - a cloak of such fineness as to leave him speechless. This one was dyed a dark red, lapped and fully bordered on all edges with yellow cord, and gathered at the top to fall in slight folds, unlike his plain off-white woolen cloak that just hung as a plain vestment. No noble officer, however high his rank, could have had a pallium that was superior to the what the woman was holding. Now he realized the reason for the mother to have taken the cloth when he arrived. She had used it to measure and fit the new cloak, and sewing the holes that were placed over the studs of his armor to allow it to hang.

The older woman walked behind him, then attached it by the stud-holes on his shoulders, then stood as he looked back, pulling the cloth aside to examine its fineness. Trying to find words to express his feelings, he said, "I almost fear to wear something of this elegance among such rough company as I will join." Covering his feelings with a jape, he said, "I will be mistaken for a noble officer, newly come to the army."

With sadness on his part and tears on the young woman's face - and hidden water in the mother's eyes - he had departed for his household to make ready for the morrow.

It was a long walk, but enjoyable. The citizens that were encountered stood aside to let them pass, but in respect rather than fear. All knew that soldiers and the army were all that were between them and pillage by the waiting bands and other cities all across the land and many of the men that they passed had been under arms in the past. The day being unseasonably warm, they stopped at an open air kiosk for a light repast and drink. The vendor refused to take coin from the two men until they insisted on giving payment. By midday they had come to the gate in the far eastern wall and in the distance, between the waters toward the mountains and the near grain fields, they could see the stockade of the officers camp. Shortly, they were being saluted by the Optio at the entrance, and being asked for their names.

"Tribune elect Lucius of the house of Junius and his Adiutor, Marcus of the house of Pythes."

Taking a wax tablet from a small table, then another, the man saluted again and said, "Salve, Tribune. You are expected." Turning, he shouted to a soldier standing behind him - one of three. "Legionary! Escort the Tribune to the Centurion of the Legion."

Marcus reviewed what he had learned from Dursus. The Roman army, since King Tullius had taken the Throne, had begun to take the shape by which it would be known for almost two millennia. Legion, now meant the entire army rather than the later use for large divisions within it, but he knew that a Centurion was the highest rank of an officer that was not of noble birth. To be the Centurion of the Legion meant that he was the highest of even those. Under him would be secondary Centurions, commanding around sixty men each, all assisted by their own Optio, the second rank down. Below those were a plethora of ranks and specialties far too numerous for his memory as yet.

At the top of the heap was the Legate, sometimes called the Dux, a noble in charge of the entire army, and under him the Tribunes, each with their Centurions in command of their responsible unit. Marcus was still somewhat dazed at the level in which he, a barely fledged man, was beginning his life.

During the walk to the camp, Lucius and Marcus had been more like boyhood fellows, their talk being a give and take between equals. Now, within the confines of the camp, Marcus was careful to match his step to his new Commander, following behind and to the side of the off-hand. Carefully, and without being apparent, he looked around. Unlike the camp in which he had trained under Dursus, being only a sandy field with a few permanent structures, this one had brick buildings and cobblestone paths and far more of everything. It also had a man-height stone wall circling it, rather than the palisade of wooden posts at the other.

But, like the far camp, this one had few soldiers in evidence. None in fact - Marcus finally decided that he was seeing working slaves in the distance, rather than men of the army. The main headquarters was evident - a stately building not much smaller than the house of Pythes, but they were apparently headed to another, set against the wall and some distance away. It was evident that the exercise that he and Lucius were about to enter was for the routine induction of future officers, rather than any preparation for war.

At the front of the building, again made of brick rather than wood, they stopped as their escort announced them to the guard at the door.   In turn, he disappeared inside for a few heartbeats then returned to his post beside the door.   Shortly, a soldier appeared, looked at the newcomers, then strode forward to stop in front of them.

In theory, Marcus was immune to orders from any officer besides his own, not including, of course, superiors to the Tribune-Elect.   He had already decided, in an instant of time, never to incur the wrath of the soldier standing before him.   The man was obviously the senior Centurion of the Legion.   He was massive.   And old - probably having seen more years than the two young men together. Marcus had seen many large and fat men in the city, but they were merchants, enjoying a life of food and drink, but this one had no indication of an indolent life feasting on his body.   He had no doubt that the man could pick up both of the young men - with one hand each - and toss them across the parade ground.

But, aside from his god-given bulk, the soldier radiated authority.   His helmet was gold trimmed, with the red brush reaching from side to side, rather than from front and back as in most others. His leather armor was dyed red and gold studded, polished to a shine that reflected the sun like a bright oil-lamp flame.   Lucius, as a member of one of the most powerful Patrician houses in Rome, was of a social position far above this old soldier, but even he, Marcus suspected, would take the words of this veteran as a tablet-writ from Olympus.   That evening, as he thought about the encounter, he realized that only a man supremely confident in himself, and one with uncommon ability, could have possibly risen to that exalted rank from a lowly pleb.

The Centurion looked over the two young men for a heartbeat or so, without giving any indication that he was impressed in any way by the sight, then said in his gruff voice, "Welcome, Tribune-Elect. The Legate is not in residence at the moment, but he will receive you after his return.   For now, you may settle into your quarters until the evening gong for assembly."   Turning to the escort, he said, "Take the Tribune-Elect to his quarters."   Without waiting for a salute or reply, he spun on a heel and disappeared back into the building.

"This way, Tribune," said the Legionary.   "Several of your comrades have already settled in."   Following the man to a moderately sized structure - this one of wood - he stood aside as Lucius walked through the open door, followed by Marcus.   Inside was a... well, it was just a long room with sleeping platforms down both sides, separated by tables - no two which were alike.   Dividing the room in half was a partial wall, through which could be seen more of the same.

At one end, was a long table, lengthwise as to the building, and at it sat four men, all young nobles, from the quality of their garb.

The group noticed the newcomers, and rose, one saying, "By Mars and his stash of secret whores, the fair Junius has been suborned." Marcus recognized two of the men as being close friends to his Commander, the young nobles Publius Publicola and Lucius Collatinus, He remembered the names from that day - and others - when he had taken Lucius home in the cart. "Salve, and welcome to the halls of glory and fame."

Lucius snorted, then said, "If your presence was accepted, Collatinus, then I would say that the King is planning no action against more than a rebellious brothel."

Both greeted each other with arm grasps and shoulder slaps as Lucius continued, "And Publicola, and you, Varinius - your families decided to send their wayward sons to war, also."

It wasn't a question, and one of the young men answered with a grin, "In my case it was for glory, but, sad to relate, for Varinius here, it was because of far too many slave girls of his house being incapacitated with fat bellies."

Lucius pointed to the fourth youngster. "And who might this be?"

The young man bowed, and answered, "Keteus, of the family Mikkos, in Capua."

The man, Collatinus, pointed and said, "Our resident Greek, although he insists that his family is Mycenaean. We have told him that his claimed lineage disappeared before the dawn ages, but he insists." The tone was a jape, and all laughed.

Lucius turned to give an order to the escorting soldier then saw that the man had disappeared. To the others, he said, "This is Marcus, my aide. Where does he barrack?"

Now, the other young man, Varinius, pointed to the other end of the building. "Through there, with the others. And, Marcus, I can tell you that your quarters are as exquisite as ours."

Without words, Marcus saluted, then turned and walked down the bare wooden floor to the opening in the middle of the building. Inside was a single man, very young, lying on the mat of a sleeping platform. The lad rose and stood, waiting until the newcomer stopped before his area. "My name is Marcus, Adiutor to Lucius Junius."

Nodding, the lad said, "Maxentius. The same to Lucius Collatinus." He waved his hand, then continued, "Pick a mat that has an empty table, and drop your gear." Marcus nodded, then dropped his belt and loculus in the next sleeping area. Carefully, he set the bow and quivers in a corner, then pulled his gladius to inspect it, then resheathed it, confident that it still had a thin film of oil protecting the metal.

Settling onto what would be his bed, he asked, "Is it just us for this big room?"

The young man - Maxentius - said, "I do not know. We only arrived a short while before. I have seen no one else." He bent over to look out the doorway at the young nobles at the far end, now all seated at their table. "The other Tribunes would have aides, I assume, but they have not arrived, nor is there any baggage elsewhere that I can see." The room - just this half of the building - would hold forty men. Empty, it was another indication that the King was not expecting a war.

Both sat down on their mats and began to become acquainted. Each gave a short spiel on their lives, Marcus keeping his tale simple, just mentioning that he was a ward in a merchant's house. Maxentius was the son of a loyal servant family in the Collatinus household and recently was given the chance to become the Adiutor to the son of his master. In a while, they were on warily friendly terms and in the start of a possible friendship.

That afternoon, halfway to sundown, they heard a sound of tramping feet, and looking out an uncovered window, saw a formation of soldiers marching into the compound. There were forty or fifty men and two officers - the red brushes on their helmets quickly marking them as the leaders. In the front rank of four, Marcus could see a man holding the standard, a pole with an emblem at the top, and three others carrying... he couldn't tell, except that the items glinted in the afternoon sun. All the rest were carrying either long spears or the shorter javelins known as pilae, along with shields of various types.

Unlike the army of later Rome, the units in the time of Marcus were equipped as were the forces around most of the central sea, the Etruscans of Latium, the Greeks and far across the sea, the Egyptians. Swords were certainly in evidence, but few smiths could forge a long blade that would stand up in fierce combat. Imperfections and internal flaws gave weaknesses to the metal that would have fatal consequences in battle if the weapon were to strike against a hard object, such as another blade, or even the armor of a foe. A spear, with a thick wooden shaft and a flat point, was unlikely to fail, and, even if the metal blade became detached, the wielder still had a sturdy staff to defend himself until he could retreat to find a replacement. But a sword that shivered left the wielder holding a useless stub and at the mercy of his opponent.

Certainly, good blades were to be found, as in the Spartan weapon carried by himself, but the cost was such that few ordinary soldiers could hope to purchase one. The fearsome short sword - the gladius, with which Roman armies would decimate the obsolescent spear formations of their foe, would not appear in quantity for many years to come.

"Interesting," said Maxentius, as they watched. "I would assume that they are part of the training for our masters."

Suddenly, they saw the Senior Centurion striding across the ground toward the formation, which stopped at a shouted order, then turned to face the main building. At another shout, all weapons were grounded, then straight armed forward in what had to be a salute. A murmur was all that came from the officer, but shortly, the men broke apart the formation and began to move across the compound toward what Marcus assumed was their barracks.

The Centurion turned and strode rapidly toward their building, then disappeared from view through the window. Both young men stood back to watch him enter the doorway and issue a command to the new Tribunes, who had been watching the formation also.

"Legatus Tertius will receive you at the ninth hour. Might I suggest that you young gentlemen use the time to arrange yourselves. The Legate has been known to put even high-born officers on fatigue watch. I will return for you just before that time." With that, he turned and left, leaving the five young nobles agitated and wondering.

The man called Varinius looked out the window, apparently at the sun-clock, then said, "We have the last part of an hour left."

"Marcus! Assist me." The call from Lucius brought both aides hurrying into the room. His Commander's luggage had not yet been unpacked, so he opened the leather bag and found the washing cloth, which he carried to the water pitcher on a shelf. Wetting it, by pouring water from the jug, he began to wipe the dust from the armor - also sitting on the bed - then the helmet and belt, then knelt to clean the sandals and straps. He lifted the armor, then lowered it over the head of Lucius, and began to lace up the sides. The cloak was shaken out, then attached to the shoulder studs, and finally, the helmet was donned.

As Lucius stood at attention, Marcus walked around him, examining and adjusting this strap and that fold, deciding that the sword scabbard was less than desired. Removing it, he scrubbed the leather till it shone again, replaced it, then finally stopped in front of the Commander and nodded. He had seen Maxentius doing the same

for the other Lucius - Collatinus - but the other three officers were
assisting each other.   Catching the eye of Marcus, Lucius slightly
inclined his head toward the three.

Nodding, Marcus walked to the other officers and said, "Might
I be of service, Sos?" Gratefully, they accepted his help - and that of
Max - and shortly, all five were ready for their appearance - hopefully.

"My thanks, Marcus." This from Varinius. "If my man arrives
while I am away, would you show him to your quarters?"

"Aye, Sos." He bent backward slightly to look out the window,
then said, "The Centurion approaches."   That instantly made all stand
to attention, waiting, as the massive officer strode through the door.
Marcus wondered if the man ever walked anywhere at a leisure pace.

"Follow me, Tribunes.   When we enter the presence, form a
line to where I indicate, then stand to attention until further ordered."
Without waiting for an answer, he turned, and the five scrambled to
follow.

It was a long meeting - the clock was past the tenth hour and
they were still not back.   They waited and talked, watching various
groups of men walk here and yon around the compound.   Finally,
another man, unarmored but still apparently an officer, stepped in to
look.   Seeing the pair, he said, "Heard ye not the dinner gong? If ye
wish to eat, then move your carcasses to the mess tent, and hurry."

"Aye, Sos," replied Maxentius.   "Might we inquire which
building that might be?"

The man pointed. "There. With the smoke from the roof. If
Canto - the cook - claims you are tardy, tell him that Optio Sextus said
to issue your rations."   Since the officer was in garrison garb, they did
not stop to put on their armor and formal attire, but just hurried across
the compound, hopefully to a welcome meal.

Inside of what was called the mess tent, although it was a
wooden building, they walked to where the rations were being doled
out to the last few men.   There was no complaint on the part of the
cook, or the serving man, whichever he was, and they each took a bowl
of meat soup and generous slices of cheese and bread.   The building
had few men inside, so most must have carried their repast outside to
their barracks.   Marcus nodded to a table with only four men, and
they sat at one end, across from each other.

Being uneasy in the unfamiliar circumstances, they refrained
from talk - just listening to the snatches of conversation around the
room.   But the food, while plain, was filling and good, and both young
men realized just how hungry they had gotten since the midday meal.

Suddenly, from down the table came a hail, "What be your unit, boy? We have not seen you before."

It was apparently one of the men that they had seen marching into the compound, earlier. Minus the spear and armor, of course. He - they were wearing about what both of the young men were garbed in, except that the usual tunic was just rough homespun, like the one Dursus had advised that he take for rough training. Marcus had no idea how to answer the hail. He had little knowledge of what was before him, and certainly none of what unit the Tribune would be commanding. But, as the question was gruff, but not unfriendly, he just grinned and replied, "We are just arrived and have yet to receive an assignment."

Maxentius spoke up. "Our officers were called to the Legate, and probably to receive their places."

One of the other men asked, "Officers? New tiros are assigned to a Hastilarius for their first learnings. What officers do you speak of?"

Marcus replied, "Lucius Junius is my warden. Lucius of the house of Collatinus is his." He pointed his thumb to his comrade. "We are Adiutorae to both."

Both were utterly stunned by the reaction to his words. The four men looked at each other, disbelieving, then all four jumped to their feet, and at attention. The first man that had spoken stammered out a reply, "Our deepest apologies, Sos! We did not know. If we have given offense, then know that it was from lack of knowledge."

Maxentius broke out of his consternation first, and said, "Nay, nay! We are without assignment as yet and have no authority. Please, be at your ease and do not misconstrue our importance."

Marcus finally found his voice. "Aye. As he said. We are just two hungry men seeking to fill our bellies and without ceremony." Apparently relieved, the men went back to eating, but the attitude at the table had changed. Their voices were lowered to such that neither young man could hear the talk. They hurriedly finished, then left before they could fall into some other unfamiliar situation.

It was nightfall before the Tribunes returned, Lucius asking if the two men had eaten. Receiving the affirmative, he said, "We will rise at the break of day, and in full uniform. I suggest that you not wear your best tunic and cloak."

Martial Proof

The day started with the morning meal, then, the morning parade with the soldiers that had been observed marching into the compound after the arrival of Lucius and Marcus. The two young men understood that this was a new levy of potential lower rank officers, rather than just a group of farmers and merchants being turned into Miles - the name for new and untrained soldiers. These men were not doing mandatory training - rather, they had volunteered for the service in the hope of becoming more than a common soldier.

Still, to the Centurions, and especially the Senior, they were not yet soldiers, and by all indications of the Hastilarae, were to be ranked with the scum of the city, worthless and unlikely to be of use in any conflict. Many were the times that Marcus saw an officer lift his hands toward the heavens, asking for mercy for whatever sin had been committed to causing the gods to inflict such punishment on himself. The air itself rang with the curses after this march or that maneuver had failed to come up to expectations. The five Tribune-Elects were not immune from the loud and profane criticism, although the correction did not reach the depths of that given to the Plebeian soldiers. While a grizzled Hastilarius would freeze the air around a young noble after a perceived failure, he would never actually strike one with his baton.

Interestingly, the aides were as invisible as wraiths to the training officers. They stood by to assist their Commanders - another had arrived during the night, the Adiutor to Publicola - and the other two early the next morning, but no one gave them orders other than their own leaders. All spent their time doing very little for the first days, but later, they would be handling messages, maps and suchlike.

For the morning, the Tribunes would be on the field, doing exercises with the other men, running here and there to the orders of the officers. Split into five groups, and each assigned to a young noble, the soldiers would each be commanded to perform this maneuver, or that one, by their young Commander. After the noon meal, the Tribunes would gather for instruction while their men usually left the compound for some exercise or another.

The five aides would stand by, watching, fully accoutered and waiting for any assistance needed by their Commander, During the sessions in which a weapons master attempted to impart some knowledge of the sword, Marcus could hardly believe that these young nobles were to command an actual unit of soldiers, someday. Only the Tribune Varinius, seemed to have any skill at all with the blade.

Junius and his friend Collatinus were, at best, indifferent with the weapons, but the other two, Publicola and the man from Capua, Keteus, were as young wives desperately swinging a broomstick at a rodent in the pantry. Indeed, the later two had more bruises from their own wooden swords than from that of their foe - far more, in fact, since the weapons master was just that, a master whose strokes went only as far as he commanded and exactly to the point of aim.

After Marcus had made a few comments about their shortcomings - in a low voice, beyond any hearing by either the Hastilarius or his students - Maxentius asked, "You have had instruction with the sword?"

"Aye. My principal engaged a veteran in teaching me the use of the blade for most of a year, but only with a session every few days." That afternoon, as the Tribunes were at their general meeting in the administration building, Marcus brought two of the wooden swords into the barracks. Giving one to Maxentius, he began to show a few rudiments of swordplay, as the others watched. He was no fell swordsman, to stand in toe-to-toe battle with some barbarian, but the skills of the other four aides were as children to his.

That evening, after the meal and in the quiet time before sleep, Marcus asked to see the weapon of his friend. As he suspected, it was a toy, made for salutes in a parade or to prance around a court. It would not survive the first stroke against another weapon or a shield. Naturally, he was asked to show his in return.

All watched as he pulled the shining blade from the scabbard. No gilded toy this, made to impress the women or to indicate the status of the holder. The blade, glistening from the light coat of oil, and the practical and serviceable hilt gave notice that this was a weapon for use in battle. He pointed to a line of tiny Greek letters stamped into the blade just at the tang. "I do not read the language, but my friends among the smiths of the Caelius quarter tell me that they indicate the ancestry and the testing."

The aide of Keteus - for whatever reason, this one noble was called by his given, rather than family name - said, "I can read it." Looking closely at the blade, as Max held it up, he continued, "The first symbol is for the city of Sparta." Marcus nodded. "Then a name - Kreon."

"The name of the Smith, apparently," said Max.

Continuing, the aide read, "The number ten, and..." He shook his head. "The letters nu, tau, and phi. What do those mean?"

Marcus took his weapon and resheathed it. "I am told that it is proof markings, and that the blade has survived ten strokes each, against a wooden log, a shield of metal and then stone." He set it on the shelf beside his bed. "You know of this place called Sparta?"

The young lad nodded. "Aye. A famous Greek city known for its ability in war. It is said that boy-children are raised from birth to be warriors and any that fail to measure up are killed. Many are the tales that I heard of Spartan heroes in this war or that." He grinned. "Some might even have the mantle of truth, but I fear that my tutor had no scruples about making a good story even better."

A full month went by, as the Tribunes molded their skills into some semblance of the martial arts by maneuvering their individual units of about ten soldiers in this charge, or that envelopment. On occasion, the entire unit of men would be assigned to a single Tribune to lead, in the tactics of the battlefield. In the main, all but Publicola and to a lesser extent, Keteus were, at least, satisfactory in their learning. But, Marcus, watching the latter two in their orders and decisions, prayed to the unknown gods of Rome that the city would never have its fate depending on the skills of the pair. He firmly agreed with the one of the lesser Hastilarae, overhearing that worthy speaking in a low voice to his fellow and saying, "Neither of them could assault a brothel in the Oppius and have a chance of returning with their ballstones still swinging between their legs."

The aides learned much also, but not with direct teaching. Rather, they stood with their respective Tribunes as the Centurions gave their experience, For the first week, the noble officers would meet alone in the administration building, but after, the Adiutorae were as shadows to their superiors, with only a few exceptions. It was one of those afternoons when the Legatus had called for the Tribunes without escort, that gave a seasoning to their training.

Behind the barracks was a large square of sand, its use unknown, but it made an ideal location for Marcus to fend with his fellows, giving some semblance of sword knowledge, as he had gained from the old Hastilarius. In the main, it was private from other eyes, and more importantly, any japes from passersby. Marcus was engaging with Albanus, the aide to Publicola. "Nay! Do not swing wide. Remember that either your shield or your sword is between you and your foe at all times."

Backing up, the young man came at Marcus again, but now in the proper form, the wooden sticks clacking as he searched for the opening for the tip of his weapon. They moved back and forth, then came the lunge for the kill. He could have easily parried the thrust, but Marcus let the point touch his armor, then backed up with a grin. "Better! But do not over-thrust. While the mark would be dead on his feet, you are leaning forward and out of balance and asking for his comrade to separate your head from your neck."

The young man - also with a grin - lifted his helmet for a moment, wiped his brow, and replied, "Again?" At the nod of his opponent, they brought their sticks up and began anew. The shields were round bucklers, light and not something that would be used by a Legionary in the front ranks, but they gave far more protection than just the upraised off-hand. Again came the clash of sticks as the young man took the offensive and searched for a chink in the attention of his foe. Suddenly, Albanus backed up, eyes wide and mouth open, causing Marcus to fear that he had touched his comrade in a sensitive place and with unintended force. But before he could gather his own surprise, and ask the reason, the aide shouted, "Attention for the Senior Centurion."

His four comrades stood for a heartbeat, then spun on their heels to see the massive bulk of the officer standing behind them. Instantly, they froze at attention, wondering at what doom might have befallen themselves. The man looked them over for a moment, then moved to stand in front of Marcus.

"You are the Adiutor to Lucius Junius. What is your name?"

"Marcus, of the house of Pythes, Senior Centurion!"

"And you are attempting to teach your fellows the blade? Where did one so young come to such knowledge of the sword that you presume to have the measure of skill to pass it on?"

With some relief that apparently, the doom wasn't happening, he replied in a lesser volume, "My principal hired a soldier to give me the rudiments of defense, Sos. One Dursus, veteran of twenty years, Sos."

Suddenly, he saw the officer's eyes shift and widen, and he knew that somehow he had struck a... a memory?

In a much quieter tone - far less than they had ever heard before - the Centurion asked, "How long were you in his teaching?"

"About a year Sos, every third day for the morning-time."

"I was watching for a while. You have more than the rudiments of skill. Apparently, you did not entirely waste the time of that veteran." Looking at the other aides, still stiffly standing and moving only to blink, he continued, "It impresses me to see minor officers spending their time in improving their skills, rather than hunching over the play of bones in the corner of the barracks. I will inform the Legatus of such." Turning back to Marcus, he said, "You were blessed by the gods to have such a man as Centurion Dursus as a preparator." He stepped back - the inspection apparently at an end, then suddenly spoke to Marcus, "This is not an order, but if you will, when you next see Dursus, give him the greetings of Senior Centurion Tatius to an old comrade."

"Aye, Senior Centurion. It will be my pleasure to do so." With that, the officer turned and strode off out of sight around the building.

The five young men relaxed, relieved that the encounter had been without casualty, but with Marcus still thinking on the interchange. He had assumed that Dursus had been a good soldier, learning enough during his many years of service to be assigned to train new men. But a Centurion? An officer, as high as a Plebeian could rise in the fighting ranks? He now wondered at the fee that Pythes had paid to contract the service of such a high rank. Even now...

"Are you coming, Marcus? That was the gong for the evening mess."

"Aye... Aye... I was just..." Time enough later, in the unit bath, to discuss the encounter.

As they approached the end of the three-month training, the five officers, and their aides were called into the presence of the Legatus - the first time that Marcus had seen the great man at a close distance. Also in attendance, were the Centurions of the encampment, five in all, and the Senior. The reason, was for the final instruction on a long distance march, through hostile territory - at least, hostile in the putative sense.

The august presence of the Legatus was again present for only a short speech, after which he left on his carrying chair. Once again, Marcus wondered at the presence of the high noble general in a camp that was almost deserted during peacetime. He was seldom seen in the compound, and what task he performed inside the brick administration building was a mystery to the aides. Of course, through all of history, ordinary soldiers had the same wonders and the same lack of knowledge of their superiors.

The Senior Centurion was giving final instructions. "...after you decide on your route, you may leave at any time between the rise of the moon and the breakfast gong. It is up to you. No unit may leave sooner than one hour after the previous. It will be three days good march to your destination - five if you choose your route badly. Water you will find en route, but you must monitor the use of rations carefully. Your men are volunteers, superior to inducted farmers and merchants, but still, they will want to eat when their bellies demand it.

If you do not watch the allocation of their fare, you will stumble into the camp with a cohort of starving wretches."

Marcus grinned inwardly at the units being given the status of massive numbers. Usually, a cohort was a fighting unit of six centuries of sixty to eighty men each - or about half a thousand soldiers. Since the men in the camp would be split between the five Tribunes, then each "cohort" would be about ten or twelve men. The actual numbers made little difference to the training maneuver - his thought was that both Tribune Publicola and Tribune Keteus would almost certainly get lost with their units - whether ten men or an entire Legion.

"...The two Contubernae of the quester units will not be allowed to leave until the midday hour plus one, giving you a long start ahead of them." Marcus knew that a Contubernium was the smallest unit in the army, with seven men and the lowest ranking officer - a Decanus. "But I warn you that both units are veterans and the Decanuae leading them have more experience than any in this camp. They are tough, march fast and can live on what would make your men fall out and lie down to die. They will attempt to assail you on your march or to enter your night-camp undetected, to cut throats - or to show that it would have happened." He stopped to let the words sink in, then began again. "If they succeed - and they almost always do, then your unit - and you - will march back to the compound in disgrace without your weapons, to show your failure to all." He paused for a few moments to allow the information to be assimilated. "In addition, another Contubernium will be ranging out of the remote encampment looking for you. So, be aware that even if you outmarch the pursuers from here, you will still have another to avoid."

Into the night, Lucius and his assigned Centurion pored over the large parchment map of the region hanging on the wall inside the administration building. The three would gather in a corner of the room for discussion, on occasion walking back to inspect the map, or to point out a feature by the light of the huge oil lamp. In other parts of the room there were four other groups of three - the other Tribunes and their assigned Centurions doing the same thing. Marcus did not envy the task of the two officers assigned to the two inept young nobles. Between himself and his growing friendship with Max, was the quiet agreement that the junior Centurion's opinion about those two inept Tribunes assaulting a brothel greatly overvalued their abilities.

The camp officer would not be coming on the trek - none of the officers were, the intention of the exercise to determine the skills of the new Tribunes without the advice of a veteran soldier. They would give advice to their assigned Tribune, but when each unit moved out, they would be on their own. For his part, Marcus just listened and absorbed the plan that was being constructed. Except for one occasion...

"Sos, if I may speak?"

Lucius, naturally somewhat apprehensive about the coming trial, barked, "Of course. You may speak anytime you have something that needs to be said!"

Marcus pointed to the map, and the three walked over to it. "Sos, I have hunted as far as this area, from here..." Another finger point. "...to here, and I can say that these bottoms are not walkable at speed. This is a marsh, waist deep overall, and beyond it are thickets that would hinder a herd of aurochs."

Lucius nodded, and said, "And your suggestion?"

"This ridgeback... here ...is rock and stone, but firm and sparsely brushed. The effort on the legs from the inclines would be less than that expended in the swamp fighting sucking mud and insects. These water lands are about..." Marcus had to think for a moment. He was just becoming familiar with the Roman measures of distance, but he still could not easily visualize the units. "...Three stadia across to firm land." A stadium was equivalent to about six hundred human foot lengths. He had discovered that the length of the street of the Poets was about a stadium and used that to visualize across a distance.

Both officers looked for a moment then they moved back to their corner. The Centurion said to the Tribune, "Your man seems to have uses beyond handling your cloak and writing tablet." Looking at Marcus, he said, "You are familiar with the area? How?"

"I grew up in a hunting village. When I came to Rome, I supplemented my purse with meat taken from the forests around the city."

Lucius nodded as he looked at the Centurion. "Aye, and in fact, his hunting is the reason that he is in my service." He pointed across the room to the map. "And beyond that area?"

"Nay, Sos. I have not ventured beyond that point, but if I may give my experience in the woods - water in the lowlands means brush and thickets. Higher up, some watercourses make fairly good trails."

More talk went on by oil lamp into the night, until the final advice of the Centurion. "Have your men wrap any metal in cloth, so as not to clink on the trail. And they must keep their chatter down. Remember that the Decanus is of the unit trying to find you knows that this is a training mission, and there is no danger to his unit in any way. So he - they - will probably break their men up into smaller details - maybe even of one - so as to cover more of the roads. You must move quickly the first day and try to outrange them."

Lucius nodded as the man finished. "And at night, make sure your guards are posted at distance and without a sentry-go. In a normal encampment, you would have them walking the watch, but movement attracts the eye, and for a sentry at night, his ears are his weapons. He will hear an approacher long before that man will see your guard."

The next day was one of rest for all. The men were allowed to enter the city for the day, to return before nightfall. Unlike this one, most training camps for the army were a considerable distance from the city, to prevent the craving for home - or women - from being consummated. However, all of the Plebeians in the common unit were here of their own accord, hoping to win a position as a minor officer when next the army formed. All were told not to go beyond the Oppius quarter, but as long as the man returned before darkfall, no one would question his day.

Marcus was tempted to make the long walk to the Viminalis quarter. His craving to see Sabina again was very strong, but he realized that the walk would be long and hot, and would be less than a rest for the following day and the mission. Instead, he accompanied his fellows into the near quarter to the baths. They were nothing like the Apollinian Waters in the Palatium quarter, but the thermae was far more elegant than the single pool in the training compound. One of the Centurions had warned them of the less than honest watch-slaves in the apodyterium, the disrobing room, so all took nothing but their work tunics and only coin for the baths and a measure of food and drink.

That evening, Lucius called him to take a walk around the compound. For a while, they talked about the discussions with their assigned Centurion, but that soon tailed off. Marcus knew that something was taking the attention of the Tribune. Finally, the noble lad stopped, turned toward his aide and asked, "Do you think that you could guide us to the outpost through the mountains? Without traveling up the Jupiter Latiaris road that leads to the post from the city of Lavinium?"

Utterly surprised, Marcus hesitated a moment, thinking on the question to make sure he understood it correctly. The route that the Tribune and Centurion had plotted was on this road, or that one, of necessity. Few, if any of the soldiers, and certainly none of the officers had any experience in the wilderness. Even those that had traveled far had walked on the well-maintained roads that connected the entire peninsula of Latium. Should they enter the vast wilderness that spanned from the lowlands to the foothills, and from north to south, a city man would be as lost as a village boy suddenly finding himself in the Forum.

Finally, he replied, "I can point us in the correct direction - that I am sure, but I have no knowledge of what is beyond what I have actually hunted. There could be large rivers or mountains that would bar our progress." He hesitated, then added, "You wish to avoid the roads and trails, apparently."

The Tribune looked over at the barracks in the darkening evening. "The quester units will use only the roads. Speed will be their watchword and neither Decanus will flounder around in the brush for no reason. Nor will the one looking for us at the end of journey. Besides a few farmers, you are the only man on the post with a knowledge of the land outside the city."

Slaves were not allowed on the post - a rule that would be greatly modified as Rome grew in the future - so one of the men on light duty was designated as the waterclock watcher for the night. At the third hour beyond the middle of night, Marcus woke instantly as the man touched his shoulder. "It is time, Sos."

Marcus leapt out of his bed and began to gird himself in the dim light of the half moon filtering in the window. This would be a march with full equipment, as if to a real war. His gladius and pugio would travel with him as a matter of course, but also would his best bow, and a quiver. The weight was little and it would find no use for this exercise, but he would feel nothing but unease should he venture into the wilds without his lifelong weapon. Never had he entered the forests - anywhere - without a bow. He had made a leather scabbard for the weapon, to keep the morning dew and any rainfall from impairing the wood and string.

Shortly, he strode into the Tribune's half of the building to find Lucius already accoutered and ready, needing no assistance from his aide this night. Their march bags already filled the day before, they hoisted them to a shoulder and moved quickly across the compound to where their "cohort" was assembled. Unlike the work-averse attitude of the usual levy of common soldiers, these men knew that a good performance by the Tribune would greatly help them in their desire to obtain a commission afterward and would do their best to perform their duty.

Lucius stood before the eleven men and said, "We will move with all haste for the first day. Our feet need to put much ground behind them before the sun tops the sky." With that, they moved at a steady pace toward the gate, then turned toward the direction from which the sun would rise in about three hours. The waning moon gave sufficient light, and more, as they strode down the dirt road pointing toward the mountains.

This time of night, the road - not much more than a wide trail - was naturally devoid of travelers. They passed not even one encamped for the night, since this road led only to minor villages and farms and would eventually turn into an actual trail and just a path through the hills. Before they would reach the end, their feet would strike off to the south and over the untamed wilderness, their actual destination being a very remote encampment at the very foot of the southern mountains.

The sun began to show its rays over the eastern hills and Lucius called a stop for a rest and a short meal, both he and Marcus warning the men again to eat only one ration. Water was not a problem - they had already passed many flowing streams. While they sat, Marcus carefully unfolded the parchment that he carried in his pack. He had known of the concept of a map from his earliest age, although any that he had used had been made with a charred coal on the skin of the whitebark tree, or with a stick in the smoothed dirt before a hunt. Certainly, before his military service, he had never seen a drawing on the bleached skin of an animal - parchment being a method of communication for the very wealthy. The map on animal skin in the administration building would have fed a village for the winter, could it have been sold. Even Pythes sent and received his communications on wax or clay tablets.

But Marcus was impressed with the utility of the use of parchment - the small map that he and Lucius had carefully copied from the large one, with notes of this mountain and that water, was durable and could be folded to ride as a very small load in a traveling pack. And unlike the writings on the beaten and joined reeds harvested from a swamp, it was fairly proof against water and impossible to tear.

The inspection - again - was just a measure of his concern. The Tribune had rested enormous faith in the ability of Marcus to find their way through a wilderness that none of them had seen. If he failed to find the outpost, or worse yet, lost the unit to starve and stumble around the forests... He put that thought aside. Time enough to worry if it happened.

The fastest and easiest way to their destination would be to walk the vias along the coasts, then take the road inland to the outpost. The Roman and Etruscan roads were unmatched in the world, even at that early age. In fact, both of them thought that either Publicola or Keteus - or both - would do that. The pace would have to be inordinately fast to outspend a unit of hardened Legionaries, some of whom had probably moved at speed when it was a matter of living or being speared. And there was the problem of the unit waiting on the other end of the route. No doubt they would be looking for a "cohort" of city men being allowed to walk into a trap, as a spider waits for an insect.

Since time was of no consequence, the longer route through the upper hills would be far safer, although Lucius had commented on the probability of their rations only lasting a part of the way. Marcus almost commented on the absurdity of starving in a land of plenty, but held his tongue, knowing that the city man had no practical concept of living off the land. What was important was for them to leave the road. He had no doubt that the units of the opposing force had risen in the night to watch their quarry leave, and, no doubt, wonder at the sight of the unit of Junius taking a road inland, and one that did not even begin to point in the direction of their destination.

"Sos, if I may instruct the men?"

Lucius nodded, and replied, "You may give orders at your discretion. And certainly at any time on this foray."

Marcus walked to the line of relaxing men, then waited till they stood. Without preamble, he said, "At the next clear path in the forest, we will bend our walk to accommodate our destination. You..." He pointed to a man on one end of the line. "I designate you to follow to the rear until we leave the road. When I signal, thus..." Marcus raised his arm and opened his fist. "...you will carefully examine the way we have just traveled that no other eyes are watching. We want no farmer or villager to give notice of the direction we have gone." The man nodded. "Also, mark this. As we leave the way, until we are far into the forest, make care to leave no footprints in the mud or broken branches that could also give away our course." Finally, he finished with, "At every watercourse, fill your waterskins. It will become less plentiful as we climb the hills."

He nodded to Lucius, who said, "Fall in. We march."

Martial Trial

They had left the road - a broad village trail, actually - about a stadium further. Seeing a usable ridge that rose above the surrounding marshes, Marcus stopped the column and gestured to the soldier of the rear guard. That man waved a nay, and they stepped off into the brush. By midday, the column was beginning to flag, the route being mostly uphill from the point of departure from the trail. Still they made good distance, and both officers estimated that they would be far ahead of any pursuers, even should any attempt to follow.

"Hopefully, our departure into the direction of the sunrise, rather than on a via leaving the city should confound them," commented Lucius over their sparse meal of jerked meat and bread. "If the gods are with us at all, the Decanuae assumed that our action was a feint, and that we bent our course southward after we left any observation."

Marcus had just come from inspecting the area over which they had traveled, or about a hundred strides of it. He shook his head, "I hope you are correct, Sos. We have left a trail that even the son of our village chieftain could have followed and that halfwit could not track a fish flopping away from the flaying board."

Lucius smiled. "I doubt that worry is a concern. Our play-foe will try for the easiest quarry before setting off into the wilds of the hills. I suspect that poor Publius Publicola and his troop are already marching back to the compound without weapons - if, indeed, they did not set off in the wrong direction at the start." He chuckled. "Publius is a friend and a good man, but, sad to say, he could get lost in his own house. I would not be surprised, if he is still unchecked, to hear of him walking through Tarquinii and asking the way to the mountain camp."

This time, Marcus laughed. The Etruscan city of Tarquinii was to the north, and in the opposite direction of their destination. And considerably beyond the borders of the Roman kingdom in Latium.

Looking back at the men sitting in the shade - and some already napping - Lucius commented, "I fear that we have a cohort of footsore men, already. How far do you think we have come?"

Marcus thought for a moment, converting strides into the Roman foot, then into stadia, then replied, "Maybe eighty stadia - no less than seventy."

Lucius looked around. They had encamped for the midday rest in a grove of broadleaf trees, shady, and next to a clear stream trickling down the rocky hillside. "How do you find your way in this thickness? I have seen nothing but trees and sky and mountains since we left the trail."

Marcus chuckled. "Nay, Sos. The mountains are many strides...stadia towards the sunrise horizon. Even if we mounted that tall hill over there and climbed a tree, they would still probably not be in view. We will not come close to them during this travel and should we do so, your men would need the skills of the ram to traverse them."

Lucius stood and looked around. The sentry pair down the trail were not visible, being concealed in brush and with orders that one would watch and listen while the other napped. The others were relaxing, with their spears beside them - most apparently asleep but the few that were conversing were doing so in murmurs, knowing without being commanded that sounds were more likely to give their position away than being seen in the thick brush. "These are good men," he said quietly. "I will recommend Blacus and the Etruscan lad... what is his... Dulius, yes, for immediate promotion to Sesquiplicarius when we return - if we are successful."

Marcus looked over at the two men, both sitting propped up against a tree, but watching the way that they had come, their spears at hand across their folded legs. Nodding, he asked, "What will be your position, on our return, Sos?"

"As a new Tribune, you mean?" At the nod, Lucius continued. "Very little. I will have the rank and may sport the uniform at formations of the court and yearly assembly, but unless a war begins, I will still be the second son of our house. In that awesome position, I will fill out my days attending lectures at the forum school when I am not accompanying my father in his continual roaming of our farm properties. In that post, I will be much as you are now, an imitative Adiutor to my father, but without the companionship. And of course, while at home I will be listening to my mother pointing out this female and that daughter as the perfect mate for myself."

He shook his head with a wry smile. "And you, will you seek the nuptiae with the young daughter that you claim must be the child of Aphrodite?"

Abashed, Marcus replied, "Aye, Sos, if she will have me. But first I wish to establish myself as a bowsmith, if I can find a proper stall with a domicile, My little room at the house of Pythes is unlikely to impress her as a home." He hesitated, then said, "Always assuming that I have the coin to purchase such a place."

Lucius shook his head. "Money is the concern of the incompetent. If it is to be, then you will succeed. And I may be of some help in that - you have certainly helped me far beyond my worth."   He stood up, "But we are spinning silver cobwebs for the future without earning the place, yet.   It is time we were off."

Seeing the Commander rise, the men who were awake nudged their sleeping comrades.   Shortly, after retrieving the watch-pair down the trail, the column set off again.   By nightfall, the men were leg weary and were almost stumbling in their walk.   Marcus pointed to an area next to a low cliff that was open and would shield them from the cold night air that always flowed down from the higher elevations, seeking the warmer environs of the lowlands.   There was no stream here, but the waterskins of the unit were still ample.

"Sos," he said.   "A single man on that projection..." he pointed to the cliff top about three man lengths above.   "...would cover the entire slope from which any could approach.   And in this dryness, he could hear them in the brush for half a stadium."

Lucius nodded.   Turning to the men, he said, "Blacus.   Step forward."   As that man approached and stood to attention, he continued.   "I will rate you as Decanus until we return to camp. Number your men and make a watch list.   One hour each at the top of that cliff.   They will stand on watch so they can't fall asleep.   Their mission is to listen and report any noise that approaches."

The man saluted by bringing his grounded spear to his forehead, then back to a stiff arm.   "Aye, Tribune.   Do the men make a fire?"

Marcus immediately spoke up.   "Nay! Your pardon, Sos, but the nightwind is off the highlands and the smell of fire would flow down the slopes and be noticed for stadia."

"Cold jerked meat and cheese it is.   One ration."   Lucius waved in dismissal.

Marcus walked around for a while, disappearing into the woods, then returned and sat beside the officer, opening his bag and retrieving the evening meal.   "Should we have to decamp, I suggest that we go that way, Sos.   There is a valley between those hills there," he pointed,   "that fronts a ridgeback that will take us to the south. With the moon, it could be traveled at night."

Both had little worry about being followed by the pursuing units - had any tried, they had probably long given up the chase, assuming that the Tribune had been touched by the gods and was flinging his little troop into the abyss of the wilderness in his madness. From the top of the cliff, Marcus could see far down into the lowlands - they were halfway to the slopes of the mountains and far away from the cities of the coast.   A village or two might be encountered along their trek, but little else of human origin.

The second day was as the first, a long walk at a steady pace until sundown.   This night they encamped beside a stream and in a slight depression that would shield them from observation from unlikely eyes.   The land was higher and the trees taller - needle trees now, with little brush under them.   From those observations Marcus knew that they were now in the same highlands as the village of his family, although that community had been far to the north, along the slope of the mountains from this encampment.   He had little worry about their being tracked now.   The ground had been hard and rocky for the entire day - even a man from the mountains could not have trailed the little party and certainly not a man of the city.   They would have to take care as they approached their destination, but he doubted that the defending unit would expect them to descend from the direction of the mountains, rather than approaching upland from the plains.   Besides...

He stopped his reverie and jumped to his feet as the posted sentry approached at a rapid pace.   Seeing his aide rise, Lucius looked around, then he too, scrambled to his feet.   The man stopped and took a breath, then said in a low voice, "Sos! Down the slope. There is... are men."

Lucius turned and waved to his newly appointed sub-officer.   As the man ran up and saluted, he said in a low, but imperative voice. "Get the men ready to move at haste.   And quietly," he added. Waving to the sentry to lead, both he and Marcus followed the man up the shallow slope to the top of the rise.   At the crest, the man slowed, then moved forward just enough to look over the low bushes.   He pointed downslope.

Marcus could see nothing at first.   The sun had set but the evening light had not yet fully gone.   Their elevation from the top of the hillock was such that they were looking over a horizon made of the tops of tall needle trees.   Then, suddenly, he saw the rising sparks of a fire, probably as someone threw another stick or log into the flames. He estimated the distance to be at least three hundred long strides - or, he calculated, about a stadium or more - considerably more.

Lucus said, in a whisper, "It is a village?"   The caution was unnecessary - the distance was too far for a normal voice to carry.   In fact, they could barely hear the shouts and calls in the distance, doubtless coming from the vicinity of the camp - or whatever it was.

Marcus shook his head.   "Villagers do not build such infernos for no reason.   Such use would strip the area of firewood for a day's walk." He thought for a few heartbeats. "Would the Legionaries of the stalker units make such a fire?"

"Nay. Not unless the officer has been touched by the gods. It is even less likely that it is one of the other Tribunes and his unit. I can believe that a couple of them would set a celebration fire, but what chance of them getting this far, or coming this way? I doubt that any ever left the Via Latina in their march." And to himself, he thought, "And if they did leave that road, then they are now as lost as I am."

They watched for a while, then he asked both himself and Marcus a question. "Do we stay, or march away?"

Marcus thought for a moment. "The moon will give us light about three hours before sunrise. We could be far from here in that time, and still have the balance of the night for rest."

"Still..." Lucius was musing as he developed his thoughts. "We are a unit of the army of Rome and not a lechery of temple virgins to be sent running from a the sight of a rodent."

"Sos. Let me approach that... encampment and ascertain what they are. It may be something innocent like a nuptial, or the clamor of the rites of manhood." Very unlikely, Marcus thought to himself. Life in these sparse uplands was not conducive to profligate displays like they were seeing.

"Aye. Let me give instruction to Blacus and we will be off."

"Nay!" The sharp command to his officer just broached his mouth without thought. "I mean, Sos, with all respect, this is my land and I know the movements here. I need no one of the city to... to..." He stopped, trying to convey the thought that the assistance of a city man stumbling around the brush would be less than helpful.

Lucius put his hand on the shoulder of his aide. "...to thrash around like an ox in the wheat fields. Aye, and I understand your concern, but I would show little fabric as a Tribune by crouching with the men while my man scouted out possible danger. The tale would little impress my mother nor my sister. I will follow your lead and mimic your actions."

After giving the sub-officer the order to keep the men at arms and ready to move - or fight - on a heartbeat's notice, the two men slipped over the hilltop and began to work their way down the gentle slope. The dark was now complete and Marcus was moving strictly on what he felt his feet moving over and with a hand out to feel any trees that appeared suddenly in front of them. It took little time before the Tribune was completely and utterly lost and reduced to following by holding the cloak of his man. Marcus, in an unnoticed reflex, had already taken the measure of the stars above, the slope of the ground, the slight breeze - all of the natural fingers that touched his senses without his even being aware of the ability.

Besides, the clamor of the men ahead was as a signpost in the Forum. He could have made his way to the fire had he had blinders on his eyes. To the Tribune he cautioned, "Step only on the needles from the trees - they will make no noise underfoot." Lucius just nodded, unseen in the black of night and wondering how he was to attend to his footfalls when even his hands were lost in the dark. He began to realize just how skilled his Adiutor was in his own environment.

Finally, they could spot the gleam of the fire through the columns of trees. Stopping, Marcus put his mouth to the ear of his Commander. "They will be fire blind. We need only to stay out of the glare and make no haste. It is movement that attracts the eye in the forest."

The needles from the trees made a carpet wherever the tall trees grew. The dried fallings had some toxicant that prevented the growth of underbrush so there was little cover to allow them to creep up to the gathering as would have been easy in the lowlands. Slowly, from tree to tree, Marcus moved - Lucius following - and keeping the massive tree trunks between the pair and the fire. Whatever the purpose of the gathering, stealth was not a concern. They could hear talk, shouts, and good natured cursing from the men who were beginning to become apparent as they moved closer.

Finally, to the relief of his Tribune, Marcus stopped behind a very large tree and began to look carefully around the trunk. They could see many men, most sitting around the huge fire beside which some side of meat was being roasted. From the size, it had to be an animal killed in the forest, or one brought with them on their march.

And a march it had to be. This was not a permanent encampment any more than the one the Legionaries up the hill had established. This was a band of men who had settled in for the night, to leave in the dawn of the morning. Asses they could see, tethered to trees almost out of the light. And bundles piled in a heap - the burdens of the beasts, no doubt. On the far side of the fire, they could see others, but other than a man or two standing, could not tell the numbers or...

"Sos," Marcus whispered. "There is low brush yonder. We can retreat, then move around to approach behind it." Lucius just nodded, then followed as his man - again slowly - began to move back up the slope, still keeping in the shadow of the tree trunks. Now far enough away for a low conversation, the Tribune said, "A caravan of traders, it would seem."

Marcus shook his head. "Nay, Sos. Why would they be so far from the cities? Villages in the hills have little to trade other than skins, and in my life, I never saw a caravan until I descended to the lowlands. I see only armed men. Where are the drovers? And the pack servants and slaves?" He shook his head. "But for the asses, I would call these men a band of raiders, except that such would never hobble themselves with beasts of burden. Speed is the watchword of bandits." He had learned much from his trainer, Dursus, who had entertained them in times of rest with tales of his unit chasing and sometimes catching raiders that ofttimes plagued the roads of the coast.

Lucius nodded. He knew the importance of haste to men who lived by plundering the vias in the land that Rome controlled. Caught, their fate would be to hang by their heels from the city walls or be nailed up by the extremities to posts in the Circus Maximus.

Working their way around the encampment just outside of the possible vision of the men, they approached from a different quarter. The brush that Marcus had seen was hardly a thicket, but far more than sufficient to allow them to approach without danger of being detected. Now, crawling, they moved at a snail's pace until a clear vision of the camp could be seen, the fire no farther than about thirty strides.

The hackles on the back of the neck of Marcus rose as he realized that his surmise was correct - this was a band of brigands, preying on any and all that could be taken with effort. Taking a deep breath, while telling his internal self to calm itself, he realized that the chances of this being the band that had destroyed his village and his family were very remote. The homestead of his childhood was - had been - many hundreds of stadia north, along the line of mountains. Since those days as an unfledged youngster, he had learned the hard truth that the world was filled with men who would take by force if they were able. Best he consigned the memory to just that, memories of the past with no practical use in his new life.

Sitting between two guards, both armed with long spears, were at least two double handfuls of men... and women. Obviously, the unfortunate wretches that either were owners of the caravan or persons that had taken travel with it. More than half were women, and he could see several oldsters, but no young men. That was to be expected - they were probably either killed in battle with the bandits, or slaughtered after the fight for precaution. Several were in pairs, for whatever reason - a man sitting and holding a woman, usually with her face buried in sorrow or...

Lucius had tapped his shoulder. Marcus slowly retreated further into the bush as a man strode up and stopped just beyond the foliage. In a moment of alarm, the young man put his hand on the hilt of his gladius in preparation to defend against the inevitable assault. That thought only lasted a heartbeat - the man stopped and began make water against the trunk of a tree. Small wonder of it. In the distance, beyond the fire, he could see a large amphora being lifted again and again, pouring its contents into a few common bowls. Obviously, it was wine looted from the caravan - a treat of ambrosia to barbarians, no doubt. It was only a matter of time before the attention of the roisterous men turned to the women sitting in the guarded circle beyond the fire.

Lucius said in a whisper, "I count six and ten in total." Marcus nodded. The Tribune motioned to withdraw, and once on the far side of the little grove of bushes, they rose, then carefully made their way out of range of the firelight and any vision of the men around it. Marcus led them up the hill and they finally reached the top of the hillock with the waiting sentry. Again Lucius marveled at the ability of his aide to unerringly find his way in a strange land and total darkness.

The men were waiting, arms at hand and packs shouldered - ready for the order to move out quietly under the cover of darkness. Lucius could barely see them in the light from the stars, but by now the dazzlement of the fire had passed and he could count all ten - eleven with the guard at the top of the hillock. He began to give them the situation as he had found it. "Yon fire marks an encampment of men, but none of ours - neither the veterans trying to find us nor one of our sister units following the same path. They are bandits, and more, they have already struck. With them is the remnants of a caravan, including prisoners and probably servants and slaves." A pause, then a surprise for all. "As a unit of the Roman army, it is our duty to destroy that band of parasites where they camp. Utterly."

Marcus was not expecting such words, and neither were the men. There was a stirring in the line as each looked at his shoulder mates, but discipline kept them quiet and the Tribune continued, "They have our numbers and a half more, but we have the opportunity of surprise. But mark this - those men are not taburna brawlers, to be frighted by our uniforms and brass. They will kill without mercy and will neither give nor accept quarter. Well do they know the lot of raiders who are taken back to the city and few will accept that fate before death.   For now, sit and rest easy while I decide the course of our action. Sleep if you can."   With that, he motioned Marcus to follow and both moved up the hillock to the top.   To the guard, he said, "Join your fellows in rest.   We will take the watch for now."

As the man retreated, Lucius said, "Well, I have made a brave speech. I would that I had the idea of how to accomplish it."   He looked down the hill into the blackness. "Perchance they will doss out from the wine."

Marcus shook his head in the darkness. "They would be fools to do so. Their captives would be long away before any woke."

The Tribune chuckled, lightly. "Nay. For once, your ideas are in error, looked at as a man of the wilderness.   Those are city folk, and the night woodlands are almost to be as feared as the bandits who captured them.   Were you in that group, you would be gone between one breath and the next and at sunrise sitting in a taburna with a cup, laughing at your erstwhile captors. Most of those wretches would stumble and falter the night away, contused and torn by the foliage and trees, and at morning's light be barely away from the encampment. Still..." He paused for thought. "They were tipping the jug even as we watched.   We will wait for a while and see if their craving for good drink will overcome their judgment."

Marcus said, "I can stand the watch on them, to get a measure of their alertness."

"Aye. I was about to say that. You do not need myself or another stumbling in the dark to mar your stealth.   Report back by moonrise, or before, should some event warrant."

Shortly, Marcus was traveling back down the slope, much faster this time, not needing to worry about towing another behind him. Now that he knew the layout of the camp, he easily crawled back under the bushes and settled in to watch.   As he had known would happen, some of the younger women had already been taken from the group of captives and were even now being used by the laughing men. There was little protest, since any attempt at refusal would result in a cuff that the man might regard as a mere slap, but was a stunning blow to the woman.

He was encouraged by the continued imbibing from the amphorae. Even were the band not to drink itself into oblivion, their judgment and weapons skills would be impaired to a great extent and their rest-sleep would be deep.   At intervals, one guard or another would be relieved from the group of captives, the new one swaying from his bout with wine and women. Studying the unfortunates, Marcus realized that they were tethered together with ropes around the neck, one leading to another. The few times that he had seen bound criminals taken to the Circus, they were in chains - bonds that were unbreakable and inescapable, unlike a rope that could be gnawed through by one desperate enough, and in short order. After some thought, he realized that a fast moving band of brigands would be unlikely to carry a large quantity of chains - both cumbersome and expensive - just on the chance of finding slaves to bind. And anyone seen to be trying to chew through their ropes would probably be put to the spear as a warning to others.

Eventually, the urge for woman-relief was filled by all, and the amphoraea had emptied or they had drunk their surfeit - the camp settled down around the dying fire, leaving only the two swaying guards to stand over the also sleeping captives. Those unfortunates could thank their gods that the wine had been included in the caravan, else the Tribune might have decided that the large band was too much for his newly trained Legionaries. Eventually, he saw the waning quarter moon rise over the mountains, giving about three hours to sunrise, then slowly withdrew from his place of observation and moved back up the hill.

Unwisely, perhaps, the Tribune was still on the top of the hillock, not knowing that he was clearly outlined against the moon-lit sky behind him. It would not matter tonight, but was something to be aware of if they went to war in the future.

"Marcus?" came the low call.

"Aye." In a few moments he was giving the tale of his observations, and his opinion that, unless they blundered badly, they should have no problems with subduing a band of wine-sleep men. "The guards change at irregular intervals, apparently when one can no longer stay awake on his feet." Suddenly, he realized the reason for using two men on the guard duty, rather than one. A single armed man could easily control any revolt or attempt to escape by the captives, but could fall into slumber and not know it. With two, each watching the other, it was unlikely that either could sleep unnoticed for long. That was an interesting factoid that he made note of.

They conversed for a while longer, the Tribune giving the plan that he had concocted during the time that Marcus was scouting the encampment. "Now is the time when a man has his deepest slumber, even one who has not been imbibing for the night." Moving down the backslope, he called to the sub-officer, "Decanus Blacus. Rouse the men, and quietly."

In moments, the ten Legionaries were lined up in front of their sub-officer, and Lucius stepped forward. "We are not training as of now. This will be a real battle and men will be killed. If we do our task properly, then none of us will accompany those who will cross the Styx this night. Silence is the watchword. Those men will fight as individuals, and they will be desperate when they see that we are of the Roman army. Most will probably prefer to die on your spear-point than hanging by nails in the Circus. Remember your training and keep your formation. Should any ask for quarter, we will give it, but do not trust the gesture - they will, with gladness, supplicate with one hand while the other carves out your belly. Kill any that resist."

Marcus looked up and down the line but felt no fear in any particular man. Of course, their backs to the rising moon, the faces were just a black circle under a helmet, so it was just a hope that his men were in order. No matter. Lucius continued, "This is what we will do..."

It was an hour of sunrise and time to begin the action. Marcus was standing behind a tree looking at the two guards. He had wondered if they would let the fire die down - something that would be a problem for what he needed to do, but every now and then, one guard or the other would throw another stick on the fire. It was not the inferno of the early evening, but it still gave enough light to allow Marcus to see them clearly. That was fortunate, since the rising, but waning moon, was hidden behind the tall tree canopy.

He could just glimpse the line of Legionaries in the darkness, on the opposite side of the encampment. They had stopped and formed up far enough away to make it very unlikely that they would be noticed by two sleepy men, but close enough to rush into the battle if the action of Marcus went astray. Just before the quiet march down the slope, Lucius had asked, "You have no qualms about striking down unwary men?"

Tight-lipped, the young man returned his answer. "Nay, Sos. Those men, or men of their ilk, destroyed my home and my family, taking any who lived as slaves, like those unfortunates down there. I would kill such men as the kitchen cocua mashes ants on her meat table. I have done so before."

"Aye. So you have told me. May Jupiter guide your hand and eye tonight."

That night on the road, when he had first met Pythes and Valens, killing two bandits in the action, he had used the simple bow of a primitive villager and the hands of a boy whose strength was enhanced by rage. Tonight, he would use a polished weapon that was thrice and more in power, and wielded by a man - a very young man, but still, one who had reached his size and strength. Looking around the tree, he studied the standing men. From the experience of that night on the road, he knew that the point had to pierce a vital area to prevent the quarry from crying out in pain. Fortunately, the men of the band wore no armor - and in fact, many wore little but a loincloth or a ragged tunic.

He stood watching, arrow nocked and two others stuck in the ground for immediate use. The two guards needed to have their gaze in directions that did not see their fellow fall. As skilled an archer as Marcus was, he had little hope of beating a surprised shout from the man who was shaken out of his sleepy sentry-go by seeing his fellow fall with a shaft in his chest. Unfortunately, this pair stood and jawed with each other, so as to pass the time. Even were they back to back, it would be unlikely for one not to hear the thump of his mate as he...

Suddenly, he saw one of the bandits step away toward the same bushes in which Marcus had hidden twice this night. His comrade idly watched as his mate moved to the tree trunk to relieve himself of his load of wine, then slowly turned to stare into the fire. Marcus drew a full-stretch, aiming at the offside of the chest, and released.

The shaft passed over many of the sleeping band, and while the wood made little noise, it was not silent, especially in a quiet night with no wind. Neither was the impact without sound, but the man fell like an axed tree with the arrow through his heart. His watch-mate was still standing and emptying his water into the night, and Marcus had ample time and more to take another stance and aim. Once again, a shaft, barely arcing over the sleeping camp and at such a speed that the waiting soldiers could not see its flight, entered the upper back of the bandit and only stopped at the fletchings. The man expired with an audible rattle of breath and a fair amount of noise as he fell face forward into the brush, but the sound was nothing to alarm the sleeping men or captives. Marcus had little of the bloodthirsty cravings common to some men in arms, but he looked in satisfaction at the two bodies sprawled on the ground.

Looking across the encampment, he saw that the soldiers were advancing in a line, rapidly but fairly silently over the carpet of needle leaves. Knowing that a bow was useless should the encounter become a melee, he put it in its carry position across his body - still strung - and pulled his gladius and waited. Despite the still smoldering coals of his memory of that horrible night and the welcome possibility of revenging himself on the cousins of those murders, he had little taste for slitting the throat of a sleeping man. He knew that he could do so when necessary, but it gave no craving to him for the opportunity.

Suddenly, he saw movement by the fire, and a bandit rose to his hands and knees, no doubt intending to follow his fellow at the edge of the camp in his urgent need to empty his water. It took a considerable time for his wine-addled sleep to fall away enough to recognize the doom that was approaching, even now well into the firelight. His sudden bellow came far too late. As the bandits stirred to wakefulness, most still wondering at the shout that had roused them, the line of Legionaries was on them, still in a single long line and behind shields. The man who cried out, fell before he had reached his feet, a spear point in his chest.

This was not a battle. Slowly, as shouts overcame their sleep, the individual men woke without knowing why, and in their grogginess, most died before they could rise to their knees. Had they been thrice their numbers, the result would have been the same. On the far side of the fire, two men rose and realized that they were undone by assailants in the night. The first, with less of his sleep - or maybe less wine - dimming his eyes, immediately ran downslope to reach the dark safety of the trees. Still trying to look over his shoulder at the wraiths that were slaughtering his fellows, he never saw the man standing quietly just beyond the reach of the firelight.

Marcus had little need to thrust with his sword. Indeed, the momentum of the bandit was such that he had to rapidly withdraw the stroke to prevent the blade from sinking to the hilt. The following man suddenly saw the young soldier, but without weapon he had no chance of avoiding or parrying the thrust. His progress across the ground was the ally of the sword of Marcus again. In a heartbeat, the soldier was back on stance, two bodies laying at his feet.

There was no need for further swordplay. The entire encampment of bandits were either dead or dying, except for three that had cried for quarter. The action had been more like a slaughter of pigs than a battle, and the Legionaries had no trace of the bloodlust that can follow a bloody and desperate engagement, else even those three remaining would now be wharfside of the river Styx. By now, the captives had woken and were standing, as confused as their erstwhile captors as to what was happening in the night.

Marcus walked around the fire and up to Lucius, who was giving orders at a rapid pace. While spears were held at the throats of the surrendered men, several soldiers were dispatched to find ropes - either in the pile of ass-baggage or that on the captives. The four grievously injured men had nothing but curses for their foe, and were immediately dispatched to follow their fellows into Hades.

The relief at seeing the assailants from the night were uniformed soldiers was palpable among the captives. The two older men - obviously well-to-to merchants, bowed to the Tribune, then one said. "We are most grateful, Captain, for our..."

"You speak to Tribune Lucius, of the house of Junius!" barked Marcus.

Both merchants looked at each other, no doubt wondering what a noble of his rank was doing far into the wilderness. Then, "Your pardon, Noble Tribune. No disrespect was intended."

The other broke in, "Again, our gratitude for the succor from such beasts. Upon our return to Antium we would be most gratified to reward you and your men with other than words."

Lucius waved his hand. "That is unnecessary. A Roman soldier needs no reward to perform his duty." He looked past the two men at the group of captives, the women finally realizing their descent into slavery - or worse - had been stayed. Most were weeping into the dirt with relief. One was even on her hands and knees and trying, without success, to heave the contents from her empty belly. "We are on a mission of training, and it must be completed. You may follow us to our destination, two days away, or make your own way."

"Aye, Sos. And our gratitude to you. Our men of the caravan were killed by the brigands and we would have little chance of finding our way with women and slaves."

Lucius nodded and said, "Make haste to ready yourselves. We leave when the light allows. And warn your party that silence is paramount. We will abandon anyone who gives our position through either chatter or clumsiness."

With three soldiers guarding the now well-bound captives, the others began the time-honored routine of discussing every aspect of their recent victory. In time, and once back at the barracks before their fellows of the other units, the battle would become a desperate engagement, fought with sweat and steel and blood and worthy of the tale of a street bard. Marcus could hear approving comments about his own actions, and again, in time would be equated to bowmanship worthy of Apollo himself, followed by single combat in steel with two desperate bandits. For himself, he knew that the victory was the planning and execution of the Tribune - to use the darkness and the wine, and the incaution of their foe to best advantage. Had they just stormed into the camp as a charge of soldiers, the tally would have been less one-sided. As it was, no Legionary had even been touched and certainly none had been injured by the foe.

Still, he was silently satisfied with his own performance. His use of weapons he discarded as trivial. The arrows had been released over a range so short that a village boy of less than a double handful of years could have sunk a shaft to the feathers. And his sword play amounted to less than the effort to kill a pair of sheep in a thorn-corral. Nonetheless, he had approached the battle with intense alertness, but no fear, and had done his duty to the satisfaction of the Tribune. And, more importantly, to himself.

He remembered the Hastilairius, Dursus, saying many times that training, no matter how intense, does not equate with experience. "You will have no hint of your quality, nor that of your comrade until you have faced a man trying to spill your guts. I can teach you the blade, or the spear, and you may learn to wield it as though Mars himself were guiding your arm, but until you have seen hot blood pour on the ground, you will not know if you are true soldiers." He had continued. "I have seen braggart toughs run like babes to their mother's skirts when the steel glints in the sun, and young striplings stand against a horde like grizzled veterans." Of course, were Sabina present, he would no doubt preen like the men in the...

From behind he heard the Tribune say, in a low voice, "You did well, Marcus, Very well, indeed."

"As did you, Sos," returned his aide. "The Legatus will approve your commission now, without doubt." He hesitated, then said, "And we have learned the penalty for the failure of sufficient alertness."

"Aye. By the gods, that is a lesson not to be forgotten. Fortunately, the fee of the tutor was paid by others."

Marcus had also learned the value of at least two men on the sentry-go, both guarding each other against the insidious sleep-desire of late night.

The sky was beginning to lighten with the promise of a clear day and the men feasted on the remains of the looted caravan, their spirits still flying around the camp in full feather over their "triumph" in battle. The two merchants began to burden the asses with baggage - that which had not been spoiled by the pilfering of the bandits. It was evident that actual droving was far in their apprentice pasts, as they struggled to remember how to properly load the beasts. The curses flew as the remaining slaves and lackeys were pointed here and there, doing and undoing this strap and that sling. Even the women were suborned as workers, excepting the two wives of the merchants. It was obvious that the actual drovers were not in the group - killed in the ambush, or just out of hand for cause.

The sun had not yet risen when the column set foot behind Marcus as he led the now thrice-sized party into the forest. The last evening, he had garnered his directions from two mountains that had been indicated on the map. Had they not burdened themselves with the remnants of the caravan, a route step might have taken them to their destination by darkfall, but now, that pace would have the women and older men exhausted by the time of the noon ration.

Their long curving path of the previous marches had taken them close to the mountains, but this day had moved them downslope and over the lesser foothills. If the map was correct, then the Roman outpost was between them and the large two-peaked hill he could see far in the distance. The caravan members were showing signs of collapse and Lucius called a halt early in the afternoon. The encampment was in a draw with two sentries posted on the high ground on either side.

Marcus noticed that the men had realized that even with this being a training foray, they were beyond the bounds of patrolled civilization, and men could die here from steel as easily as on a battlefield in a far land. Instead of their spears being cast aside as in the other nights and rests, most had them laying at hand, ready at once should they be the recipients of that which they had given the night before.

At sunrise, they set off again, with Marcus far in front to scout out the land. With him was a Legionary to act as a messenger, should the occasion arise. And it did. Long before midday, he came to a halt, his upraised hand signaling the stop to his soldier. It took little time before he turned and quietly gave an order to the man, who then waited for the following column to reach that spot. Marcus moved on down the little valley for a distance, carefully looking ahead before exposing himself in any openings in the brush. Finally, assuring himself that his senses were correct, he moved back to join the traveling group, meeting Lucius who was waiting with the soldier - and with some anxiety.

Quietly, Marcus said, "The outpost is ahead, no more than four or five stadia. It is directly between us and the sunset."

The Tribune looked into the brush, but without seeing anything but foliage. "Did you see the post?"

"Nay. In this brush and low scrub, we will see nothing until we are almost upon them." Seeing the question in the Commander's eyes, he continued, "I can smell the cook fires and spices of the post."

At that, Lucius lifted his head and carefully sniffed the air, the gentle lowland breeze flowing up the slope towards the mountains behind them.   He could detect nothing.   "It could be a village, rather than the outpost."

Marcus shook his head.   "People of the uplands use wild onions and leeks for their cookery-flavorings.   They have no access to garlic, and I never tasted the seasoning before I descended to the lowlands.   Yon cocus is overusing that bulb to the point of reeking."

Lucius sniffed the wind and again, without detecting any scent of other than the vague forest smells.   He was astounded - and not for the first time - at the sensory perceptions of his young aide.   To smell something that was completely oblivious to a city man, and not only detect it but be able to separate the components of the cooking fires that wafted up the slope with the breeze was...   Since his introduction to the enterprising young man, his prejudices of non-city dwellers - barbarians, to use the common term of his fellows - had taken an unexpected turn more than once, and this would not be the last time.

Both of the officers doubted that any of the quester units looking for them would be on the mountain side of the outpost.   Still, they were on their mission to arrive at the destination without hinderance.   "We will leave the caravan here, with two soldiers in escort, then carefully approach and announce our presence."   Lucius turned and began to give the orders, emphasizing to the pair of Legionaries that would remain behind to keep the loose assemblage of people quiet and to allow no fires or roaming from the temporary camp.

Following Marcus, the men walked silently in single file as he carefully found the way down the gentle slope.   About four stadia along, as close as he could estimate, they reached a breach in the foliage and could see upslope to a small and rounded hill.   Lucius clapped his aide on the shoulder, as they looked to see the wooden ramparts and tall watchtower with the standard of Rome on a pole above.   This was the furthest reach of the kingdom in this direction - that is, along the foothills of the mountains to the south - to be considered under the control of the city.   The small garrison monitored the mountain pass to the east, and patrolled from there to the city of Lavinium on the coast, along a line that bordered the southern lands under the claimant of Rome.

Marcus whispered, "We can move around to the road, then march into the compound to complete our task.   I will scout for any..." He stopped as the hand on his shoulder gripped him with force.

Lucius, also whispering, said, "Look to the watchtower!"

Over the wall and toward the west, overlooking the road leading to the camp, the tall tower that was a feature of all permanent

Roman army garrisons stood as expected. "I do not see a watchman. We will be out of view even if one appears..." He halted as the significance of his first statement suddenly hit him as a blow.

There was no sentry.

Book 3

Blank Slate

Tabula Rasa   (Blank Slate)

Marcus stood watching the carpenters in their task of founding a new ship. He was still awed at his first sight of the sea - an apparently infinitely wide body of water that he knew of from innumerable descriptions over the last several years, but the view of such an expanse was far more than his imagination had expected. Some of the vessels that were afloat at wharfside were vastly larger than any that he had seen on the Tiber at Rome. He still had no idea of how such a bulk could float, and even less of the method of making it travel in the direction desired by the crew.

The woodwork he could understand. In the main it was the same as his buildings of bow weapons, only on a far larger scale. Still, the shavers and saws, hammers and hole punches and whittling knives were familiar, and he could compass what they were doing. But, his attention was on an area where long vats of steaming water were holding planks of wood. After a considerable time of soaking, two men would pull a board out of the water, then lay it on a long, wooden - and sturdy - table that was curved like a bowl laid on its side. One end of the plank would be fastened by wrapping several thick turns of rope around both the table and the board, then the other end would be pushed down to follow the curve of the table. For this last operation, several large men would be called to sit or stand on the board to make it bend sufficiently to follow the form, then the two men would quickly fasten that end with more wraps of rope.

In a pile next to the operation he could see the result of the work. Many long boards, now dried or drying in the sun, were stacked, all having the permanent curve fixed in their shape. He wondered if the shape had to be...

"Your pardon, Sos." He turned from his observations to look at the under-officer, Blackus. "The Tribune requires your presence, Sos."

Nodding, he started back to the tiny headquarters post of the town. Lavinium was a port city of little importance, and far smaller than even a single quarter of Rome. It existed strictly because of and for the sea, and as a night-stop for travelers up and down the coastal roads. Fishing and boat building and inn-keeping were the staples of work for the citizenry.

They had arrived in the afternoon, having left the hill outpost almost as soon as they had achieved it, and only upon entering the town and encountering the magistrates did they begin to grasp what was happening. They certainly hadn't known on the yesterday, when they entered the outpost...

Both had stood listening and looking up the gentle slope at the palisade wall and the empty watchtower on the western end, next to the gate. Marcus whispered, "It is not abandoned. I can hear voices."

Lucius nodded and replied, "Aye. And even I can smell the cookery now. But it is not occupied by a unit of the Roman army. A watchtower without a sentry is cause for severe punishment, either of the soldier assigned to the post or the officer who fails to notice that his man has abandoned it." He turned to his sub-officer. "I want maximum alertness and minimum noise." His man saluted, then turned and gave some quiet instructions. To Marcus, he said, "We need to move to see the gate and if it is barred or open."

Marcus nodded, then began to pick a trail, making sure that the brush was between them and the outpost. Shortly, the column was in the foliage beside the trail, the crude road that started here and led to the Roman town of Lavinium. In the other direction, the dirt track ended at the open gate of the palisade. From their advantage, they could see a goodly part of the inside of the outpost, not much larger than the compound of a prosperous merchant. Other than some structures on the far wall, nothing out of the ordinary could be seen. At least the outpost was not brimming with... with... whoever had taken possession. Bandits or villagers - either.

Turning, the Tribune said to his underofficer, "Form the men, two ranks. And spears at the ready." Instantly, they assembled, dropping their packs in the grass and taking their shields from the carrying position across the back. Standing in front of the tiny unit, the Tribune said, "Now, let us discover the facts of this matter."

The distance to the gate was only fifty strides or so, and as they approached, the angle of vision widened to allow them to see more and more of the inside of the compound. Halfway to the opening, they began to see men... and women... and children. Not a horde but, at least, thirty or more. They were gathered around a fire over which a steaming pot was cooking. As they reached the gate and stopped, a woman finally noticed their visitors. She screamed and all standing or sitting around the fire jumped to their feet or began to run in panic. Only a few had the presence of mind to find a ladder to the sentry-go at any of the three opposite walls.   The short platforms, in place to allow vision over the walls were the only way out, except for the gate. But it was only a few of the younger men who took advantage of the escape - a double man-high drop to the ground over the wall was not an option for oldsters - nor for women and children.

At a command, the men of the unit stopped in the gateway, closing that exit against a sudden rush to freedom.   The two officers halted at a distance sufficient to allow them time to respond, should a conflict arise, and looked over the assemblage of people.   No bandits these, so the missing garrison would not have been either routed or destroyed by such rabble.   Most had backed up to the wall, leaving a few crouching in the dirt, hands out and upward in appeal as the two officers stood looking over the rabble, swords out and at the ready.

"Who is the leader here?" yelled Lucius.

Immediately, the babble halted, and an elderly man raised his hands and spoke a rapid stream of words that were totally incomprehensible to the Commander.

Hesitating for a moment, the Tribune said to his aide, standing beside him, "Can you compass what he is saying?"

"Aye, Sos. Somewhat."   He asked a question in the dialect of his own people and received a reply that was somewhat understandable.   For a time, he conversed until he had garnered an idea of what had happened, then turned to the Tribune.   "These are people of a local village, and this is their headman.   He says that the garrison decamped two days ago, suddenly, marching out with all accouterments."

"Did they give a reason...   No, the Commander would not make a villager privy to his orders.   Why are they here?"

More give and take before Marcus said, "Some of them are hired as workers for the garrison, clearing brush from the walls, cutting and stripping new timber, and so forth.   And hunting game-meat for the outpost. He says they are not looting - they were given permission from the garrison Commander to partake of the food that was in the storerooms, else the outpost would be quickly befouled by animals.   They brought their families to feast on the largess."

Looking around, Lucius nodded.   "It may be true. I see no evidence of plundering.   But it still gives us no reason for the garrison to decamp."

Marcus asked more questions, then translated.   "They have no idea of the reason.   He says that, while there was agitation in the men, they marched with weapons slung and not with the haste of an attacked unit. The men loaded all into the wagons, leaving only the rations that could not be carried."

The Tribune thought for a moment, then said, "We have more to worry about than feasting barbarians. Tell the man that they may continue their repast without fear." As Marcus translated to the relieved headman, the Tribune made a quick inspection of the outpost, inside the wall. Satisfying himself that the post had not been despoiled, he walked back to his waiting Legionaries. "We will not tarry here. We march for Lavinium immediately and in battle order. Until we have more knowledge of what has happened, we will assume that we are at risk." He thought of something, "I would have you bring the caravan here. I fear that my men would be far too likely to lose themselves, even at that short distance."

Marcus nodded and turned to hurry back to the little draw where they had left the remnants of the trader column and the two soldiers to guard it. In a while, the long string of animals and people were assembling on the road outside of the outpost. Lucius hurried up and waved the two merchants to attend himself. "We have some unknown happening that can not be explained, but I have decided to march immediately for the city of Lavinium. You may camp here till the morrow and rest, or follow us at your pace, but we cannot moderate our march to yours."

The two merchants looked at each other, then one spoke, "We will follow, Tribune. Even at our pace, the city should be in view by darkfall." Lucius turned to leave when one of the men said, "Tribune. You have our gratitude for the most courageous reprieve from the thieves and murderers of our people." The Commander nodded as the man continued, "We have no means of rewarding you and your men at this time, but know that I am Lartes and this, Bithenus." He waved his hand at the other merchant. "We are merchants of some repute in the city of Atium, and should you find yourself in that area we would be most gratified to host your stay. If I may say, our domiciles will be far more comfortable than any taburna in the city. Be assured that your actions will not be forgotten by us."

The Tribune nodded, and replied, "Well said, merchant. And I will avail myself of that offer should I find myself in your fair city. For now, farewell and good traveling."

The two men bowed, and Lucius turned and walked to the head of his column of men. Shortly, they were marching at a route step down the road. Marcus had given orders to the villagers that they would care for the outpost in their absence, in payment for the food stores in the storehouse, then joined the unit as they set off down the trail, en route to the port city. As they walked, both discussed the strange occurrences. Of course, with absolutely no knowledge of the happening, their conversion was merely a method of passing the time as the stadia passed under their feet.

"If war had suddenly come while we were on the march, one would think that the garrison would have been enhanced, not abandoned." The Tribune shook his head in puzzlement.

Marcus knew nothing of war, nor politics, nor the give and take between cities and kingdoms. His opinions on the subject would border on the ridiculous, so he refrained from wondering on the cause. Rather, he asked questions of the Tribune, to add to his knowledge of the situation.

"There is a garrison in the port city for which we are headed. I have the hope that we will get the reason for this strangeness from them. Of course, if that fort is abandoned, then we may assume that the gods have removed Rome from the earth." He looked back at the following men, then continued, "Lavinium is not a city of importance, except for being the southernmost reach of the kingdom that is claimed by the King. It is connected to Ostia by the Via Laurentina - a road of much commerce, so it is a resting place for merchants. Many inns and taburnae are present within the walls."

Since they had a trail to follow that gradually widened into a passable dirt road, rather than finding their way through forests and around ridges, by late afternoon they had reached the environs of the city. The road followed the wall around to the southern gate, where they encountered the sentries at the portal. All four Legionaries stood to attention as they saw an officer of rank approach and stop before them.

"I am Tribune Junius, from Rome, come from a training march across the land."

"Salve, Tribune," answered one, with the helmet brush of a minor officer.

"We have been days in the uplands. What are the tidings from Rome?"

The soldier hesitated, then replied, "I am uncertain, Tribune. Many stirrings are happening, but little of the reason has reached us. I could tell you the myriad stories that have passed through this gate, but it would take the gods themselves to sift truth from tale." He hesitated, then said, "May I suggest that the Tribune inquire at the garrison post?"

"Aye. Where would that be?"

Turning, the gate officer gave the order to a man to guide the Tribune and the unit into the city. Shortly, they were marching down the dirt streets toward the port. At the small compound that acted as the headquarters for the city post and the magistrates of the port, they were met by a the Centurion in charge.

"Salve, Tribune."

"Salve, Centurion. We have come from the highland post at the top of the Jupiter Latiaris road and have news of import."

They could tell that the news was a surprise to the man. "Sos? The garrison of that post was ordered out and back to Rome two days ago."

"We are a unit on a training march from Rome, given that outpost as a destination. Now, what is the reason for the sudden... whatever is happening."

"In truth, Sos, I have little official information, but word on the Via indicates that the King has been deposed." That was an eye opener to Lucius - his knowledge of history gave reason to think that the change was not voluntary on the part of King Tullius.

Thinking on the astounding news for a moment, Lucius asked, "Is the city in turmoil? Or with fighting?"

The Centurion replied, "In truth, Sos, I can not say and it is not from my lack of desire to discover the truth. But any news that I give you would have no backing of knowledge behind it. Tales and stories are flying around this city, changing with every drip of the water clock."

Lucius nodded and said, "Aye. We will need rations and cover for twelve men for the night. On the morrow we will march for Rome." He thought of something, then added, "We also have three bandit prisoners. May you take them in charge?" The answer was in the affirmative and men were dispatched to take control of the captives.

A barracks was secured and Marcus, having nothing to do for until the morning, walked around the small city, stumbling on the carpenters by happenstance. There he stayed and looked at the sea, and the ships and the shipwrights in their building until the summons came to attend the Tribune. In the small barracks, he found Lucius standing with a messenger and the Centurion. Turning as his aide walked up, he said, "The stories have been given credence." Marcus waited as his Commander scanned the wax tablet. "Indeed, the King is removed and Lucius Tarquinius has assumed the Throne, and not peacefully, it would appear. Most units were recalled to Rome for support in the... change, which explains the empty outpost." He mused for a while, then finished with, "I am making the assumption that the recall includes us, although we would have returned in any case. Tell the men that we will rise at first light and march. Have them supplied with marching rations - will bypass Ostia and not stop until we arrive in Rome."

Marcus nodded and left to give the orders. He was less than comforted by the words and his hope was, that the city was not in chaos, with bloodletting among the people. His worry was for the house of Pythes and the occupants, and... mostly, it must be said, for a small household on the street of the Poet.

Lucius did not even wait for the first light of dawn. The gates were still closed, but the authority of a Tribune was sufficient for the sleepy guards to crack them enough for the unit to pass through. The usually busy road was theirs alone at that hour, and they rapidly put the stadia behind them as they walked the hard surface by the sliver of the almost empty moon. After sunup, and a short break for a ration, they were off again, but now passing other travelers here and there. It was soon evident that the others on the road knew of changes in the city to the north. Normally, a caravan, or wagon, or just foot-walkers would move aside respectfully for an army unit as it moved up the road. Now, they moved entirely to the grass and stopped, watching as the soldiers passed. There was a sense of... of... not fear, but uneasiness as to what might be happening and most had no desire to become entangled with any principals of the matter.

Rome, by way of the coastal via, then up the Tiber road was over half a thousand stadia. A forced march would find them at the city by dark, but exhausted and possibly unable to cope with any unusual situation that might arise. The Tribune made the decision to break the march at the Roman port of Ostia, about halfway. However, as they approached the walls, the tales from the travelers having just left were in the extreme, and he decided to camp in the woods, out of sight of the walls and the road. To Marcus, he said quietly, "It would be unwise to enter a city that resembles a disturbed hornet's nest and in a situation where we might have to take one side or the other, without any knowledge of the circumstances."

At morning time, they skirted the walls and acquired the via leading to Rome. By mid-afternoon, they had reached the environs of the city, and again, scouted around the walls to reach their training compound. But, before they could reach the gate - indeed, they had just caught sight of it - they were accosted by a man in a flowing robe and hood. He stopped before the two officers and looked up.

"Maxentius! By the gods," exclaimed Marcus. Indeed, it was the Adiutor to the Tribune Collatinus.

Lucius was about to demand news, when the man said in a low voice, and in haste, "Sos! I have an urgent missive for you." Then, in a whisper, he said, "Out of ear range of your men."

This could not be a gladsome message, they both realized. The Tribune turned and said to the men, "Compose yourselves and rest in the shade of the wall."

Waiting for the men to move away, Maxentius said, "The Tribune Collatinus bade me wait here on the chance that you would return. Lucius Tarquinius has usurped the Throne, killing the King in the process. And many others, as of my last knowledge. Your life is in peril and my master asks that you stay away until I can give word that you are back."

Both Lucius and Marcus looked at each other, unbelieving. "Why would I be in peril? I have no standing in court nor have I..."

"Please, Sos. My master begs you to leave here in haste and that I should immediately tell him of your coming."

"Leave for where?" demanded the Tribune.

"To the villa of the banded lady, he said. I have no idea of what it means, but he insisted that you would." He hesitated, then pleaded, "Please, Sos. Go at once. If you are seen, your life may end. My Tribune will join you at... that place." He paused for a heartbeat, then said, "You shouldn't be seen as a high officer wandering around the outside of the city. Tribune Collatinus suggested that you remove your armor and pieces of authority."

Lucius mulled the astounding request for a moment, then said to Marcus. "It appears that I may have angered the new King in some unknown way. I would not have you share my fate, whatever it is. Dismiss the men - send them home until called, then take yourself to your domicile."

Marcus nodded, then walked over to the men and gave the orders to disband until called again for service. He assured them that their superiors would receive a good report of the excellent conduct of the soldiers - whenever the circumstances allowed. The Legionaries were not amiss to return to comfortable quarters, after several days in the wilderness - and a battle. With salutes, they walked along the wall toward the southern gate.

Watching them go for a few heartbeats, Marcus moved to join the other two men still talking in low voices. As he walked up, Lucius said, "I will retire to a villa of the Collatinus family, where my friend and I once... entertained ourselves. Hopefully, he will arrive to make clear the muddy waters that I seem to be swimming in. I wish you farewell, Marcus. And with my gratitude for your excellent service."

Marcus shook his head. "Alas, my service is not over, yet, Sos. The Dominus of the house of Junius, gave me charge to watch over his son. I have not allowed you to become lost yet, and I would most dislike having to inform your pater that you were mislaid on the way to some remote destination while I was comfortably slumberous on my mat." He grinned as he said it, to rob the words of offense.

Trying not to allow his face to show his sudden emotion, Lucius nodded and said to Maxentius, "Go, and tell my friend that I will do as he asked. But to hurry - this unknowing is worse than any possible facts."

As the man turned and ran toward the direction of the gate, the Tribune pointed and said, "Come, we will need to move to the Gabious via and that is on the eastern wall." First, they moved to a broken wall from some long past structure and looked around to see if they were under observation. With no person in sight, they both removed both their helms, armor, and cloaks. Shortly, both were garbed in plain tunics and sandals. The armor and helmets were covered with stones and branches, hopefully to be recovered at a later time. Both naturally kept their belts, to hold their blades, waterskins, and man-purses. Of course, Marcus would not be separated from his bow, and it was in its usual place - carried reverse strung across his body,

Scouting the outside of the wall, but away from the eastern gate as they passed it, they finally came to another cobblestone road. This one was far less developed than the coastal roads that connected cities north and south, and much less traveled. Still, it was no forest trail and was easy to walk.

"The villa of which he speaks is about ten stadia away. Lucius and myself had our first experience with a woman there, and together, one springtime. She was a trollop from the temple of Venus, but clean and young and willing. Unlike most of the jaded whores of the temples, she had not yet been worn down to a mere receptacle for a man's svans." He smiled at the memory. "By the next day, neither of us had either the strength to walk back to the city nor the fortitude to allow our sore pouchstones to swing under us for the distance."

Before sundown, they had reached the villa, a stadium from the road, deserted in a forest of young trees and in fairly poor shape. Apparently it had not been used by the family nor kept up by servants for many years. Sweeping the accumulation of leaves and dust from a stone bench, Lucius sat down and said, with a grim expression. "So, here I am. Either an outcast or a fleeing criminal, and with no knowledge of my crime." He looked around. "If Collatinus does not arrive soon, I fear we will starve and be left for the crows."

Marcus had dropped his belt on the floor and was stringing his bow. "If I may say, Sos, this is my kingdom, crowned to me from the time I was weaned. I can assure you that we will not want for food. If you would gather some sticks for a small fire before the sun is gone, I will return with our repast."

Lucius nodded, then cleared the fire pit of loose leaves and debris. Then he walked around the overgrown courtyard, gathering sticks and dried branches, making several trips until he had a pile of kindling far more sufficient than needed for a cook fire. Dark had almost completely fallen when he heard a rustling in beyond the door, turning to see Marcus enter with two coneys in his hand. Watching his aide place his weapons against the wall, then kneel to skin and strip the meat, the Tribune said, "My association with you has made me question my sense of worth."

The statement made no sense to Marcus, who just said, "Sos?"

"The lessons of my tutor always gave we Romans as the epitome of civilization - the rulers of the lands and the keepers of the knowledge. And my place, in the House of Junius, at the top of that heap and far above the barbarians who had no knowledge of the ways of the civilized world." He paused for a moment, then continued, "Old Tiberious would have named you as one of those primitives to be looked down upon."

Marcus moved to the fire pit, then taking his flint from his man-purse, struck it against his pugio to shower sparks into the dry leaves. Quickly, there was a growing flame that he nurtured until it was safely alive. Lucius continued his musings.

"You can find food where my cultured and superior friends - including myself - would starve, probably scrabbling for worms in the leaves. Your senses can find your way through any wilderness, although how I can still not fathom. I would yet be wandering in circles, lost and beyond help." Another pause. "You do not grub for wealth, which my tutor would call unfathomable, yet you seem to be satisfied with your life." Marcus speared some of the pieces of meat, then jabbed the stick in the ground to hang over the fire.

"Sos. I think your brooding over what has happened in the city has depressed your spirit. As my mother said to my family many times, do not vex yourself over what has not yet come to be. If a friend is bringing news of ill, it will not be lessened by tormenting oneself over the unknown during the wait." In a short while, the thin strips of meat were bubbling their juices with heat and Marcus handed his friend a steaming slice, wrapped in a green leaf. From his man-purse, he removed and opened the little bag of salt, carried by all who travel through the wilderness.

Lucius nodded, and said, around a mouthful, "This is good hare, even with hunger giving garnishment to the taste." They sat and ate in silence, listening to the low crackle of the fire and the noise of the insects and creatures beginning to rouse for the night. As they finished, licking their fingers of the last taste, the Tribune finally spoke again. "Marcus. You have been a good friend, from the time that you succored me after my upsetting ride. Nay! Let me speak. I know, in fact, that you would make the better Tribune, if our society would allow it. But, know that whatever happens to me, or has happened, my feelings will not change. Should our lives return to normal, our first task will be to find you a merchant shop of some significance, that you may follow your skill in bowsmithing. And, to assist you in decorating that dwelling with a particular girl, the likes of which the world has not yet seen - or so you have told me."

Marcus just smiled in the dark at the mild jest, but kept his silence. He had no idea of what to say. To himself, he had just done what was necessary for the task at hand. The idea that his worth was enhanced by help to an injured stranger, or that a best effort put forth as an aide was something to be praised, was... well, those were actions that were over, successfully concluded, and not something to spend time on in relating.

To get the Tribune's thoughts to move from worry, or praise for his aide's actions, he said, "I am deficient in knowledge about the clans of Rome, but the mother of Sabina has told me of your relationship to... Tarquinius is the name?"

Lucius snorted, "I hope that our sojourn is not long enough to explain the gens of Rome, else we are in need of far more than two coneys for our sustenance." He stood, walked to the door opening, looking and listening, but apparently in just a thoughtful mood, rather than expecting to see anyone. "The tale is confusing, but we have little else on which to spend our time for now. My mother was the daughter of King Lucius Tarquinius Priscus, who was on the Throne before Servius Tullius assumed it. She is also the sister to Lucius Tarquinius, the man who is apparently our new ruler." He hesitated. "What is amusing?" he asked.

Just a shadow in the now dying cook file, Marcus said, "I mean no disrespect, Sos, but do all Roman nobles carry the name of Lucius?"

This time, the Tribune laughed out loud. "Aye, it would seem so. Romans seem to have an affinity for only a few choices for the praenomen - the first name. Most of my friends are either a Lucius or a Spurius, Julius, or Publius. Or Marcus. And on that theme, how do you come to carry the praenomen of a Roman noble? Do highlanders often copy from the cities to name their children?"

Marcus shook his head in the dark, explaining his actual name and the apparent bending of it to a more recognizable form by the ear of the merchant, Pythes.

Nodding, Lucius continued, using the tale to pass the time waiting for... "This Lucius Tarquinius that apparently claims the kingship had a wife that was the daughter of King Servius Tullius - a good woman by my mother's saying, but she had a sister - named Tulia - who was as the gorgon come to plague the land." Marcus had no idea of what the word indicated, but assumed that it did not describe a wonderful girl like Sabina. "By accounts, Tulia murdered her own husband, and then her sister, as to allow for her nuptials to Lucius Tarquinius. In any case, both were killed, and Tarquinius took the freed Tulia to wife."

He took a stick and poked the fire absently, then continued, "This was before my manhood, and the tale is from my mother, but I have no reason to doubt her veracity. By her accounts and many others, I suspect that much of what has happened during our absence may be laid to her feet. A more ambitious woman never trod the cobblestones of Rome. Had she been born with a svans, rather than a venter, I could easily believe her to have slit the throat of King Tullius long ago. And that of anyone else that might bar her lust for power."

Marcus mulled over the story, then said, "The mother of Sabina gives good words to King Tullius. That Rome has been prosperous and in growth since he took the Throne - apparently many years ago."

"Aye. The people are happy, and there is little strife with neighboring lands - at least, not since his youth. He allows for little graft in the magistracy and criminals have long learned to take their trade elsewhere..."

Suddenly, both jumped to their feet, automatically reaching for their blades. Whatever, or whoever was walking from the road was not attempting to approach undetected. In a few heartbeats, they could see a torch, held high, and moving towards them. Stepping through the gate-less stone wall, two shadows stopped, and they heard a call.

"Junius?"

Stylus

"Salve, Collatinus!" The two friends ran together and embraced. "By the gods, the night was getting oppressive with my friend trying his best to keep my mind from the news that you might be bringing." He pulled the newcomer by the arm. "Come under the roof and out of the dampness." The other man, of course, was his aide, Maxentius, holding the torch. Marcus nodded to his Adiutor friend, then took the bag from his hand. Inside, he threw some sticks on the coals, and soon the empty stone room was alight with the leaping flames.

"Have you eaten?" asked Collatinus. "We have brought provisions as I knew you hurried here with haste. Wisely, I must say."

"I need no food. What I desire is the tidings of what has happened since our leaving of the training post. My family? They are well?"

Marcus knew instantly from the averted eyes and expression, seen even in the dim flickering light, that the missive was not gladsome. Junius knew it also. "Tell me! What has happened?"

His noble friend swallowed a few times, then said, "Your mother and sister are well, and send word for you to stop elsewhere, rather than return to Rome at this time." Another hesitation, then, shaking his head, he continued, "I would promise the gods any offering not to have to deliver this news. Your father and brother were executed by men in the charge of Tarquinius." Seeing the stunned expression on his friend's face, he hurried to expand on the evil tidings. "They were accused of resistance to the new reign, and other accusative complaints, all of which were constructed from nothing. Other Senators were put to the sword, also, for giving unkind words to the usurpation - Atilius, Lucianus, Aurelianus, Scaevola. I have not the entire list. The city is as a disturbed nest of bees, and some may be in hiding rather than killed."

Lucius sat down on the bench, looking at the ground. "My father? And Titus? Why?" The crushing hurt to his being was evident in his words.

Collatinus sat beside him. "The Senator was not a man to hide from duty - all knew that. He attempted to forestall the murder of King Tullius, but the small unit of protection was overwhelmed by the force sent to make the deed. Tarquinius has planned this from the time that he stormed the Senate-house and lodged the complaints against the King. Or even before that, likely."

"King Tullius is dead?" Another blow that was unexpected.

"Aye. He had gone to the Senate-house in response to the news. Tarquinius, himself, threw the King down the steps and ordered his men to strike. Your father, and others attempted to intervene, but were set upon by the bullies of the usurper and killed. But hear - the body of your father was not violated and lies in repose in your atrium waiting for the auspices of funeral."

The Tribune felt his fury and his gorge begin to rise. "What of my brother, Titus? Was he there? Why was he killed?"

Collatinus shook his head. "The reason is unknown as of now. His body was found in the street, off the Pavian way. My assumption is that Tarquinius is eliminating any nobles that might oppose his reign. Your brother, too, is now reposing in your household."

There was a period of silence, the other men allowing the distressed man to roam in his own thoughts. Then, Lucius pulled his gladius and laid it across his knees. "I will cut the heart from this murderous arrogant. If I lose my own head, I will avenge my father and brother. Before the next sunset, Tarquinius will..."

"No!" The sharp call from Marcus brought the Tribune up short. "Sos. The action that you seek must not be planned nor attempted in a state of furious sorrow."

Hotly, Lucius replied, "My family has been destroyed by a murderous claimant to the Throne of Rome. Do you suggest that I honor his actions with my oath of allegiance. Or, commission a statue of my uncle for our atrium?"

Knowing that he had no authority to command a Tribune, nor any member of a noble house, Marcus plowed ahead. "Nay, Sos. That is not my meaning. I will assist you in your retribution, but it should be done only as a military mission - after much thought and planning."

"To Hades with that! I have lost my father - my Father - and my bother, and for what? Do you have any idea of what that is..." He stopped and dropped his eyes to the floor. Taking a deep breath, he said, "Forgive me, Marcus. Of course, you know of this exact sorrow. And yours was even greater than mine. I, at least, have my mother and sister, still."

Realizing what the aide of the Tribune was trying to do, Collatinus broke in. "Consider this... Any retribution will be sweet, but you are the last scion of your family. If you die, then the house of Junius is ended."

Lucius threw a stick at the fire. "So? Do I just ignore the actions of our new and accursed ruler? Affect that it never happened? I cannot just let the murder of my family go without some action."

"Nay, Sos." Marcus was relieved that his noble friend had been persuaded from storming back to the city with a swinging sword. "But let us find what has happened, and what might be a future course of our agency.   We cannot bring your family back from the dead, no matter what our haste, but considered action after a course of planning might resolve your need for vengeance."

"Your aide speaks with wisdom, Lucius," said Collatinus. "And you must not return to the city for now. It would be too easy for the Tarquinius cronies to kill you in the turmoil, and if in your household, your mother and sister also, just in the bloodlust frenzy." He held up his hand as Lucius was about to reply. "Wait. You must retire to some other city, and stop there until we find the best pathway for your return."

"To run, you mean."

"Nay, Sos." This from Marcus. "Remember the words of the Senior Centurion. 'A retreat is sometimes the best strategy when the battlefield is uncertain. It allows for a period of rest and planning before rejoining the action. And ofttimes a new outlook after considerable thought will turn the battle.'"

Collatinus grabbed the moment, hoping that the tide was running in their favor. "As long as you are alive, the house of Junius stands. Tarquinius cannot take your lands and possessions while a legal heir exists.   And, do not forget, he is the brother of your mother and unlikely to call for her murder for no reason. A usurper he is, and willing to dispose of any who oppose him, but he has no streak of bloodlust for the satisfaction of pleasure. Now, let us eat and plan the morrow. Maxentius, unstopper the wine and lay out the bread and cheese."

While Lucius just sat and looked into the fire, brooding, the other three made the motions of preparing a repast. In fact, while Marcus was less than hungry, he realized that a cup of good wine would not come amiss. Maxentius poured a goodly portion into the four wooden bowls and handed two of them to his Tribune. Marcus took another, then froze as he saw Collatinus discretely - and expertly - turn a hand over one of the bowls as he reached for it. In the dim light, it was only a brown powder that fell from the palm and was quickly gone as the vessel was moved in a small circle to agitate the liquid. Marcus caught the eye of the noble, realizing what was happening, then quickly looked away.

The sun was three handspans above the horizon before Lucius awoke. Groaning, he sat up and looked around. The other three had been up since sunrise, talking and making plans for the day. "By the god of slumber!" Lucius put his hand to his forehead. "Between the wine and my sorrow, I have spent the night and the morning in the domain of Hypnos, and without the dreams that I feared. I do not even remember reposing for the night."

Collatinus handed him a bowl, this time half filled with unadulterated wine. "Marcus speaks of a pair of merchants for which you performed a good deed during your march. And the offer of habitation should you enter their city."

Looking up from the wine bowl, before he had even sipped from it, Lucius replied with some heat, "I know your thoughts. But I will not rusticate in some far city while my house and family sit unguarded in Rome." He took a mouthful, swished it between his teeth, then spit it on the ground. "And for what? Will Rome be more accommodating in another season, than it is now? Why would it?"

"Nay. It is only for the time to allow for the hot blood in the city to cool. Think on it. At the moment, Tarquinius is sleeping with one eye open and his hand on his sword. He knows that now is the time to expect resistance from any that intend to confront his usurpation. It would only take a dropped word by a merchant in bad humor to focus his suspicions on you. Or from one of his lackeys, wishing to ingratiate himself to the Throne by exposing you as a traitor." He hesitated, then continued. "In any event, be careful of Caeus."

"Caeus? The guard Captain of King Tullius?"

"Aye, but he switched allegiances quickly enough. He is now the Plenipotentiary Custodis of the Throne. Murdering throatslitter would be a more fitting attribute for the man. Unlike Tarquinius, he would kill his mother just for the pleasure of the act. He was the sword arm that did the deeds - or at least, ordered them. It would have been his lackey, the foul Patronius, that culled the blood."

Lucius sat in silence, thinking on the advice of his friend. Looking up, he asked, "What of your father? Is he well? Or in the same danger as I?"

Collatinus shook his head. "Nay. You have known the Dominus as long as I. You certainly have spent as much time at my house as I have at yours. My father is a good man, but as a Senator... You know as well as I that his thoughts are on his scrolls and study, not in stirring the pot of intrigue in the Senate house. Tarquinius could never see him as a threat. Besides, to maintain legitimacy of his Throne, he cannot dispose of the entire body."

The talk went on through the morning and into the midday meal as the strategy was planned. It was agreed - to the relief of the others - that Lucius would travel to Antium and take the offer of host from the merchants, Lartes and Bithenus. Marcus would be the messenger for whatever news that Collatinus might learn.

Antium was a port city under the dominion of the Volsci, a people claiming the lands to the south and of a territory that dwarfed that of Rome. Despite years of disputes of the exact border between the two lands, thus far the disagreements had not descended into strife and trade freely flowed between the two. At a question from Marcus, Collatinus stated that the distance from Rome to Antium was about three hundred stadia in distance - an easy distance for a good walker over two days.

Finally, there was nothing else to say as the friends stood to bid farewell and the favor of the gods. "Inform my mother and sister that I am well, and hope to return soon."

Collatinus nodded and replied, "Aye. It will be my first stop on reaching the city." He had enhanced the purse of Lucius with a double handful of coins that would allow for his repose in comfort for any amount of time.

To Marcus, Lucius said, "And you, friend. I want to see you with news without much time in passing."

"Aye, Sos. You may be assured of that. And I will obtain greetings from the Domina and your sister before I leave to find you."

In the plain tunic and robe of a merchant traveler, Lucius made his departure. Collatinus made to return to the city, while Marcus retraced their footsteps in the walk to the villa. At the stone wall, where their military uniforms had been hidden, he regarbed as an Adiutor of the Roman army, then set his path to the training camp.

As he walked up to the gate, he had no problem in noticing that much had changed. Instead of an almost empty post, it was now considerably more occupied. The grounds were not packed with soldiers, but still, far more men were within than had been there when they left. Identifying himself to the guards at the gate, he set foot for the administration building. Unlike before, two more guards were standing in the doorway of the building.

"Adiutor Marcus, aide to the Tribune Junius, reporting to the Senior Centurion." Inside, he stood for a moment as the word was passed, then stood to attention as the huge man approached.

"By the stinking verpus of Jupiter. It is one of the wandering waifs of the forest." The statement needed no reply, and Marcus just stood. "Where is the Tribune? Where have you been hiding all this time? The other units returned three days ago."

Assuming that the Centurion wanted a report, Marcus said, "Our march took us away from the roads, Sos. In the journey, we encountered a band of raiders, with prisoners from a caravan in tow, and engaged them." That sparked the attention of the officer, but before he could break into the account, Marcus continued, "The Tribune Junius executed a masterful plan, that resulted in the bandits being killed and three given quarter. The captives were freed and accompanied us to the outpost, necessarily slowing our pace, as they had women and asses to drive."

"And your losses?"

"Not a Legionary was touched, Sos, except for the Tribune. In the lead, he received a blow to this head from a spear shaft that stunned him considerably." He paused, expecting a question, but none came forth, and he continued with his tale, "We continued our march to the outpost, but it was deserted. We immediately set out for the post at Lavinium, where we received the news of the... happenings in Rome. From there, to the city where the men were released until called."

"But where is the Tribune Junius?"

Marcus shook his head, "In truth, Sos, I do not know. When I woke this morning, he was gone, leaving only his military garb, which I have brought with me."

Now the Centurion was agitated. "Could he be planning retribution to the King?"

Marcus was now entering the dangerous territory that he knew would be coming forth, and again carefully monitored his response. He had little experience in dissembling, but his responses could not be flawed. Were it unbelieved, not only would Lucius and his family be in deadly danger, so would he.

"S...Sos? I do not understand."

"Did you not know that the Dominus of the house of Junius was put to the sword for treason?"

With a dropped jaw, and what he hoped was an expression of consternation on his face, he opened his eyes wide and answered, "Nay, Sos! We have had no news in any form except for a stream of tales in the city of Lavinium, but nothing to that matter! Why... What..." He seemed to realize that a newly minted soldier did not demand answers from a lofty superior, then just closed his mouth and waited, keeping his dismayed expression on his face.

The old Centurion stood for a considerable time, in thought, then ordered, "This must be reported, else we all may be undone should the Tribune Junius take violent action against the King." Yelling to his own aide, a small detail was instantly formed and very shortly Marcus and the Centurion were striding for the gate of the city, followed by four Legionaries. Thus far, Marcus could assume that he was still just a messenger, and not in the path of the swinging blade. Were he considered culpable in any way, his gladius and pugio would surely have been taken from him.

Through the Mons Oppius they marched, then the small Velia quarter and across the empty Circus Maximus toward the Capitolium quarter. The hair rose on his neck as he realized their destination - the Palace! As he walked, he desperately reviewed the story that they had concocted that morning. And the wise warnings of Collatinus. "Any falsehood must contain a goodly measure of truth to be believable. And, above all, it must be simple, else you will find yourself caught in your own trap from a defective memory of the tale."

He had seen the Palace many times, but only in the distance across the Forum. Except for passing through, or his few sojourns to the house of Junius, he had little reason to enter that noble quarter. Now, however... Surely he was not to be questioned by the King himself!

The Senior Centurion was apparently still in his old rank, even with the change of authority. The guards at the Palace gate saluted, but said nothing and gave no hindrance to the small party as they strode through the openings in the wall. Keeping his head straight, but letting his eyes roam from side to side, he looked at the unbelievable sights that he was passing.

The courtyard - if that is what it was - was of slabs of blindingly white stone. Marble, he remembered Sabina telling him, when, during one of their many walks, they once examined the Temple of Vesta in the huge concourse of the center city. The buildings on either side were of the same material and the frontal portico roofs held many man-lengths above by fluted columns. Under them were milling people, all dressed in finery, but as to their reason for being he could have no idea. Ahead was the Palace proper, the largest building fronted by four pillars that must have taken a cohort of men to have raised. Everywhere were soldiers, all in like garb, but not that of the usual Legionary. These had to be the Regius Defensoris - the elite guards of the King. Certainly, the worth of any soldier's habiliments - armor, helmets, and accouterments - would keep a Plebeian family for years.   Marcus fleetingly wondered if the position was obtained through martial skill, or with the championship of wealth.

Stopped at the entrance for a few heartbeats, they were met by a ridiculous individual in colored and heavy robes, and carrying a... gilded staff with a wooden animal on top.   This was the Chamberlain, although Marcus had no concept of the position - court protocol and ranks not being in any lesson that he had received since coming to the city.   Once inside the gilded entrance, Marcus was almost blind, his eyes still adjusted to the glaring whiteness of the outer yard.   It took a short while before his vision began to discern the riches inside - tapestries, statues...

Rather than continuing straight into the huge arch, again guarded by spear-carrying soldiers, they turned to a side room and were announced at the doorway.   Inside was a man in the ordinary toga of a highborn - definitely not the King, although Marcus had never seen that worthy to his knowledge, but somehow he knew that this was not he.

Stopping and raising a hand, the Centurion said, "Salve, Praefectus."   Marcus froze as he realized that the magistrate was the man against whom he had been warned, Caeus, second to the King in his rank of Warden of the City.   "I have received word of Junius the Younger, from his Adiutor, Marcus."

The man rose and looked at the young man.   He was stocky, and no oldster, himself, although many years older than Marcus.   In his white Toga, and with only the hilt of a pugio sticking from his belt, he looked more like a magistrate of the accounts, than the second most feared man in Rome.

To the Centurion, the man asked, "Where is the noble Junius? Has he not accompanied you?"

"Nay, Dominus.   He has not returned from his Tribune activity - one in which he encountered bandits and was apparently injured in the battle." Turning, he ordered, "Adiutor!   Give your tale to the Praefectus."

It took only a short time, after which the man just stood and thought for a few heartbeats.   Suddenly, he asked, "And Junius has no knowledge of the treasonship of his family?"

"Nay, Sos... Dominus.   We had no word of the happenings in the city - or none that could be given credence to.   I myself only found out upon reporting to the Centurion."

"Why did you travel to this... villa after releasing the men?"

"I know not, Dominus.   Luc... The Tribune continued to say that he was called by the Oracle of Dodona and in need to consult on her behalf. I am unfamiliar with the meaning. There was only myself with him and no man to share the guard. As I woke at sunrise, he was gone, leaving his Tribune habiliments and even his weapons. I searched the road in both directions, and queried the few travelers, but found no trace."

The Praefectus looked in disbelief at the aide. "The Oracle of Dodona? That entity is a Hellenic myth, told to children at bedtime. He would have to journey to Olympus itself to find that spirit." He paused, thinking. "So he is apparently addled from the blow during the fight." It wasn't a question, just a musing for a moment. "But, still, he will find that his father and brother were brought to justice for their crimes and may wish vengeance."

Carefully, Marcus weighed his response. "If I may respond, Praefectus. I doubt that the news will weigh heavily upon the Tribune. Certainly, he will not rejoice in the deaths of his family members, but he was not enamored with his place in the house." This had been carefully plotted by both Lucius and Collantinus and recited to Marcus to repeat if the opportunity arose. "His brother was to take the place of the Senator in time, leaving young Junius as secondary, and not even with authority to assist in the family lands." He hesitated, for effect, then said, "In truth, Sos.... Praefectus, he was somewhat embittered with his place." He gave more hesitation for show. "He may even welcome the changes - both in his family and the Kingship. Should his infirmity be lessened with time, he could represent the house of Junius in support of the King."

The official just stood and thought for a long time. "Hmmm. In any case, an addled man is no threat to the Throne. Should he recover, then we will determine his place. The King has no interest in removing the family name of his sister from the tablets of the city." He looked at the older soldier. "Report to me when and if you find further news of the Tribune. For now, we will assume that he is wandering as a mind-lost. I have other duties than to worry about a single man touched by the gods - no matter from what family." A nod of dismissal, and the audience was over. They were escorted back to the gate.

As they stood in the street, Marcus said to the Centurion. "Sos, despite the future of the Tribune, I wish to report on the conduct of his unit. All did well and two, especially, were marked out for further advancement."

The Centurion nodded, and thought for a moment. "Aye. For now, I expect that you wish to make the acquaintance of your family after all the time. Come to the compound on the morrow and I will take your report."

Marcus stood to attention and saluted. "Salve, Sos." That was the exact order that he wanted. He had been far too long from the house of Pythes - they might even be wondering if he was still alive. And of course, he was craving to see Sabina again. That desire was paramount, but in propriety, he had to give his presence to his warden first.

Marked

Marcus almost laughed out loud at the expressions on the faces of Sabina and her mother. He had left this very doorway two months before, garbed in what almost seemed - to him - to be a costume for the acting-boards of the Forum, on the way to a new experience and uncertain as to the future. Now, the same young man - standing tall and tanned and confident, garbed in shining helmet, waxed armor and the red cloak, and with the signature of an officer at his breast - stood in the same spot and waited to be noticed.

With one long scream of "Marrccuusss," the young woman launched herself at him and would have propelled the both to the cobblestones of the street, were he smaller and she not so slight.

"Ah. I see that this household has not forgotten its student, in the long absence." The jest was lost on the sobbing Sabina but was smiled at by the mother. In only moments, they were seated at the familiar table in the front room, with the mother bringing wine, and cheese and bread. As she set the containers on the low table and prepared to leave, Marcus waved and said, "Please, Matrona. Sit with us. I have not come only to see your daughter." With widened eyes, the older woman spread her stola and sat on the opposite side.

For the while, Marcus gave his story of the last pair of months and even a sanitized version of the battle. And the news that his officer had apparently become unstable in his thinking process. He had no qualms about giving the prevarication to the two women - in no way would he put their lives at risk by including them in the still undone plan.

The same had happened earlier in the house of Pythes - the first place that he had stopped on his return from the Palace grounds. No less than the two women would be, Darius had been stunned when the young man stepped through the door of the storefront. Mouth open, he took several heartbeats to realize that what he was seeing was not an apparition, then with a massive grin, walked up and almost squeezed the life from the young man. Then, yelling at the top of his lungs, he pulled Marcus down the long hallway to the atrium. There, both Pythes and Valens, wondering what misfortune had befallen their storekeeper, received the same stunning vision. Then the open area became chaotic, as all were pounding the young man on the back and shouting questions that had no chance of either being heard nor answered. The two house-women were standing and watching but soon would be trying to fill the young man's belly far beyond its capacity.

Over the sumptuous meal, Marcus gave his tale, accurately, with the exception of the plot with the Tribune. For his part, he asked about the news of the usurpation. "I have only pieces of the tale, and not even sure of which of those are true."

Between the three older men, they pieced together what they had seen or heard. Pythes started the tale. "Do not take our stories as writ from Olympus as we have received them through many mouths. As it is told, the man Tarquin stormed the Senate-house with his men and placed himself on the Throne, then the Senators were summoned to the presence of the rightful King, as he called himself. Upon their arrival, he recited a list of grievances that he claimed to reduce the legitimacy of the Throne of King Tullius." He looked around in hesitation, more in habit than any fear that agents of the new King were listening.

Valens spoke quietly. "The actual accusations are difficult to trust. Every tale has new items and none seem to fit that royal person. There are imputations that Tullius was the slave of a slave, which is absurd, and that he was given the Throne by the machinations of a woman yet unnamed. And many other tales of no repute."

Pythes shook his head. "What is not a tale, is the fact that the King was murdered by the men around Tarquin, led by the Praefectus of the old regime. I forget his name..."

"Caeus," said Marcus.

"Aye. He took little time to switch his affiliations, which was probably done long before the deed. Many Senators were put to the sword - any who looked at the new changes with less than enthusiasm. Some of the story is as a tale from the bards - we are told that as the body of King Servius was laying in the street, his daughter refused to allow his transit to the temple, and indeed, threatened the drovers of the mortician cart with arrest should they linger. She herself slapped the asses with her whip and the cart wheels ran over the corpse as if it were offal."

Valens shook his head. "I fear that our times are in turmoil. If the tales of the past kings are in truth, then much blood will run before the succession is confirmed."

Now, with just an hour on the sundial to dusk, he was at the house on the street of the Poet. Again, the women wanted to feed him far beyond his need or even the capacity of a young man, but he made a masterful try at appearing to be hungry. Finally, with Sabina leaning against him - the position that she had not changed since his arrival - and the mother sitting across the low table, he began the spiel that he had practiced for the two months of his absence.

"Your pardon, Matrona. Like Sabina, I have no pater, and must act as my own surrogate. I am of legal age, even though not having made the rituals of manhood of the city. But, I am now an officer in the Roman army, callable at need, and in the patronage of the house of Junius. And I have a skill that I will augment into a vocation." The woman knew what was coming, but she allowed Marcus to fulfill the protocols. "As you are the maternal patron of Sabina, it is you that I must ask. And that is, to enter the nuptial ritual with your daughter."

Sabina was wide-eyed, not daring to breathe, and unlike her mother, astounded at the sudden discourse from Marcus. The older woman, knowing almost from that day that he had first stumbled into their dwelling that this conversation would come, was happily waiting for the event. With little dowry, other than the rental on the scribe school of her late husband, the prospects of her daughter were to become the wife of this fat charcoal merchant, or that stinking fish monger. To be beaten during the day and used at night and being turned into a termagant shrew before her paps had fallen. This boy - this young man, Marcus - was far above that which her little girl could have possibly hoped for, had circumstance been unchanged.

Smiling, she replied, "I give you my permission and my blessings." With that, the girl broke down completely - so much that she had soon wept herself to sleep, her arms still around his neck.

Trying to hide his discomposure at the reaction of his wife-to-be, he carefully disengaged himself from the girl. "Sabina seems to have taken my words with some dismay."

He mother just smiled. "That statement alone gives notice of your inexperience with the upbringing of a young girl. I can assure you, Marcus, that her reaction is one of an overburden of happiness." She stood and pointed. "If you would bring her, we will put her to repose on the sleeping bed." Carefully, Marcus picked up the slight girl, and in just a few steps, lay her down on a soft mat in the back room.

As he began to strap on his belt, in preparation for departure, the woman said, "The happiness does not just extend to my daughter. I give thanks to the gods that caused your feet to enter our dwelling on that first day." Without any comment - indeed, he could not even think of one in that situation - he merely bowed to the woman and made his exit.

His walk back to the household was in the failing light, but unlike a previous evening, he had little fear of any street toughs that might be lurking. He walked in uniform, a hand on his gladius and his ears open to all sounds - his thoughts, this time, not placing him in a haze of indifference to his surroundings.   He was not a veteran of desperate battles, but he could use his weapons with far more ability than would be needed on the streets of Rome against the sticks of street brawlers.   And, more than once in the near past, he had been given the lesson of the dangers of inattention when moving through unfamiliar territory.

Twice, this night, as during the previous day, he passed small squads of soldiers patrolling the streets to keep the calm, although, to the average citizen, the days had not changed from one to the next. Any of the resistance to the regime change was at far higher ranks than would be found in the lesser quarters of the city.   The leader of the squad, usually a junior officer of the rank of Sesquiplicarius, would examine the coming stranger, then suddenly shout a halt to his men, then salute Marcus with a "Salve, Sos!"

Marcus would return the salute with, "Salve, soldier. Continue your patrol."   With another salute, the men would walk on, leaving Marcus still bemused at his status - raised by chance from an orphan from the mountains, to a man of the city to be saluted by inferiors in rank.   The gods of Rome might be wealthy and powerful, but they were also apparently blind to a man's antecedents.

During the following days, he had much to do.   First was to call on the house of Junius to give his news of Lucius.   The plan had been that Collatinus would call as soon as he returned, and should have done so, but Marcus wanted to assure himself that the household was not in frantic worry about the son, should something have prevented that noble from his planned visit.   Knocking on the door, he waited for the servant... yes, Nonus was the name, he remembered. Not daunted by the greatness of the house on this occasion, as he had been on the last visits, he immediately announced, "Marcus, Adiutor to Tribune Junius, to call on the Domina of the house."   His tone and appearance were such as not to be questioned by a mere door slave.

Led into the atrium, he waited, resplendent in his freshly laundered uniform, armor wetly glistening with wax, and his helmet polished to a mirror shine.   Even the horsehair brush that indicated his rank had been replaced with new.   And of course, he wore the wonderful pallium, the red cloak that had been made and given to him by mother of Sabina.

Suddenly, and with shock, he realized that he was looking at two biers, on which were two wrapped... they were obviously bodies, and he instantly knew who they were - or had been.   He was aware of the Roman ritual of burial but had never participated in any of them as of yet. In his village, a person who had his or her life ended, was buried immediately, with wailings of the womenfolk and the chanting of the village shaman, then life moved on. Here, he knew that the ritual was long and involved, even if he had little knowledge of the details.

In a few moments, he saw the Domina walking across the floor, in that steady but unhurried pace of the upper-class woman. Stopping in front of Marcus, he could tell that she was still in the throes of sorrow, but she was composed and said, "Welcome, Marcus. Your presence gives this house honor."

"My thanks, Domina, and my pitiful regrets for your losses." He looked around to see if they were alone, then into the face of the woman. She knew the meaning of his intense stare.

"Come, we can converse in the garden. You are just back from the encampment?"

"Yesterday, Domina. I gave notice to my warden and my future wife, that I had returned."

They stopped in the middle of a large flowered area, an actual garden in the midst of the house. Next to a pool was a stone bench toward which she gestured, then both sat to face the entrance to the atrium. "We can talk here without the fear of wandering ears. Collatinus was here on the yesterday and gave me notice of the plans - and the absolute need for secrecy. In that, even my daughter does not know the true story. Only I, Collatinus and his aide, and yourself - besides Lucius - have the tale."

Marcus nodded, "Aye, Domina. Then I have little to say. I was concerned that the Tribune Collatinus might have been delayed and wished for you to have real news of Luc... the Tribune."

"Tell me of your journey on that march. Collatinus had no knowledge of it."

Once again, he gave the story, except, in this case, assuring the woman that the alleged injury to her son was a total fabrication. "By now, he will be in Antium, relaxing at the house of one of the caravaners. I will leave to take messages to him when the Tribune Collatinus determines the true situation in the city. And of course, I will stop here, before I leave, to receive any missives that you may wish to send."

The talk went on for a while, but there was little to be said that both did not know. Finally, she asked, "And you, Marcus, what are your plans?"

He smiled shyly. "There is a beautiful young woman whom I have asked permission to wed, and have received it from her mother.

And I will look for a merchant's shop to purchase, that I may begin my career of bowsmith. That is, of course, assuming that my purse will stretch to make a payment on a suitable dwelling." He paused, then said, "But my warden, Pythes, is knowledgable in the city and will assist me in finding what I need without fear of usury. And, of course, when Luc... the Tribune returns, and should there be a war, I will assume my place as his Adiutor."

The Domina smiled through her grief over the two bodies in the atrium. "You will not begin the nuptials without informing this House of the whereabouts and time. A present to the bride-nuptae is the least this house can do for your services."

"It is not necessary, but you have our thanks, Domina. And you have my dwelling place at Pythes, should you need my services, or if something... untoward might come to the front." He paused, "But for now, I will engage in none of my plans until the situation of your household is resolved."

The woman dropped her head, then stood. "The house of Junius has a good friend in Marcus. We will not forget it."

Leaving the household, he walked back to the Palatium quarter, then up the street of the merchants, visiting his many friends along the way. Once again, he was offered breads and sweetmeats, fruit and cheeses in quantities that would have fed two handfuls of soldiers. Many were the comments from the stalls on the looks of the handsome young soldier, so recently come to the city as a waif. Several of the merchant wives gave good natured japes at the wish to be many seasons younger and unwed - and in his single presence.

At the bakery of Porcia, the widow baker, he was commanded, as if a child, to sit and partake of her finest cake, just removed from the oven. At her insistence, once again, that such a young man needed a mate, he shyly told her of his request for the match to a girl. Astounded, the woman called to her neighbor, the wife of an oil vender. From her, the news spread up and down the street as a gossip from the gods.

The widow filled his cup again, and laughed. "You will bring the lucky girl for our perusal, Marcus. We must make sure of her suitability to be your partner." He knew that she spoke in jest, but also in the obvious desire to see the young woman.

He smiled. "Aye. I will do that, but know that she is not a street urchin, but learned in the art of the marks, and in chronicles of the world. Her pater was a... schola... an instructor to students." He had forgotten her father's actual title, but his description was close enough.

Finally, with his belly protruding from all the viands and drink that had been offered, he made his escape and bent his path to the eastern gate, and the training fields where he hoped to find his Hastiliarius, Drusus. As the post of the Tribunes, this one was now less deserted, with several groups of men scattered around the field, all running, or thrusting or parrying in concert with the profane shouts of the training officers. Again, he wondered if the new King were planning a military campaign - the number of soldiers being called up was far in excess of any needed to quell unrest in the city, and thus far, there had been none whatsoever from the peoples.

He saluted, and received the gesture in return at the gate then entered to look over the field. There, in the distance, he saw the familiar bulk of his Hastiliarius. Drusus the Centurion, he reminded himself. Walking across the dusty ground, he stopped behind the officer and waited for his curses to end. It was obvious that the wait might be considerable since the young men under his training seemed to be not conducive to learning. Not for the first time, Marcus wondered at the existence of the gods. Should they exist, they obviously turned deaf ears to the training grounds of Rome - the number of obscene references to the gods themselves and their private parts and even their choice of mates, should have long since have been sufficient to condemn the city to the far reaches of Hades.

Finally, with a shake of his head and the obvious conclusion that these farmers and charcoal burners would be nothing but sword fodder to any enemy of Rome, the Hastiliarius turned to leave. Then, suddenly seeing an officer standing behind him, automatically began to assume the attention pose, then recognized the man.

"Marcus! By Mars and his syphilitic whore-wives!" He looked his previous student up and down, obviously approving of what he saw. Turning, he shouted. "Attention for the Adiutor of the Tribune of the house of Junius!" Instantly, the training unit of men, probably thrice ten or more, stood to a ragged attention, in two ranks. With a wink, the Hastiliarius said to Marcus, "Care you to examine the tiros, Sos?"

Going along with the jest, Marcus assumed a stern expression then walked to stand in front of the man on the end - the standard bearer. Then slowly, he walked down the rank, looking up and down, finally reaching the far end without comment. Turning to the training officer, he said, "One hopes that these are not scheduled to engage with enemies for the while."

"Nay, Adiutor. This compilation is just started their training." To the men, he shouted, "Go for your midday mess. Then return here at the end-hour gong."   Smiling at Marcus, he motioned for the young man to follow.   Theoretically, Marcus was of a considerably higher rank than the old soldier, being an adjunct to a high-placed noble officer, but he well knew that in the practical sense, he was as a babe to the ability of the old veteran.   The gods themselves could not have ordered him to presume to give commands to the old soldier.

Dursus stood aside and gestured for Marcus to precede him into the officer's building.   Inside, the tables were empty, with all officers either on the training field or other duties.   Shouting to the tent-slave, he pointed to a bench then sat himself down across the table.   A slave entered with two bowls and a jug and a platter with cold foods, which he set before the veteran, then vanished back through the doorway.

Pouring a generous portion in each bowl, he began with, "As you have the signature of an officer on your breast, I am to assume that you have survived the trial of the Tribunes."   It wasn't a question, but a statement.

Marcus nodded and gave the tale of his training.   Of course, Dursus was interested in the encounter with the bandits and asked questions from every aspect of the fight.   The noon hour went by, with both asking and giving, until Marcus remembered the request, given one afternoon behind the barracks.

"The Senior Centurion Tatius sends his greetings to an old comrade.   One, whom I might add, never chose to reveal his actual rank to his flock."

The Hastiliarius set his bowl down, then nodded.   "Aye.   Those were the days.   We chastised the Eturians thrice, in battles that would send these farmer's boys running to the skirts of their maters.   Tatius was the Centurion of a sister cohort, and many cups did we drink to the spilled blood in those days."   He stared into nothing for a moment. "I have not laid eyes on my comrade since he assumed the baton of Senior - and no man deserves the rank more than he."

As the hour wore away, Marcus brought forth the question that had been the actual reason for his coming, besides the desire to visit his martial tutor.   "Sos, you may have heard of the disability of my superior, the Tribune Junius."

"Aye, some measure of the tale has been passed around.   And from a blow to the head, it has been spoken."   He nodded.   "I have seen men addled by such, and in all degrees of harm.   For most, it is a slow end to life, as they seldom recover their reason."

"Aye... But I feel that... for my Tribune, the illness will not be forever."   His hard stare at the officer was not unnoticed.

"Methinks you have more of this tale than is apparent." He waited for a reply, then continued. "Loyalty to a superior is a mark of desirability in a soldier. Break no confidences for me, but you have a reason for the statement?"

"Aye, Sos. Despite my lofty rank, given to a homeless waif of little worth, and as a gift from the gods it must be assumed, I have little actual understanding of how the army is constituted. I understand that I am now a legal Adiutor, but with my Tribune in a state of silentium, and for a time that is unknown, what may my status be? Do I stand down the uniform and enter my life as a citizen until called. Or become an aide to another?"

The old veteran shook his head. "You are the legal Adiutor to a Tribune, and as long as he is in that rank so may you be. Unless the Tribune is removed from office, your status will not change. And, until he is called to Army, you will not be subject to service." Looking around to make sure they are still alone, he leaned over and said in a low voice, "And that may not be far into the future. There are... tales on the wind, that this new King may wish to cull out a triumph or two for the storytellers. In that event, we may yet serve together should war come. And there is still much swordplay left in this old arm."

With much to think about, Marcus retraced his steps to the household. Finally, removing his military garb for the first time since coming to the city, he donned his simple tunic and sandals and was about to ask Darius for any work with which he could help. In the storefront, he saw the fat storekeeper conversing with another uniformed man, apparently a...

"Maxentius!"

The soldier turned, and raised his hand. "Salve, Marcus. You are prompt as usual. I was just asking this good man if you were in residence."

"Had you come earlier, I would not have been. What brings you to the realm of the Palatium?" He knew what this visit had to be concerned with, but it was important to keep up their veiled curtain to all.

"I have not had the chance to speak to a friend since the training marches. Have you time for a cup or two?"

"Aye, but we need not retire to a taburna. Come, the wine of Pythes is as good as any."

Leading his Adiutor friend through the maze of the house, he stopped by the kitchen to procure two bowls and a jug, then led them out the back door to his workbench in the stable. Here they could be alone - even Cleo apparently had gone with Pythes and Valens on their... wherever it was that trade had taken them for the day. This was far more private - and secure - than a table in a taburna, surrounded by other cups. And ears.

Pouring the wine, Marcus said, without preamble, "What news?"

Nodding as he accepted the bowl, Maxentius replied, "It is not all bad. Apparently the Tribune Junius has dropped out of the consciousness of the swine, Caeus. And of the new King's. They have far more problems to deal with than one addled young noble."

"That is what we were hoping, is it not."

"Aye. My Tribune and the Domina have met and concocted a plan for which you are to be the courier, as was expected." He reached into a bag that he had carried and pulled out two leather purses. "This is for the Tribune Junius. The Domina was assured that her son was given enough gold by Collatinus, that night at the villa, to sustain him well for many months, but she is a mother - and mothers have to be sure of the welfare of their sons." He handed the second purse to Marcus. "This is for you and any expenses you incur on their behalf. Any that is not used, is yours."

The small bag was heavy - very heavy. Marcus looked inside with disbelief, then said, "What expense do they expect that I will have? This would buy my own house in the Capitoline quarter!"

"Aye. I think that is her thought. I overheard some talk of your buying a household on the merchant's street? Apparently, the house of Junius lists you as a person of value."

Marcus just thought for a moment. And again, on the apparent favor of the gods to a nonentity from an unknown village. Before he could comment further, Maxentius continued. "You must remember the plan. Nothing is to be written down, for obvious reasons. "First, you will...

And as with all plans, nothing is guaranteed without a writ from the gods...

Three days later, he had entered the gates of Antium, enjoying his first sojourn to another place that wasn't a wilderness, and by himself. As a relatively extensive port city, he had some small effort to locate the houses of the merchants, but finally was walking up to the compound of Lartes. At the door, a slave saw the spotless tunic and expensive sandals and asked Marcus of his need. Shortly, he was escorted to the atrium where he saw the fat merchant, swaddled in far more finery than he had worn on the trail. Bowing, the man greeted, "Welcome, Sos. Marcus, is it not? Aide to the officer that delivered us from the brigands in the wilderness."

"Aye, and good day to yourself, Sos."

"What brings your goodself to our city. One hopes that you might tarry a while and allow myself to repay part of your courage."

Marcus gave a dismissing gesture. "No repayment is necessary, good Sos. The dislodgment of rabble that preys on citizens is a duty. I come to speak to the Tribune."

Instantly, from the expression on the face of the merchant, Marcus knew that something was amiss with his journey. The reply underscored that fact. "The Tribune? Alas, I have not seen that good man since our parting on the trail from the mountain outpost."

With a sinking feeling, Marcus said, "Perhaps he is at the dwelling of Bithenus?"

The merchant shook his head. "Unless he has arrived this day, that would not be the fact of the matter. I, myself, spoke with Bithenus on the yesterday, at the forum. He certainly would not have failed to mention the presence of our savior from death or slavery, had he arrived." Lartes realized that the news he was purveying was not gladsome. "One hopes that his absence is not of great concern."

"I... I do not know. He was expected to reside here until I came with news."

"This concerns the exchange of leaders in your city, does it not?" Without waiting for an answer, the merchant continued, "Whatever the fact or reason, the Tribune is welcome in my household, either as a guest or a fugitive, although I pray to the gods that the last is not the case."

Taking his leave of the merchant, Marcus wandered around the streets, thinking on his next actions. Antium was not a city on the scale of Rome, but neither was it a small village. Searching the alley and streets for a single man would be an exercise in futility. Especially, one who was probably careful not to be apparent as a noble of a high house. He would have to return to Rome and consult with Collatinius.

The day was almost gone, and leaving for Rome wasn't practical, even if his weary legs were agreeable. He walked until he came upon an inn, apparently prosperous and with the scent of good food wafting from the door. He would stop here tonight, and determine what to do on the morrow.

His choice of lodgings was good. His room was clean and the food in the common room, plain, but filling, and served by a wench barely older than Sabina, and as tasty to the eye. He just sat in a corner, contented with the repast and the agreement of his legs to be finished with the road for the day. The other guests, to a man, were all merchants traveling the coastal roads, and their conversation was confined to the cost of this and the value for that. A few comments were made on the turbulence in the big city to the north, but only in the context of the effect on the trade routes. Even though his association with Pythes made him quite literate in the subjects of the men, he had no interest in joining the conversations. It was enough to sit quietly, sipping the good wine and thinking on the morrow.

Obviously, he could not travel up and down the roads, looking and asking about the missing Tribune. Such a search would be as looking for a grain of sand in the training field. In the back of his mind, was the fear that his officer and friend was planning a retribution, despite his oaths to the contrary. But, still, Lucius was not a stupid man, and Marcus knew exactly the path that the thoughts of a man would take after such a horrible tragedy. He, himself, had the same reaction, blindly and furiously following the trail of the marauders of his village until the hot blood cooled enough to allow him to realize that even should his quest be successful, the result would just be his death at the hands of many.

Lucius had gone through the same natural thoughts, and should have reached the same conclusions. But why would he not be here in the city as agreed upon? And, it appeared, he had not even come to the place. It was as if...

Any of the men watching Marcus would have reason to assume that he had suddenly seen the Gorgon, and was now a figure of stone, immovable forevermore. As the sudden thought expanded and filled his mind, he looked at it from all angles, then finally, after much time nodded to himself...

Noted

Marcus looked through the foliage at the abandoned villa, listening and waiting for movement. Hearing and seeing none, he slowly approached, invisible to anyone in his stealth. His skill in stalking, learned from the time of a babe, made him invisible to any who were not concentrating on an approach from the forest. At the wall he slowly - very slowly - raised his head just sufficiently to look inside, past the decaying board shutters of the window opening.

Nobody.

From here, it could have been abandoned and not visited since that time - about seven days before - when the four conspirators had left. Inside, however, was a different tale. The fire pit was fresh, and warm, with hidden coals under the ashes - probably from a meal to break the morning fast. In a corner was a sleeping mat, and two jugs. Nodding in self-congratulation on his guess, he walked to a corner and sat down, his back to the wall.

The walk from Antium had been long and fast, and even his young legs were protesting about both the distance and the pace. But, he had made the journey between daylight and dark - and in fact, it was still the half part of an hour by a sundial, had there been one, until full darkfall. Also, his belly was complaining mightily about the abuse during the day, so he opened his pack and retrieved the bread and cheese that he had hurriedly purchased as traveling rations as he passed through a minor hamlet on the way.

The light was almost gone when he heard the footsteps in the direction of the road. With his hand on his pugio, he waited, then saw a shadow figure enter the door portal. He relaxed when the outline resolved itself into the expected man. He watched as the Tribune scratched the fire pit to expose the dying coals, then toss a handful of leaves to bring it to life. Shortly, a small fire was blazing, casting a small light into the far corners of the room.

"It is gladsome to know that even a city man has the wisdom to bank his cook fire before he leaves for the day."

The Tribune froze, his hand automatically reaching for the hilt of his gladius, when the recognition of the voice stopped his action. He turned and stood up as Marcus strode toward him. "By the gods! Marcus! Once again you have proven that sharpened wits are not the exclusive property of the city-born." They grasped each other's wrists, then at a motion from the Tribune, sat facing the small fire. "I knew that you would build a structure of the right conclusions."

"It took me a while, but as you have never been seen in the city of Antium, this place was a possibility. Unless you were meaning to disappear from all sight, this was the only private spot known to both of us." He hesitated, then said, "I am hoping that your proximity to the city is not an indication that you wish to fulfill your original desire."

The Tribune shook his head. "Nay. The memories are still green and should the chance permit I will carve the hearts from the King and all around him." He held up his hand to stifle the protest of his aide. "But, I will wait. And for a lifetime if necessary. I would never initiate an action that might rebound on my mother and sister."

Relieved, Marcus answered, "It relieves me to hear you say so. But what is your purpose of remanding here, rather than in the comfort of a merchant house in Antium?"

"Before I answer, have you the auspices date of the pompa funebris?"

Marcus had little knowledge of Roman funerals but guessed the meaning. "Aye, Sos. The auguries have specified the second day after the Kalends to be favorable for the funeral procession."

Lucius thought for a moment. "Four days hence."

"You will not attend, Sos? That will destroy our plan completely."

The Tribune smiled as he replied. "Ease your liver, Marcus. I will be there in spirit, if not in body. Now, tell me of the words from Collatinus, as to our scheming. And, by the by, do not tell my friend of my whereabouts. He would inevitably wish to visit me, and a noble of his rank cannot wander up and down a remote road without comment being made by all whom he passes. You will be the only man who knows the complete truth. Now, what news?"

"Well, Sos. On my return, I will report..." The talk went on until both bedded down for the night. Early the next morning, Marcus was striding through the Capitoline.

Unlike the Senior Centurion, the mere aide of a Tribune did not just walk through the gates of the Palace. To the guard Captain, he gave his mission. "Marcus, Adiutor to the Tribune Junius, with information requested by the Praefectus." He stood, waiting for the request to flow up the channels and then, the permission, back down to the gate.

Soon, an officer walked up and gestured, "Come," and Marcus followed him to the same area of the Palace as the last time. "Stop here." Inside, he waited in the empty room, using the time to recite once again the report that he was about to make. In a while, two men appeared from a curtained doorway.   One was the Praefectus Caeus, but the other was unknown to Marcus.   But, not for long...

Caeus looked at the young man, obviously trying to remember one of many faces that he had probably encountered in the busy days of last.   Nodding, he said, "Ah...   This is...   Marcus, Adiutor to the Tribune Junius."

The second man was tall, and by not any means old, probably having seen thirty seasons in all.   Dressed in the traditional toga of a noble Roman, he was unbearded, tall and muscular.   But, other than being the obvious superior to the Praefectus, Marcus had no idea of his identity, unless...   The fantastical idea had only just been conceived when it was delivered as true.

"This is the Regis Tarquinius.   Make your report."

Inside, Marcus was frozen in shock, but knew that he had to respond.   Unfortunately, in all of the education that he had received since his arrival in Rome - from Pythes, Valens, Sabina, and even the people of the street - nothing had been given that would allow him to know how to address a king.   The idea that he would experience the need would have been laughed off as a ridiculous jest - young barbarians from the mountains were not brought into the Royal presence - anywhere.

"Aye...   Sos...   Regis."   He had no idea of the proper honorific to use in this circumstance, but as he wasn't called down, he continued. "I have the gladsome news that the noble Lucius Junius is recovering from his malady and is improving by the day."   A pause.   "His spasms are decreasing as is the swelling to the side of his head."

"Where is he residing?"   The King had a surprisingly deep voice, but Marcus had hardly expected the ruler to be soft-spoken.

"He is taking the bathing cure at the Oracle in Epidaurus. The hot waters of the brimstone pools are curative for the vertiginous malady. And he reaches to a chirsurgeon in the city of Anagnia who is cleansing his body with medicinal herbs and elixirs."

"And has he made you privy to his plans, should he become well?"

"Aye. So... Regis. He will return and assume his place as a Tribune and head of his household."

The Praefectus spoke up. "What are his feelings as to the passing of the members of his family? A man must resent the deaths to an extent."

Marcus breathed a sigh of relief, or would have had he not caught himself. That was the question that he - and his fellow conspirators needed to be asked. "As I surmised in my earlier report,

Sos, the Tribune is certainly heavyhearted about the deaths but realizes that in any... change of leadership some sacrifices may occur. As the action elevates himself to the position of the Dominus of the House of Junius, then he will not gainsay the past. And, he looks forward to being of service to the King Tarquinius."

The King nodded, apparently satisfied. "As you may be aware, his mother is my sister, and she has suffered enough. I would not have her lose her only son, and the lineage of the house. When may he return?"

"Alas, Regis. The chirsurgeon speaks of a cure, but his explanations are so steeped in his practice that I get the meaning of only one word in three. Should I attempt to ordain the future, I would say by the third Kalends from now he will be cured to a state that will not chance the shaming of his family by... his malady."

Tarquinius thought for a moment, then said, "Very well. Give my wishes to the Tribune for his complete restoration to health, and that he should call upon me when he has returned."

With that, he nodded to the Praefectus, who said, "Dismissed, Adiutor."

After informing both the Tribune and his friend, Collatinius, of the encounter, and taking a covered wax tablet to the mother, Marcus was suddenly without need for any immediate service anywhere but the house of Pythes. And of course, his lessons at the little shop on the street of the Poet.

Now that Marcus had become the de-facto Dominus of the house of the two women, even before the ceremony of the nuptae, Sabina could accompany him at will, and often did. To maintain her propriety of a virtuous young woman, and so as not to alarm her mother, he always returned her to the house well before the sun would set behind the buildings. One of her first outings was to the street of the merchants in the Palatine quarter. And naturally, the wives and female merchants of the street were effusive with their praise of the choice of Marcus for a mate. Many were the gentle jests about the luck of the young man to find and win such a jewel. Porcia, the widow baker, shooed away the street urchins, hanging around for a crust of bread, and offered her best chair to the young woman.

The morning turned into a festive occasion, with Sabina the center of attention for all on the street. Had Marcus allowed, she would have been burdened with gifts of such quantity as to have required an ass and cart to convey them to her home. Still, the fruit, sweetmeats, warm breads and cakes and suchlike were offered in a quantity far beyond the capability of the young woman to consume.

Marcus just relaxed and let the womenfolk talk and jest. By the midday bell of the Crier, she had fully captured the hearts of the street.

Afterward, they spent the remainder of the day in the atrium of the house of Pythes. Once again, the women of the house attempted to fill the young woman with delicacies delivered in heaps. All agreed later that Sabina was a jewel beyond price and wondered in jest at the feats that Marcus had done on behalf of the gods to be blessed with such favor. By the time that she had been escorted to her house, the young woman was almost exhausted. This had been a day beyond belief for a girl who had seldom ventured beyond her own threshold, and who had previously considered a walk - with a handsome young man - to the boot-maker and back, to be a high point of the season.

The next day, Marcus was assisting Cleo in loading a train of asses with pelts, to be taken to the port at Ostia for shipment to... some far-off port of which he had never heard, when Darius called from the back door. "There is a Conciliator here to see you in the front of the store."

The young man had never heard the word before and asked, "What would his wants be with myself?"

The fat storekeeper just shrugged. "He is a land agent of the quarter. I assumed that you had summoned his services."

Perplexed, Marcus followed the older man through the house and into the storefront. There, stood two men - one obviously a servant - or slave - but the other in garb that made him a prosperous tradesman of some type. Seeing the young man approach, the man bowed and said, "You are Marcus, of the house of Pythes, I presume?" At the nod, he continued, "I am Parmensis, property factor and Conciliator in the hire of the Domina of the house of Junius."

This was interesting. The Tribune had mentioned being of assistance in his selection of a suitable property for his own, but... "You have me at a disadvantage, Sos. I have not discussed any such with the good mother of the Tribune."

The man waved his hand in dismissal. "I am not privy to your arrangements with that noble house, but I have been specified to make your acquaintance with a property that is in..." He stopped as Pythes walked up behind Marcus.

"Parmensis!" Marcus turned as his warden walked up to the guest. "You old thief! My youngster does not need your vermin infested swampland or whatever worthless properties that you are trying to vend." His actions belied his words, as both grappled in a massive hug that left no doubt that this was a meeting of two old friends.

"Your youngster, as you say, would seem to be a man of his own accord.   He can determine his need for swampland."   At the questioning look from the merchant, he continued, "I am in the compensate of the house of Junius, to show your ward a selected house in the Viminalis quarter."

Surprised, Pythes looked at his ward. "You have not spoken of this.   Are you now in the utility of that noble house?"

Marcus shook his head, vigorously. "Nay, Sos.   Only in my position as the aide to the Tribune. I would certainly have made you aware of any contract with another party.   It is a wonderment to myself, also."

Now it was the turn of the guest to be surprised. "This is interesting.   At the auspices of the Domina Junius, I was to show Marcus a property that might be suitable for his use.   I do not understand why he has no knowledge of it."

"Is this in response to your assist of the young Junius, that day in the wilderness?" asked Pythes to the young man.

"Aye, it must be so.   I had mentioned to the Domina my desire to one day begin my own bowsmithery." He hated to keep his knowledge from his mentor, Pythes, to whom he owed so much - in fact, everything he was today.   But, in the interest of the safety of all concerned, he could not blurt out the many other instances in which he had given assistance to the noble house - and that in fact, still was deep in conspiracy on their behalf.

"Well.   The gratitude of a noble house is not to be despised. Let us examine this property that they have apparently selected for you."

The three, along with the merchant's scribe, set foot for the center of the city then up the street of the Poet, despite the protestations that the proper direction was still two avenues further along.   Pythes said in response, "Hold your protests a moment. Marcus is wishing to gather another person who will, no doubt, have an opinion on what you are to show us."

Surprised by the group that suddenly appeared at her door, Sabina readily agreed to attend them to a place that might well become her home.   Both she and Parmensis knew the quarter much better than their guests, and led them to a cross-street, rather than back down to the Crier's Circle where the main avenues joined.   Thus, the distance was short, and they quickly attained the street that they sought.

This thoroughfare was a street of craft manufactories and the houses of prosperous tradesmen.   Suddenly, Parmensis stopped at a gate, speaking briefly to a man sitting under an awning just inside - apparently a watchman. Marcus just stood there, stunned and speechless. Not much less wide-eyed were both Pythes and Sabina. This household, inside of a stone-fenced compound, was smaller than the assemblage of buildings that made up the domicile and merchantry of Pythes, but this one was much more opulent. Instead of wood, this one was of brick and even had two massive pillars at the front door, holding up a tall portico as shelter to those entering.

"By the gods!" exclaimed Pythes. "By what issuance of the fates makes claim that you could purchase this palace!"

Marcus shook his head. "I am as taken aback as yourself, Sos." Unknown to anyone but himself, the Domina Junius, and Collatinius, he could easily purchase this domicile and more. Hidden under the boards of his room was not only his own stash of savings, but the bag of gold given him to help his Tribune - none of which he had used, or saw any reason to use in the help of Lucius. Still, he had planned on a small and cozy house, in the Palatium quarter, with a workshop in the back that he might practice his craft. Should he take this dwelling as his own, he would be seen as one of the major merchants of Rome - something totally at odds with his true status.

Parmensis waved to him. "Come. Inspect the household."

Inside, the dwelling was clean and spacious, and Sabina looked with longing at the atrium with the center sun-hole and small pool and garden underneath. And at the spacious kitchen, the loft with bedrooms - one larger than the entire house in which she had been raised. And... A stone bath easily big enough for two, with an undercove for heating of the water.

To Marcus, it was all just a presumptuous display of wealth. The house of Pythes was bigger, and with only one floor, but every section had a purpose, only a small part being for living, the rest mostly just storage. Of course, left to himself, he would be completely satisfied to live in a workshop, with his bed-mat in the corner. But, even in his state of youth, he realized that a women - a wife - needed something more than just a room with a bed to call home. He was about to tell the agent that the idea of the purchase of this house was beyond any possibility when the party wandered out the kitchen to the back of the compound. There, he saw a large and low structure - this one of wood - with open bays and a large center workshop.

Eyes wide, he wandered around the building, giving a far more intense inspection than he had bothered with in the main house. Trying to keep his expression neutral, his eyes sparkled as he looked at the workshop of a luxury that he had never imagined. Seeing his interest behind the feigned indifference, Parmensis said, "Do not take my words as writ, but I believe that this was the works of a carver... Cateronious or Caterenous, or some such name. He made votive statues for the lesser houses that could not find the means to visit the stone carvers." That explained the balks of wood stacked in two of the bays and the many pieces scattered around. There were no tools - apparently the previous dwellers took anything of value when they left.

Pythes asked, "What was their reason for leaving?"

"Again, I am not closely privy to the tale, but I am told that the principle passed on to his ancestors, and the male siblings, having no skill in likeness carving, soon lost their clientele and could no longer make the rent."

As the two old friends talked about... this old time and that, Marcus and Sabina walked around the compound. Out of hearing of the others, Sabina said, "Marcus, the stories of your past, during the lessons, gave me no indication that you were wealthy enough to purchase such a manse. Have you a part of your life to which I am ignorant?"

He looked at her, then shook his head. "At the time, my tales were true, but much has happened since the death of the old King. But, ask me not about that. I will give you the story in full, but at a time when the actions are old and not of danger to report. I have told you about my succor of the Tribune Junius..." She nodded. "Much of this stems from that, but there is more that you may not know as yet." Looking up at the imposing brick backside of the house, he chuckled and said, "Would you wish to be the mistress of such a monstrous dwelling? One with at least ten rooms, to my count."

She smiled also. "I would feel like the Domina of a great house, needing to purchase many fine clothes to keep up my position above my inferiors."

Now he laughed, but she continued, "I know that you have little interest in this dwelling, and I would be happy with being your wife if we lived in a village hut from your youth. But... I can see in the eyes of a man when he looks upon something with longing, be it the body of a woman or, in your case, the manufactory in which you are trying not to demonstrate interest." She hesitated, then, "Marcus, when we wed... my mother..."

He knew exactly her concern. "She will live with us, wherever we are put down. Your good mother will not live out her life as a lonely woman in an empty house." At that, Sabina just hugged her man and said nothing.

Seeing all that could be seen from the outside, they walked back to the two men, now sitting on balks of wood and reminiscing over old times, apparently - or maybe, just discussing the prospects of trade under the new regime. Looking over his friend's shoulder, Parmensis said, "What is your idea, Marcus?"

"I am still astounded at the suggestion that I should purchase such a... place."

"Nay, your purchase is optional - and apparently not expected. My assumption is that you would undertake a permanent lease... Although from the attitude of the Domina I have the feeling that you may make your own decision."

Pythes spoke up. "So, this property is in the ownership of the house of Junius?"

"Aye. They own many properties in the Viminalis quarter - and others. I am only one agent that they contract with."

"Hmmm. What is the amount of the conducio for the property?"

Parmensis shook his head. "Now you are entering the strangeness of the offer. I do not know. My task was only to get the satisfaction of Marcus for the transaction. The Domina will discuss the details of the payments." A pause, then, "It is most unusual. It would appear that your ward is somehow in the good graces of that noble house."

Indeed, Marcus knew that to be true, but he had no expectation that the graces would extend to his domicile. After the noon meal, he and Sabina set foot for the Capitoline. She was nervous about visiting a noble house, something that she had never done, and never expected to do. "I would not like to bring shame upon you, in my ignorance of the rites."

Marcus smiled. "There are no rites any more than visiting a friend, other than politeness and respect for the household. She is to be addressed as 'Domina' and that would be the only difference."

At the doorway to the impressive house, a knock brought Nonus, the door steward, or whatever his task was. The slave well knew the young man by now, and that he was welcome in this household. Looking at Sabina as they walked into the atrium, Marcus could well remember his first entry into the world of the wealthy, and knew her of awe at the sights. They stopped and waited, as the girl looked around, trying to appear as if she were not. "Had I visited Olympus," she whispered, "I would not have expected such wealth." Marcus just nodded, seeing a woman and a girl approaching from the far doorway.

"Marcus. You honor our house with your presence. And this is your bride-to-be."

It wasn't a question, obviously, and he replied, "Aye, Domina. May I present Sabina, of the house of Nikias, a well known and respected Rhetor, he being late of the Viminalis quarter." Turning, he said to the girl, "This is the Domina of the house of Junius."

Sabina curtseyed, dipping deeply in the feminine fashion, as the older woman looked at her intently. "My, my. You said you had become affianced to a young woman, Marcus. You failed to mention that she is indeed as beautiful as the daughter of Venus."

At the complement, the pure white complexion of the girl turned to a red that rivaled the clay on the river bank. "You are most kind, Domina," returned the girl, still looking below the face of the woman.

The Domina waved a hand. "Sabina, this is my daughter. It would seem that both of you are of a like age. Iulliana, would you please keep the company of Sabina while I converse with Marcus." To the young man, she said, "Come. We will speak in the garden."

As they settled into a stone bench, once again out of hearing of any of the many household staff, she asked, "And you Marcus. News of my son is what you bring unexpectedly?"

Marcus shook his head, "Nay, Domina, else I would have come alone, and instantly." Looking around for wandering ears, he lowered his voice and said, "The Tribune Collatinius has given me no indication of any change in our... situation."

The woman nodded and smiled. "Then I am to assume that this visit is in reference to the property that my agent was to have offered you."

"Aye, Domina. And I am grateful for your efforts, but..."

"But you were astonished at the sight of the dwelling, when you were expecting a modest merchant abode."

He nodded. "Such a household would seem to be... overly magnificent for my... our needs. And of considerably cost for a young man just starting out in a trade that he has not even mastered yet."

"Nonsense. As to the cost, that is of no importance." She looked through the open arch at the two girls carrying on a lively conversation, then back to the young man. "Marcus. The house of Junius at a cusp in the history of our family. Only one male is left to carry on our gens into the future. And he is a good man, as you know, but young, and much may happen that he will have to sustain." She looked off into the distance, then back to him. "My brother is not a man intent on saving Rome from the clutches of an illegal monarch, as he says.   Tarquin and Tullia, his wife, are greedy and will do anything to increase their power and presence.   This I know and have known since we were children playing in the Palace garden."   Marcus just nodded.   "Should he decide that Lucius, or I, or any of the people of Rome, however noble and high, are obstacles in his way, then he will eliminate them without mercy."

"Should that come to pass, I hope to flee in safety with my daughter and son, but such a future is not conducive to planning. Still, I have gradually moved...   various assets to safety, in the event, and so that we will not become not only a family in flight, but also not one of penury.   The house in the Viminalis quarter is one of those assets.   By happenstance, it has become empty during this time of stress."

Another look into the distance as she gathered her thoughts. "Your efforts on our behalf have far more than earned a mere dwelling, but my thoughts are beyond that.   My intention is to vend the property to you."   She raised her hand, "Hold, and let me finish. Should my fears come to pass, the property would have been sold and beyond the notice of Tarquin.   And even if our family falls, it will still be safely yours and beyond seizure.   At least, as well as anything in the city is safe from a king with megalomania."

"Domina.   I would be purchasing the property with your coin. The bag of gold you gave me is far..."

"Shush.   I do not intend that you pay anything for the household.   We will, of course, register the vending and the price with the tax magistrate, and pay the appropriate fees, but you will only pretend to the annual payments to our house.   Should better times return, then we will reconsider the transaction, but know this, it will be yours to live in as long as you wish."

"But..."   Marcus was having trouble with the concept of accepting what was actually a gift - and a magnificent one at that.

"The gold that I have given you will support the house for many years, even assuming that you do not succeed in your craft, and that is very unlikely for such a resourceful individual as you."   She leaned over and said in a low voice, "And I would ask the boon from you to also hide a portion of our treasury in the house, buried somewhere in the grounds."   Straightening up, she continued, "The house of Junius has friends, and good friends, such as Lucius Collatinus, but he and they are nobles also, and at this time we cannot know which families will be considered a danger to Tarquin.   Already, old and good families have been decimated for no reason than they were less than enthusiastic about the change of royalty.   You, are not in their vision, and just another citizen of Rome and no possible threat to the succession."

She paused, then, "As I have said before. All others are the friends of the House of Junius.   You are the friend of Lucius."

Funeris   (Funeral)

For the first time since he had returned from the trip to Antium, Marcus was back in his uniform.   He had just come from the funeral of the two male members of the house of Junius and feeling more tired than had he worked a day in his shop.

The rites had been extended to the bulk of the day and interminably to Marcus.   There were rituals before the march that took an hour by the sun clock, then a slow march across the city to the cementerium outside the walls.   By then it was after noontime.   Then the laudiato funebris were spoken one after another as this man and that eulogized the two departed men.   Then more chanting by the priest and his acolytes, followed by still more eulogies.   It was late afternoon, with the horns and paid mourners at full crescendo, that the pyres were finally lit.   Then he got a surprise - the guests began to leave with the flames still high.   He knew that the lamantae would hold vigil all night - indeed, for the full seven days of mourning - but for the family and citizens of the city, apparently the rites had been satisfied.

Walking Sabina back to her house, both were quiet.   She was a daughter of Rome and he did not wish to offend her by giving his opinion of the supposedly sacred customs that, to him, seemed more like - well, the Forum on feast days.   Tired, he gave his regrets to the mother at her offer of food, then left for his own bedroom in the merchant's house.

Two days later, he filled a bag with viands and a jug, then set off out the southern gate, on the way to Antium - at least, that is the story that he gave to the vendors and casual friends.   All knew that he made the journey twice during the month, to putatively search the extent of the Tribune's recovery.   At the gate, he stopped in surprise, looking at the guard officer standing alongside the portal.   Seeing the smile on the face of the soldier, looking back at him, he stepped forward and saluted, although Marcus was not wearing his uniform, only a traveling tunic.   "Decanus Blackus!   I see that you have been seen fit to enter the rank permanently."

The man saluted, and said, "Aye, Sos. And my gratitude to yourself and the Tribune for the recommendations.   But, as of now, I am a sub-Tesserarius for the nonce."

Marcus nodded, with a grin. "It suits you. A sub-guard officer is a good step on the journey to Centurion."

The man grinned in return. "Aye. One hopes the gods are in agreement with the travel."   He tilted his head slightly, then stepped away from the men, into the grass. Marcus followed and when they were out of hearing of the gate, the Captain continued. "One hopes that the Tribune is progressing well."

"Aye," replied Marcus. "In fact, I am on the way to check his progress now."

The soldier hesitated, looking back at his men standing on either side of the gate. In a low voice, he said, "Sos. I would make you aware of a possible danger to yourself or the Tribune." He waved, then pointed to the training post half a stadium down the wall towards the east, but it was just misdirection should someone be watching. Marcus nodded, and pointed with a hand, himself, keeping up the farce, then the officer continued. "Know you of the guard Captain, Petronius?"

"I have been warned of him, but nothing else."

"He was here on my last duty, and asked when and how often you left the gate. Of course, I had to tell him of what I had seen of you, that your travels seemed to be twice in a month." He looked at Marcus and simulated a laugh, that was returned. "There is a man, even now, keeping watch on the gate. He has been there for several days, but when you appeared, I noticed that he had gone. To inform that you are on another journey, one assumes."

Marcus waved his hands toward the city - more indirection. "That is interesting. I have it from the King himself, that the Tribune is not in bad graces with the Throne. Why would..." He paused, furiously thinking about the ramifications of the news.

"Sos. If I may say in our privacy, I know nothing personally about the Captain Petronius, but the talk in the barracks is that the man with the three-fingered hand is one of which you may wish not to be noticed by."

Marcus nodded. "Aye. He is the butcher arm of Caeus, another man not to be offended." He thought again, then said, "My thanks, and that of the Tribune for your warning, sub-Tesserarius Blackus. It will not be forgotten."

They saluted each other, then turned to walk back to the gate, but the Captain suddenly said, in a low voice and without turning his head, "Sos. Through the gate, at the wine stall. The watcher has returned and with friends, it seems."

Marcus could see four men, through the wide opening, all sitting at cups. He had no idea which was the sentry that had been apparently watching for him, but obviously, the man had called for assistance and for a reason. He looked around at the masses of humanity outside the gate - many were coming or going, but enterprising merchants had booths and tents set up along the road, serving both drink and viands to the travelers. Many were the efforts of the sellers in the city to have the venues closed and forbidden, but custom had long decreed that land along the roads to the city were free for use by any, unlike the rents on a kiosk in the city, and the prices of the merchandise were lower as a result.

Marcus found a small canopy under which an old couple was serving both wine and bread and took his seat at a table. Before leaving for Antium he needed to think on the information just given him by the sub-officer. He was not bothered by the idea that the powers of the city were attempting to follow his actions - all rulers in all lands, he was sure, wished more information about their subjects. But why would he be followed? They knew his destination - or rather, they thought they did. The only persons who knew differently were the four conspirators, and none of those would break the confidence. The proper action for the watchers would be to wait at the city gate of Antium, and follow him from there, safely anonymous in the crowds of the city.

Casually, and out of the corner of his eye, he looked back at the men who were supposedly to tail him down the road. They had returned to their cups, apparently confused that Marcus had stopped just outside the gate, rather than setting foot on the journey. The cutthroat Petronius had set the men to action, but that did not mean that the order did not come from on high. After all, it would be ridiculous to expect the Captain of the Guard, Caeus, to personally engage the men.

He was in a quandary. If he should abort his journey now, after being seen speaking to Blackus, it would put that good man in danger of being suspected as a fellow conspirator. But if he...

A long drink later, he was still asking himself questions. He knew that this King was not adverse to eliminating anyone on the slightest pretense of threat. Therefore, the ruler did not currently harbor any doubts about an unimportant person such as Marcus. Had he done so, there would be no reason for stealth and following to another city - Marcus would just be taken to the Mamertine and put to the torture to tell the story. Therefore, this had to be an action by a subordinate, looking to raise himself in the eyes of his superiors. But once again, why follow him rather than wait for...

Suddenly, he knew. The men had no intention of following him to the city of Antium. Once out of the sight of the city, and assumably when a less traveled part of the road was reached, they would accost him for answers to their master's questions. Marcus knew that any questioning by those men would not be a pleasant experience, nor one that he was likely to survive. Again, neither the King nor Caeus would bother with the subterfuge - this HAD to be a plan by the scum, Petronius.

"Know what you plan, before you engage in combat," was the oft-given advice of Dursus, his sword-trainer. "A surprised foe is half defeated before the metal even meets." He wondered if the three or four men were veterans of the army, or just street toughs in the hire of the butcher. It made no real difference - Marcus could not, with confidence, engage four men of any skill - four to one might as well be as one against fifty. Even the most skilled fighter cannot parry four blades at once. Swordplay was not an option. And any action that he took would have to be most definitely out of the sight of any other eyes. Should a report be returned to Petronius that his four men were slain on the road while following Marcus, the next attempt at questioning would be with an entire Contubernium of soldiers.

Finally, nodding to himself, he stood and placed his coin on the table, wishing the old woman a good day. With that, he set his feet on the road to Antium and stepped off. At any turn in the road, or at the times that a loaded wagon gave cover, he looked back to see his followers. There were three - apparently one had just been the sentry to watch the gate. They kept a good distance, about a stadium or more as they walked abreast down the road. Marcus slowed his gait - he needed for them to be close enough to see his next action.

At the little hamlet that was no more than a few huts and an open-air vendor of bad wine, he suddenly turned his steps to the small road that skirted the Pontine marshes. No doubt, his shadows were surprised at his leaving the main road, but the action probably reinforced the idea that the journey of Marcus was indeed a sham.

Far fewer travelers were on this minor road - mostly farmers going here or there. Marcus maintained a vigil behind him to make sure that the men didn't suddenly rush forward to accost him for the questioning. Still, they had to be close enough to see his next turn. That came at the eastern end of the marsh when he suddenly turned onto a path leading away from the waters. This followed a dry watercourse between hills and led to one of his most productive hunting grounds - back in the time when his life was much simpler, and he had the time to enjoy hunting for game, he told himself, wryly. Now he hurried, almost at a run and out of sight of the following men. They would have no problem following the trail - it was bordered by the steep hills on both sides. And that was the reason that Marcus had chosen this route.

Three or four stadia along, he came to the part of the watercourse that he remembered - and wanted. Now he climbed the steep embankment, then, at the top, walked quickly back toward the way he had come. Shortly, he was at the top of a cliff, overlooking the trail that he had followed. In mere heartbeats, his bow was strung and several arrows were stuck in the dirt, ready for use. Again, it was only a short time before the three men came into view - hurrying to gain the sight of their quarry again, but not actually running as Marcus had been. By necessity, on the narrow trail between the rocks, they were following in single file but not expecting any strife apparently, as their blades were still sheathed. Of course, three ruffians would have little to fear from a just-grown stripling, no matter that he was a soldier.

That attitude was a mistake on their part, and was never realized by the second and third men. Marcus waited as they passed below, the cliff protecting him from a rush by the three, should his plan fail to be decisive. He stood up and drew the string to his ear...

The last man in line fell on his face, dead with an arrow in his back and through his heart. Death was so sudden that his comrades did not even hear him fall. The next man fell in order, and not quietly, but just as quickly dead. The surviving man, turning to look, was stricken at the sight that he could see on the dry stones that he had just trod. That answered one of the questions of Marcus. The man was just a ruffian, hired from the streets for his rough work. A veteran of the wars, or even just of the training fields, would have already reacted by instantly moving this way or that - not by standing and gawking like a fruit vendor who has dropped his basket in the mud.

The man had not even raised his eyes to the cliff when the third arrow found its mark, but unlike its fellows, this one did not enter his upper body. The unfortunate bellowed and fell, the shaft sticking out of his knee with an equal portion on either side of the red wound. But his hurts were just beginning. He gave another scream as an arrow entered his other leg, this time halfway between ankle and knee. Safe now from any rush by blade-wielding men, Marcus walked along the cliff top until he could descend to the watercourse. He was in no hurry, wanting the shock of the encounter to subside, and casually strolled to the spot where the third man was cursing to every god in his knowledge, but just as had been true in the experience of the young man, none made an appearance to alleviate his pain.

Walking up to the man, laying on his back and writhing from side to side as he tried to pull the arrow from his knee - stopping as the pain overwhelmed the action, then beginning again in his desperation. Finally, he noticed Marcus standing and looking down at him, the bow still in hand and strung, but no arrow on the nock. Deciding that his mark had mostly gathered his wits from the surprise assault, Marcus said, "Who gave the orders for you and your men to follow me?"

Through gritted teeth, the ruffian attempted a futile defense, made totally ineffective by the pain destroying any in-borne deceit that he might have. "We took no orders from any..." His attempt at a tale was completely submerged by the pain from his lower members.

"Then, without an ordered purpose, you were a party of bandits, preying on honest travelers between the cities."

"Nay! We had no.."

Marcus halted the flow of falsehoods by gently kicking the shaft sticking out of the knee of the prostrate man. "Your life is at an end, and you need no coverings of your duties. Answer truthfully and I will give you a swift and clean death. Confound me, and I will leave you to your own devices. No doubt the wolves will find the feast on the fall of dark, but..." He stopped to let that sentence take effect. "...Unlike the cocus in her kitchen, they do not wait until the meat is dead before consuming the meal. You may be entertained by watching your own entrails being enjoyed by the pack before the riverman calls you to the boat of Hades." He was parroting words that he had heard since his descent from the mountains, actually knowing little of Roman gods or the concepts of such afterlife. Marcus stooped to bring his face closer to his human quarry. "Answer now! Who gave the orders for myself to be questioned on the road?"

"In truth, I know not his name." More grimacing. "The leader of the Sucusa caetus offered us coin for the location of the Tribune Junius."

Marcus knew of the existence of gangs that gave some organization to the bottom of society, but he had no familiarity of one in the small Sucusa quarter, a section of the city given to transients and laborers in the work yards and granaries.

The man broke into his thought with desperation, "Sos. I have metal in the city. It is yours if you allow quarter and my succor in..."

Marcus broke into the plea. "What of the guard sub-Captain Petronius? These orders came from him, and you well know of that."

"Nay! I know of no such person. Any bidding would have come to the caetus leader."

Marcus stood and thought. It was probably true. Petronius would not have dealt with the hired men who would do the deed - he would have contracted the mission to a man with known experience in unlawful activities, the gang leader or other. But this still gave no indication of how high the orders originated. Petronius, he knew, was at least the enabler, if not the instigator - he had the word of Decanus Blackus at the gate, who had been questioned by the Captain.

Suddenly, Marcus demanded, "Who was the forth man at the gate? And do not lie - I saw you with him at your cups."

Weaker now, from the loss of the lifeblood pouring from both wounds, the man answered, "He is Tartarus, it was said. Also of the Sucusa quarter. Hired to watch the gate and make an accounting of your movings." Marcus made a mental memory of the name - possibly a visit to the watcher might give more information as to the depth of the knowledge seeking. But for now...

The man had settled back with his eyes closed - not unconscious, but drifting into the haze of weakness caused by his bloodletting. Marcus had no intention of allowing this scum to further plague the house of Junius, but he had no pleasure in watching pain in another, however deserved. Suddenly, and quickly, he pulled his gladius and thrust it directly into the heart of the man. A long sigh of breath was all the noise that the criminal made, as his body suddenly went limp in death. Marcus pulled the arrows from the other two men, then from the leader, except for the one that had directly penetrated the knee. It was locked into the bone, so he broke it in half and pulled the ends free. It was very unlikely that the three would be discovered before they were nothing but bones bleaching on the rocks, but should some hunter or other rambler find them, he did not want the method of death to be exposed by leaving the shafts with the bodies. By the morning, all would be just loose ends of bone and meat, fought over all the night by the creatures of the wilderness.

He hurried back down the watercourse to the trail, then to the main road, putting his feet on a course back to Rome. Just before coming into sight of the city, he cut through the grainfields to skirt the wall to intercept the road into the foothills. He was very careful about any person - few as they were - that he met on the minor road, watching for uniforms or carrying chairs that would indicate a noble. He did not expect to see either - this was, after all, just a minor trail leading to a few equally insignificant hamlets in the foothills. Just before he came to the turnoff onto the abandoned track leading to the villa, he looked up and down the road, then disappeared into the brush. As before, he crept up to the stone building, listening and carefully looked through the rotten wood to see Lucius standing in the doorway, looking back toward the road.

Now, he skirted the wall and walked into the vision of his officer. Lucius shook his head, and said, with a wry smile, "You are a wraith, Marcus. A court lackey listening at doorways is like an oxen stumbling through the Forum compared to you. One day, you must give me lessons in stealth." As his aide did not join, as usual, in the banter, he asked, "Methinks you have news that is not gladsome."

"Aye. But I have not completely fathomed the impact, as yet." He began the tale of the day, taking the food and jug from his traveling bag and cutting the bread for both of them with his pugio. Lucius just listened, and ate, until the end of the narrative was reached. Then he sat back and mused over the happenings while Marcus just relaxed and let his road weary legs begin their rest.

Both sat for a long while, Marcus almost dozing against the wall, when Lucius suddenly said, "The time for my skulking around the city has come to an end." Marcus just opened his eyes and listened. "My family will be safe as long as I am not in the vision of the King, and the house of Junius will continue as long as I am alive. So..." A pause as he drained his cup. "I will decamp for other lands for the near future. In a year or so, my perceived threat to the safety of the regency should be lessened considerably." His aide just nodded. "You will give it that I am still unstable and in search of my total reason. You might also claim that you tried to change my desire, but I left without notice."

"Aye, Sos." He hesitated, then said, "I must inform the Domina, at least. We cannot leave her in wonderment as to your fate."

"And Collatinus, but no others." He stood and looked out the broken door into the weed infested courtyard. "I will visit Athens. The family has an old relation who befriended my pater once, during his young travels." Turning, he nodded and said, "Yes. That will be my destination. I will send you word of my staying-place so that you can inform me of anything that might change my situation. And I will entrust any missives to my family to you." Walking over, he stooped and took his aide by the wrists. "I regret that I will not be there to support you in your nuptials to the young woman. But, you have been a friend without equal, Marcus. I hope that the gods permit me to repay even a small part of your noble assistance... someday."

Nuptia (Nuptials)

The Domina had sent a steward and several slaves to the new household, to clean it and prepare it for living. She, herself, came to see the dwelling for the first time and to give advice about its repairment. And, of course, in her enclosed carrying chair, her daughter, Iulliana, would be another passenger, gladly welcoming the chance to leave the confines of her own household.   It must be said, that Sabina and the young noble woman used the occasions to extend the visit as long as possible, and a few times, actually getting permission from the Domina to stay for the entire while, taking her own chair back to her household.

Marcus had delivered messages from Lucius and made her privy to his plans.   She was sorrowed to know that her son would be gone from her view for the long time but agreed that it was a good plan.   Especially, since the King was still murdering the odd person on occasion, trying to ferret out any resistance to his assumption of the Throne.

Marcus had no interest in filling the house with slaves, and indeed while he recognized that the custom of owning others was ingrained within the society, and, in fact, the world, the idea of purchasing another as if he were an ox, was still an anathema to him. Unlike Roman slaves of later times, these could actually own property, if allowed by their masters, and even earn wages that might be put toward the purchase of their freedom.   And once freed, they could enter Roman society as a citizen although they were barred from certain municipal occupations.   Still, many of the families of the city could trace their roots to some sire or dam who had served in bondage at sometime in the past.

It was with that knowledge that Marcus approached Pythes with the request to buy the freedom of Cleo, so as to have at least one non-stranger in his household.   It would have been very easy to have just given the slave the required coin to purchase his own liberty, but Marcus owed everything he now was to the old merchant, and the idea of betraying the man was not even to be thought of.

Pythes was mildly surprised at the offer, although he well knew that both had become friends, despite the social custom against it.   He had ignored the efforts of the two young men to hide the friendship. He even knew of the distaste of Marcus to the idea of slavery - something that might cause him trouble in the future, but the young man was not one to fit his ideas into the mold of another.   The old merchant knew that a good part of the strength of character of his young ward was that he grew up outside of the matrix of Roman society, and could see and notice things that were as invisible to the citizen as water to a fish. He also knew that Marcus would probably become a powerful figure in the Roman hierarchy if not actually founding the beginnings of a noble family.

Smiling, he replied, "Cleo will be my wedding gift to you - do with him as you wish."

Marcus had approached the slave with the news of manumission and the offer of a place in his household as the steward. In utter disbelief, the bonded young man just stood, obviously trying to determine if his ears had actually heard correctly. Stammering, he said, "Sos. I would be honored to... for the place as your man."

Marcus just smiled. "Pythes will give your freedom on the date of my wedding, but you are not obligated to accept the position. You may just leave as your own..."

"Nay, Sos!" The interruption was abrupt and without thought. "I will take my place in your house, gladly."

"Then it is done. Pythes will be acquiring another man for his work. You will spend the days making him familiar with your tasks until that day. I do not wish to leave our master with a man of no ability for the duties."

Cleo nodded vigorously. "Aye, Sos. I will make sure that the new man has all knowledge for his needs."

Marcus and Sabina and her mother, Decima, had visited the temple of Juno - a lesser one in the Palatium - and made sacrifice to obtain the knowledge of a proper date for their wedding. The priests then chanted their mumbling nonsense - as it seemed to Marcus - and pronounced a day in the near future. Pythes would not hear of the nuptials being presented in the street, as was done by the lower classes, but insisted that it take place on the grounds of the temple. Marcus protested at the cost, but again, Pythes was adamant - the young man was as close to a son as he would ever have, and he would not be denied the pleasure of seeing him take a wife.

The day dawned, bright and clear as Marcus arose to his fate, and to the gentle jests of the gathered men about his taking a new master of the distaff variation, to rule his life from daylight to dark - and after. The tabulae nupiales had been presented by the priest on the yesterday and was signed by the proper number of witnesses. Marcus had no idea why he needed a marriage contract, but again, he had no intention of disparaging the rites of his adopted city.

A sumptuous wedding breakfast was laid out and eaten in the courtyard of Pythes, and gifts were given to the groom by all. And more.   Given the popularity of the young man in the Palatium quarter, the presents from well-wishers up and down the street were of a magnitude to almost overwhelm Cleo, who had the task of storing them in the building until the newlyweds called for their transport to the new home.   He was not displeased at the task - on the day before yesterday, Pythes had issued a certificate in which the ownership of the slave was transferred to Marcus, who immediately contracted a scribe to issue a proclamation of manumission, freeing the lad from his bondage.   Properly registered in the archives, the young man was both ecstatic and free.

The procession of men walked the distance to the temple and at that point, Marcus lost all track of the day.   The rituals were both confusing and involved and had Pythes not been at his elbow, he would have probably brought disgrace to the entire day of ceremonies. As he entered the gates of the temple, he saw Sabina, lovely as always, standing next to her mother, Decima - waiting.   The elder woman being a weaver of great skill, the garb of Sabina could have decorated a noble bride of the highest houses.   Her flammeum, the flame colored veil, left her face uncovered, and allowed her specially coifed hair to show, with its six ritual wedding locks fastened in a cone shape.   She wore a pure white muslin tunic and a cingulum - a girdle - that was encircled by a belt with a single knot.

After many rantings by the priest, calling down blessings from innumerable gods, Pythes nudged the young man, who then stepped forward and untied the knot at the girdle of the young woman.   At that point, Sabina turned and clutched her mother's arms in fear, as Marcus picked her up and forcibly pulled her away.   Of course, it was all play-ritual - Sabina would have plunged her little ceremonial dagger into the breast of any person who tried to interfere with the abduction-act of her man.   Pythes had explained that the ritual was enacting the scene of the seizure of the Sabines, which tale Marcus actually knew, having learned it from the like-named young woman.

Now, with good natured obscenities and japes thrown by the party, Marcus left the procession to hurry back to their new household, in accompaniment of his new steward, Cleo.   It was important for him to precede the woman to the place of their consummation, although he could not have told the reason.   At this point of the day, all he desired was that the farce come to an end, and the mob leave the couple in peace.   But, it was not to be, at least for the bulk of the day.

The bride procession took long to make the journey, having to stop at every well-wisher to receive blessings and goodwill.   Finally, he saw the parade moving up the street, singing and with the procession leaders carrying torches, even though it was midday. As he stood in the doorway, he said quietly to Cleo, standing beside him, "I would that I was still in the mountains. There, our first child would be well on the way in the time it takes for Romans to celebrate the wedding day."

Cleo just grinned - happy for his master and himself. He was holding the jar of oil and the pot of fat that the bride would need to anoint this house as now being a joint domicile. As the procession reached the doorway, the torches were extinguished, and the young woman stepped forward to take the brush from the new steward. She stroked the doorway with the brush, painting oil onto the sideboards, then with her hand, took a globule of fat and smeared it on the threshold. At that point, Marcus jumped as the crowd suddenly shouted and chanted. Two young men, selected by Pythes as each having two living parents, carefully lifted the bride and carried her over the threshold.

They were married.

But the day was not over. Well-wishers came and went, bringing even more food and gifts. Only as the sun touched the buildings in its setting did the guests depart, leaving only the newlyweds, with Cleo and the Decima standing in the atrium. Marcus had given the mother authority over the running of the household, and directed her to hire a cocua - a cook - and a maid. That was no problem at all, the city being full of young women anxious to earn some small coin for their dowery, or wives wishing to support their own household with another income. He would have no slaves in his house - that was made plain.

By Decima's order, a simple meal was prepared and served in the atrium, from which both the older woman and Cleo retired to take their own repast in the kitchen with the cocua and the maid, leaving the two newlyweds to themselves.

The night had finally arrived, on leaden wings, as it seemed. To Marcus, the day had seemed to be as the length of a month, but now they were alone, and without need to protect the innocence of the young woman. Neither had any experience with the Venereal couplings between a man and woman, but even in the clumsiness of their ignorance, both were enthralled with the act and each other. It must be said that much activity, if little sleep, was taken by both between the setting and the rising of the sun as they explored each other by the light of the dim oil lamp early in the night, and after, by the rising half moon shining through the gauzed window.

The next morning, with the mother warning her daughter about the risks of appearing too happy before the gods, both women began to examine their new household. It was far too large for the use of a childless couple, being more suited for a family with many children and relations, along with a staff of size. But, rooms unused could be left idle until another time. For now, only the large bedroom for the master and mistress, and one for each of the other four in the house were needed. The atrium and kitchens and bath would be used, of course, but several of the side rooms had no reason for the moment.

Pythes and Valens arrived early, giving their well-wishings behind grins, as they unloaded the cart holding the previously given presents. Sabina and Decima happily assisted Cleo as they were stacked in one of the unused rooms until they could find the time to examine their use. Marcus was glad to let the women do, well, women-stuff in the house. After the departures of his warden and helper, he and Cleo examined the work area in the back of the compound but had barely even walked the length of the structure when the young maid came running up, breathless. "Your pardon, Sos! The mistress sends word that there is a noble woman at the door!"

It could only be one person, Marcus knew, and he was right. Sabina had already greeted the Domina of the house of Junius when he strode up and bowed, "Greetings, Domina. You honor our new house with your presence." Her daughter, Iulliana, was also present, with both her and Sabina exchanging happy grins with each other.

"My felicitations at your gain of such a jewel, Marcus. Your good wife has already asked us into your abode, but I told her that I would never enter without the approval of the master of the house."

Marcus smiled. "You are welcome at any time, Domina. We would be dire ingrates to deny entry to one who has performed so much for us." He waved, "Please, seat yourself in the atrium."

She nodded and turned to her daughter. "I would speak with Marcus, alone, Iulliana. Perchance, Sabina will show you her new home."

As both young women happily bounced up the stairs to the bedrooms, Marcus said to Cleo, "Bring us wine, then see that no one is privy to our conversation." The steward just nodded and stood aside as the two walked into the atrium and reclined on the raised platforms.

"I will not ask if word has arrived from my son," the woman began. "It would take a messenger on Pegasus to deliver a missive this soon."

Marcus nodded. "Aye, Domina. And be assured, I would have immediately set foot for your door had one arrived, be it any time of day or night."

She waited for Cleo to set down the two cups and a jug before retiring, then said quietly, "I have... certain family items to be hidden. I would be gladsome if you would find a place that they could be secured as soon as possible."

"I have a good location, but the items must be placed when my steward is set to some task elsewhere. Might I know of the bulk to be hidden?"

She thought for a moment. "Some scrolls, folded parchments and some heirlooms of little size, sealed in pots. A few bags of coin."

He nodded. "Not large, then." He looked around to make sure they were alone. Cleo was standing at the door of the kitchen, far out of hearing if they kept their voices low. "There are many stone blocks left by the previous merchant - pedestals for carven likenesses, I believe. Large and heavy. Your pots can be placed, then the stone stacked around and over them. Neither fire nor rain will threaten them." She nodded and he continued, "But, anything can be found should its existence be known. The strength of the hiding will be that no one should know that they are stored here - or even that they exist." More thought. "It would be better if they were delivered to the house of Pythes as though they were items for trade. They could then be placed on the cart with my possessions and brought here, just another load for a Plebeian household."

The Domina just nodded, as both Sabina and Iulliana came into the room. Sabina stopped and said "Husband. Iulliana has many ideas on the adornment of our household, with your permission."

Her friend nodded with a wide smile, happy to not only be doing something away from her own home but actually accomplishing something of value. "Mother, if I might tarry here until later? You could send the chair back for me in the afternoon."

The older woman looked at Marcus and replied, "If the master will allow for a young female to have the run of his household, then you may do so."

Marcus just smiled and nodded, and both young women ran back out of the room, chattering girl-talk to each other.

Quietly, the woman said, "I will send word when the delivery will be made to your warden's house. It will be in the guise of the present from the household of Junius to the married couple."

"You have done much for myself, Domina. It will be an honor to assist you in your time of need." The woman just smiled and took her leave. Marcus watched the carrying chair move down the street, the pedestrians giving a wide berth to the gilded lectica, obviously of a wealthy and powerful house. He turned and walked back in. Until some word came from Lucius, his days were his own.

The first weeks of their new life, it must be said, saw less activity in making the house their own than might have been. Marcus would be measuring his work area for a new table, or carving a long stave from a plank, when Sabina would appear, her work-a-day stola carelessly arranged so that a breast could be inadvertently exposed as she leaned over to examine his work. Or as she bent to examine a tool, the hem of her woman's tunic might ride up her thighs, giving a suggestion to her man's eyes of the pleasures that could be found further up. Shortly, they would be in their soft bed, exploring the various items that had been barely glimpsed by him in the work yard.

Still, he began to experiment with his craft, daily. Remembering the ship builders of Lavinium, and their bending of boards to fit the curve of a ship, he contracted to a tub maker for a small, but long tray, sufficient to hold water and a stave of length. He began to try different woods, soaking them in boiling water for a while, then, bending them over a form to take a shape as they dried. Long hours he spent, finding the proper time for the hot water soaking, and which woods would take the bend and which would not. Many bows he made had the look of the curved foreign weapons, but were less potent than his first attempts as a boy, but gradually, be began to find the measure of the wood. It was a slow, gradual learning process, rather than any sudden insight of thought. Still, he was happily engaged with both his craft in daylight and his lovely wife at night. He produced enough of his normal bows - thought to be excellent by the weapons merchants of the city - to keep his household in good order, and without having to tap his stash of saved coin, nor the vastly greater amount given to him by the Domina.

A few days after the wedding, he journeyed back to the Palatium quarter, and up the street of merchants. Greeting all, and purchasing a few items of food for their house, he stopped by the bakery of Porcia. With pleasantries, and after delicious and freshly hot bread was enjoyed, he asked, "Have you seen the boy, Flavis?" This was a street urchin - half grown - that he had used for minor tasks before, beginning back when he had paid the boy to inform Sabina of the assault on the day of their meeting. Porcia had seen him, but not that day. Marcus said, "Tell him I have a copper piece for a task."

That afternoon, the youngster was standing at the door of his home, with Cleo unwilling to have such a filthy urchin despoil the new rug that Sabina had just put in the door hallway. Knowing that the youngster was expected, the steward led the boy around the house to the work yard, there to leave him with the master of the house.

The boy's eyes widened as he was handed a copper coin. His usual payment was a snippet of metal, or at most, a droplet of copper - this was riches indeed for a homeless street rat. "...name is said to be Tartarus and he is from the Sucusa quarter, but I last saw him at the southern gate on the Antium Via. Let him not know that you are searching for his whereabouts. The secrecy is more important than speed. Should you find news of this man, I will pay you with this." Marcus held up a small silver coin - a Greek obol of minor denomination. Stunned at the prospect of such wealth, the boy nodded, and at a wave of dismissal, turned and ran from the yard.

Sabina was the mistress of the house, by right of marriage to the master, but in actual fact, she had little experience in running a household of that size, even one with only two servants. Her mother was the power behind the feminine half of the property, at least until her daughter learned the art of managing more than a two room hut. Marcus did not care, nor did he interfere. The inside of the house gave no interest to him. It was enough that the food was cooked for meals, the bath was hot in the evening, and his wife was warming the bed at nightfall.

Decima had moved all from her household into the new domicile of her daughter, and the old house was put up for vending. After asking permission of Marcus, she set her weave table and loom in one of the front rooms and began her work again. With the fine materials bought for her by her new son-in-law, she could produce much finer thread and cloth - materials that now matched her skill in weaving. And she gave up no rights of teaching her daughter. For the first month, she indulged Sabina as the girl tempted her man into the marriage act at all hours, and as often as he could be drawn. However, as time went on, the mother began to insist that her daughter become a good Roman wife - and those did not play at coupling with her man at all hours of daylight, nor dally at ease during the day. Soon, Sabina was back under the tutelage of her mother and working at the thread table and loom.

All was not work, however. At least one day a week, her noble friend Iulliana would visit for half a day or more, or Sabina would walk to the house of Junius for the same purpose. Decima was, at first, hesitant about the friendship between the two girls. It was unusual - almost unheard of - for a Plebeian woman to be admitted to a noble household as a friend, but her innocent beauty and poise - and education - made her virtually undetectable as a girl from the lesser classes. Since the friendship apparently had the auspices of the Domina, she held her doubts as the young women grew closer together. Between them, the two young girls began to transform the house into a home, limited only by the thriftiness of the mother as to purchasing this rug and that curtain. The only disappointment in the life of the newly wedded girl was that her husband had no interest in her adornment of their home - indeed, he would not notice a new rug, or painting, or statuary even if it were set in a place of prominence. Mentioning his disinterest to her mother, Decima just looked at her with a dry expression, saying, "Daughter, if that is the worst that you can find to say of your husband, then you will indeed have a life of bliss seldom experienced by a wife."

Marcus met with Collatinus on occasion. With Lucius far away and any messages taking months in the travel, there was little for the friends of the Tribune to discuss. And, no missive had arrived as yet. He learned from the noble that the new King was altering the ages-old hierarchy of the city by refusing to replace the Senators that had been murdered during the assumption of the Throne. By refusing to take even advice from that body, he had greatly diminished the authority of the Senate. In addition, he was acting as Judicial Imperatous - judging capital crimes without seeking opinions from the counselors and magistrates. The result was a fear of the monarchy by any who might be hesitant to support the new regime.

His Captain of the Royal Guards was as a representative from Hades, itself. Many were the citizens taken into custody, and never seen again. By accusing this noble family or that merchant of treason, the man and his kin would not only be put to death, but their estate would be taken into the royal coffers - and much of the coin stuck to the hands of the Royal Captain. Collatinus had told Marcus that the excesses of the man were such that even the King was repelled and put some limits on his reach.

In the light of that uncertainty, Marcus had taken possession of a quantity of sealed jugs that had been delivered from the house of Pythes - the documents, certain heirlooms, and much of the coin wealth of the house of Junius. Now the stash was buried under a huge stack of limestone and marble blocks beside the workshop behind his house. And, for good measure, he had moved the baulks of lumber and stacked them around the stones. To any questioners, the pile was the leftovers from the previous owner and craftsman. No one had any reason to think that the mound was anything else, especially as Marcus replied to questions about the material, that he would have to have it hauled off someday when he needed the space that it occupied.

To his knowledge, only the Domina and himself knew of the stash and the contents.

For the ordinary people, the Plebeians, the days were much the same - for now. The intrigues and maneuverings of the royal court and nobility were far above the vision of the street folk. To the common man, one King was the same as another, unless the royal overreach began to touch their lives.

Curious as to the new tenants in what had been the house of the woodcarver, the other occupants of their street made tentative visits to find out as much as possible about the handsome young couple. Names were learned and new friendships began to take root. Indeed, the atrium of the house became an occasional meeting place for several of the young women on the street - daughters of the merchants and craftsmen.

Marcus had come back from the weapons merchant, Aetius, after delivering a finished bow for vending, to find that Sabina had two visitors in the house. In addition to Iulliana, there was another young girl, all in the weaving room with Decima. Sabina stood up as Marcus looked in the door in wonder at all the woman-talk. "Husband. This is Lucretia, of the house of Tricipitinus and a friend of Iulliana, and affianced to the noble Collatinus." The young woman was standing as Decima knelt and measured the cloth falling from the shoulders, apparently building a stola for her use.

She was obviously another highborn woman - a given if she was to become the wife of Collatinus. He half bowed, and said, "My greetings, Femina. And my welcome to our house."

"You are gracious, Sos," replied the girl. "The mother of your wife has a rare gift with her weaving." And it was true - Decima could make garments with a style and goodness seldom seen across the city. The cloak that he had been presented on his induction into the army had been commented on by men and officers alike, all assuming that he had paid a fortune for such a fine piece of apparel. Until the taking of her daughter to be the wife of Marcus, Decima had been in the philosopher's quandary, as to their garment making. They had been unable purchase quality materials with which to make beautiful garments, but without such merchandise to vend, they could not accrue the coin to purchase the raw materials with which to make finer clothes. A few months before the wedding, Marcus had ordered, through Pythes, bags of the finest white wool from the flocks of Tarentum and, unbelievingly to the women, bundles of exquisite linen fiber from Egypt. The woolen fabric that Decima - and Sabina as her apprentice - now wove on their vertical loom was as good as seen in the city and better than most. But the linen was of such a fineness as to approach the sheen and feel of that rarely seen fabric that was sometimes imported from somewhere toward the sunrise - silkium, it was called, made from the spinnings of a worm in a tree. At least, that is what the traders said of the origin - it might even be true.

Decima had made Sabina a woman's night-tunic, for her consummation evening, from the finest linen fiber. It was unremarked - indeed, even unseen - by Marcus that night. Of course, no man, just come from the nuptial rituals, and about to take his young bride for the first time, would have observed the fineness of her maiden garments had they been made of spun gold and silver thread on the looms of Olympus itself. But, the young woman's friend noticed it - Iulliana had remarked that the linen tunic made her own night-garments look as if made from rag-cloth. Then and there, she requested a like piece for herself. Then, after that, a stola, of the pure wool that Marcus had obtained.

From there, the reputation of the house of Marcus began to grow - and not as the abode of a bowsmith, as he expected, but as a producer of exquisite garments for the noble-born. The Domina of Junius, seeing the fineness of the new clothing of her daughter, ordered a stola for herself. Of course, her friends and acquaintances naturally asked from where they came.

Now, Decima and Sabina were weaving and fitting a set of clothes for the friend of Iulliana, the girl known as Lucretia. Knowing that a man was unwelcome in a situation where a young woman was being dressed, Marcus bowed and retreated out of the back of the house to his work area. He had recently made several forays into the wilderness east of the city, bringing back wood of every type of tree that he could find. These were to be seasoned and carved into staves that might someday be a weapon. For the moment, he was not building bows, but just trying different joining of woods to test their usage for such weapons. He had just extracted a long length of stave from the boiling vat, when Cleo walked into the covered work area, followed by Valens. Behind them was a young man of about three and ten years. Maybe a year more.

"Welcome Valens," boomed Marcus, wiping his hands on a rag, then tossing it to the table. "By what blessing of the gods brings you to my new abode?"

"I bring you the greetings of Pythes, and his hope that your new mate has not completely drained you of vigor to wield your carver blades."

Marcus grinned. "Nay, not as yet, but she has made the effort often and again. Sometimes I must add to my sleep on yon table in the daytime." He pointed to the boy. "Who is your follower? I assume that he is in apprenticeship as a drover for the good Pythes."

Valens turned and said, "Come here, boy." Then to Marcus, "This is the son of a merchant who has fallen on evil times, but to whom Pythes owes a debt of some magnitude. He suggests that you might use the boy for an apprentice, so as to free your time for actual improvement-finding, rather than just day to day carving. He was tested by Darius for some months and reports that the boy is not entirely deficient in wit."

Marcus looked the subject of their talk up and down. He seemed to be an active young lad, with a bright expression and looking around at the work yard. "Do you have a name, boy?"

The young man started, then nodded. "Aye, Sos. I am called Ennius, if it please you."

Valens spoke up. "He need not be paid, other than his food and a plank to sleep upon. At least until he can produce more worth than he consumes."

Marcus nodded. "And you, boy... Ennius. Do you wish to work in this house, learning the art of wood?" He added, "It is your choice. There are no slaves in this household - anyone may leave at any time they wish."

The boy vigorously nodded his head. "Aye, Sos. I would be gratified for the chance to prove my use."

To Valens, he asked, "Has he eaten, this day?"

"Aye. We broke our fast before coming."

"Then, boy, Take that bucket and fill that vat..." he pointed to the large wooden water tank. "The fountain is up the street toward the sunrise." Turning to Valens, he said, "Come, our cocua has made some cakes for the day. They are not of the excellence of those of Porcia, but good enough. We will have a cup and you can tell me of the happenings in your household. By the gods, I sometimes miss the days of simplicity, and working with Darius and yourself."

"But, then you would not possess that jewel that you found on the street of the Poet."

Marcus grinned. "Aye. I would not give that up should the gods permit me to fly back to that night on the trading road."

The time passed, Months went by as he settled into his new life as a man of means and with a wife. Since he had no need of self-aggrandizement before his friends and acquaintances, the earnings from his bow making and the greater income from the weave table were far more than enough to see to their needs. Their house became a center point for the prosperous merchants of the street - all were in agreement that the handsome young couple was a welcome addition to the neighborhood.

Their steward, Cleo, allowed no failings among the small staff of the house. Indebted to his master for freeing him from bondment, he became doubly so when Marcus brought the mother of Cleo - Cordia was her name - from her dingy hut on the bank of the Tiber and gave employment to her as a textorius in a small cubicle next to the weaving room. There she spun the wool and the linen into threads, then wound them onto wooden thimbles, freeing Sabina and her mother from the tedious, but necessary work. During the day, except for the meals and times that a female had to tend to her needs, the woman wielded her spindle and distaff, turning the raw wool and linen fiber into fine threads and yarns. After seeing his mother brought to a place of safety and comfort, far from the dirty and crime ridden alley of her previous home, Cleo let no criticism or disparagement fall upon the house of Marcus within range of his hearing.

The young boy, Ennius settled in happily also, doing this and that around the work yard. Soon, he was doing the rough carving of staves, and even some learning of work on the bending press and laminating table. It was a happy household, untouched by the turbulence that was disturbing the nobility, after the usurpation of the Throne by Tarquinius.

Finally, months after seeing the Tribune Lucius for the last time, a messenger arrived with a scroll from that noble. Knowing that it was expected, Cleo immediately brought the runner to the backyard to the attention of Marcus. Realizing what it was, he shouted to Cleo to remunerate the man with goodly coin, and immediately set off at a run to the Capitoline quarter, not even thinking to tell Sabina of his going.

Being shown into the atrium, the Domina looked up in surprise. "Welcome, Marcus. This is a pleasant..."

"Your pardon, Domina, but I have just received a scroll from Lucius... the Tribune." He held out the scroll to her.

Her face growing pale, she asked, "What does he say? Is he in good stance?"

"I have not opened it, Domina. Immediately on its arrival, I ran to your door." She took the spindle and slit the wax with her thumbnail, her hands trembling. Reading quickly, she twisted the wood so to let the material unwind for her view. Marcus just waited, trying to see an answer to his questions in her face.

She handed the scroll to Marcus. "Read, and tell me what it means." He was barely able to stop his astonishment from appearing as an exclamation. Was it possible that the Domina was not literate? No. He had seen her mark on tablets before...

Taking the scroll, he suddenly realized her confusion. The missive read like the tale of a drunken street bard. Lucius had interlarded the message with many of the agreed on mis-directions that they had concocted before his departure. He nodded as he read out loud. "He is well, as you can see from the preamble. He is staying in the abode of... the old man of the vases?"

She nodded and said quietly, "An old friend of Titus - Aristides by name. Their friendship extends even further into the past than my marriage to the Dominus."

He continued, translating the words in to the real meanings. "The city of stone means Athens, and he is spending his time in the... Ac... Acropel..."

"Acropolis," she corrected. "I am told that it is a magnificent city within a city on top of a mountain. It has many temples and libraries by the tales."

Most of the missive was just a warm greeting to his long missed family, and little was of any importance as to the future of the household. Still, to a mother, it was a statement that her only son was alive and well. Marcus finished and rolled the material back on to the spindle and just sat as the Domina thought about the words from her son. Finally, she rose and said, "You must eat before you return. It is long past the time for the noon meal."

Suddenly, Nonus entered and bowed. "Your pardon, Domina. A young man has arrived with some missive for... your guest." She nodded, and the man turned and motioned for the man to attend. In surprise, Marcus saw that it was Ennis, breathless from apparently having run across the city. Suddenly, the hackles rose on his neck at the idea that something might be... that his household might...

"Ennis! What..."

Taking a deep breath to gather his wind, the boy said in gasps, "Pardon, Sos. A missive from the noble Collatinus has arrived requiring your immediate presence at his house. A summons from the army, the runner said."

With relief that the boy was not bringing news of problems with his household, he turned and said, "I fear that my repast at your table must give way to my summons, Domina."

"Of course. You must attend to your duties." She pointed to Ennis. "But, your young man would probably not look amiss upon some drink. Nonus! Take... Ennis, is it?" The young man nodded, still breathing deeply. "Take Ennis to the kitchen and have him refresh himself with liquid."

With more regrets to the Domina, but with his mind now on the strange missive, Marcus set his feet to the cobblestones of the street.

Conspiratus

Immediately upon receiving the summons, Marcus hurried to the house of Collatinus. Without the Tribune Junius as his senior, he had no idea what would be his duties when the officers assembled. The noble invited him into the atrium and, over cups, they discussed the matter. "The King wants Lucius represented, and I believe it is from the insistence of the Domina. You know, of course, that she is the sister of Tarquinius?" Marcus nodded. "Should he not attend a formation called by the King, he would be dropped from the rolls, thus, with your presence, you will be Lucius in absentia."

"But what would be my duties?"

Collatinus just shook his head. "At the moment, even I do not know the reason for the assembly, except that it is not for a war - no units of the army have been called up. For now, you will attend me, along with Maxentius." He smiled. "That will give me two Adiutorae - I should be able to sleep late in the day with two men such as yourselves attending to my affairs. Come to my house on the morrow - we will march to the assembly together."

The next morning, the three men - the Tribune and two batmen - left the household of the Patrician and walked to the Palace. Inside the gates, Marcus could see the other three Adiutorae that he had trained with, and many more that were unknown to himself. He counted, at least, twelve Tribunes and their aides, plus several other officers of high rank, including Senior Centurion Tatius and many more Centurions and Optios. Marcus and Maxentius excused themselves from Collatinus and walked to greet their friends from the training regimen. After the well-wishing and jests were over, each asked the other for information as to their assembly. Of course, none knew anything that the others did not - which was very little in all.

The soldiers - officers and men, just milled around in the courtyard till, finally, an over robed individual appeared on the speaking platform. "The court Chamberlain," muttered Maxentius to his friend. With his gilded staff held high, he announced the arrival of the King, but not in such brief words. Instead, he rambled along with flowery statements about the "Keeper of the sacred Throne of Rome," "The High Commander of the Army of the Tiber," "The son of Mars, and the power of the people of Rome..." And more such blatherings, until Marcus wondered if the sun would set before the King would show himself. But finally, the fat court lackey either ran out of verbiage, or breath, and the Regal Person appeared, flanked, as aways, by the Plenipotentiary Custodis - the Commander of his personal guard, Caeus. As the King stopped at the edge of the platform, the Chamberlain tapped his staff on the floor three times, signaling for silence into which the monarch might drop his words.

Tarquinius had discarded his regal robes for the uniform of a soldier - a high officer with polished breastplate, the lorica segmentata, and the pteruges, the petal skirt to protect the legs. His gladius was on his belt, in a scabbard of gold and silver and jewels. Greeves protected his lower legs, just above the caligae, although these boots would be useless in the field, being of felted wool. Finally, a purple cloak - the pallium, and also outlined in gold thread - and a helm topped with a purple brush finished off his garb. In all, Marcus estimated that the cost of such a display would be enough to purchase a Plebeian domicile and merchant kiosk with coin left over. Of course, the equipment of the King was utterly useless for real combat, being overly adorned and heavy, but its purpose was to decorate the Monarch of Rome and the Commander of the Army. Besides, Tarquinius would never be in actual combat in any event save the unlikely fall of Rome itself.

But, the display meant that this assembly had some martial meaning.

"My fellow soldiers - comrades in arms, and the protectors of the city of Rome. This day I am announcing a gathering of the Chiefs of the Latium cities, to renew the bonds that link the peoples of our lands. With our forces combined we will be far more secure in our persons and properties, from the forces of plunder and pillage that encircle our lands..."

As he continued in his flowery speech, Collatinus slightly turned his head to his companion, Publicola and said in a low voice, "He has already mapped out a war - I will wager two gold pieces on it."

Publicola shook his head and whispered back, "I would rather skip the gold across the Tiber, to see if the Sirens return the coin, tenfold. My chances would be improved."

Behind them, the three aides - Albanus was still the Adiutor to Publicola - just looked at each other, having heard the low wager-talk of their seniors. As young men, they were not entirely adverse to gaining the experience of a war - indeed, they could have been called eager. Of course, any sage could have told them that their zeal stemmed from a total lack of knowledge about the reality of warfare between armies. Of the five men in the little group, only Marcus had seen actual conflict, and cutting down road-bandits from the range of a bow, or blading brigands rising from their drunken sleep was only a shadow of actual combat. Of course, as Tribunes and their Adiutorae, far in the rear, it would be a desperate battle, indeed, if they were required to draw steel at any time.

"...this day messengers will be sent to the various assemblies of the cities and towns. Our meeting has gained the auspices of the gods for the Ides of the month." He spoke for a while longer, but the reason for the assembly of Tribunes had been given.

Finally, the Senior Centurion stepped forth as the King disappeared into the doorway. "Tribunes will follow the Plenipotentiary Custodis to the Apollo Atrium. Aides and soldiers will come with myself to the guard barracks." In a mass of about thirty men, Marcus walked across the cobblestone courtyard to a building nestled against the tall stone wall. Inside was a table with scribes, and several centurions. The Senior shouted for quiet, then waved a man forward - apparently the head of the scribes - possibly a Procurator or even a Ratiocinator. His garments certainly were not that of a slave or hired scribe.

"Each of you will be given a tablet with the King's seal. When you have it, step to that table there..." he pointed, "...and give your name. You will be given a scriptus with the city and the chief for which the tablet is destined. When you deliver it, you will wait for a reply which you will bring back here. The scribes along that wall will give you the directions, should you not know where the city or town of your mission is located."

A ragged line formed, and one by one, each was handed a baked clay tablet and pointed to the end table. There Marcus gave his name, which was marked on a wax tablet, then the scribe said, "Caldonius, Chief, in the city of Aricia." He had an glimmer of the location, somewhere along the Illium Via leading south. A scribe in the back of the room pointed to a parchment map on his table, showing him both the direction and roads that he would take. A long day was what he estimated. At least, he would be back to his domicile this day, if late. Finally, in small groups, the men were lectured and given the protocol to use in greeting the rulers that they were to attend. At the door, leaving, he was surprised to be handed a small staff, wrapped in purple and gold ribbons.

Outside of the gates to the Palace, he found Albanus waiting. Stepping up to him, Marcus asked, "What is this for," he asked, holding out the staff.

Coming up behind him, Maxentius replied, "That is your baton of appointment, giving credence to your authority. It will ease your path to your destination." Looking at Albanus, he asked, "What did you get from that theatric performance?"

The young man was reading the tablet, then looked up and replied, "As he said, this is an invitation to meet the King for the purpose of a closer bonding between Rome and the Latium cities. It mentions the need for a united front against the gathering menace that threatens the peace of the land."

"He can only mean the Volsci - Rome has been trading insults with that land before we were born," said Maxentius.

Marcus had little history of the cities of the plains. "Does this mean that he plans an actual war if the chiefs of the other cities join?"

Maxentius just shrugged. "It is obvious that Collatinus and Publicola think so." He looked toward the Palace then continued, "But, the city of Fregella is a long walk from here, and I must be going if I don't wish to spend the month on the road. What city were you given?"

"Aricia," replied Marcus.

"Piranes," said Albanus.

Maxentius made a grimace. "It is obvious of whom in our group has the ear of the gods. Marcus will be feasting and sleeping with his ravishing mate tonight, while you and I are laying on a cold ground and eating equally cold rations." He paused for a moment, then said, "Well, we will all have to exit the Caelius gate - shall we begin our journeys?"

They walked together to the edge of the city, then Marcus turned onto the inland road, wishing farewell and good speed to his friends. He set a fast pace, as the city of his destination was only somewhat more than hundred stadia away. He would be there before the midday meal time. His friends would be fortunate were they back in the city by the third day.

He was in full soldier regalia, it being an official mission called by the King. In addition to the tablet in his bag, he was holding the baton in one hand - its purple and gold ribbons denoting that he was carrying an official missive from the Palace. However, he felt almost naked, this being the first time that he had left the city without his favorite weapon. Collatinus had advised him to leave the bow behind, at least until the official assembly was over. "It is never a good thing to draw attention to yourself by appearing different from your fellows when before a superior." He could have retrieved it before leaving the city, but that would have necessitated a long walk to the far side of the city and then across again to the southern gate. On the short journey to Aricia, he had no expectation of having to defend his life, so he put it out of his mind. In fact, the travelers on the road, seeing a man in a uniform, and carrying a regal baton, gave him way and nodded as he passed. Apparently, the King's symbols were respected by the citizens, despite - or maybe because of - the irregular assumption of the Throne.

At the gate of the city of Arica, the baton caused a certain amount of disturbance. The guards sent for their Captain, who then dispatched a runner for his superior. Shortly, a magistrate arrived and asked the purpose for a uniformed Roman to appear at their gates. Marcus gave the greetings of the King of Rome and announced that he was traveled to deliver a missive to the... ruler of the city. Arica did not have a King as such, but rather a Chief, who ruled with the aid of a counsel. To the young man, the difference was as comparing each of his hands to the other - different, but still the same in actual form and use.

The Palace, or rather, meeting hall was a large stone building in the middle of the city. Marcus was escorted inside and told to wait. At the door in each of the four walls was a decorated guard, obviously as a matter of form, or courtesy, maybe. Certainly, they could not have looked upon one lone soldier as being a threat to an entire city. Looking around, all he saw was a large room, with some stone benches and not much else. Not even the plain walls were decorated. Obviously, the people of Latium did not seem to contain the need to fill a room with rugs, curtains, and statuary. In actuality, their thinking was more in line with his - he still had not absorbed the idea of living in smothering comfort, even with his several years of time in his adopted city.

Finally, he saw a group of elderly men approaching - all robed and obviously the rulers of the city. They stopped in front of Marcus and the magistrate from the gate said, formally, "This is the message bearer from Rome."

One of the men, the Chief, or Elder - Marcus had no idea of his rank - spoke. "What is your mission, Roman?"

Marcus thought for a moment, remembering the instructions given at the Palace. "I bring greetings from the citizens of Rome, and their pledge of friendship is renewed with the peoples of Latium. The King sends his words for your perusal, in the hope that the city of Aricia will join the city of Rome in a bond." He took the large clay tablet from his traveling bag and held it to the Chief. Instead, the magistrate took it, but without any attempt to examine the writing.

Another of the men spoke. "Is this boon of a... bond, limited just to Aricia, or do other Latium cities also become allowed to receive the beneficence of great Rome?" Marcus was not a politician, nor did he have any idea of how the administration of a city was actually accomplished, but he had no problem at all recognizing that this man was not overly enthused with the prospect of any intercourse with their much larger neighbor.

"I am just the messenger, Sos," he replied, "but I can say that heralds were sent to many other cities. Might I also add, that the King respectively requests a reply from the leaders of the city, whether yea or nay?"

The Chief spoke. "Then, Roman, we will need time to examine the message and offer. You will be our guest while we assemble and peruse the tablet." To the magistrate, he said, "Show the messenger to a comfortable abode, and provide him with drink and viands." The man nodded, and waved for Marcus to follow. Shortly, he was relaxing in a small, but well lit and airy room overlooking the... he assumed it was a forum, since people and merchants roamed here and there amongst the tables and kiosks. Now he began to realize that his ideas of the course of his mission were ignorant of the realm of diplomacy, assuming that the leaders of the city would give an answer when given the offer, and let him set foot on the road again. Thinking on it, and on the learnings from Sabina about the Roman Senate, he realized that he could be here for days as the offer was scrutinized and studied. And indeed, the night approached and fell without word from the council.

He could not fault the hospitality of his hosts. Food and wine were offered in plenty, and, at darkfall, the Magistrate called on him to inquire if a female bed-warmer would be desired for the night. He declined, and prepared to take his sleep, wishing that a bath was available - something that a Roman would consider to be essential but which custom apparently did not exist in the other cities. At least, he was not offered one.

As he prepared for the evening rest, he looked up at a tap on the doorway. The magistrate was standing in the dim light of the fading sun, with two men behind him. "Your pardon, Sos. Would the Roman allow a visit from a council member?"

Marcus stood and said, "Certainly. Might I ask with whom I am given the pleasure to converse."

The second man waved, and the Magistrate disappeared. The man said, "My name is Turnus, of the family Herdonius. And you might be..."

"Marcus, of his own house and Adiutor to the Tribune Junius." The second man was obviously his servant - he could see that now from the habiliments.

"Ah. And has the young worthy returned to his place of birth, if I may ask?"

Marcus was shocked. How would an official in a far city know of the absence of a noble of Rome? And more, why would he care enough to wonder? Carefully constructing his words, he replied, "Nay, Sos. He is still traveling while his infirmity is lessened."

"And you are not of the nobility, yourself? I ask because of your garments are considerably above what the Plebeians of Rome - or any city - would have access to."

"Nay. I am not even born of Rome but in a village in the mountains. The tale is long, and not for this time, but my garments are the result of a happy marriage to the finest weaver family in the city - nothing more." He paused from the verbal fencing, then said, "And what would bring a councilor of the city to speak to a mere messenger?"

"I would ask you some questions, if you agree. You are, of course, not required to answer, or even speak to me, as it were." Marcus just nodded. "What is your idea of the bonding that is offered by your King? Is he looking for allies in a war against... maybe the Aequi? Or the Volsci. Or even to throw off the influence of the Etruscans... Nay, that cannot be. Even Rome and all of Latium together would have trouble in subduing that land."

Marcus saw no reason to speak untruthfully. He knew little, but... "In truth, some of the Tribunes think that war is the reason. But, I can say, having close knowledge of the training fields of Rome, that no conscription of men has been made to form an army. As to the true purpose of the King... I have no knowledge of the workings of the governance of the city, and even less interest in the subject. Personally, I think that engaging in war, without the purpose of defending one's home, is foolish and wasteful."

"And yet, you are a soldier."

"Nay. I am an Adiutor, a position taken to prevent myself from being conscripted as a soldier in the ranks. As such, I have a position in the army that keeps me from sleeping in the mud. Furthermore, I have a desirable wife and household and do not wish to see those disturbed by unnecessary strife merely for the aggrandizement of lands or wealth."

The counselor just stood for a moment before he replied. "You are an uncommonly intelligent young man, if I may say. Most of your age would be seeking glory, or wealth, or women in combat. But, to my questions. What is the attitude of the people of your city as to the affiliation of Rome to Latium?"

"There is no talk at all amongst the common folk, Sos.   I, myself, only heard of it upon my summons as a messenger."

The man mused over that for a while, then said to no one, "Hmmm.   This is a strange occurrence, but kings do not request alliances for no reason.   And, in my experience, always for gain."   He nodded to Marcus.   "My thanks, Adiutor, for your insight on this happening.   And I wish you a pleasant rest.   I am sure the council will have an answer on the morrow."   With that, he bowed and left, his man trailing behind.

The morning brought no answer, but a very good meal to break his fast.   No matter if they decided to become friends or enemies with Rome, their hospitality could not be faulted.   With nothing to do, he wandered around the forum for a while but saw little to peak his interest.   Few weapons were in evident that would be of any use in warfare, and the few bows he saw did not even equal his first efforts at bow making.   Then, suddenly, he turned as a voice behind him said, "Pardon, Sos.   Your presence is requested in the meeting-hall."   It was the servant of Turnus.

Marcus nodded and followed the man to the building.   Inside were the same individuals that he had met on his arrival.   As he entered, the Chief rose from the stone bench and said, "Welcome, Marcus of Rome.   I would hope that you passed a pleasant night."

"Aye, Sos.   Your hospitality can not be faulted in any way."

The Chief waved to a scribe standing by one wall.   That man walked over to hand Marcus a tablet, somewhat larger than the one he had brought to the city.   "We are interested in conversation as to the bonding of our city with Rome, but do not wish to commit at the moment without further intercourse.   The counselor, Turnus, has a proposal that we think would be wise for the King to consider.   Rome is larger than any city of Latium, but in the total, we far outnumber by population.   Therefore, we will propose a neutral meeting place, so as to show all that none are being put in ascendancy or lowered below their place.   The suggestion is to meet at the sacred grove of Ferentina - it is central to all, and the goddess is one that must be propitiated for any bonding of our peoples to be successful."   He pointed to the tablet. "All is enumerated on the stone and we wait the pleasure of your King as to its suitability."

This was obviously a prepared speech, probably constructed by all present during the discussions of yesterday and this morning. With his mission accomplished, he gave his appreciations for the hospitality that he had received, and bowed his way out of the building.   Without escort, now, he was shortly through the gate and walking the road to Rome.

Book 4

Martial Slate

Martial Rasa   (Martial Slate)

As far as Marcus could determine, the reason for his mission, months ago, had been forgotten.   Nothing else was said, to him, and according to Collatinus no meeting had been arranged, although many messengers made their way between the Palace and the Latium cities. That was fine with him - he settled back to his bow making and testing of this wood and that lamination.   With Ennius, his apprentice, doing the rough carving, and even some involved work, Marcus could concentrate on his designs and testing.

He had produced a reverse curved bow, using two woods with a bone sliver for the center, all laminated together after being water-bent to shape.   It was powerful - vastly so, and within range of the magical weapon he had seen at the merchants on his journey to Rome. But, the power of the woods overcame the glue of ox hooves that held the laminations together.   After a handful of shafts, the glue would fail, and if used beyond that, the wood would shatter upon release. Now his search moved from finding the right materials for the bow, to a method of binding the thin staves together.

The broken bow, which he had been given by the merchant in the Palatium quarter, used fine wire wrapped at the ends for strength. Marcus had no access to the material - called electrum - that the ligament was made of, and fine copper wire had not the strength, although tight wrappings would extend the life of the weapon considerably.   Still, a bow that was anticipated to fail, even after an entire quiver of shafts were nocked, was less than useless to a warrior - or even a hunter.   Thicker copper wire did produce a bow that was long lived, but the weight of the metal, at the far ends of the staves, greatly inhibited the spring of the wood.

Still, his laminated bows, even if not of the strangely curved build, were greatly sought after by the weapons merchants of the quarters.   Ennius spent most of his time in the production of the weapons, learning to make one from raw wood to polished and shining bow.   Even so, before any were delivered for vending, Marcus inspected the work with a critical eye, and any defect would require his young apprentice to apply a correction, or even to reject the bow entirely and place it in the kitchen tender box.

Between his work in the wood yard and the weave table of his wife and her mother, their house was gaining considerable wealth. Not that Marcus cared for riches, even now - if he was in possession of enough to support his house and wife, and their professions, that was enough. Any more was just... excess with no use. Indeed, his indifference to wealth was the topic of amused conversation up and down their street. All agreed that the young man was unique in his outlook as to life.

One afternoon, Cleo escorted the urchin that had received a commission, after the strife on the road to Antium, into the back yard where Marcus and Ennis were working. The boy might have been a little taller, it having been a few months, but certainly no more clean of body. "Ah... My emissary of the streets. Have you brought me any news of importance?"

The boy grinned. "Aye, and it will be of goodness to you."

"Watch your tongue, boy," barked Cleo. "The Master is addressed as 'Sos', and he will decide if your blatherings are of importance."

A tongue lashing was of little threat to a homeless street waif, who faced far more perils every day of his uncertain life. He just grinned and continued. "The man, Tarta, as he is called, is the leader of the Ratus band, in the Sucusa quarter. He has his room and mat in the Taburna of Sweet Vintner. On the street of the Capella."

"Goodsome so far," said Marcus. "Anything else?"

"Aye... Sos. His band is four handfuls strong, and he controls the prostitutae of the street." He waited for a moment, then asked, "Will that earn the argentum coin?"

Marcus nodded. "I would say so. Stay until my steward gathers it."

"I can offer more for more."

Subduing a grin at the obvious attempt of the urchin to hike his wage, Marcus just nodded.

"Tartus was unhappy that several men that he had sent on a mission were paid, but did not return. He engaged another to travel to a city... the name is... Anum or some such sounding. They were to travel the road asking of the missing party. He returned with nothing."

"Your fee is enhanced. Continue."

"Tartus, himself, traveled across the city to the Palace of the King not long after, and more than once. He reports to a high man of the King's guard who is called Petronius. That man is also of the Sucusa quarter, but he was once known as Sudoniaus until he was taken by the magistrates for making false coin. They removed his two fingers for the crime. Should I continue?"

At the obvious nod, he finished with, "Sudoniaus, or Petronius as he calls himself, does not enter his old realm but meets with Tartus at an open wine kiosk by the Caelius gate. I have seen that twice."

Marcus just stood, almost frozen with astonishment at the lad's tale and the volume of information coming from a street rat. In the future, he would refrain from measuring a man - or boy - by their appearance. "That is a good duty, lad. Might I enquire as to how you discovered such information?"

The boy grinned. "I am the pisspot boy for the taburna where Tartus resides. I can come and go with ease among the rooms, and without being questioned. The pay is little, but they allow me to graze on the kitchen leavings. The spot was an easy one to get, and I asked after your hirement of myself."

Marcus gave a word to Cleo, who disappeared into the house. "You have earned your wage, this day, boy. I have another proposal for you, if you wish."

The boy grinned. "I am yours as long as you have coin."

Cleo came from the house with a small bag. Marcus waved a hand at him and said to the urchin, "This is my Steward. If you will report to him on the Ides of every month, he will give you a copper coin and possibly a new mission. Even if he has no task for you, then you may keep the fee. For now..." He opened the bag and selected two of the small Greek coins - silver - and a good many of copper, and placed them in the boy's hand. The denominations needed to be small - giving the boy a large Drachma, or such heavy coin, would just get the youngster's throat cut when he tried to vend it. Eyes wide, the lad's hand closed on more metal than he had ever dreamed of possessing. "Hide these somewhere before your friends know you have coin, else you may not wake from your sleep. And get yourself a bath, before coming again."

Grinning again, the boy ran from the yard and disappeared into the crowds of the street.

Another missive came from Lucius. In response to the first one, Marcus had sent a reply, giving acknowledgment that the original had been received, and sending word from his mater, the Domina, that herself and daughter were well and praying to the gods for his safe return. Marcus added to the scroll, giving the news of the city, some words from Collatinus and an account of the mission on which he had been sent.

Then his quiet home-life changed...

A messenger arrived, giving orders for his presence at the Palace. With a feeling of unease, he girded himself in his best uniform and walked to the assembly the next morning. There, he found the group of men little changed from the last time. The difference was that the King was not in evidence - their instructions being given by a Senator. Marcus could not recall the official's name, but knew that he was high in the trust of Tarquinius.

Across the crowd, he saw Maxentius standing behind Collatinus. Walking through the men, he was greeted by both. After the salutations, Marcus asked, "Do you have news of this gathering, Sos?"

"Aye," replied the noble youth. "According to my pater, the King has managed to get the cities of Latium to agree to meet. It will take place the day after tomorrow at the grove of Ferentina." Before Marcus could ask the obvious, the Patrician said, "We are just the decorations for the King, with little to do except stand and look Roman."

Marcus nodded as he assimilated the news. Then he said, "Ah... Sos. Might I congratulate yourself on your marriage to the beautiful daughter of the house of Lucretius? That was a prize nobly won."

Collatinus grinned. "As you should know, from your wooing of the veritable daughter of Venus. Aye, and thank you. Lucretia is indeed a wonderment to my house." He shook his head in mock dismay. "I fear, however, that my fortune will be funneled away to your household with the garments that she purchases from your women. I agree that a wife should be garbed in the best, but I fail to understand the need for more habiliments than a bevy of wives could wear in an entire season."

Now Marcus grinned. "Sos, if you are asking me to interpret the needs and desires of womenfolk, then you are as one coming to the fishmonger to purchase bread. I cannot leave the house without returning to find some useless bauble or adornment has been installed on my wall or taking room from the floor."

The noble nodded. "Aye. And I fear that Lucretia is guilty of conspiring with Sabina and Iulliana in separating you from your coin to obtain those baubles. And in that, you have my apology."

Now the orders came from the platform as to the march to the meeting place. As it turned out, a Century of Legionaries would accompany them for the assemblage. Again, this would be for show, rather than a need for any protection, except that they would also provide a guarding force to the person of the King. The Tribunes would march as a unit, rather than at the head of their cohort or Legion - units that did not exist at the moment. The accompanying force of about sixty soldiers - a Century - would be commanded by an older Tribune and his Centurion - actual veterans of the Army. The security of the person of the King was not to be given over to newly fledged boy-Tribunes. Another unit of support would follow - cooks, tent-quartermasters, drovers and such.

They were given their positions in the column, and instructions for the arrival - and the warning to make certain that they, themselves, and their men were turned out to perfection. "Woe unto the man or leader who brings disrespect upon the King." The Senator was insistent upon that topic. Publicola made the remark that the worthy's head would be on the block also, for any actions that impaired the success of the meeting with the Latium leaders.

That night, Marcus informed his household of his duties, and the fact that the length of the service was unknown to him. In private, he gave instructions to Cleo to deliver - immediately - any missives from Lucius, to the Domina. The Steward was left with more than enough coin to sustain the house for months, although the meeting would take only a fraction of that time.

The next morning, he was at the Circus Maximus field, with the hundreds of men who would make the march. There was a period of formation, then the King and court arrived on their steeds and they stepped off. The meeting place, the grove of Ferentina, was much less than a day's march, and their arrival should leave much light in which to make camp. Side by side with both Maxentius and Albanus, the young men spoke quietly as they walked - low-voiced murmurs that could not carry far enough to raise the wrath of any seniors that might insist that young officers should march in silence. Both of the others, having noble tribunes as their principals - or rather, principals that were not in hiding in the outerlands - had much knowledge that Marcus lacked.

"Tarquinius is wishing for an allied army so as to expand the reaches of his power," said Albanus, quietly.

"So he is looking for war, then?"

Maxentius made a sound of derision, then looked around to see if it had been noticed. "He wants to put all the lands within reach under the hegemony of Rome." That word was a new one to Marcus, but he understood the idea. "From the Alpines in the north to the southern cities on the Great Sea. Collatinus says that if he gets what he is seeking from this meeting, our children's children will be marching with the army."

"Will Latium join with him? What is the thinking of your Tribunes?"

Albanus answered. "Nay. You are looking at the construct from a defective vision. Latium is not a single entity, such as Rome. Rather, it is made of many independent cities, each with their own rulers and laws. They can be considered as a whole only because of their affiliation with each other in the face of an outside enemy. Since there is no overall ruler, each will make their own decision."

"Aye, Collatinus says that it depends on how many will join at the first askance." Maxentius paused and looked around again. "If it is many, then the others will do so out of self-interest. None will want to be left out of the booty of war, nor become plundered themselves by being treated as an unfriendly who did not join the common cause." He suddenly lowered his head with a "Ssss. Here comes the Senior Centurion and staff."

Marcus just walked along, thinking on the information that he had been given, as the several horse riders passed, moving to the front of the column where the King was riding his great white equine. The young man had much yet to make out of his span of years, and having it ended by a war was not a pleasant prospect.

Since the grove was only an hour away by midday, the column did not stop for the meal but continued until they entered the field designated for the encampment of the Romans. This was outside the sacred area where the meetings would take place, and with its usual efficiency, the quartermasters and Optios of the army had the area surveyed, and tents were being raised even as the commissary train began the late midday meal. Marcus was still traveling under the auspices of Collatinus, so his mat was unrolled in the shelter of that noble and Publicola. For now, both the Tribunes and their aides had nothing to do but stand and watch the sub-officers of the unit call and give orders for the encampment.

Until a man walked up to stop in front of the two aides.

Marcus had seen the man somewhere but did not dredge up the memory until he spoke. "My pardon, good Sos." The young aide nodded. "I am Theodus, you may remember? The servant to Turnus Herdonius." Now the memory came flooding back, although he had never known the name of the man. Another nod. "My master requests the boon of sharing a cup with the noble messenger from Rome. He awaits at his villa over yon hill."

Marcus was utterly taken aback. Before he could formulate an answer, Collatinus walked up, wondering at the snatches of the request that he had heard. The noble said, "What is this?" Then, looking at the young aide and pointing to the stranger, asked, "Rather, who is this?"

Marcus gathered his confusion, then answered. "This is the servant to Herdonius, a counselor to the Chief of Aricia, and who made me welcome on my mission to that city. I believe that I have been invited to wine at the domicile of the noble."

To the servant, Collatiuns asked, "Where is this villa? What is the distance?"

"About a hippikon on the road to Aricia." He pointed, then at the puzzled looks from the four Romans, he said uncertainly, "...about four stadia?"

"Not far then. Wait here. Marcus, I would have a word." Both men walked out of hearing, and the noble turned to the young man and said, "Who is this Herdonius?" Marcus explained all he knew was that the man was an elder - probably an important one - on the council of the city, and told of the queries that had been made of him that evening of the message delivery. Collatinus thought for a moment, then said, "You have no duties here, today. You should go, but come to me immediately upon your return. It may be that you will be made privy to the undercurrents that have to be swirling around this meeting place." The young aide nodded, then the noble continued. "Marcus. You are as intelligent a lad as I have known, and I have no worries about your conduct. But... Intrigue is a way of life in these cities - something that you will have no cognizance of in your honest life. Do not take any wording as meaning what it says. And give no statement that will be attributed to the King or his court. Listen and praise the wine, and that is all." He paused, then, "Of course, you are entitled to your opinion if asked, but just assure that it is known to be yours - not that of Rome."

Asking Maxentius to look after his kit, Marcus followed the servant down the road and out of camp. Few people were in evidence on the road - apparently, the common folk were wary of the presence of a foreign military unit in the vicinity, however peaceful the proclamation. After a hill or two, they turned onto a groomed path made of flat white stones. Just beyond the foliage, and out of sight of the road was the spacious dwelling - a villa, as it were. Marcus had come to know of such as a place for a Patrician family to escape the sometimes smothering household of the city, filled with slaves and servants and busyness from daylight to darkfall.

Herdonius was waiting at the marbled doorway. "Greetings, Marcus of Rome. It is gladsome that you have accepted my poor invitation for company."

"My thanks to yourself for the relief of just standing and waiting for some assembly, somewhere. But... I suspect that you have other reasons than company to offer a poor unknown aide access to your wine jar."

The elder smiled, and said, "Ah. The young man sees through the machinations of the old sage." He waved. "Please, let us recline in the Roman fashion and partake of a cup between friends." The villa was small, of only three or four rooms and would have easily have fit into his work area in the back of his own domicile. As he could see through the openings of the doors and wide windows, the structure was sparsely furnished and empty of all inhabitants besides the three men... No, suddenly, he could see a young woman in what had to be the kitchen, moving here and there. Still, the villa was obviously not used as a dwelling by the old man at this time.

Inside, and on a raised dais so that a garden could be seen through the large opening in the wall, was a mensa flanked by a pair of lectuae - a table and two reclining couches with fat pillows. It was, as his host had said, in the fashion of a noble Roman household. At a wave, Marcus reclined on an elbow and waited for the old man to do the same, although not with the facility and speed of the youngster. Immediately, a young girl entered with two cups and an ornate wine pitcher. She filled the cups and disappeared.

"Despite your doubts as to the genuineness of my invitation, let me say that your presence is welcome - I seldom have the enjoyment of speaking to a young man who is not concerned in the main with either mischief or the pursuit of women. Still, you hit the mark. I can say that I have other thoughts than just converse, as pleasant as that may be."

Marcus paused, then said, "Before I partake of your wine, let me say that no amount of probing will gain you any information as to the plans of my King. In truth, I know less of them than most, which is to say, almost nothing."

The old man nodded. "Aye. I am not such a fool as to think that a young man not long inducted is called into the privy counsel of his King. Still... You are intelligent, with a skill that is admired by the citizens of your city. And you have somehow amassed enough coin to purchase a household that even the most prosperous merchants would have to commit into major usury to obtain. In addition, you are brave and skilled with weapons, as the actions of your training have shown." Marcus was frozen in place, holding the cup to his mouth to hide any expression that he could not contain. "But - and this is rare in a young man - you have no enthusiasm for war that is not in defense of your home." Marcus took a sip, then casually set the cup down, trying to maintain his composure. How in the name of all the gods, existing or nay, did the man know so much of his life - and again, why would he make the effort to gain knowledge of a non-entity of the city? He decided to ask just that.

"You have me at a disadvantage, Sos. Why would an important elder, such as yourself, collect the story of a man, not even of the city in which he lives and certainly of no importance in the strata of the rulership."

"Ah. Now you are wide of the mark. It is true that I have learned much about you, and your missing Tribune, but not from any concern or fear of either. Rather, I have sons and daughters, and they, in turn, have progeny of their own. It is the fate of them that fills my heart with concern. I would that they live out their lives in comfort and enjoyment - not perish in a fire that might consume the entire land. I would assume that you feel the same way about sons and daughters yet unborn." He paused for a few heartbeats. "Let us stop our sparring, then."

"Ask what you will."

"Your King, Tarquinius, is set foot to a path of conquest and wishes allies to begin the journey. That is my reading of the events."

Marcus liked the forthrightness of the old man. He hid behind no walls of pomp, or gens, or oblique statements - saying one thing but meaning another. In the experience of the young man in the city, falsehoods were the norm among high and low alike. About wealth, ancestry, skills - any and everything. Thinking for a moment, he nodded. "As I said, I am the least person to have knowledge of the King's plans or actions, but I will say that your belief is also that of several of the Tribunes - educated men and of families high in the ranks of the city. Now, my question. Will the cities of Latium join with Rome?"

The old man frowned and drank from his cup for the first time. "Aye. I believe they will - most of them. A few, such as the city of Gabii, will not. They have even refused to attend the meeting in the grove."

Marcus pursed his lips, thinking on the days ahead. "That might be evil news. This King is unconcerned about the lives of his citizens. Already, he has murdered many of the high ranking nobles of the city and the Senate."

"Including the Pater and Brother of your Tribune." He clapped for another filling of wine, startling Marcus who had not realized his cup was empty. "I know not if you are a student of history..." A shake of the head denied that. "...But I can claim to be somewhat of a scholar and one lesson from the scrolls of the sages, is that power, once grasped, is always used. And never released." Waiting for the girl to pour and leave, he continued, "I fear that your family and mine may have a future that is less than... optimum."

"May I assume Sos, that your city has decided in the King's favor, but that you argued against it?"

"You are astute, Young man. I would tell you aye in both questions."

That evening, Marcus told Collatinus of the conversation. There was nothing in it of any surprise, and the Tribune had already ascertained that the city of Aricia was in favor of the union - even enthusiastic about the bonding. There was little more to say and nothing to do, other than relax in the cool evening and speak of this and nothing to his fellow aides.

The next day - one before the meeting of the King and Chiefs - a formation was called and an inspection performed by the Senior Centurion. Once again, the old soldier showed that absolute rank was not... absolute. In theory, any Centurion, no matter how senior, was far below a Tribune in authority. But, few of the noble officers would gainsay a man who had seen - and survived - a multitude of wars, skirmishes and conflicts over a lifetime of service to one King or another. Especially in light of the fact that most had never cut at any opponent beyond a dummy of straw, and had never seen blood spilled beyond damaged noses in boy-battles of their youth. A few of the elder Tribunes were veterans of war, but they, even more, knew of the competence of the man and that only the fact of his being born a Plebeian kept his rank from being Senior Tribune of the entire kingdom.

Striding up and down the ranks, he barked at this wrinkled cloak, and that tarnished brass - once even pulling at the belt of an officer to demonstrate the rottenness of the leather. Marcus just stood with his eyes straight ahead as the man stopped and his intense gaze looked him up and down. The relief of the young aide was considerable when the Centurion moved on without comment of his uniform.

That afternoon, a messenger arrived at their tent with a summons to Marcus to report to the Senior Centurion. Utterly surprised, he quickly donned his best garb, with the other two aides inspecting him for any flaw. With their words of encouragement, he hurried to the guarded enclosure of the King and his counselors.

There, he found himself with three other young aides and quickly called to a short formation before the Senior.

The old officer looked them up and down, adjusting a scabbard on one and the helmet on another, then said, "You have shown superior skill in your deportment and have been selected to attend the King tomorrow in his assemblage. In truth, your mission is to appear as elite young officers of the King - we will not tell them that your blades, as yet, have hit nothing but air and straw-men." He stopped in front of Marcus and looked him up and down again. "Except for one among you, perhaps." To all, he ordered, "Report here at daybreak."

On the following morning, the four aides were standing at attention outside the Royal Pretorium - the huge tent that was the quarters of the King. Also, milling around the entrance were the Senators and nobles of the Roman party, all jabbering about this and nothing. At the sounding of the morning music from the camp of the Legionaries, some distance away, the tent flap was opened by two servants and Tarquinius appeared, dressed in his military garb, and behind him emerged the Senior Centurion. He stopped in a few paces, and looked to the sky, apparently enjoying the fresh morning air and the bluing light of another perfect day. Looking around, his eyes swept over the four young men, then came back to stop on the small formation. He stepped over to the front of Marcus, looking him up and down with his brow crinkled - obviously trying to remember something. He looked around at the Centurion, who stepped forward and said, "He is the Adiutor of the Tribune Junius, Regis. He reported to your highness after the skirmish in which the noble Junius was injured."

The King nodded, and said, "Ah. It comes back to me now. And what tales of the son of my good sister?"

Frozen in place, Marcus replied, "I have had no word from the Tribune for many months, Regis. But the last missive gave that he was cured of his malady and needed only for his strength to return to his body."

The King nodded. "We hope that the good Tribune returns to our service soon. You will inform me of any news of his being, Adiutor."

"Aye, So... Regis."

The conclave was a massive affair. In addition to the primary leaders, each had their counselors and advisers, and even those numbers were filled out with self-important drones having nothing to bring except outlandish garments and an attitude of superiority. King

Tarquinius was the center of the assemblage - a given since the reason for the meeting was his and Rome was, by far, the largest entity represented. The leaders sat in a large circle, to accommodate their numbers, with their advocates arranged behind them, all maneuvering for room and to be in the first rank. Behind the King of Rome were the Senators and nobles and behind them were four senior Tribunes, each with a small Contubernium of men formally arranged in a column. This was supposedly for the purpose of pomp, but Marcus knew that, in actuality, they were there in the instance that the assembly became... unruly, or worse. He had no reason to think that the King was a coward, or even overly worrisome about his own skin, but prudence required that a supreme ruler have an outlet for surviving a sudden threat. Behind each Tribune was a Centurion and ten Legionaries - all with well-worn scabbards and oiled blades. These were blooded veterans, not conscripts from the ranks of farmers and merchants.

The sacred grove of the goddess Farentina was a pleasant and shaded place, with large pools - almost small lakes - surrounding the temple. Naturally, the priests had to query various auguries - flights of birds released by the acolytes, the entrails of lambs - even counting the number of seeds in a carefully selected fruit. Standing idly in his role of decoration to the King, Marcus wondered at the reason for a goddess, powerful enough to point the fortunes of man from the top of Olympus, in needing such arcane devices to express satisfaction or nay, rather than just causing the words to issue from her stone mouth. But, the tall statue with the beautiful likeness of the patron of the grove did not speak, instead allowing the birds and lambs and seeds to issue satisfaction in her name. He wondered - suppressing a grin - what would happen if she had decided to cast a vote of displeasure on the assembly - and if the priests would have the courage to report that the count of seeds was deficient, or that the entrails were blemished.

The babbling of the priests over, King Tarquinius stood in the middle of the circle and gave a long litany on the honorable pasts of both lands, and the fruits that had been gathered from their friendship with their brothers on the Tiber, all the while praising the wisdom and astuteness of the leaders of the Latium cities... Marcus finally turned his attention elsewhere, looking at the guards of honor for the Latium chiefs. Unlike the semi-uniformed Romans, those soldiers wore... apparently whatever was at hand. A few had helmets as those of Marcus and his comrades, and those had colored brushes or plumes indicating some rank or specialty. Other than those, and the many spears and few blades, they could have been ordinary citizens.

On and on, the King droned, for at least an hour by the huge sun clock in the temple courtyard, still praising the wisdom of the leaders assembled before him. Finally, he reached the end of his preamble - or ran out of praises, most likely - but the hopes of Marcus, for a beginning of the real meeting, were dashed. The leader from this city or that, rose and began his own paean to the leaders of the group. In dismay, he counted the assembled chiefs and calculated that they would be standing here until the next Ides before all ran through their encomiums of praise. Fortunately, with many of the leaders being advanced in age, a pause was made every hour for the benefit of those whose bodies were insisting on making water without delay. A break for the midday mess was made, then the laudations began again. The sun was only the part of an hour above its resting when the assembly agreed that the meeting was of friends and had the auspices of the goddess, Farentina. The real work would begin on the morrow.

It was a legsore Adiutor that made his way back to the tent and fell back on his mat. To the questions of his fellows, he just shook his head and jestingly cursed the day that he had left the mountains. "My belief that the sophists in the Forum have the advantage of long-windedness is in need of adjustment." Looking at the tent flap to make sure that no ears were nearby, he continued quietly, "The King and his new friends could talk those graybeards into silence before their morning cups." There was little to tell, but he gave them a short description of the day.

Fortunately, the following morning saw the leaders far less garrulous, and seriously discussing the matter at hand. As they had suspected, the King was desirous of a combined army to "defend" the borders of the combined lands. "With the Legions of Rome, and the armies of Latium at their right hand, no power in the world could subdue us." Practical matters were worked out. Tarquinius would, of course, be the supreme Commander, but would take high officers of Latium into his council. Glory and prizes would be shared equally, as would the suzerainty over newly conquered lands.

As the day went on, Marcus wondered if the Chiefs in the circle were so shallow as not to notice that the proposals that had been made in the morning - for the defense of both Rome and Latium - were now transforming into talk of conquered lands. Even of loot and slaves and all that came from successful war. Probably, he decided. It was obvious that most were looking at the proposal as the opportunity to gain riches, or even to settle old scores. Then...

As the right of speaking moved around the circle, it came again to the council of Aricia. On this rotation, Marcus saw Ternus

Herdonius stand and arrange his robes, waiting for the silence to enfold him. Then he spoke. "My friends. We have heard many proposals today from the honorable leader of our large neighbor to the north. I note that many of the speakings note the prosperity and wealth of both, Rome and our Latium lands. And indeed, it is so." He looked around for a moment. "I would ask, would the sacrifice of our young men bring prosperity of a quantity to assuage the loss? And would the gain of treasure exceed the coin required to wage war - a war that we would have no idea of the extent nor time?"

Marcus looked over at the King to see his reaction. It was immediately obvious that, among the abilities that the man might possess, hiding his feelings behind an indifferent mask was not one of them. Still, it was highly unlikely that he would take physical action against the naysayer - such a response might easily cause a war between Rome and the cities he was wooing. Marcus had begun to realize that Herdonius was a man of great import and respect in his land, the more so for refusing to translate that importance into any rulership in Latium.

"And if I may say," the elder continued, "the ability to gather allies is not confined to Rome and Latium. The appearance of a lumbering beast in the guise of our armies might cause the Volsci and the Acqui to decide that in numbers, there is strength. And what of our powerful neighbors to the north. Should the Etruscans become wary of our martial moves, they alone could inflict severe harm on our bodies, and if allied to another, even possibly grind both our lands to powder." He turned a full circle, then finished, with, "I will ask that you look in askance at any move against our neighbors, without legitimate reason in defense of our homes."

Tarquinius had managed to hold his temper, and in fact, made his face resume a look of interest. He stood and held up his hands for quiet. "I give respect to the honorable elder from Aricia. He is indeed the cloak that tempers the wind to our desires. Certainly, his speakings need to be brought into the fold of conversation, as one who has learned much from a life of years and wisdom gathering. And be assured that, all caution will be taken in our choice of paths into the future. But as one..."

"Your pardon, Regis." A man from the city of Tripontium had stood and spoken, interrupting the King in his attempt to season the nay-saying of Herdonius. "There is much in what is said by the honorable elder from Aricia. Our cities would be less than dust under the feet of the Etruscans, should our desire for aggrandizement begin to make them uneasy as to our intentions."

Another man rose and gave a nod and a wave to the speaker. "Aye. Great Rome has a wall that could protect them should our plans have less success than we would hope, but our city is small, and would be as a puffball under the treads of an enraged alliance."

Marcus realized that Herdonius had punctured the dream-gathering of the assembly, and forced them to examine their proposals in the light of reality, and not just in the hope of land and gold. He could see the colic of Tarquinius rising and wondered if it would be contained, or if he would stride forward and cut down the next speaker that raised voice against the long plotted adventure of the King.

Now a young man stood and pushed his voice into the fray. "Let one speak who has not seen his beard turn gray!" In surprise, the conclave quieted. "I hear many words from men who have seen their productive days long ago. Old men have wisdom, and all should listen to their admonitions, but it is the young men who will enact any plans that are decided by this assembly. When I am old, I may also have doubts in risking all that I have obtained in my life, but such caution is not for the young, else we would still be grubbing for our food along the floor of the forest and the shores of the sea." He looked around, then pointed to Herdonius. "Did not you, as a general in the combined armies of Aricia and Colarali, subdue the Albains with such fervor that only their name exists today?" Another pointing finger. "And you, Yodius - in your youth I am told that you had no qualms about the war with the Attriede - a war that brought you most of your wealth and status that you enjoy today." Now, many of the young men in the assembly were nodding. "Do not consign us to dream weaving with our womenfolk, when our blood wishes to us to be men."

Tarquinius was staring at the young man, then as that person had to draw breath, broke in with, "You are a young leader with spirit. Might I know your name?"

The young man turned and bowed, saying, "I am Dexterus, great Regis. Son of Sardomines and heir to the leadership of the city of Signa."

"Aye. It warms my blood to see that the spirit of men is not extinguished in the lands of Latium. Should this assembly decide on the approval of my plans, you will be an asset for our success."

Now the orderly assembly became as the Forum on feast day, with everyone having risen and attempting to insert his comments into the stream of the arguments. Finally, Tarquinius rose and shouted for quiet, which was slowly obtained. When the cry of voices tapered off, the King held his hand up and said, "My friends! We should not descend into dispute over this statement or that. Let us adjourn for the night to let our facilities rest and begin again on the morrow with a fresh beginning." Without giving time for anyone to answer, he turned and marched out of the circle, back to the Roman camp. Behind him, in the guard of honor, Marcus could tell that the King was not walking with a regal stride. Rather he was almost in a run, hurrying along and looking to neither side.

Sorrow

Marcus and his friends sat on a log, outside their tent, as he answered their questions as to the happenings of the day. All were interested in the rage of the King at the less than total dedication to his idea of alliance. Across the compound, they could see the far larger and more ornate tent of the Royal enclosure, with men coming and going with some haste. Not all were Romans - several were officers of the Latium contingent that Marcus could recognize after standing around the meeting circle for two days.

"Will Latium withdraw from the proposal?" asked Albanus.

Marcus shook his head. "I believe not - there were more chiefs with interest than without, but it is maybe that the King will not get his whole serving from the meeting."

Maxentius was looking over to the King's tent. "It would appear that he has no intention of just waiting to see if you are correct. Much is being planned, I would wager."

Marcus nodded. "Aye. He was red with anger at the opposition - that was plain - but he contained it well..." He stopped as a group of men strode by, led by a tall man with a black beard - unusual for the normally clean-shaven Romans. But the man's face was not what was noticed. Rather, the sight of the missing two fingers on the primary hand froze Marcus in place. So this was the hired cutthroat in the service of Caeus, the Praefectus to the King. Petronius. Or Sudoniaus, whichever name he was using at the present. "I believe some evil is afoot, this night." He explained the identity of the man - not the facts of his apparently being the instigator of the three men that Marcus had killed in the foothills - but that he was the blade in the hand of Caeus.

Then, he rose and watched a small group of men - not Romans - approach the King's quarters and wait to be admitted. Even in the dim light, he could see that one was the young man who spoke against the elders. Dexterus, he remembered as the name of the speaker. Marcus wondered if he had been summoned as a potential ally, or if the young leader was there under his own auspices to collude with the King in his plans.

Darkness fell, and there was nothing else to see, and they retired to the tent for the night.

Morning began the assembly again, and the King had apparently corralled his anger during the night. Following the usual opening chants of the numerous priests, calling down the blessings of the goddess, he was his normal self, taking and answering questions, interjecting his points into the conversations. Marcus noticed that Herdonius was still in his place, sitting on the little stool that he had brought. At least, he had not been murdered by the King's rage during the night - something that Marcus would not have wagered against the evening before.

This day started calmly, with the proposal from Tarquinius for a combined army, with himself as Commander, but with a generous allotment of Latium nobles in positions of authority within his staff. The men of Rome and those of Latium would be as separate units, to alleviate the problems of differences in training and tactics, but would maneuver as a one toward a combined goal. Again, some of the elders, led by Herdonius, asked sharp questions as to the future use of such forces, but their protestations were as questions, and not in confrontation as had been the method on the previous day. Still, Tarquinius was less than patient with such nay-saying, and more than once, cut into their words with sharp language of his own.

At the midday meal, one of the Adiutorae was summoned to the King's tent. Marcus and his fellows then saw the man leave in haste, moving into the trees toward the part of the grove that held the Latium contingent, returning in a while to the Royal quarters, then resuming his place among his young fellows. That evening, at their own mess, he was asked by his fellows about the mission. The aide, one Gordianius by name, swallowed his bite of meat, and replied, "It was a verbal message to that fellow that spoke for the King. Dextus or some such. The missive made no sense, just 'The tall trees are a shield to the wind.' The man returned just an 'Aye.'"

The other three examined the inscrutable message in their minds, with one saying, "That makes no sense. It could be the ramblings of a taburna patron in his cups."

"Aye," said another. "I suspect that the wine in the Royal tent is of a goodness that beckons one to excess."

Marcus just looked over at the Royal tent for a time, then said, "The missive has obviously a hidden meaning to the other party. As such, no amount of thought on our part will find the significance."

He well knew of such misdirection. The messages that he received on occasion from the Tribune Lucius had such nonsense, for protection in the case of the tablet finding its way in front of the wrong eyes. Agreed on that night before the noble disappeared, many words meant other than they read. "Land of the sunrise," meant Greece, while "sun city" was Rome itself. "Fishing the waters," was to indicate that he was taking a berth on a ship. And so on. He had an entire list hidden in his work area.

The day concluded with a general agreement, with many of the obstacles overcome, and understandings agreed to. The assembly of nay-sayers around Herdonius were more vocal, but were overridden by the mostly younger leaders, looking for a change in the sameness of their lives, or even dreaming of wealth and glory on the field of battle. And again, the next day started as the others, the scribes busy noting all decrees and agreements of the assembly. But, here was an... undercurrent, this day, to the proceedings that Marcus could detect, although there was nothing that he could have pointed to had he been asked. The King was still moderating the negotiations, but the young aide noticed that he would quickly look in this direction, or that, for just a heartbeat, as if he were expecting news. Or some event.

The noon meal came, and the circle reassembled, then suddenly, Marcus noticed a tall black bearded man appear beyond the rank of Roman guard of honor - Petronius! Now the young aide was sure that something was afoot, and probably an event that would not be gladsome. The man with the missing fingers spoke to another officer, then turned and disappeared. That officer, casually walked around the circle, nodding to the various Latium officers until he was directly opposite the King. Stopping, he waited - apparently to be noticed - until he caught the eye of Tarquinius. A brief nod, and he turned and was gone.

Something had happened, or had been accomplished, Marcus knew. But what? The assembly went on without any change until, across the circle of leaders, Marcus could see a detail of soldiers marching at a route step up the road toward the circle, a young officer at their front. With them was a familiar man - in servant garb, but... Finally, he could see that it was Theodus, servant to Herdonius. Just outside the circle, the soldiers stopped, but their officer strode through the mass of Latium leaders and their counselors. All looked in surprise at the interruption, but Marcus was certain that the King's astonishment was unreal.

One of the Latium leaders, being interrupted in his speaking, said, "What means this? You disturb a meeting of importance."

Tarquinius rose and said, "Wait, good Hermansis. For one to disrupt our consultations, the reason must be dire." To the soldier, he asked, "Your name, Sos. And your meaning for this intrusion."

The officer saluted, and replied, "Darminues, Regis. Guard Captain to the city of Ardea. I bring warnings of malfeasance and conspiracy."

Now a babble arose at the startling words, and Tarquinius raised his hands for silence. "Your meaning, Sos?"

The officer turned and gestured and two soldiers pulled the servant, Theodus, into the circle. "This man has come with news of a threat to the lives of the King and many in these surroundings." He pointed to the rumpled old man and barked, "Speak your tale!"

The old man almost fell in the dust when the two soldiers pushed him forward and released his arms, but he bowed and said in a quivering voice, "Your pardon, great King. I am devastated to give the words that my master, Herdonius, has a regimen to stop the plans of this assembly, with the deaths of yourself, great King, and many of the leaders of the Latium tribes." Now there was complete silence all around as disbelief fought with the hearing of the words of the servant. "In the villa of Herdonius, considerable arms have been stored for many months, waiting for this event, and men hired to wield them. It is to happen at night, when all are at rest and throats are most easily cut."

Marcus was as astounded as the rest of the gathering, but not at the words of the servant. He, himself, had been in the villa of Herdonius on the evening before the first assembly, and knew that it was a small and clean country dwelling no different than those owned by many nobles of Rome. And certainly not filled with arms, and even less with men hired for rebellion. That the man was lying was obvious, and he wondered if the betrayal of his master was for wealth, or in response to a threat to his own life. He also wondered if the cutthroat, Petronius did the plot, or if that man was just the instigator and the actual deeds were being carried out by a Latium contingent, possibly assembled by the leader, Dexterus, or one with the same desire for the success of the meeting.

He looked over at Herdonius, but the old man was still sitting, an expression of normalcy on his face. Marcus realized that he was looking at a brave man, even one knowing that he was staring into the face of his own death from a plot of lies meant to entrap himself. Tarquinius looked also, then said, "I cannot believe this tale. An honorable man such as Turnus Herdonius does not stoop to the slaughter of men in pursuit of service to their people." He pointed a finger at the shaking servant. "You are giving falsehoods, and will pay the price for such."

Now the man dropped to his knees, both hands clutching each other in his fear. "Nay, great one! The arms and men are there. And now. I can lead you to the villa and your eyes can see the truth of my words."

The babble rose as each man tried to give his ideas and beliefs or disbeliefs of what he had just heard. Tarquinius, playing the part of the astounded man, let them shout and gesture for a while, then stepped forward and raised his hands for silence. Slowly, the chatter died away, and he said, "This is a nefarious plot, indeed, if true, but it would be unseemingly for a contingent from Rome to march across the lands our allies in search of any treachery. I would suggest that a Latium assemblage be formed to investigate the tale of this man." He looked around, then spoke across the circle. "Dexterus, may you march to this villa with a group of your citizens and determine the truth or nay of this man?"

The young leader, keeping a solemn look on his face, bowed and replied, "Aye, Regis. I will do that as you say, but I also disbelieve that the good Turnus would betray his people." Marcus knew that this man also was certainly knowledgeable of the plot. He wondered how many more were privy to the scheme. And, he remembered the sardonic statement of Collatinus that "One man, alone, has difficulty in keeping a secret, and two certainly are too many for its security. If three are privy to the information, then it might as well be announced by the Crier of the quarter." This plot had to have many actors. He wondered how long it would remain concealed and what would be the uproar when the men of the circle came to know they had been cozened.

The assembly adjourned for the moment, waiting for information to return as to the truth or nay of the accusations. Marcus knew that the weapons would be found, and the men would be encamped at the villa. He wondered if those men knew of their roles in this farcical play. Almost certainly not, he decided. They were probably hired on some premise as workers, waiting to load a grain caravan or such. It would be a great surprise when they found themselves accused of treason as a hired band of assassins.

The two tribunes were at their tent, speaking of the astounding revelations of the last hour. As Marcus strode up, Collatinus said, shaking his head, "By great Jupiter, this day has made alleviation of our boredom. Little did I know, when you were bespoken by the elder of Aricia, that you had been invited into the lair of the serpent."

"And I was not, Sos."

The two Tribunes looked at the Adiutor in surprise, with Collatinus saying, "I myself heard the request for your meeting with the elder, Herdonius."

"Aye, Sos. I found him to be an honorable and intelligent man, and the meeting at his villa was pleasant and without acrimony between two men of different lands." He paused to make sure they were out of hearing of any other ears. "And, his dwelling was utterly devoid of weapons - not even the ceremonial spears that I have seen in noble houses. Blades might be found in his house now, but they were not there for the month, as his servant has claimed." Another cautious scan around, then, "And there was certainly not a band of cutthroats inhabiting the grounds or rooms - only a single girl was present."

Publicola began an exclamation, then looked around guiltily to also check for wandering ears. Marcus made a mental note not to trust the noble with secrets of any importance. "You are saying that this tale is a fabrication? By whom? Tarquinius?" The last word came out in a whisper, again with a look around that would have indicated a conspiracy to even the most casual watcher.

"Aye," replied Marcus. "The weapons will be found, as will men to wield them, but the plot was not concocted by Turnus Herdonius. He has no interest in violence as a means - quite the opposite."

Both men looked over at the Royal tent. Finally, Collatinus said, "Aye. I can believe your tale. Tarquinius is one to bend any truth to his needs. This reeks of his plotting."

And it was as Marcus had predicted. The soldiers came back to the grove, herding a group of about four and ten nondescript men, all bearing armloads of weapons - mostly spears, but some blades and such. Indeed, even some of the soldiers were carrying the odd weapon as burdens. The young chief, Dexterus called a halt to the procession, then walked into the middle of the grove, waiting for the Elders and Tarquinius to hurry back from their rest. When they had assembled, the King spoke. "Speak of what you have found."

Dexterus bowed slightly, then spoke in a loud voice for all to hear. "It was as the servant, Theodus, has said. The villa was the meeting point of the evil plot to disrupt these meetings by the selective murder of certain Chiefs." He turned and waved to his soldiers and barked a command. Several took armloads of the weapons and brought them to the center of the circle, dumping them in a pile at the feet of the young leader. He pointed to the pile of metal. "Here is the proof, taken from the rooms of the villa belonging to Turnus Herdonius, himself." Turning to wave at the cowering group of men, squatting under the pointed spears of the soldiers, he said, "And the men to wield them. All encamped in the yard of the villa, awaiting instructions to strike."

It was obvious to Marcus, that the men being accused were completely bewildered at the situation in which they now found themselves. Even now, they had not understood that the accusation of treason was being foisted upon them. He wondered if any of the elders saw - or would admit - the absurdity of the accusal - that a more unlikely band of assassins could not have been found elsewhere beyond the acting-boards of a farcical play in the Forum.

Tarquinius looked this way and that, then called, "Where is Turnus Herdonius? Why does he not attended the circle at this unfortunate time?" Marcus looked all around and saw that, indeed, the man was not in evidence. "Dexterus! Examine the tent of the elder and demand that he present his person to the assembly." All waited until they saw the elder striding toward the circle in the front of the small detail of soldiers. The elder had regarbed himself in robes of fineness, but his habiliments were not what Marcus was noticing, but rather, the total lack of fear on the face of a man who must realize that he was condemned before even asked to speak. The young aide wondered if he himself, or anyone at the assembly would have the same courage to stare into the face of his own death.

Tarquinius waited until the chatter died down, then held up his hands for silence. "Since my person is a mark for which this treachery was fully aimed, I must claim the right to demand punishment for the traitor. Do any here dispute my right in this matter?" Marcus looked around among the circle of men, wondering if any had the courage to balk the monarch. As he would have wagered, none did.

As the detail, and the man that they were escorting entered the circle, Tarquinius raised his voice again. "It is unfortunate that a voice of treason has entered this common circle of friends. A voice of caution, or even of alternative strategy would be considered - nay, even welcome. But..." He looked around the circle, apparently judging his audience and their level of acceptance of his words. "But to attempt to alter the desire of the leaders of the lands by the sword is a most despicable act." Raising his voice, and pointing to the old man with his hand, he said, "Turnus Herdonius - You are accused of treason against the proper leaders of the cities of Latium and also against myself, the lawful King of Rome. It is fitting that your crime be adjudged by your peers of this circle." Turning, he looked at the young leader of the band of Latium soldiers. "Dexterus, Son of Sardomines, I ask that you take this man into your custody to hold until the pleasure of this circle requires his presence."

With that and not another word, the old man was led off, surrounded by a dozen armed men. But as soon as the party had left the vision of the attendees, the circle erupted with shouted questions and statements. Finally, and after much hand waving and gesturing, the King managed to quiet the leaders enough to make himself heard.

"My friends. We have come to a door that will lead to a different future than our previous footsteps would have taken. We must now - all of us in this assemblage - decide if he will enter that doorway. Let me say that Rome will enter - it would be a disservice to my people if I were to allow the natural course of life to take command - to stand by in comfort and sloth as the world grows around us, someday to be swallowed by a peoples who did not take the idea of pleasure and leisure to be guiding spirit of the land. Rome will march to our future glory." He looked around for a moment. "I will say nothing to any leader who indicates nay. I will let his people decide on his actions. But now is the time for decision and I would hear from all."

There was an immediate series of shouts from the younger leaders, then nods by most of the others. Then everyone desired to talk, to put his voice before the assemblage, to enter words that might be quoted by bards and historians down the path of the years. Marcus could see the King relax, obviously satisfied that he had received what he had desired. Now the path to war was assured - some war, somewhere. Aggrandizement was the whole purpose of the King's meetings.

Finally, Tarquinius raised his hands for silence. As the group quieted, he said, "Now we have the displeasure of giving an action to the despicable act that we were given notice of by the alertness of Darminues, Guard Captain to the city of Ardea. By his swift actions, we have avoided bloodshed to our persons and harm to our people. The traitor Herdonius must be adjudged before our adjournment." There was an attempt by several of the older leaders to interject, but the King took no notice. "As the traitor is not of Rome, then is would be unseemly for the men of that city to pass judgment. Were he Roman, I would have him thrown from the Tarpiean Rock, but this matter must be tried and taken by the cities of Latium. I would ask Dexterus, son of Sardomines to take the matter as the jurist for the decision."

Marcus saw the young man walk to the front of the group, giving a slight bow to Tarquinius, then saying, "As you wish, Regis. It is not a task that brings me gladsome desire, but as necessary act to cleanse our assembly of such despicable actions, I will comply." Turning to the group, he said, "In the customs of Latium, I will need a body of ten persons to act as adjudicators. I would ask you, Darminues, and you, Simoneas..."

Tarquinius interrupted the young man, saying, "This matter is for the men of Latium to resolve, and it would be indecorous for we men of Rome to be a part of such important deliberations. Therefore, we will retire until the morrow, when, hopefully, this matter will be decided."

As they marched back to the camp area, Marcus knew that the decision of guilt or innocence of Herdonius had already been decided in the tent of the King. This was nothing but a farce that should be playing on the boards in the Forum, not in a meeting of leaders of cities.

Morning time brought the leaders together again, and after the usual clamor for the auspices of the gods, the group waited for the decision of the fate of Herdonius.

Tarquinius stood and waited for the group to quiet, then asked, "Dexterus, son of Sardomines. Have you and your jurists reached a conclusion regarding the actions of Turnus Herdonius, of the city of Ariccia?"

The young man stepped forward and bowed, then turned to face the assembly. "We have, Regis. We find that the despicable actions of this man of Latium are an affront to all civilized men, and especially to this gathering of honorable representatives brought together for an assembly of reasonable debate." The assembly looked at each other, but none spoke. "As the malefactor is a citizen of Ariccia, we have asked the members of that city to call the punishment..." He gestured toward several men. "...and they have decreed that Turnus Herdonius shall be cast into the pool in the grove of Ferentina, and that goddess may dispose at her will, the body of the man who has brought dishonor upon her domain."

Now the man was brought forth to stand before the assembly and was given his sentence by Dexterus. Marcus admired the oldster, standing apparently unafraid and with much dignity, even in the face of his own doom. He said nothing, without doubt realizing that even a summoning of testaments from the Twelve Olympians and delivered by Mercury himself would not turn the intentions of his accusers.

Now came an action that was far more debasing of the men who were leading the despicable proceedings - at least to the thought of Marcus - than of the man accused of putative treason. A large wooden cage, made of widely woven reeds, was brought - tall and made to hold a man standing. Attached close to the top were two large poles that were used for bearing the enclosure from here to there as if it were a tall carrying chair. Without further ceremony, Herdonius was placed in the cage and his ankles tied to the lower members to prevent any chance of climbing out. Then, six men hoisted the reed cage by the poles and carried it to the bank of the deep pool in the center of the grove. Wading out into the water, they reached a depth where the cage would float of itself, then dropped their burden and return to the shore.

With the two large poles attached, and the natural buoyancy of the reeds and the body of a man, it floated with the head of the unfortunate still out of the water. Marcus looked away in detestation, but immediately returned his gaze, to honor the man who was refusing to be degraded, himself, by this obscene ritual. He wondered if the man was just to be left as he was, allowing the reeds and wood to slowly sink from the immersion in water, but it was not to be. Tarquinius would not allow such a man to pass without attempting further punishment.

"If I may give advice, good Dexterus..." A nod from the young man and he continued, "...the men of Latium should give symbolism to the extirpation of treason by casting a stone, each, into the cage. In this way, they will assure all that their city has condemned the actions of one of their own, and receive the accolades of all who see their actions."

Now, with looks and glances at each other, the men of that city came forward and selected a stone, each, then one by one, cast it toward the floating cage. It was obvious that the rock throwing talents of their boy-youths were far behind them. Only one stone in four even touched the cage, and half of those bounced and were lost in the water. Still, with the three or four that did enter the opening, the weight was enough. Suddenly, the cage reached the critical point where the buoyancy of the wood was overcome by the stones and it slowly sank out of sight.

Now, with haste, the assembly was called together and an agreement was made for the armies of Latium to combine with that of Rome. Then, with another chanting by the priests, the meeting of the cities was called to an end.

Marcus was almost ill with disgust at the events of the day. The reason for taking the life of a man was something that he understood - indeed, even in his young life, he had sent several men to an early sojourn in the domain of Hades, but this farce was despicable by any determination. He knew that the King was a man who used murder as a way to gain his means - the list of innocent men put to death by his hand was known by all, but the actual deaths were tales told by others. This taking of the life of an honorable man had been seen by his own eyes.

Then, as the Tribunes and their aides entered their tent for the last night, the events of the day were washed from their minds by the apparition that appeared in front of them. Standing by the center tent pole, as if he were waiting for some person of acquaintance, was Lucius Junius.

As the men stopped, stunned, at the flap of the opening, he assumed an air of surprise and said, "You appear to have discovered a vision of some startlement. Am I so forbidding, so giving of affright to make you good men into statues this evening?"

Return

With Albanus on guard at the tent flap, the two nobles plied their long-missing friend with questions. Lucius first took the arms of his Adiutor and said, "You are looking well, Marcus. How is the goddess that you managed to convince to live with you?"

"Very well, Sos. It was her regret, and mine, that you could not attend the nuptials, but the good Domina came to bless our house the next day."

The first query of his friends was to the outlandish attire in which the newly returned Tribune was garbed. For an actor of a farce on the boards of the Forum it would have been sufficient for a laugh, but on a noble officer... In place of a tunic, he wore leg coverings that consisted of two tubes that joined with a waist band like a soldiers subligacula, except that this was not underclothing, but worn as an outer garment. His upper clothing was as a tunic, sheared off at the belly. Above his shoulders was a band of cloth with the ends dangling fore and aft, as if it were a loincloth for the neck. His footwear was as sacks of grain, emptied and tied at the ankles.

And the colors were striking. In Rome, clothing was usually shades of white, with decorative stripes or lining, depending on the station of the wearer, but the garb of Lucius was... as the rags of children, playing in a dye manufactory after the work day had ended.

"I thought my clothing to be of worthy as conversation, at least," replied Lucius.

"As a traveling bard, I would agree." Turning to his Adiutor, Collatinus said, "Open my kit, Maxentius. We have no extra armor, but we should be able to extract you from those tatters that would even offend a stone statue."

Lucius shook his head. "Nay. My garments were chosen with great care and device as to the future." At that statement, the two noble Tribunes just looked at each other in confusion, wondering if the jest was for them, or if their friend had actually lost his reason by the fictitious blow from the bandit. "Now, sit and hear my intentions..."

Late that night, Collatinus had finally called a stop to their conversations. "It is past the mid of night, and we are unlikely to impress the august members of this grove meeting - or, indeed, the Senior Centurion - on the morrow unless we get a modicum of sleep." With that the three Tribunes and their Adiutorae settled on their mats for an attempt to rest.

For Marcus, sleep did not immediately come. His worry was the encounter with the King in the morning, and the reaction to the sudden appearance of the long absent son of a popular Senator that he had murdered. Or had ordered such, which was the same crime to the young man. Still, there was wisdom in his Junius returning at this time. It was unlikely that any such retribution would be performed on a Patrician son in front of the notables of the Latium nations.

Morning time came, far too early, and at the second sounding of the horns, the five men, as turned out and polished as possible in such a primitive encampment - and accompanied by a what appeared to be a traveling bard - marched to the Royal tent as a group. As they took their places in line, the Senior Centurion and upper officers of the camp lined the other side of the walkway. Marcus had to bite his tongue to keep his expression in the proper military form, rather than laughing out loud as the eyes of the officers widened as they suddenly recognized the extra Tribune that was standing in line.

Even the Senior had an expression of disbelief at the sight - a man who would normally keep a steady countenance even with news of barbarians pounding on the gate. He took a step forward, possibly without realizing the action, then the Chamberlain appeared through the flap of the Royal tent - the man overdressed and carrying his ornate staff as usual. All stood at attention as the King appeared in his finest attire - this morning being the conclusion of his successful gathering to join all the cities of Latium into a single force.

Marcus had to admire the control of the regal person. As the King saw the new Tribune standing at attention in the double line, he raised his eyebrows in surprise and stopped his walk, but otherwise made no spectacular reaction. "Ah, Lucius, son of my sister. Your return is as blessing from the gods to underscore our noble undertaking, just concluded by the leaders of the lands. We hope that your wounds and maladies have taken flight."

Lucius saluted, then replied. "Aye, Regis. Indeed, with the assistance of the Oracle at Dodona, and the cleansing vapors of Trophonius, I have recovered to return and serve my King."

Tarquinius just looked for a moment, then put his hand on the shoulder of the young noble, saying, "After the conclusion ceremonies of the morning, we will return to Rome. Ride with me and tell me of your adventures." The statements of Lucius had meant nothing to Marcus - the study of ancient gods and miracle workers not being in his education since coming to Rome.

The purpose of the meetings in the Grove of Ferintina now finished, and apparently to the satisfaction of the King, the camp was broken, and the Roman contingent marched back to the city. Along the way, the two Tribunes and the three Adiutorae discussed the return of Lucius and his strange manner. Even with his explanation, his conduct was fantastical in the extreme.

In a low voice, and watching the Adiutor guarding the tent flap he had given his reasons for what he had planned. "I am not as worried at the reaction of the King to my return as of his advisors. They will alway tend to take the path of removing uncertainty rather than waiting for proof of allegiance or no. Caeus, his Praefectus, would kill a newborn babe rather than take a chance of it being a future threat." He looked at his friends, then continued, "So... It is known that I was taken with a blow to the head. If all should think that I have come from the recovery as addled somewhat, then I am no longer a danger." Now, even quieter than before, he said, "But know this. I will avenge the murders of my family. By Jupiter, I swear it."

The procession into the city, only an hour before sunset was a triumphal profession. Obviously, word had been sent back to the Criers of all the quarters, and they had announced the successful conclusion of the amalgamation of the Latium forces, under the command of Rome. The streets beyond the southern gate were lined with cheering citizens, clamoring about a matter of which they knew little, and completely unknowing the significant changes that it would bring to their lives.

As the major festivities were scheduled for the morrow, along with the formal report to the Senate, the procession dissolved as it entered the streets of the Capitoline and all moved to their homes or domiciles. As the house of Junius was just down the street, Marcus escorted Lucius to his door. The scene in the atrium, as the Domina and his sister, Iulliana, fell into his arms with floods of female tears was not a scene for an outsider to behold. Marcus just smiled, and quietly made his way into the street and along the avenue to the Viminalis quarter and his own home.

His entry into his household was no less of a female tumult than that of his Tribune. Four persons were reclining at the table - along with Sabina and her mother, was also Cleo and his dam. With little noise he strode forward until his Steward suddenly saw an approaching figure in the dim light and was about to jump to his feet in alarm, when he recognized his master, gone for these many days. His sudden exclamation caused the others to look and their expressions were taken with as great an astonishment. Wide-eyed, Sabina jumped to her feet, her action tossing a platter of viands across the table, then ran to Marcus as if she were assaulting a foe.

The night, suffice it to say, was far more satisfactory than those of the mat and tent of the Tribunes in the Grove of Ferentina.

As Marcus had not been released from duty, he was at the main Army encampment beyond the walls the next morning for the celebrations called by the King for his new alliances. Mostly, it consisted of standing behind Tribune Lucius as this unit and that marched past the platforms of the watchers. On one side and with the Royal party, were the Senators and upper magistrates of the city. On the other were the masses of citizens, standing rather than sitting, but enjoying the unexpected festival. Finally, the interminable day ended, and he was able to return to his home for another night of bliss.

On the morrow, not being needed until called again, he garbed in an old tunic and entered the work yard in the rear of the compound. Ennius, his apprentice, was already at work, bent over the bench and moving his shaving tool back and forth over a long stave. Seeing his master approach, he stood with a greeting. "It is gladsome to have you back, Sos." He grinned and continued, "Aetius says that Rome has enough soldiers and far too few artisans that can tell stick from stave."

Marcus grinned back. The merchant was opposed to anything that interfered with his commerce of weapons. "When you see him next, request that he inform the King of his concerns." He walked to the storage area and examined the wood that his apprentice had worked in his short absence. The young man was diligent and hardworking and would ask if he was in ignorance of a method or need. And his work followed the instructions of his master to the utmost degree.

Suddenly, the young man stood and said, "Sos. I forgot. Aetius sent a bag for you. It is there." Marcus walked over to the indicated shelf and lifted a large cloth bag, tied at the top with string. It was heavy, and he heaved it to the top of a workbench and untied the closing fiber. Inside was a plethora of... bones? He turned the sack to empty the contents and both looked at the different objects that clattered to the bench top. Both realized that the pile was of horns of animals - antlers and spikes, straight and curved, thick and short, long and narrow.

"It would appear that Aetius is overanxious for our goods. I asked him about procuring an assortment of horn. It would seem that he has definitely completed the commission." Lifting a long piece of animal headpiece, he looked closely at it then said, "I will stop and thank him for the effort. Have you any completed bows ready for vending?"

Ennius pointed. "Two, Sos. But they should stay under the rocks for at least two more days - four would be better."

Marcus nodded. It was very important that the weapons complete the drying of the binder, before the heavy stones that compressed the laminations were removed. "Aye. I can, at least, inform him that he will receive them soon."

For the next several days, as his apprentice continued his work on the staves, Marcus shaved the various horns into thin slices. Rather than waste the boy's efforts by experimenting on finished bow staves, he glued the different shivers of horn between long pieces of unformed wood. For the trial of strength and resilience, fineness was not needed - only bendable wood that enclosed the white animal material. In a few days, he had many laminations of wood with various examples of the stiff horn slices between, slathered with binder and pressed by many man weights of stone. For this, the stone blocks left by the statue carver were excellent, being regular in size and with flat surfaces, and very heavy.

The work was both satisfying and went far to erase the unpleasant memories of the last days of the meeting of cities. He hoped that his military obligations were over - preferable for all time, but certainly for the balance of the season. Alas, it was not to be...

Both young men looked up to see Cleo running into the back yard. "Sos. In the atrium! The Tribune and Domina of Junius!" Looking at his work tunic, ragged and stained with splotches of binder fluid, he knew that Sabina would be appalled if he were to appear in such a state, and in front of such noble guests, but he could hardly make the Tribune and his mater wait while he bathed and found new garments. Both the Steward and apprentice dusted his clothes as best as possible, then he walked into the house, using the rear kitchen entrance. Inside, the cocua was hurrying in her attempt prepare some sweetmeats to go with the wine, no doubt already in the cups of the guests. Marcus did not tarry, but strode past and into the atrium.

Sabina was obviously ecstatic at being host to such noble guests, and he saw that her friend, Iulliana, had also come. He walked up to the group, none having reclined yet, in observance of the custom that guests need the presence of the master of the house for acceptance. "Our house in indeed honored by your entry, Tribune and Domina. And you, also, Femina. I would cast my sorrow for my lack of attire, and I must confess that I was engaged in my work at your arrival." In the back of his mind were the thoughts of wonder at his change from the ignorant mountain boy into a city dweller, able to formulate such flowery excuses in an instant of time.

"Nay, Marcus," replied Lucius. "A man does not need a defense for honest labor, done in his own domicile."

Seeing Cleo nod in the far entrance to the privy, Marcus said, "Please recline and refresh yourselves. I will return in a few moments." Moving across the room and into the alcove, he immediately pulled the soiled garment off and stood as the Steward and the house girl washed him down with warm rags, then hurriedly dried his skin. He pulled a new tunic over his head and waited for it to be adjusted by his helpers, then strode back into the atrium.

Reclining in his place as head of the house, he accepted a cup then said, "As this is the first time that we have been honored to host your presence, Sos, I wish to welcome you to our household. And one that your family played the major part in our taking it as residence, if I may say."

The Tribune held his cup in a salute, then replied, "Nay, good Marcus. What you have done for our family shrivels our deeds to insignificance. And while you are my Adiutor, by law, first and foremost I consider you and your family as friends, even with my noble colleagues of the Capitoline." He gestured to his mother, just reclining with a smile. "She has told me of your kindness - and your willingness to take risks for our house. And I certainly know of your actions for my account. These are not the acts of a retainer, nor are they to be regarded as something for which remuneration can service."

Marcus hoped that he was not going to speak of the details of the hidden property and riches of the Junius family. His was a trusting household... still, the fewer hands that stirred the soup, the less chance of a spill. But, he need not have worried. Lucius moved on without further mention of the secret. After some polite inquiries as to his profession, Lucius came to the matter at hand.

"I would speak to you of a matter of importance. I wonder if Sabina would show my sister the latest fashions that they have produced?" The intent was obvious, and the women, with the exception of the Domina rose to leave.

Marcus also stood and waved to Cleo. To his Steward, he said quietly, "Make sure that we are not overheard." The young man nodded and retreated to stand by in the hallway to the kitchen.

Looking around at first, Lucius began, "On the day after the morrow, we will have an audience with the King. I would that you accompanied me as uniformed Adiutor. I will receive my Tribuneship as a permanent member of the army, along with Collatinus and Publicola - and several others."

Marcus smiled. "Excellent, Sos. None will deserve it more than you." He hesitated, noticing that his happiness was not mirrored in the faces of either Lucius or the Domina. "It would appear that there is more to the ascension than mere promotion."

Leaning over, Lucius nodded. "Aye. I have... friends in the Palace and they have told me that, while Tarquinius seems satisfied with my presence, his advisors are adamant in removing even the slightest danger of rebellion from the streets of the city. Thusly, I will act out my part, started when I joined the meeting in the Grove of Ferentina."

Marcus was taken aback. "You will continue to act as though you are suffering from the... supposed blow to the head?"

"Aye. In fact, one of the mentioned friends overheard a conversation with the King in which he stated that the son of Junius is obviously touched by the gods, still, and presents no danger to the Throne. I must keep him with that impression." Now, quietly he said, "Until it is time for my vengeance."

Alarmed, Marcus whispered rapidly, "Sos. You are not planning an assassination of the King? That he deserves it, I have no doubt, but the retribution on your family and friends will be total! Even to your friends Collatinus and Publicola and Tripciptinius. The Praefectus, Caeus, would make the streets run red, then assume the crown. Of that, I have no doubt. If there is actually a god of evil, then that man is his chief priest."

The Domina leaned forward and put a hand on his arm. "Nay, good Marcus. Be at ease. My son is not so reckless as that. Any act of his - on our part may not happen for years and will not be as crude as a blade out of the dark."

Marcus nodded slowly, relieved that the threat to all in his life was not suddenly imminent. It was one thing for himself to be involved in the intricacies of the manipulations of the nobility, but totally another to risk the being of Sabina and her mother - even Pythes and all of that house to which he owed so much. He asked, "But what will you do?"

Now Lucius smiled. "I wish it to be a surprise to yourself, as to all my friends. In the King's presence, you must not stand with the countenance that gives notice of your knowledge of my plans. Instead, you will react as the others, as they form their thoughts as to my... being."

The Domina looked around, then said quietly. "There is, however, another concern of ours. It would appear that the men of the King are attempting to enter our household. For what reason, we can only guess, but of late there have been several instances that have caused concern.   Apart, they are just happenings, but taken together, make one think of a concerted effort."   At the puzzled look on the face of her host, she continued, "Centus, a servant that has been with us since childhood - indeed, his father served us for his whole life - has been acting..."

Lucius put his hand on her leg, then continued as she paused. "He will be found in a place with no reason, and always when a conversation might be overheard.   At any other time, the actions would not have even been noticed, nor cared about. But, the Domina happened to overhear our steward, Nonus, as he chastised the man for eavesdropping on myself and Tripciptinius one late night.   After that, we began to notice the actions.   And possibly of others."

The Domina finished the thought.   "It is a perilous path that we must trod in these uncertain times.   You have been shown to be a man of infinite resourcefulness.   It was our hope that you might suggest a way... through the wilderness, so to speak."

Marcus just sat, staring into nothing.   Once again, he was amazed at his life and the path he had taken after he had walked out of the mountains as an illiterate youngster of a village with no name.   His belief in the gods could still be called nebulous, but he wondered if the idea of a life guided by some deity on Olympus might be...

He began slowly, as the thoughts formed.   "There would be no advantage in dismissing the servant. If his actions are just those of a curious and bored retainer, then the dismissal would be a disservice. If he is indeed in the service of another, the removal would just indicate that you have become privy to the observations.   And, besides, there would be no way to know if any newly engaged person was in the pay of an adversary."   He paused as another idea came to the fore.   "And, it may not be a matter of subversion for coin - knowing the character of the men around the King, it may be an object threat to the man."

"Aye," replied Lucius.   "We had already determined not to let our suspicions become known, but this must be countered in some way."

"But not by yourselves. I ask your pardon if I cause offense, but as nobles of the city, there is no possible chance of you finding the cause of the action against you at the level of the servant and slave. All would cease any covert activities on the instant that they saw you or the Domina.   Or, even any of the household.   Even myself." He thought for a moment more, then nodded to himself and said, "We need an entity that is like the sprite, or the forest imp, that my mother always set milk out for."

He stood, waving them to continue their recline. "Cleo!" As the steward ran up, he ordered, "Tell Ennius to wait on me, now." As his man ran out of the atrium, he sat back down. "We must have our own ears within your house. I will engage a message boy, to travel between our houses with important missives between Tribune and Adiutor. He will stay at either, depending on the direction of the communication, but mostly at yours. You may have your steward give him an alcove somewhere with a mat, but it needs to be with the other servants."

"...Aye." Lucius was in thought, beginning to see the purpose of his aide. "Continue."

Now the young apprentice ran up and stopped, uncertain in front of guests far above any that he had ever been in the presence of before. Marcus stood again and quickly gave instructions. "Go to the Taburna of the Sweet Vintner in the Sucusa quarter. The street of the Capella. Ask at the cryer's square for directions, as I cannot tell you. Then..."

Early the next morning, Cleo escorted an urchin into the back yard. Now the boy was considerably cleaner than before, but his clothes were mere rags, still. He gave an order to Cleo, then waved the boy to follow him to a covered shed. Here was a working table, with tall stools and the youngster was waved to sit across from the man. "Flavis is your name, is it not?"

"Aye... Sos." Marcus assumed that he had learned to give an honorific when talking to a grown man - the painful way.

"I have a proposition for you that will change your life, should you wish it." He stopped, realizing that the boy did not understand the word for the proposed work. "A mission of some importance." The boy's eyes widen, but apparently not in fear. At that moment, Cleo brought the jug of fruit water and a plate of sweetmeats - soft rolls covered with honey-sugar. The urchin looked at the food with craving - such treats he could have had only rarely, and then only after stealing them on a run. At the gesture of his host, he grabbed one and began eating as if starved for days.

"Easy, boy. They will not disappear, and you will get much less pleasure if you dump them in your belly so fast that it wishes to empty itself by the same route." Letting the youngster savor the honey for a while, he began again as the last of the roll disappeared. "Should you finish your work with satisfaction, you will be given a warm room of your own and a position as a servant apprentice in a house. And be paid in coin every half month. Do you wish for me to continue, or to find another?"

A vigorous nod came from the boy, looking at the plate and wondering if he dared reach for another.

"Excellent. Finish another roll and we will find you something besides rags to wear."

Jester

The Throne Room of the Palace was of a majesty to match the grandeur of the greatest city on Earth. At least, that is what Marcus had been told. And, indeed, it was a spectacle the likes of which he had never seen, nor had ever imagined. In his usual sense of practicality, he wondered at the reason. After all, a King was still the ruler, whether in a Palace made of logs or one of gold-trimmed marble. This was more like a parade in the Circus, with the court hangers-on in their over garbed attire, and the officials looking like fantastical figures with colored drapery. Even the King looked to be twice his usual bulk in his robes and finery. Only the Palace guard was in normal attire, with bossed armor and helmets.

In fact, even with this being a military occasion, the guard unit was the only one in uniform. None of the actual soldiers present were in their military habiliments, in standing with Roman law - although that statute was apparently bendable on certain occasions that Marcus did not quite understand as yet.

The room was exceeding large, the vast expanse of the floor broken only by a triple line of stone pillars to hold up the vaulted ceiling, far above. Centuries later, the walls would have been adorned by large tapestries, and the floor with equally huge carpets, but the arts to produce those decorations would not come about - in Rome - for another two hundred years. For now, other than a few small rugs in front of the Throne, the floor was of bare white stone, and the walls were pierced at intervals with openings to let in the daylight.

Now the Chamberlain droned his speeches to the glory of both Rome and the King, praising his actions in diplomacy to strengthen the security of the city - nay, the entire whole of Latium. Various senators also took the venue to extol the actions of the Regal house, then finally, the Dux of the army stood forth. Rather, it was the current leader and one of whom Marcus had never heard. Apparently, Rome had a plethora of Generals, callable at will and all of the noble class, of course. He wondered if any had the slightest knowledge of war, or if they would learn with the blood of their Legionaries.

The new Tribunes, nine in number, stood forth to receive their ivory batons of rank. Several of them Marcus knew, and some well. Lucius Tarquinius Collatinus, was among them, of course. And Publius Valorous Publicola. And also the nobles from the training venue, Keteus, and Varinius. Spurious Lucretius Tricipitinus was present, but not as a new Tribune, he having received the rank years before. The others, Marcus had seen but knew little of each.

All were in the attire of a noble citizen, flowing togae, but with the obligatory belt and weapon underneath, needed for the ceremony to proclaim their loyalty to the city of Rome.   Behind them, in a standing audience, were the families of the young men, come to see their own receive his reward.

To Marcus it was all a sham.   Lucius Junius had done well - very well - and had returned with not only his training mission completely successfully, but with the report of a bandit troupe destroyed and three captives taken for the punishment ritual in the Circus.   The other Tribunes, however, had failed to approach even their destination before they were putatively destroyed by the regular force out to inhibit them.   Publicola had not even made it to the first night's encampment before being ambushed and sent back to the compound without weapons.   Thus, it appeared that any effort was sufficient to succeed, for one of high enough nobility - even one that ended in abject failure.

Each man stood forth, was blessed by the priest of Jupiter, then by Tarquinius himself.   Then, with baton in one hand and drawn sword in the other, the new Tribune pledged his service and life to Rome.   As the time approached for his officer and friend to approach and receive, Marcus became more nervous at the thought of what he might be planning.   Certainly, Lucius looked no different than his friends - indeed, the very epitome of the noble young officer.   At least, he did not arrive wearing the outlandish garb that he had worn on his return - on that next to the last day of the meeting of the Latium cities. A glance across the stone floor told him that the Domina of the house of Junius was beset with the same worries.   Her expression was neutral, and not at all what one would expect of a proud mother at a time of honor for her son.

Now, Lucius stepped forward and received the same droning platitudes from the priest, then the welcoming speech from the King. Receiving the polished rod, he held it up and pulled a long weapon from his flowing robes.   Planting the haft onto the stone with a clang, he announced, "I, Lucius of the house of Junius, receive and confirm my duty as Tribune to the Army and to King Tarquinius.   From this day, my life will be in service to the glory of Rome."

A ripple of disbelief ran through the crowd and more than one gasp, but not for his words, which were the same as the other young nobles.   Rather, it was for the... weapon that he had revealed.   To Marcus it was a... he did not know. It looked like a pronged tool that he had seen in the stables for moving straw and fodder for animals. But...

Behind him, he heard a low whisper among many, "By the ballstones of Orcus! Why is he brandishing a fish lance?" Another, "It is a trident, I believe."

Again, Marcus marveled at the ability of the King to hold his expression in the face of any surprise. As the young man's declaration ended, the monarch said, "Most elegant, young Tribune. But, we have wonder at the display of the tines of Neptune. Have you perhaps dedicated a quest to the god, or a need for supplication?"

"Nay, Regis," came the loud reply. "The Oracle of Dodona gave me fair warning of a threat to come from the sea. I have prepared myself for that day, to turn back the scourge that will give attempt on the walls of Rome."

Now even the King seemed to be nonplussed. "Ah... Aye... We would hear more of this threat. As Regis, it is my duty to counter all enemies of Rome, from whatever element they may spring. Come tomorrow, and we will discuss it. Bring your good mater, my sister, along with you."

Marcus noticed little of the ceremonies after Lucius had bowed and retreated from the room, to join the other newly appointed Tribunes in the receiving room. As soon as he was able, he also exited the Throne Room through the buzz of low talk that was discussing the incident in an otherwise placid ritual. In the street, he waited, then walked to join Lucius and the Domina, with Collatinus and his young wife, Lucretia in trail. Seeing his aide walking to them, Lucius called, "Welcome, good Marcus. Join us at the household of my friend, if you will. We will discuss the events of the day over his good wine."

It went unsaid, that the household of Collatinus was less likely to house spies reporting to the Praefectus, or his toughs.

The walk was not far, and all settled around the large mensa in the garden. Here, if their voices were kept low, there would be no chance of being heard by servants or slaves. Collatinus opened the conversation. "I have to say, you certainly know how to interest a crowd. This is one investment that will not be forgotten for a while. The trident was a startling feature of your acceptance. It certainly caught me by surprise. And you, Marcus?"

"Aye, Sos. Even knowing that something untoward was planned, that was a startlement."

As Lucretia was not privy to the plans of the Tribune, the conversation had to be limited to the day's happenstances, rather than planning for the future. She asked, "Was that a jest for your return? A play on your injury in the strife of the forest?"

Her husband nodded, knowing otherwise, but unwilling to allow another into the secret. "Aye. You have known Lucius all your life. He likes nothing better than to jape with his friends and startle acquaintances." To the new Tribune, he asked, "What is the desire of Tarquinius to speak to you on the morrow, do you think?"

Lucius shook his head. "I do not know. That was not expected by myself, either."

The Domina spoke. "Knowing Tarquinius and that wife-bitch of his, I do not have a goodsome feeling for the morrow." Then, knowing that the men needed to speak of actual needs, she said to Lucretia, "Let us retire and refreshen ourselves. I would cleanse myself of the presence of neutered senators and aspiring court lackeys." Both women rose, gave their regards, and disappeared into the house.

Now, Collatinus, watching the women disappear through the doorway, said, "The line you must needs walk is narrow, my friend. You have to give the impression of a gadfly, without appearing so addled as to be worthless to both the army and the Senate."

The eyes of Marcus widened and he asked in a rising tone, "The Senate?"

"Aye," replied Lucius. "When my father was murdered, the mantle devolved onto my shoulders. I will have to stand for election in the next cycle, but for now, I am actually a Senator of Rome."

Collatinus shook his head. "It matters little for now. Tarquinius has so neutered the legislative assembly as to be nothing but a crier's platform for his needs." He took a long drink of wine. Then, "I look to the day when the Senate will be an actual body of the people, and not a puppet of whichever copper-plated ass is on the Throne." He gave a grim laugh. "Of course, it will probably be my grandchildren that see such a change."

Marcus thought of something. "Did my boy, Flavis, become settled?"

Collatinus repeated, "Flavis?"

"Aye," replied Lucius. "Marcus has once again taken it upon himself to solve a problem that is vexing me - to cleanse our household of spies. Or, at least, verify or deny of the existence of such. A very young boy will act as the missive bearer between myself and my aide. At least, that is the story of his arrival. In reality, he will keep his eyes open when residing in my house."

"A boy? What kind of boy?"

At a nod from Lucius, Marcus answered. "A street urchin. Of course, he has no knowledge of the conspiracies of both ourselves nor of the King's and in fact, would not understand them if they were explained. But he is no dullard and has served me well enough in the past to receive a retainer each month."

Lucius nodded. "Marcus has told me that the boy was the instrument that ferreted out the plots to find my location - schemes that led through the Sucusa quarter and from there to the Praefectus."

"Schemes?" Collatinus looked around to check the empty hallway. "Did something happen at the villa that I am unaware of?"

"Just that the right-hand man of Caeus - by the name of Petronius..." Collatinus raised his eyebrows at the name. "...engaged a group of toughs to waylay Marcus on the road to my supposed lair in Antium."

Eyes wide open now, Collatinus looked back and forth at the men. "And..."

"They were unsuccessful."

Now the noble just stared at the young aide for a moment. Shaking his head, he said, "Marcus, you are the very proof that still waters run deep. Would that you had entered my service rather than that of my friend, whom I am sure fails to appreciate your talents to the full."

The talk went on, but without much being planned. For now, the watchword was wait. As the guests gathered themselves to leave, Lucius said to Marcus, "I would favor it should you accompany me back to the Palace on the morrow. Then I will have another set of eyes to give opinion of any happenings."

Morning time found the family of Junius and the Adiutor of the Tribune entering the gates of the Palace again. No special activities were planned that day, but still the grounds were crowded with supplicants and wishers of Kingly favor. And of course, the crowds were filled out with hangers-on and the many court functionaries - including Senators needing to assure the monarch of their loyalty. It was just another day in the life of a King.

After a while, the Chamberlain banged his stick on the floor and announced, "At the command of the King, Lucius, of the family of Junius, is called to the Presence." Marcus stood with the crowd as the young Tribune and his mother walked to stand in front of, and bow, to the pair of curule seats on which sat Tarquinius and his wife, Tullia. He wondered about the presence of the woman, having been told that she seldom presented herself at the court.

The King accepted the obeisance and said, "We welcome you, Tribune Lucius of the house of Junius. And your honorable mater, our sister in blood. We have the hope that you have recovered fully from the injury taken in the service of Rome." Lucius just bowed again. "As I have been informed of your satisfactory conduct in your induction training, you will have the honor of command of a mille in the army of the combined cities of Latium that is forming for the defense of our peoples." There was more praise of a general nature, for which Marcus could see no need that could not have been satisfied on the yesterday. It was the smirk on the face of the King's mate that worried him.

And for good reason.

As the King ended his praise, Tullia spoke loudly and without looking at the two people presenting themselves. "My Regis." A pause and a look that told Marcus plainly that this was a rehearsed utterance. "Without doubt, the Tribune is a valuable addition to your realm, but it must not be forgotten that the pater and frater of himself were guilty of the blackest treason against your assumption of the Throne." Now the hair on the back of the neck of Marcus rose, and his skin began to prickle. This was the most blatant of lies - the father and brother of Lucius were murdered on the public streets by the agents of the King for no other reason than a perceived dislike of a usurper.

The King pretended to consider the matter for a few heartbeats, then said, "Aye... that is true. But the actions of the Tribune show that he has no likeness trait of his gens. This pomi-fruit has fallen far from the tree of treason." Again, he dropped to silence in thought - still an act, Marcus was sure. His view of his Tribune was from behind, but the young noble seemed to be just listening with calmness. Apparently, the King was not so sure of the expected reaction, as two guards were stationed at the end of the seats, with ready spears, to counter any sudden acts of rage on the part of the unfortunate receiving the jape of the Royal person.

Then the King raised his head with a look of decision. "We would not want our loyal subject to be tainted with the past actions of kindred, therefore we will decree that the family will take a new cognomen that we will assign. So as to not deny past loyal citizens of the family their due, the family name may be retained as the new nomen." Marcus barely followed the line of the King's thought. From his tutoring with Sabina, he knew that the noble Roman usually followed the convention of the tire nomina, or three names, the praenomen, nomen and cognomen. These elements and their choosing were important - to a noble - but of such disinterest to Marcus as to not even cause him to wonder that the family of his Tribune had apparently been satisfied with a mere pair of names for each member.

The King was still presenting and Marcus could see the satisfaction on the face of Tullia. "We will assign and allow the family of our Tribune to accept the new family name of Brutus." There was a series of audible gasps by the audience, all cut off in the hope that the outburst was not noticed. Marcus was unbelieving, his fury barely contained as he tried to believe what he was hearing. Looking around, he could see that the crowd was also disbelieving, and from the expressions, most were disapproving as well. He could not understand the motive of the Throne. If the King - if any King - disliked one of his subjects, the direct path to removing the irritation was usually to have them imprisoned or killed. Why bother with this... this humiliation of giving the family the name of Foolish?

Just as unbelieving, Lucius seemed to be taking the new cognomen without rancor. Indeed, he merely bowed and turned to leave as the staff of the Chamberlain tapped the floor to indicate the interview was ended. Even in the courtyard, as they approached the lectica of the Domina, he gave a calm aspect as if the events of the day were uninteresting. Not so, his mother. As she approached her carrying chair, she could not hold the distress from her demeanor - and in fact, had not both her son and Marcus been walking beside her, she would have fallen to the cobblestones in despair.

Shortly, they were at the entrance to the house, and both men helped the older woman into the household. Inside, Lucius said, "Mother. Perhaps you should seek your bed for a rest before..."

"Nay!" The reply was sharp and immediate. "I may be in the throes of womanly emotions at the happenings, but I will not run and hide in my rooms as if I were a spurned femina!" Looking around, she saw the steward, Nonus, and commanded, "Bring wine to the atrium. My son and our friend will take our cups in private."

Not long after they had reclined at the long mensa in the atrium, the steward began to admit visitors. Word had obviously spread rapidly, and Collatinus arrived, breathless, obviously having run from his own house. Then behind him was Tricipitinus and Publicola and several others that were nameless to Marcus. Then, obviously taking the longer path of walking or carrying chair, several women were admitted, including Iulliana and Lucretia, who had been away on some girlish foray to the Forum.

"Domina. Lucius," said Collatinus. "I cannot begin to tell you how deeply my own grief runs."

The two young women had no idea until now that something had happened, and naturally insisted in being told at that moment. And since no others were present besides Marcus, all wanted news of the... whatever had happened.   Marcus admired his Tribune, as he calmly explained the happenings in the Throne Room, without rancor and apparently without concern.   Then, explanations finished, he said simply, "I will make the house of Brutus a renown name in Roman history.   A name is nothing - it is the quality of his worth and actions that make the man."

Book 5

Bellum (War)

Quo fata ferunt   (Where the fates bear us)

To Marcus - to any man, the sight was impressive.   From their
low hilltop, across the bare plain they could see the vast bulk of the
combined army - rank after rank of men standing, their spears
grounded and pointing to the heavens.   The gods had finally relented,
and the torrential rains had stopped, giving way to a day of moderate
temperature and clear blue skies.   In front of the ranks and, at least,
three stadia distance, was the city that had become the destination of
Tarquinius.   These were not the massive and tall stone walls of Rome,
but still, they were not to be leaped over by mere mortal men.

Turning, he could see the calvary still in their encampment
and apparently not forming to assist in the day's work - at least not yet.
As Lucius had just explained, horses do very poorly when trying to
charge through mud, and... "besides, if the Volscians remain behind
their walls, then the horsemen might as well have stayed home with the
women."

The city was named Suessa Pometia, the capital of the first
peoples to feel the wrath of the King of Rome, although Marcus could
not have named the actual sin that brought those people in front of the
spearpoints of the combined Romans and Latins.   Of course, he knew
the named reason - that the opposing king was guilty of horrific crimes
against innocent traders on the road to the city, and citizens of the
good peoples of Latium unfortunate enough to live in the borderlands
between the two cities.   Marcus wondered if other wars had been
started - or would be started - with lies and fomentations.

Directly ahead of them was the unit under their command -
about a thousand men, the bulk of them armed with Grecian-type
spears and large curved shields.   The unit had no formal name of
structure, but would be called a Legion in the future.   But as of now,
the word applied to the entire army, so the group under the Tribune
was usually called a Mille - or simply, a thousand.   The Roman
contingent had nine of these Millae, in addition to another two units of
Rorarii - lightly armed men of foreign extraction serving in hopes of
gaining citizenship with good effort.

Finally, in another encampment were about a half thousand
Equites Celeres, or cavalry, recruited strictly from the noble and

wealthy families of the city - those who could afford the huge expense of a horse and equipment for the rider.

The Latins had their own formations but numbered about half of the Roman army. In all, Tarquinius had about sixteen thousand men in the field under his command - a huge army for the time and larger than any ever seen in the land of Latium - or so he was told.

They had been standing for most of the morning as the King and the Dux sat on the back of their steeds and gazed, as staff officers rode back and forth trying to look as if they were carrying important missives. Finally, Marcus asked, "Since we have brought no ladders to the field, I assume that the King intends for the men to vault the wall?"

Lucius just smiled. "It is shown by that statement that you have not studied war under a Roman tutor. There will be no bloodshed this day. Our formation is as the stance of two brawlers in the taburna. Each is displaying his sinews to encourage the other to back down without conflict." And indeed, he was correct. At midday, the tubae sounded the recall, and the men returned to their encampments. Thus far, war had been nothing but an exercise in boredom, although the year leading up to this day had been full...

A year ago, and more, not long after the family of his Tribune had received their new cognomen by jape of the King, the recruitment of the city began. All men of military age were called to stand for possible induction, although only the younger were pulled into the training encampments. Marcus had attended Lucius daily, as they began to receive men into their mille, first as a trickle then a steady stream. As few were veterans, the shouts of the training officers were constant and profane. It was only a day or so into the training, and Marcus was praising the god, or gods, that had allowed him to become an Adiutor - else he would be sweating under the curses of the Hastilairius assigned to Lucius - or another. As it was, he stood around in his clean uniform holding a scroll or tablet, ate with the Tribunes in their mess, and slept on a clean mat under a roof - in his own household, normally.

His homelife was confined to bedding with Sabina at night, and he had no time at all for learning the bowsmithing of exotic weapons. But still, most evenings that he could spend at home, he would examine the work of his apprentice, Ennius, and give advice or commands for the next days. Then on leaving, he would have to reassure - yet again - his young wife that an Adiutor did not stand in the line of battle. Thus it went for the half year, without much to differentiate the passing of time. Until one evening...

The evening meal done, Marcus was looking forward to relaxing on the terrace with Sabina. The night was clear and cool, after a hot day on the field of training. He was immune to the sweating and running, but not to the hot sun and ever blowing dust from a field of marching, running and fighting Legionaries. Cleo had come to the foot of the stairs and called, "Master. Flavis has come. With important news, he says."

At that, Marcus jumped to his feet, and telling Sabina to wait, hurried to the ground floor to meet the youngster in the atrium. The boy would not be recognized by his fellow street urchins, now. He was now unsullied by the usual dirt of a rat of the street and wearing plain and worn, but equally clean garments. As the boy opened his mouth to speak, Marcus held up his hand for silence and led the youngster to the work yard, now in complete darkness but for the quarter of moon. Then, far enough from the house not to be overheard, he said, "Now. And quietly."

The boy was just a blur in the dark as he began, "Nonus will be unhappy that I have departed and him untold, but your orders were to report if I found a... a listener."

"Aye. I will intercede with the Steward. Worry not about that. What have you found?"

"The servant, Centus... Know you of whom I speak, Master?"

"By name only. Continue."

"When Master Lucius is there, that servant will sometimes go to the kitchen store - silently. He will not come out until the Domina and the Master rise for their night's rest. The room as it is contains only... cocua things and foodstuff." Marcus nodded, unseen in the dark. "I have watched him go in that room several times, but tonight, after the cocua went to her mat and before the Master and Domina came in the atrium, I entered the storeroom and hid behind the stovewood pile. And, again, Centus entered..."

Marcus knew what was coming, if not the way it was actually performed. "He is listening to the conversation in the atrium."

"Aye, Sos. There is a little hole in the wall, hidden behind the statue of... of... a man in the atrium. In the quiet of the night, it is muchly easy to hear two people in converse only a few paces away. Even from my crouch, I could hear the sounds of the Master and the Domina."

He paused and Marcus thought furiously. It was as he feared... or rather, as Lucius and the Domina had suspected. There was a spy of the King, or his cronies, in the household. On the morrow... "That is a goodsome work, Flavis. I will see that you..."

"Pardon, Sos. There is more." Marcus waited and then, "When the listening is done, and the patrons have gone, Centus leaves the house, going along the wide street... I know not its name, but the one that goes to the Circus. There he enters a taburna... the... the... Carpentenum... or Carpenti... I have only heard its name spoken once - it has a wagon and horse over the door..." Ah, the taburna of the Chariot of Apollo, thought Marcus. "...Then, in a short time he returns to the household." A pause, then, "That is all I have seen, Sos. I need to return, so as to not cause the Steward to..."

"Nay. Your mission has ended. You have done what I asked. Come." In the house, he found Cleo and said, "Flavis will reside here for the nonce. He can help Ennis in his work beginning on the morrow. See that he has a cubiculium for his own. And a clean tunic for else than his work in the yard." To the boy he said, "My gratitude to you, boy. And you have earned a place to sleep and food. And work." He thought a moment, then said, "Do not speak of this to anyone other than myself or the Dominus of the house of Juni... Brutus, should he ask."

Not waiting for the Steward and the boy to leave, he turned and hurried back up the stairs to the terrace. By the flickering dim moonlight he could see that she was gone - obviously to bed. He sat down for a moment to collect his thoughts. There was indeed a spy in the house of Lucius, and no doubt in the hire of one of the men of the King. He wondered if the reports made it to Tarquinius, or if they were just held by... Caeus, or Petronius - or whichever person was behind the surveillance. In any case, the task of the boy was done, and for the safety of all, he would not be returning to the house of Lucius. Should someone suspect him of being a witness to the deed... A young street urchin would be disposed of with the indifference of a cocua mashing an ant on her meat cutting board.

Across the balcony, he hurried to his own cubiculium and entered, immediately seeing his beautiful mate reclining on the mat, but with the oil lamp still burning. She said quietly, "You have a hidden side to yourself, husband. Might I know of the importance of a boy out of the night?"

He hurriedly stripped off his tunic and lay beside her, saying, "Military messages, my little street flower. And of a nature that I hope means that I do not be called to service for a long while. But, the boy, Flavis, will be with us as a servant for a while. He can help Ennis in the woodyard or do tasks for you if needed."

She nuzzled her face in his chest, then replied. "That is goodsome. I may need an assistant to my mother in a while."

He reached under the light covering and tweeked a nipple, gently. "And you wish to become like the Domina of a great house, and sleep until the noon meal while others make the work?"

"Aye. A life of rich ease would be goodsome to try, but that is not my meaning." She leaned over and blew out the lamp, then settled back against her man. "My woman's moon has stayed itself these two months."

Female happenings meant little to Marcus. Natively intelligent as he was, he knew less of women than the history of Babylonia - and nothing of their bodies except for the use that every man learned. "Is this news that I must needs concern myself with? I would think that the cessation of the monthly flow would be a goodness to a woman."

Sabina was amused but kept it to herself. As a husband, he was far above the norm, but she was sometimes astounded at the depth of his ignorance of matters that she took for granted were known by all. "Aye, husband. The ceasing is a goodness to a young wife, but not for the matter of inconvenience. Rather, it means that you have planted your seed in fertile ground, and the harvest is in sight."

It took a moment for the indirection to settle into his thoughts, then the realization of what she had said broke on him like a sudden storm. "An infantulus? Ours..." He grasped for words. "A son? Mine?"

She put her finger to his lips to stop the stuttering thoughts. "Only the gods know beforehand as to the sexus of a child. But if it is only an infantula, she will be welcome in our house, will she not?"

Struck with the sudden news, he took a heartbeat to respond to her words, then with a grin unnoticed in the dark, said, "If it is a girl, we can sell her to Egyptians and try again. The nightly work with you is pleasant." Then, even his unsophistication told him that a mother-to-be might not welcome such a jape. He pulled her to him with firm arms and said, "If she is her mother's daughter, then she will be the little jewel in this house, outshone only by her dam." With that, he rose above her and began the act that was now useless, but all the more pleasurable for the results that their previous efforts had brought.

Marcus rose much earlier than usual, even before the first rays of light were evident. He then walked on fast paced feet to the Capitoline quarter and waited in the street outside a large and opulent house. His timing was good, and it was only a short time before he saw Collatinus emerge from the building, the door slave bowing and then retreating inside and out of the cool predawn air. It was just a moment before the young Tribune noticed Marcus standing in wait.

"By the gods, Marcus! What has happened?" Just the fact of the unusual and deliberate encounter gave notice that something was amiss.

"I wished to speak to you before I gave my news to Lucius." The statement showed how far a young waif from the mountains had risen since his arrival at a strange city. After his return, Lucius had insisted that the Adiutor use his given name in private and told Collatinus and the Domina of his desire. Neither had any objection to the unheard of idea of familiarity between a high-bred noble and a man of the street. Both well knew of the quality of the man and his loyalty to a household that had been earned at the start. "On the last night..."

The sun was well up, and the Legionaries of both Tribunes - and several others - were engaged in their mock thrusting at each other with cloth blunted spears, when Collatinus walked up to the two men. "Lucius, a word with you and Marcus in private, if you please." This had been planned by the two men on the walk to the training fields that morning.

The Tribune knew instantly what this had to be, and turned to the Centurion and ordered the exercise to continue in his absence. Across the field, in an open space away from others, the three stopped and Marcus told the story given to him by the young street boy. At the conclusion, they stood in silence as the Tribune thought over the tale. Finally, he muttered, "Centus, himself. The man as a boy was my playmate in the household from my earliest years. And his father was almost a brother to the Dominus in his youth." He looked across the vast field of moving and sweating men without seeing, but visualizing a happy childhood, fighting barbarians with wooden swords in the atrium. Or assaulting the fortress of the upper balcony until the house matron chased them into the stables before the wrath of the Dominus descended upon all in hearing of the tumult.

"And he is there now, in the house with my Mother, and no other man to oversee it. This night I will carve the heart from the man."

Marcus looked at Collatinus, as Lucius had reacted just as he feared. The Tribune looked back and nodded.

"Nay, Sos. It must not be." Before the retort could be formed, Marcus hurriedly continued. "To dismiss the servant will give instant notice that we are aware of the surveillance."

Lucius returned his answer with heat. "The man is a traitor to our family, after a lifetime and more, of shelter by the household! Would you have me induct him into the family?"

Collatinus held up a hand. "Nay, Lucius. You are transfixed in the heat of the news. Listen to Marcus."

The Tribune nodded and Marcus continued his spiel. "We know not why the man has betrayed your family, but think of this - it is more than possible that the threat was to your mother, or sister, unless the cooperation was gained, and the man, out of loyalty to you, has agreed to it." Lucius pursed his lips as he contemplated the idea. "Or even to himself. The men around the King are not likely to ask for the service of a retainer with politeness and deference - some dire threat must have been made."

He looked around to make sure that no one had approached, then, "But, this is not a blow to us - it is an opportunity."

At least he had gotten the interest of the Tribune, even through the red haze of fury. "Speak."

"You wish to continue your charade of being addled by the blow in the mountains." He received a nod. "Now you can reinforce that trickery easily, and believably. And, it will not have to be done in public, risking ridicule to your family and name." Lucius nodded to continue. "The Domina must be informed of course, as she will be a player in the farce. But now, at night you may interlard your conversations with nonsense, such as the need to visit the oracle of... of... Dorama..."

"Dodona."

"...Dodona again. Or the need to pass a law in the Senate requiring the people to eat turnips before every Ides. Or any such absurdity. All will be reported and your addleness will be confirmed."

Lucius nodded slowly. "The good Sabina needs to continue your lessons - I doubt that is a word. But, you make a good crux of the matter."

"Eventually, we will find the truth of Centus," added Collatinus. "And at that time you may make the determination. But for now, the worth of the man as a conduit to the men of the King is too priceless to remove."

The training over by the end of the warm season, the men were released to their homes and work until the budding of the year brought the ability to move an army across the land. Except that no conversations of a serious nature were held in the household of Junius, now Brutus, the lives of the three men were back to normal.

Marcus happily worked on his bow-learning, while giving direction to Ennis and the boy, Flavis. His nights were even more pleasant as he lay with his wife, watching her belly slowly grow from inside until she seemed to have engulfed a melon. His concerns were such that he would have had a midwife installed - months ahead of need - in the room next to theirs - but for the intercession of the mother of Sabina. The woman politely, but firmly gave to Marcus that woman matters were not the concern of the man of the house. Sheep faced, he nodded and withdrew from the attempt to become the mistress of the situation, but not before pressing a purse of gold into her hand with the order to obtain any item of need or comfort for her daughter.

Still, the days were golden. In the yard, he tried every conceivable method to fix the curved laminations of the wood and bone slivers that they might not shatter upon release. Often, their work on the standard weapons well along, the two young apprentices would assist, giving this advice or that. Upon the idea of Ennis to pin the layers together with bronze studs, as was used to fasten leather, several staves were made to test the matter. Alas, while the studs certainly prevented the shattering of the lamination, it also inhibited the release of the wood and greatly reduced the power of the bow.

Remembering the magical bow that he had seen on that first caravan with Pythes, the ends wrapped in fine wire of unknown material, he tried the same with a cord. Hemp was unsatisfactory as it soon loosened and lost its use. The cords that Sabina and Decima used for chafing a rug or curtain did not have the strength. Finally, he visited the coriarius - the leather maker - in a tannery of the quarter and ordered a spool of fiber, cut long and very thin.

Back at the work yard, pieces were cut that were long enough to allow a tight wrap of the leather cord from the end of the stave and toward the center for about two handspans. Then the fiber was soaked in water overnight and, in the morning, stretched to its maximum, with Flavis and Ennis pulling on each end with gusto. It took a few tries before they learned the proper amount of force to use without pulling the cord apart, but then, with one man holding the bow stave, the other wound the cord around the end of the wood, pulling with force to maintain the stretch and to wind the leather as tightly as possible. Then the other end was done. After that, the bow was hung up to dry.

All three were anxious to see the results of their efforts. During the days and nights, even though cool and cloudy, the leather had finally lost its moisture and changed color from wet-dark to the usual shade of dirt color. The leather cord had attempted to shrink back to its normal length, and in doing so had tightened to a state that almost seemed to be as if it were a cord of iron, had there been such a thing.

And, unlike any metal wrapping, the fiber added little weight to the bow.

Marcus was hoping that the wet leather, drying all day and night, had not compromised the binder that held the laminations together - in this case, two thin lengths of nut-wood with a sliver of animal horn between, and all inside surfaces liberally slathered with the oxen-hoof glue. In any case, he would soon know.

The bow was a piece made to test an idea, not a polished weapon for use or vending. As such, it lacked the shine and finish of his usual work, but still, it was a serviceable bow - as good as any and better than most even for the lack of finishing that had been made on it. That is, assuming that it worked at all.

At one end of the compound, at a ridiculously short range, even for a novice bowman, was a bale of old leathers, suspended by a rope from an overhead beam. Still, it was the greatest range they could have without leaving the city - a considerable distance to walk just to shoot an arrow. Marcus tried the bow with some practice stretches, then all looked at it for signs of failure.

Then, with a ragged arrow from the pile that they used to test the worth of their buildings, he nocked, drew and released. At that short range, even with a strange and newly made weapon, there was little chance of his strike being more than a fingers breadth off the mark, and it was not. The bow certainly worked, and was powerful. But how long lasting? He handed to Ennis. "Use it for a while - both of you. I would know the enduringness of it."

A half month later, the bow was still in use, and Marcus was encouraged. He had several more made, with this curve or that, longer and shorter, thicker and with differing laminations - all to determine the optimum size and shape of the weapon. Then, suddenly, all was forgotten.

"Master! Within!" Marcus turned to see Cleo standing and waving his arms. "The opstitrix! She says the time of the mistress has come!"

Marcus ran through the kitchen, almost trodding on the little kitchen maid, then across the atrium and up the stairs, three at a time. Then, breathless, he stopped at the door to their cubiculum, not knowing what to expect. What he saw, was Sabina laying on the mat and the midwife kneeling beside her. At the other side of the low bed, Decima was gently patting her daughter's face with a wet cloth. At the table, and squeezing water from a rag, was Cordia, mother of Cleo. It took a moment, but then he realized that, rather than being engrossed in the dramatics of childbirth, they were discussing some garment that had been seen being worn on the street!

Sabina saw him standing wide-eyed in the doorway and called, with a smile. "Husband. You are early. Our youngster has not yet been convinced to leave his comfortable abode."

"I... I... Are you well? Is anything of a... a...?"

Decima stood and walked to the doorway. "She is well. Her waters have flowed, but the time is not yet." That meant nothing to Marcus. "Say your blessing to your wife, then leave us. This is not the place nor the time for a man. When the urchin arrives, you will be the first to be informed."

He walked to the mat, and knelt, taking her hand in his. No words flowed. He could think of nothing to say. It was as if the gods had stopped the flow of time. Then, the young woman said, "Husband. Will you send word to Iulliana? I made promise to inform her when my time had come."

Relieved to be able to do something - anything, he squeezed her hand and ran from the room, wondering if he would survive the ordeal. In the yard again, he shouted for Flavis and gave him a set of instructions.

Now was just the time of waiting. In the work yard he whittled on a stave, with Ennis watching at his work, perplexed, as Marcus shaved the wood to splinters, then put it aside and gathered another, his hands and thoughts having no connection with each other. Pythes arrived, giving notice that Flavis had delivered part of the missive. He offered his optimism for the delivery of a healthy boy, then sat with Marcus at the eating table of the yard, knowing of the agony of the waiting of a man for his first child. "Women make their own time, Marcus, and all are different. Some produce with as little effort as squeezing the meat from a grape, and others will lay for half the day before delivering. So worry yourself not, should Sabina not rush to increase your family."

Marcus nodded, then jumped to his feet as Cleo hurried up, but the message was not of a birth. "Pardon, Sos. The Domina and daughter have arrived in the atrium."

Waving for his old friend to follow, they walked through the kitchen then into the atrium and bowed. "Your presence blesses our house this day, Domina. And noble Femina." Had his other guest not been present, the greetings would have been much less formal.

"Good Marcus. This is a memorable day for your household and I give you thanks for including us." He bowed again. "My apologies for the absence of my son, but he and his friends departed early this morning for the Forum and have not been seen since."

"Nay, Domina. As has been pointed out to myself, and with some intensity, this is not the day of a man until it is over. The Tribune will hear of the results in good time." He turned and gestured to the older man standing behind him. "Might I introduce my warden, Pythes, without whose help and guidance I would still be wandering the mountains as a lonely hunter."

"You may indeed." Looking at the older man, she said, "A friend of Marcus is a friend of our house, good Sos. And my thanks for whatever encouragement you gave to produce a citizen of the quality of your ward."

She looked up the stairs, then back at Marcus. "With your permission, we would visit your wife to deliver our hopes and help."

"My thanks, Domina. She was indeed wishing for the presence of your daughter at this time. And to have come with her mother will be of even greater pleasure. Please..." He held his hand out toward the stairs.

Now the men just sat in the yard, all pretense of work forgotten. The cocua and kitchen maid came and went with drink and pastries, and they just spoke of this and that, waiting for word from the house. Listening to Pythes speak of another incident with bandits, in the uplands of the city of Rusellae, Marcus had almost forgotten the reason for their idleness, when the kitchen maid appeared. "Master. Your presence has been requested in the atrium."

Jumping to his feet, Marcus demanded of the little girl, "What is the reason!? Is Sabina of good being? Do you..."

Pythes put his hand on the young man's shoulder. The older man well knew of the danger of the ordeal that the wife of his young friend was enduring, and the woe that sometimes came from the process, but he could see from the smiling countenance of the maid that she had not come from a birth-bed of tragedy. "Be at ease - Sabina is in good straits. The maid is trying not to burst out with happiness in the presence of her master."

At the foot of the stairs, Iulliana was standing, holding a bundle, of... of... He bent over it as the woman pulled back the swaddling cloth. "You have a son, Marcus," she said with a broad grin. "He is small, but of good color and form."

Marcus just stood, wide-eyed as the three men practically shouted their congratulations. Even the two apprentices dropped all semblance of propriety between master and servant and joining with Pythes in hearty slaps to the backside of the young man. He looked up the stairs, then back. Then again. To the noble girl, he asked simply, "Sabina?"

"She is well, if tired. You should go to her now."

Again, taking the steps three at a time he arrived at the cubiculum and peered in the doorway. Sabina was laying quietly, speaking to the Domina, sitting in a chair on the other side of the mat. The noble woman pointed, then Sabina looked to see Marcus standing wide-eyed and uncertain - as out of place in a birth-room as a fisherman in the forest. "The gods have delivered our wishes, Husband. You have a son."

"Aye. But more importantly, you are well and..." Suddenly, the countenance of her face changed to a grimace. "What is wrong?" She arched her back with a groan and an outburst of breath. To the midwife, he shouted, "What is happening!?" The woman totally ignored the man in the room, something she had learned to do in the many years before. Feeling of the abdomen of the prostrate Sabina, she probed and prodded. Decima knelt and again, wiped the brow of the young woman with the warm and wet rag. Marcus was becoming frantic - a son was a god given gift, but he would not trade it or any others for his beautiful wife. Stepping forward, he demanded again of the midwife, "Curse you woman, what is the matter with her?"

The opstitrix just looked up at the Domina, who immediately rose and walked around the mat to the other side. Taking Marcus by the shoulders, she said - no, commanded, "Leave us, Marcus. You will learn what we know when we do. This is no place for a man and you will mar the work of the opstritrix." With that, she pushed him backward and out of the room.

Now, in the atrium again, the festive mood had turned to gloom, the worse for not knowing the cause. He sat beside Iulliana and looked at his son, then up the stairs, then back as if in a trance of the gods. The kitchen maid came and went, at a run, carrying hot water and...

"Let us not despair as yet, Marcus." Pythes had sat down beside his young ward and put a hand on a shoulder. "First births are sometimes a trial for a wife. And many times a woman has a more difficult afterbirth than the actual borning. She is young and of good health."

He just nodded, still looking at his son. Iulliana was bobbing him up and down, and the newborn seemed to be enjoying his first foray into the world. Then, unbelievably, she extended her arms and held the bundle to Marcus. Aghast, he just froze, the idea of holding an infant completely beyond his understanding. The woman smiled and said, "He is not a fragile wine cup, Marcus. He will not break even if held by a man."

Steeling himself as if he were to hold an object of great weight, he took the bundle. Trying to emulate the actions of the woman, he moved it up and down as he had seen her do. The infant was not to be fooled - he immediately gave indication of his displeasure in being manhandled by a clumsy male. Almost panicking, Marcus held his son out to be accepted by his temporary nurse. The infant approved the switch, by becoming calm and returning to his contemplating of the new world his eyes were seeing. It was obvious to his father that a new-born was partial to females.

Time passed. Hours. Days. It seemed to Marcus that entire seasons had gone by as they stood in the atrium waiting for word. And yet, for all the time, their bodies seemed not to need sustenance. Had the water clock been registering the hours, he would have seen that, thus far, not even a whole hour had passed. But, this day, the household staff had other pressing duties than refilling the water container of the clock. The infant was showing signs of unhappiness - probably from a need to dine at the paps of his mother, according to Iulliana. But he would have to wait with the rest of them.

Finally...

Pythes jumped to his feet as he saw the Domina appear at the head of the stairs. Then did everyone else. "Iulliana. Bring the boy. It is time for his meal. And you come also, Marcus. And your warden as witness."

At the doorway to their cubiculum, Marcus saw that Sabina was still with the living, and laying on her mat with a smile at her man. Silently, he began to praise the gods - any god - all of them - for the life of his mate, and for the... Suddenly, he noticed that she was not laying alone. Beside her was another bundle...

"We have another son, Husband. And this one was even more reluctant to leave his warm domicile than his brother." Marcus just stood, frozen as if having viewed the Gorgon - although knowing nothing about Greek mythology, he would not have understood the reference. He had never heard of multiple births - at least, not of any other than the animal kingdom. But it was a fact, and he was looking at the proof.

Iulliana kneeled and placed her burden to the opposite side of the mother, who cradled him in her free arm. Sabina was pale and obviously tired, but as content as a newly made mother can be, with a husband in attendance and two warm and healthy sons to display.

The Domina knew that the actual person in the room needing relief was not the mother. "My good man, Pythes. Perhaps you could take Marcus into the atrium and ply him with some wine. Otherwise, I fear that he may not survive the birthing process. And besides, it is time for his sons to dine and it is not meet that it should be done in male company."

Grinning, the older man pulled Marcus toward the door, having to support his charge when the feet of the young man failed to move with him. "Aye, Domina. We will try with diligence so as not to let the father expire on this fine day."

Downstairs and in the kitchen, the cocua had already had outdone herself for the celebratory meal. Wine and sweetmeats, pastries and all manner of foodstuffs were brought. Marcus made Ennis and Flavis sit at the table with himself and Pythes. Even the cocua and her maid were invited to take a cup with them. At the moment he could have not cared a broken stave about what his proper neighbors would have said about master and servants sitting together. The congratulations and jests flowed as freely as the wine - some gently obscene, referencing double-yoked eggs and his unerring aim with any type of weapon.

Before the last light of day, the Domina and Iulliana took their leave, with the effusive and wine-lubricated appreciations from Marcus. The midwife departed, more than satisfied with her fee, as it had been doubled by the father in his joy of the day and her work. Then by the light of the oil lamp, he sat beside Sabina and his new sons, talking until she drifted off into an exhausted sleep. Rather than disturb her, he pulled an old mat from another room and laid it beside their bed. With the effects of the wine, and mostly, the events of the day, he was asleep before he had removed his tunic.

In the following days, guests arrived from as far away as the Palatium quarter, bearing gifts and congratulations from the neighbors that he had befriended in his days at the merchantry of Pythes. Porcia, the widow baker, sent loaves of fresh bread and from Legos, the fruit peddler, a large basket of his best. His neighbors lined the doorway to see the new additions to the family, proudly displayed by their father as if he had had a major role in their birth, rather than just the one unknown night of bliss.

Theirs was a popular household on the street. Marcus was both generous and friendly to all who returned the feelings. Many a young boy on the street had received a copper piece for this bit of work or that, carrying water or hauling refuse away. And more than one young girl had received a large silver piece on her wedding day to eke out her meager dowery. Or a muslin tunic and girdle for the ceremony, vended at a very low price and of a quality far beyond any to be expected by a Plebeian bride. All agreed that the household of Marcus and Sabina had been blessed by the gods.

Now his life was a different as between that of a fish and a fowl. Coming from a happy household, with a beautiful wife, and now two sons, and a profession that he loved, he stood now as a soldier, across the fields from a city that had done him no wrong and men against whom he held no ill will.

Urbes constituit aetas   (Ages erect cities...)

The evening brought a long meeting at the tent of the King. Marcus stood with the other sub-officers at a distance, all wondering at the strategy being discussed.   With him was Maxentus, and Albanus, the aide to Publicola, along with several others.   One said, "Since the Volscians seem disinclined to emerge from their city to play with us, I wonder at the strategy.   Do we knock at the gate and ask them to attend us?"

Albanus replied, "Aye, or stand and hurl names at their maters, in hopes that they strike in their fury."

Marcus thought the jesting not in keeping with the seriousness of the matter - one in which many men would fail to return to their homes.   "We have brought many ladders, but I fail to see their use.   A kitchen maid with a broom could defend those walls before the long climb could be made."

"Aye.   I give my thanks to the gods that I am not among the ranks of the Rorarii that will be tasked with the mission."   Maxentus was of the same thoughts as his friend.   "Merely dropping stones from those heights would clear the rungs of men, no matter how armored."

"Maybe Marcus could stand and clear the heights with his bow of Cupid."   This from an Adiutor that he had only just met.   The jape was in good manner and delivered with a friendly grin, but was based on ignorance of the strange weapon that Marcus carried.

Unlike that first conversed bow - the first successful one, that is - that he had made while waiting for his wife to deliver his sons, this one was a finished and polished work of art.   It was one part of three shorter than the normal and to the eyes of any man who had any knowledge of the art, looked strange and... and almost fantastical. Even with the shortness, it had far more power than a simple stave weapon, and, thanks to their discovery of the power of tightly wound and dried leather cord, it was as long-lived as any.   This one was dyed in the dregs of wine, then polished with the finest sand until it fairly glistened, and finally dipped in hot wax to give protection from the elements.   Then polished yet again.   A leather-maker was commissioned to make a sheave for it to give even greater protection should the day turn to rain.

One discovery - and a painful one - that he had made while practicing with his new weapon was that his arrows had to be made of a straight and hard wood, else the violent release might cause a lesser shaft to bend and shatter before it left the nock.   Fortunately, the lesson was not disabling, and Decima removed the long splinters of the broken arrow from his arm without leaving permanent injury.

Only Maxentus knew of the skill of his friend, with a missile weapon, or the quality of his bowsmithing.

"We already have a hundred and a half of bowmen, although what they will do against such walls is beyond my knowledge. They will be at a major disadvantage with their foe shooting downwards and from behind stone." Marcus had no idea of how an army of foot soldiers would reduce the massive stone walls across the field. Unfortunately, the morning brought sufficient evidence that neither the King nor his Dux had the knowledge as well.

After the break of their fast, the men were arranged in the fields, with some smaller units investing the city from the other walls to prevent sallies by the defenders. The long ladders, carried by five men each, were arranged along the front of the ranks, pointing toward the destination for their use. Behind their Mille of men, the Tribune and the Centurion of the unit stood, having distributed the orders that had been received from above to the lesser Centurions, and from them to their Optio, to be given to their men. Marcus, like all of the Adiutorae, had few tasks, and just stood with his Tribune. Unless there were an important missive to deliver to the headquarters, he would have little to do in this fight.

Then, this tuba sounded, giving an order for readiness, and that one, then the trumpets began the march. Marcus had an empty feeling in his belly, the more so as the men walked across the wide field and became even more ant-like in relation to the size of the wall. The officers followed their unit, but even so, remained far outside of the reach of any weapons of the city.

As the marching soldiers came within range of the bowmen on the walls, the arrows began to descend - not with much effect, as the Legionaries held their tall curved shields ahead and somewhat above their heads. Still, here and there, a shaft found its mark in an unprotected foot, or calf. Then came a double blast on the tubae. The ladder carriers, and the men assigned to each to ward off missiles with a shield, began the run to the base of the wall. Reaching it, the forward men dropped the end into the dirt and two set their feet to prevent it from sliding, then the ladder was rapidly walked up and over to impact against the wall. The carriers then stood behind the wood and pulled with all their might to prevent the ladder from being tipped away by the defenders above.

All had gone as in the months of training, and had the precision of the ladder placing been the crux of the battle, it would have been shortly won. But, the soldiers tasked to take the city from their foe had a long climb before reaching the fight. And all advantages accrued to the defenders. Falling stones, boiling water and steaming oil were just three of the obstacles to be overcome before reaching the top, and those weapons could be wielded by the oldsters of the city - even the women, leaving the men ready for battle in the event that an enemy actually attained the top of the wall.

Few did. The bowmen of the Legion stood along the ranks and shot their quivers skyward, but to little avail. The height robbed the shafts of a considerable amount of power, and their foe could only be seen as glimpses as a torso leaned over to drop or pour or ladle.

Ladders fell, pushed with long poles, despite the attempt of the steadiers on the ground to hold them in place. And they fell with soldiers, and onto other soldiers, only a portion of whom returned to their feet. The ground was covered with Legionaries, with heads bashed into mush, or scalded by water, or screaming with the hot oil clinging to their skin under their garb. Few were cut with weapons since few actually made it within the range of a blade or spear, and those did not return to their comrades. In places, a man or two, and in some cases, a handful gained the top of the wall - although only the gods knew how - but in every case were immediately overwhelmed and cut down by the real soldiers of the city, waiting for the chance of battle. The noise of the strife - as all battles - was a cacophony of shouts and screams and curses, but muted somewhat at the ears of the three officers, standing some two hundred paces from the wall.

There was no sound of recall on the horns, but gradually, the men began to drift back from the wall, realizing that even with the assistance of the gods, no Roman - or Latium - would reach the top of the wall and remain alive. In addition, there was a swell of men, crawling or stumbling away, blinded or burned or crippled.

Lucius just shook his head, watching the appalling spectacle. "What a waste of good men, this is to be." Marcus quietly and wholeheartedly agreed. Only the Centurion kept his peace, his thoughts on the competence of his leaders unknown.

Finally, the horns of the recall were sounded, and the attackers retreated from the city wall. Marcus noticed that they did not turn and flee, but reversed their steps, holding their shields for protection, and in some cases, assisting a sorely injured comrade to retreat from under the rain of arrows. Their spirit had held, even in the face of being given an impossible task - and worse, one that could have been seen to be hopeless before it was started. Marcus did learn a lesson - that a good scutum was a necessity in warfare - without their shields, far more men would be covering the ground, lifeless, pinned by the deluge of shafts sent down from the heights.

Marcus stood, looking at the city as the men streamed back around him, wondering how men could be so courageous, and leaders so ignorant. The actual battle had only lasted a short time, maybe an hour by a water clock. That was fortunate - had the men themselves not had the realization that the assault was futile, they might have lost one part in three of the army before the piles of bodies prohibited any approach to the walls.

The soldiers had done as well as mortal men could do, in the situation. But... That attitude was not shared by all. It was at this time that the son of the King, Sextus, began to emerge as the irritation on the skin of the Roman people - a vexation that would eventually change the course of history.

In the afternoon, another officers call was sounded, but, this time, were accompanied by their aides and Senior Centurions of each Mille. The King was not present, still in his tent and out of sight. The leader of the Legion - the Dux - was at this time, one Senator Domitius Gallus. According to Lucius, the man had no military experience whatever, but as the law required a General Superior, he was honored with the position. In any case, the King would be the guiding hand of the army. Still, the Dux was required to pretend at least that he was the military Commander. His words - in the estimation of Marcus - removed any doubt of his lack of qualifications to command even a troop of men removing mud from irrigation ditches.

"This day has been a disgrace for Rome. Our ancestors must be cringing as they look down from the slopes of Olympus and see their sons and grandsons flee from an impotent enemy like children running from the storm." Brave words from a man who had sat in a padded chair, drinking wine under a canopy, while his men were facing stones and blades. "All have felt shame at those who did not carry through with their duty, and instead favored their own being over that of the city." If he was meaning to stir emotions in his officers, he was succeeding. Marcus heard the murmur of the Tribunes - none remembering with pleasure the stupid charge of footmen against a stone wall many times the height of a man. "Tomorrow, the attack will continue, and the officers of the Millae will answer for any such disgraceful failure as seen today."

He turned as a man and several staff officers walked up. It was Sextus Tarquinius - the son of the King. Bowing, the Dux asked, "And what is the pleasure of the King?"

The son of the King was a large man, of age, but somewhat younger than Marcus. Intelligent he was, from the gossip in the group of aides, but a man with an overwhelming sense of entitlement. It was said that no Plebeian woman was safe from his approaches, his attitude being that it was the duty of women of the inferior class to service him at will, making no matter of their own feelings or family. Some of the tales of the man were discarded by Marcus as being... just tales, told by men to enhance their own stature among their fellows, then amplified by others as they were passed along. Nonetheless, the son obviously considered the city of Rome as his personal property, and himself superior to all, other than the King, by reason of his rank as the successor to the Throne. Even his words, fairly dripped haughtiness.

"The King is most disappointed in the conduct of his army, and the failure to even come to blade length with the enemy. On the morrow, another assault will be made, and any failing to perform his duty will receive just punishment for a coward."

Now, any lingering respect for the man was gone from the mind of Marcus - and, he suspected, from all in the gathering. Equating failure with cowardliness was an indication of an officer with little use. Rather, the Dux and his staff should be evaluating their plans for the morrow, rather than wasting time and breath on such useless words. More of the same worthless judgment was given, then the officers dismissed.

That evening, as the Tribunes met in their own session, Marcus walked around, seeking the Centurion of their Mille - a man that he knew was an experienced campaigner in the wars with the Samnium. That, and the fact that the name was Rutilius, was the entire knowledge that he had of the sub-officer. He found the man walking between the tents, with several of his subordinates, doing... whatever a man of his rank had for his duties. Seeing Marcus, he and his following came to attention.

"Salve, Sos."

"Salve, Centurion. Might I discuss a matter with you?"

Turning to an Optio, the officer handed off a wax tablet case, giving the order to proceed with the activity, and then replied, "Aye, Sos. I am at your duty."

"Come. We will walk to the hilltop." It was only a short distance, and from there they could see the city walls across the field - a field now planted with the bodies of many of his adopted citizens. Other than several outposts of men on guard duty, the open area was empty of movement.

As they stopped, the Centurion asked, "Have you orders from the Tribune, Sos?"

Marcus shook his head. "Nay. I wish to query your experience as to the happenings of the day. But first, what was the tally of the losses for our mille?"

The man nodded, refreshing the numbers in his thoughts. "We were blessed, this day, Adiutor. As our unit was in the second wave, and did not reach the ladders, our losses were limited to mostly arrow-points flung at random from the walls. Two have expired from their wounds, and five and twenty at the medicos for patching of holes and will not be in service for several weeks. An additional fifty or so have minor hurts but are placed for duty."

Marcus nodded. He knew that the good fortune of their men was balanced by the losses of others - at least three hundred dead and many more in and around the medico tents.

He pointed into the distance. "How would a Commander - one in the campaigns of your experience, have treated the situation this day?" He paused, then, "I know that Rome has handled herself well in wars of the past, else the city would not still be, but in no way could those battles have been fought with such idiocy as today."

The Centurion hesitated - no underling in any army in any land - past or future - lightly criticized his superiors to which he was bound, and certainly not to a man of whom he knew nothing.

Marcus saw the uncertainty, then turned to face the man. "Centurion - Rutilius, it is?" A nod. "I am no virgin to bloodshed and have killed in the past when necessity demanded it. Still, I am not a willing soldier and have no wish to be. But today was a stupid waste of good men, and there will be women in the city who will have no understanding of why their husbands and fathers were lost. I wish you, as a real soldier, to give me your ideas and thoughts about what could be done on the morrow to prevent the slaughter that we saw today."

He looked down the hill at the camp, then back toward the city of the enemy. He knew that the Centurion was an experienced campaigner - a professional soldier in an army of half trained citizens. From the first, when introduced to his new Tribune and Adiutor, the man gave a sense of confidence in his own ability. Lucius, too, knew well of his own shortcomings and relied on the man for advice and knowledge. From early on, when faced with an unexpected decision, the Tribune would ask for the opinion of the Centurion. The man would, without overstepping his place in the ranks, reply that in the past, this was done by that officer, or that was a method that was found to be successful for a unit. The Tribune would almost always follow the lead of the sub-officer, and if in the presence of others, would pretend to consider the 'suggestion,' then nod and give the order.

The Centurion, for his part, was relieved that he had been assigned to an officer who knew his limitations, rather than a haughty noble who assumed that his birthright was the equivalent of experience and intelligence.

Marcus continued. "Centurion Rutilius. I give you my oath before the gods that anything that you say will not be heard by ears beyond this hilltop. We both want to succeed in this battle and with the loss of as few men as possible."

The older man - at least twice the age of Marcus - looked at the Adiutor for a moment, then nodded. "Aye, Sos. Today was... planned with less... experience than one might hope for." He pointed aimlessly at the city in question. "The assault that you saw, works well on lesser cities, and I have climbed many a ladder over the ramparts. But, those were far less of height, and some even no more than a wooden palisade. The walls of this Sussa... Suess... whatever the cursed place is called, are of a breed as of Rome itself."

Marcus nodded. "The height is daunting, even for a man not under the falling rock and boiling water."

"Aye, Sos." Again the look down the hill, automatically looking for anyone approaching to hear. "But it is the combination of tallness and the width of the top that makes the obstacle." At the questioning look from the young man, he continued. "We scaled the walls of... of some city of Samnium - I forget its name. They were tall - almost as these be. But the upper rampart had no depth and the defenders had no room at the top for more than a single line of men." He pointed. "Like those of Rome, these parapets above allow for a defense in depth, and are probably even wide enough for almost an entire contubernium to stand shoulder to shoulder - eight men or more. With such a mass of defenders allowed at any given assault point, I have misgivings if our force could succeed even if they were allowed to climb the ladders unhindered."

Marcus saw the point he was making - it was as plain as flowers under a noonday sun. Even he knew that the key to winning a battle was a matter of bringing greater force against lesser. In the case of yon city, with a wide platform on the top of the wall, allowing for the enemy to mass at any point, the Romans and Latins would be feeding a man at a time against many. As soon as a soldier stepped off of the top of the ladder, his head would be lopped off by any one of multiple foes, probably vying with each other for the pleasure.

"Aye. You make it clear. So, what is the answer."

The man was more comfortable now, being able to give his misgivings to an understanding officer. At least to his mind, the young man was his superior, given that he was the right hand of a Tribune. In actuality, an Adiutor had no command authority, being in essence, a runner for his officer. Still, a man that accompanied, and ate and slept in the tent of a Tribune, was no ordinary soldier and was imbued with unofficial authority, even if that was not recognized by the organization of ranks.

"If a battle is wanted, then we have to enter the city in the normal way. Through one of the gates." Marcus nodded. "But, again, unlike the cities of Samnium, where the portal doors are flimsy and easily battered by a ram, these are massive. I have a man of the ranks, whose pater is a traveling merchant, and as a youth accompanied him on his trades - and some to this city. He reports that the gates are of hewn logs of massive trees, and take fifty slaves to remove the bar that secures them in the nighttime. Such a mass could not even begin to be broken by a ram before the wielders were slain to a man from above." He pointed. "Notice that the portal is recessed, and flanked by the wing walls that allow for archers to shoot directly down on any who come to knock for entrance." He hesitated, then, "The builder of that structure knew what he was about."

Marcus looked at the portal in the distance. Even in the fading light, he could see that the man spoke as it was. He had no knowledge of the worth of the doors themselves, but no doubt that any approach to them close enough to test, would be fatal for any below. Finally, he asked, "What else, then."

"A sapping attempt would be futile, both from the location of the city and the season."

"Sapping?" Marcus had never heard the term.

"Digging a tunnel to the wall, then along it. The wall is held up with timbers during the work, then brush is placed around the poles and fired. An entire section of wall will collapse into the hole." He shook his head. "But, here... even as the men dig their latrine pits, they encounter water no more than three foot-lengths below the surface."

"Then there is the siege. We outnumber the city-folk by... I do not know the numbers, but it is large. We could invest the city on all sides, leaving them with the choice to leave their protected confines and do battle, or starve within." Marcus could tell that he had no enthusiasm for the idea, but before he could ask, the Centurion gave the reason. "Sieges are... arduous. Without knowing the storage of food in the city, we have no idea how long they could hold against us. And... the men become... difficult. Marching to battle is a thing, and fighting is another, but with a long beleaguerment and little to do but wait for months, and sometimes, years... Desertion, mutiny, drunken fighting over this and nothing. It does not add polish to an army."

Again, Marcus just stood in thought, looking across the now darkened field, but not really seeing. Surely an army with the history of Rome had other methods for taking a city than... "On the morrow, I assume they will try to scale the walls again - possible at another spot."

"Nay, Sos." The head shake could barely be seen now, on this cloudy and moonless night. "At least not on the morrow. Unless there is a store that I am unaware of, we have no scaling ladders."

"But the ones at the wall were not damaged, that I could see. Those can still be..."

"Nay. Even now the city-folk will be sallying to retrieve them. That is another reason for my... fear of the... worthiness of our leadership. Whatever the knowledge of the Dux and the... others, the Senior Centurion is no fool, and has been fighting the foes of Rome longer than I have been alive, but I cannot understand why he did not post a unit at the gates to prevent the sallies. And other units to recover our ladders."

Looking back toward the camp, Marcus said quietly, "I have no knowledge of such, but would wager good coin that the son of the King may have a hand in the matter."

They walked back to their section of the encampment, the Centurion to check his posts, and Marcus to the tent of Lucius - now empty with the Tribunes gathered around a fire, no doubt discussion the aborted attack of the day. He sat against the tent pole, thinking on the problem of entering a city in which one was not welcome. How did one destroy a gate, made of wood - huge balks of wood - against the will of the owners? Lucius returned, late, and they retired, still without his finding an answer.

Morning brought the usual horns for assembly, then the formation across the field. Marcus had asked if the plan was to attempt the same climb of the walls, this day. Lucius nodded. "Aye, but we will group the ladders so that a soldier that attains the top will not be fighting alone." That made better sense, but Marcus doubted that men reaching the parapet five or ten at a time would have any different result than if singly. On the yesterday, he had seen the enemy moving in far larger groups, back and forth, as they marched to the need for repulse.

They stood, the sun in the now clear sky growing hotter as the morning progressed. The midday time came, and still the order to advance had not come. Finally, in mid-afternoon, the horn to disassemble was sounded. Then, in the camps, Marcus and Maxentius walked to meet their respective Tribunes, coming from the headquarters table. In disgust, Collatinus mentioned that the reason for the lack of action was because of the equal lack of ladders. They had disappeared during the night, collected by the soldiers of the city, and no doubt, now being broken up as firewood. Apparently, the order to collect them in the night failed somewhere between, "I ordered it done." and "We received no such orders."

Both of the Tribunes stopped at the tent of Collatinus, sitting down heavily on the grass in front of the flap. Maxentius poured two generous cups with wine, then, at a gesture from his Tribune, one for himself and Marcus. The Tribune shook his head. "The gods must be laughing today. The mighty army of Rome, and allied with most of the cities of the land, acting with less skill than a band of street urchins trying to steal sweetmeats from a vendor."

Lucius almost emptied his cup with one swallow, then wiped his lips and said, "Why the King allows that id..." He stopped and looked around for any wandering ears, then finished the sentence quietly. "...that idiot son of his to give commands is a mystery to myself - and probably to the gods, as well."

Maxentius asked, in an equally low voice, "Sextus was in command, Sos? I saw the King on his steed most of the morning."

Lucius shook his head. "Nay, I was not meaning the battle - or the formation for the battle that did not happen. Last eve, the Senior Centurion gave notice to Sextus that the climbing gear would need to be recovered, and a unit set to watch the gate to prevent the sally of the city. The Tribunes, Bibaculus and Marullus were attending him and heard. But, apparently, the illustrious son of the King, was interested in dallying with his female tentmates first, and forgot. Of course, this morning, he made claim of his direct orders to the effect, but I doubt that even the King believed him."

Collatinus waved his cup. "More ladders are being made by the quartermasters. Supposedly, they will be ready for the morrow."

And they were. And the grouping was tried, and with the same success as before - none. More Roman and Latin bodies attracted the vultures in the following days, and the tents of the medicos had even more broken men laying on mats in the grass and under the sun awnings. Then, realizing that continued thrusts by flesh at stone would deplete the army of men in short order, the King ordered the full investment of the city. Camps were moved, patrols set to prevent smuggling into the city and major forces encamped at both of the two gates in the event of the soldiers of the city suddenly making a foray in surprise.

Again, Marcus sat on the knoll, as he had done the nights before, looking across the field, thinking of his Sabina, and two sons whom had not yet even received names, but also of the huge gate and the fact that it was keeping him from his family. After several days, even Lucius noticed his preoccupation. Coming up behind his aide, he said, "It is an evil thing, to be separated from a family, and one that has just increased with sons."

Deep in thought, Marcus started and jumped to his feet. "Aye, Sos. But I was pondering on yon gate, and a method to ask our foe to open it."

Lucius shook his head. "If I live as long as a Sumerian king, you will never cease to surprise me with your thinkings. Do all Plebs spend their lives in the construction of this and that? I ask, because I can say that noble men do not - they seldom even wonder from where the devices that they use on a daily basic are derived, and they - I certainly could not bring one into existence."

Marcus just smiled, not really listening. "Sos. On the training field at the Oppian gate..." Lucius nodded. "There was a huge log at the armorers - with a head of a goat with horns attached to the end."

"Aye. It is called a ram. Used to batter through... well, city gates and walls. It and its fellows were used in the Samnite wars, and with good results." He shook his head. "But, do not think of its use on yon city portal. You might well ask your Sabina to push the gates open for us, as to use such a toy against such a barrier." He pointed. "And with the inset walls, the men carrying the weapon would be feathered and crushed before they could even heave it against the wood."

"Aye, Sos. But what if it were much larger, and the men did not have to lift it to strike? And if the wielders could not be seen from the wall?"

Lucius looked at his aide in puzzlement. "You have the power to call down the auspices of the gods, to use the very Aegis shield of the Greek Zeus? Come, what are you thinking?"

"Your pardon, Sos. But the idea is incomplete in my mind..." He thought of something. "Do you send a missive to your household with the courier?" A nod from the Tribune, then, "Then might I include a tablet to my home?"

"You know that it is unnecessary to ask. Of course. I will tell you when the pouches are being collected."

The days went by, one after another, and other than a few sallies at the wall by bowmen, there was little happening in the way of battle. Eventually, Lucius came to the fire circle of the young aides and called, "Marcus. I have some gladsome news of missives from home."

The young man jumped to his feet and walked to the Tribune, who handed him a leather pouch. "My thanks, Sos." In his tent, by the oil lamp, he read the long missive in wax from Sabina. "Dear Husband. Your missive was as a message from the gods. I give thanks that you are well and unharmed, and hasten to inform you that all in this house are in health as well. Your sons have taken note of their smallness and are hurrying their growth by demanding to be fed at all hours of the night and day. Even our neighbors have awe of the..." It was a long message, in small lettering and stopped only because the woman could not fit more words onto the pair of wax surfaces. He read it to the end rapidly, then again slowly to savor the meanings. And yet the third time before closing the tablet and setting it aside. Only then, did he examine the odd items in the leather pouch - items that he had requested Ennis to procure and return to him as quickly as possible.

The next morning, Lucius asked about the missive, and the hope that all was well. Then wondered at the small pile of items that were laying at the foot of the aide's mat. "A roll of leather. String... And, what?" He held up a small block of a white substance.

"Binder made of the hooves of oxen, Sos." He grinned, knowing that the Tribune was totally perplexed. "I will demonstrate the use of these items when I have finished my thought." A thought came, and he asked, "Might I ask to be excused from the morning formations for a few days? I wish to work on my... my idea."

Lucius just looked at him, knowing that whatever the reason, something solid would come of it. He had long learned that actions by Marcus always had results. "Aye. There is little happening, so you will not be missed. If you should look out and see the Volscians galloping towards us, you might take up your bow and assist us." With that parting jest, he left for his watch duties for the day.

Marcus set his steps for the forest on the far side of the encampment, passing through the quartermasters area to procure an ax. For the morning, he gathered a goodly assortment of green wood and sticks and, after the midday meal, sat in the shade of their tent and began to carve with his pugio. As he worked with his hands, he thought, refining the design over and over. With the binder melted in water over the oil lamp, he glued this stick to that, sometimes breaking it apart and starting again. The results he put under his kit, so as not to have to answer questions when Lucius returned in the evening. At the moment, he himself was not sure of the result that he was trying to approach.

Finally, in a few days, he asked Lucius to invite his friend, Collatinus to the tent. Maxentius was already there, knowing of the reason for the invitation, as he had sat, at times, with Marcus during the making. Inside, on the floor they found a small grid of sticks woven together as a frame, with some worn leather stretched across, to make a surface about two-foot lengths in either direction. On it, they could see a fairly good representation of a part of the wall of the city, easily seen across the fields. Marcus had made it close to the look of the actual, with the indention holding the gate, and the wing walls protruding out from it. At the base, in front of the little gate, was what looked like a... a tent. But, if the size was in relation to the wall that it was in front of, then a tall tent it was.

"What in the name of the gods has your man been doing, by himself and out of the sight of his fellows? Will he throw a spell on yon foe, or call down the wrath of the demons on the image of the walls, to curse their standing?" The jest of Collatinus was only partial.

"Aye," replied Lucius. "If I could tell you that, then I would be the master bowsmith, and not he. Very well, Marcus. You have our attention."

The young aide began to speak, pointing and demonstrating, even sometimes opening the flap of the tent to point across the field toward the city. The two Tribunes were astounded at the detailed thought that the young man had put into the project. They were even more astonished, almost to speechlessness with the audacity of the idea.

Finally, the lecture came to the end and the Tribunes just stood and looked at the little construct. Finally, Lucius spoke. "By the gods, Marcus. Sometimes I do not believe that you are actually real. You claim to be a waif, come down from the mountains as a homeless orphan, but you create webs of complexity that even the sages would attribute to Minerva." He turned to his noble friend. "I see no flaw in his arguments, assuming that this... this fist of the gods can be built. What say you?"

Collatinus looked at Lucius, then back at the small diorama. "He makes a good argument, I will say that. Of course, anything that

might end this interminable encampment would garner my approval."
He looked at Marcus. "And you can build this?"

"Aye, Sos. Well, not by myself, but there is no difficulty in constructing such from wood. If..." He emphasize the word. "If I have the supplies and sufficient men."

"You may say so, Marcus, but if it were put on me, I fear that the end of time would close down the world before I could make such." Looking at Lucius, he asked, "Should we present it to the Senior?"

The Senior Centurion had to listen to the two Tribunes, who theoretically outranked him by reason of status, but he had little time in his days to waste with listening to schemes from - to himself - an almost newborn soldier. Still, as Marcus set the model onto the table, the eyes of the old officer looked with interest. Halfway through the explanation, he suddenly said, "I remember you now. The aide that assisted Tribune Brutus on the training exercise then accompanied the King's guard to the meetings at the grove of Ferentina." Marcus answered in the affirmative, then continued his spiel.

At the end, they knew that an ally had been made. The man nodded, and said, "Aye. It could work. Come, we will present it to the King."

Marcus and the Tribunes waited as the Senior walked to the Royal compound, then reappeared, waving for them to attend. Inside the huge tent, one in which a half a Century could have stood, Marcus found himself inside a small room with a long table. Surprised, he realized that the tent was actually a full domicile, cut up into sections by internal walls of fabric. And for the moment, the room was empty of all but the four soldiers. At a gesture from the Senior, Marcus set his diorama on the flat surface, then just stood. Now, he was wondering at his audacity to bring forth suggestions that might affect the entire army. A Plebeian who annoyed royalty in any way wasn't paraded to the Tarpeian Rock and thrown off to the accompaniment of ceremonies of trumpets. Instead, he was nailed up to a convenient crossbeam - or just speared and tossed to the fish in the Tiber. Still, he had thrown the bones, and the tally would be...

All stood to attention as Tarquinius entered, dressed in a simple, if elegant, tunic and sandalae. Behind him followed Sextus, the Dux and another robed Senator, looking ridiculous in the thick purple striped city garment. That last was a stranger to Marcus, but as a Plebeian had little interaction with such nobles, that was not unusual.

The Senior pointed and said, "Regis. This is Marcus, Adiutor to Tribune Brutus."

The King looked at the young man for a moment, then nodded. "Aye. I remember." A pause, then, "And you have a plan to conqueror the Volsci without needing the bulk of the army." Turning to the Senator, he continued, "I would that we had known of such a son of Mars in our ranks before disrupting city life with our inductions. Much time and effort would have been saved." Marcus was about to answer but stopped as Collatinus jabbed a finger into his back, unnoticed. A Plebeian did not just break into the discourse of a King without call. "Well. Show us of this plan that the Senior has given notice of."

Marcus stepped up to the table and began to talk. "...and on the word of a man in our unit, who has visited the city with his pater on trade missions, the gates are thick and solid. So massive as to require an equally huge ram to breach them. Alas, any such tool would have to be of a size that the men would expend all their strength in hefting, and have little left with which to strike the blow."

"And this little tent that you display here will alleviate that?" The King was noncommittal, but not hostile. As yet.

"Aye, Regis. But it is not so small." From a pocket of his tunic, Marcus took a small carved piece of wood. Setting it beside the model of the ram, it became obvious that it represented a soldier. Now the scale of the diorama became apparent - and that the proposed structure was very large and tall. He then extracted a long rod from the same pocket and set it next to the little figure. "This shows the size of the ram itself - almost three foot-lengths in width, and almost forty foot-lengths from end to end. The largest tree that we can find."

The Dux spoke up. "That would be almost impossible for men to lift, without consideration of wielding it."

"Aye, Sos. And if green, the weight would be even greater. I doubt that any barrier made by man could withstand blows from it. But, the men do not have to hold it to be used against the gate."

Sextus spoke up, with audible disdain. "A weapon that can not be wielded, no matter how powerful, would seem to be a..."

The King held up his hand, instantly cutting off the words of his son. "You have our interest. Make your explanation - and without other interruption."

The little model was a triangular structure, with a much taller apex at the top than the width across the bottom. Marcus had no such words in his vocabulary, but the toy weapon filled in for his ignorance. He removed the flap of cloth that covered it, allowing the underlying structure to be examined. "The body is as a tent made of wood, but much taller than wide." It was framed with sticks, representing the logs that would be used in the real thing. "There are no wheels, which would greatly complicate not only the building, but the use, as I will show."

"Firstly, the structure is moved to the gate - on a dark night with no moon, I would recommend. It would give the defenders much less chance of knowing what was coming to their city. Notice the poles that span the bottom from side to side, leaving just enough room between each for a row of men. The wooden tent, if I may call it that, would be lifted by the men inside - forty or so - then walked to the gate and set down, touching it." He looked up at the King, and received a nod to continue.

"Following behind it is the ram, carried by as many as can gather around it. If the structure were moved with the ram in place, the weight would be too much for even the number of men that could be gathered inside it. In this way, we can use the largest tree-wood that can possibly be wielded." He pointed to the model. "The reason that the ram structure is much higher than wide is twofold. With such a steep slope to the sides, any large stones that are dropped on it from above will just slide to the ground, unlike a cover with a flat top that could be smashed with a sufficient weight of stone. Also, any boiling water or hot oil will just run down and off."

Another look at the King and he continued. "Notice the small strings that I have attached to the inside of the tent at each joining of the poles?" He picked up the stick that represented the actual ram, and maneuvered it to lay, suspended by the loops of string. "This is the other reason for the height to the top. It gives the weapon a much longer and more powerful swing." He moved the stick back and forth on its little slings to demonstrate the action. "The huge log is pierced at intervals along the length, then thick poles are inserted into the holes to give handles on both sides to allow for the men to thrust in a natural manner, rather than trying to manhandle a tree into movement."

He was encouraged to see that there was interest in the eyes looking between him and his display. Maybe he would get out of this presentation with a whole skin, after all. The Dux said, "With your permission, Regis." The King nodded and the General asked, "What of burning oil? We have seen no use of it by the city as yet, but would not such a rain of flame turn your structure into a bonfire."

Marcus nodded. "Aye, Sos. It would indeed." He put the little flap of cloth over the ram, covering both sides from apex to the ground. "This is just cloth for my showing, but on the ram itself, it represents green hides. These would be procured from the commissary unit not long before the action, and continually soaked in water until the night of use. Then they would be spiked to the sloping roof, in a thick blanket and constantly watered until we approached the walls." The man nodded. "I am sure that you know, Sos, that a fresh hide is almost impossible to dispose of in fire - any that are not given to the leather makers are carried to the putrid pits, or buried. I fear that the smell will be exceedingly offensive, but the men will have their attention on other matters than their nose."

The King spoke up. "If the noses of our men are the only casualty of the assault, that can be borne with ease."

The unknown Senator finally spoke. "Should not the ram be pointed, the better to pierce the gate?"

"Nay, Sos." That came out sharper than Marcus had intended, and his following words were tempered. "A sharp point, on such a heavy ram, would certainly pierce the gate, or anything in its way, but I fear that it would just make a hole, after which further blows would hit nothing. The flat end will deliver the entire force of the blow against the structure of the gate."

He pointed to the stick that was the ram. "Once the gate has been breached, the pushing poles are withdrawn and discarded. Then, men with blades will cut the sling ropes, allowing the ram to fall to the ground." He reached into the model, removed the stick-ram and set it under the slings. "Now the tent structure becomes a tunnel, allowing for the assaulting soldiers to pass the walls that jut out from the portal, and into the city, without threat from rock or archers overhead."

With that final statement, he stood back and waited. The King reached down to pick up the stick-ram, and set it back into the little slings of the model. He pushed on it, then just watched it swing to and fro until it came to a stop. He was obviously deep in thought.

Then, Sextus spoke. "Your accent is not that of Rome. How it is that you hold the rank of Adiutor without reference to the law?"

Marcus knew he had to tread carefully. In actual fact, he was not a citizen, but just a wanderer who had found his way to the city by fate. Or some whim of the gods. Or... "I was an orphan, Sos..." He had no idea if the son was to be addressed with the royal 'Regis', or the usual greeting, but as no one in the room objected, he continued. "...taken in and adopted by the merchant, Pythes, as his son." Not really true in the legal state, but definitely so in the real sense.

Sextus looked at him for a moment, then asked, "Pythes?"

"Aye, Sos. A man with a respected merchantry in the Palatium quarter."

The King, broke out of his trance, and stopped the queries with a sharp, "Nay. The Adiutor is as Roman as any and more than most." Looking across the table, he asked, "And you, Senior Centurion. Your opinion of the... instrument?"

"It is certainly worth the effort, Regis. Nothing will be lost if it is a failure, and if it succeeds..."

Tarquinius reached to push the little boom again, watching it move back and forth, then... "Senior Centurion. You will instruct the quartermaster to supply anything that the Adiutor needs to make this... device. In this, Marcus has the authority of the Throne." Looking at Lucius, he said, "Tribune. Since the man is of your unit, then you can supply any manpower needed by him for the construction. And for the thing in battle, when it begins."

"Aye, Regis."

"Then make it so."

...hora dissolvit (...an hour destroys them)

As he looked at the growing pile of logs, dragged to the construction area, Marcus had no presentment of the start of an era - one in which the Roman army would grow and power until it engulfed the entire world.   It would do so, in no small part with the engines and machines that would grow from his idea.   To himself, and all who would see it, his covered ram would be a spectacular engine of war. But had the gods, in a moment of diversion to their long lives, allowed him to see the into the future, he would have been stunned at the power and size of the machines to come, and the soldiers - numbering into the many thousands - that would be charged to build and use them.

Such imaginings were beyond him - his thoughts were more pragmatic. He doubted that the King would excuse failure, with the expense and manpower being used on this idea.   Rather than spending his time in dream weaving about nebulous futures, he walked to and fro, trying to see problems and to correct them before they were built into the... contraption - a word that he had just learned from a builder of housing.

Lucius had put out the call, of the soldiers in his Mille, for men who were from the construction trades, then Marcus had spoken with each, choosing forty men with which to work. Many others were used for the work details, chopping trees and hauling them through the forest to the work area. Also, he 'borrowed' the Senior Centurion of the unit - the man with the name of Rutilius - as the sub-officer of his work detail.   The man was honest and spoke truly - one whom would give criticism and agreement with equal emphasis. A professional soldier, he knew the art of commanding men to get their full potential - something that Marcus still had to learn.

Marcus had pointed out during the meetings that occurred while the supplies that he had ordered were being gathered, that the ram needed to be built out of sight of the city. "...else, with advanced knowledge given to our foe, we might find that the gate has been backed by another wall of stone, even of whole buildings torn down to make an obstacle."   Thus, he walked through the forest, marking this tree and that, then followed by the work crews, they were felled then stripped of branches and hauled to the worksite - a flat area on the opposite side of a low hill from the city.

The major structural members were first spiked with long iron nails, then wrapped with thick rope to secure the joining doubly. Many were the groans of the quartermaster over the cost of the metal fasteners, but with the orders of the King behind the young aide, he delivered the type and amount requested.

Marcus learned as they built. The shape of the ram cover had been determined because of the need to gain height for the sling ropes, and to give immunity from heavy stones dropped from above. But, as the wooden tent, as it was called, began to take shape, he realized a basic truth about the structure - that the three sided shape was the strongest configuration that he could have built. Educated men, in a future unbelievably remote from his time, would use that shape to build massive structures that would not even have been conceivable by the gods of the time, had such deities actually existed. As it was, Marcus had not even the word for triangle in his vocabulary, but his native sense of invention gave him the realization of the fact, even if he could not give the reason.

At the same time, a massive, tall and straight needle tree was selected - one that even the largest man could not encompass with his arms. Until it was felled, then cut to length, Marcus was not sure that any number of men could actually move it, let alone manhandle it into slings. And in fact, it was beyond the strength of the forty men as it fell. With nothing to grab or hold, it could not even be budged, so he had the holes for the handles cut in place. Drills being unknown at the time, a man would use a long sharp iron rod, and a mallet to slowly chip a hole the width of a man's hand all the way through the massive log. These holes would be about a long pace apart, giving about twelve in the entire length of the log. As each hole was finished, a long pole would be inserted, sticking out on both sides far enough for two men to grasp - one on each end. His plan, should the long ram pole be too massive to move, even with the lifting poles, was to cut the log shorter in steps, until a reasonable weight was obtained.

The structure was not complicated, and even with some changes that Marcus had made during the construction, it was finished in a span of five days, not counting the weeks that they waited for heavy ropes and long iron spikes to arrive from Rome. As the work ended, he put more and more men on the arduous task of holing the log. That task took twice as long as the structure, but eventually it was completed and the lifting poles inserted.

Now, he would see if it could actually be moved. There were twenty-four men on the poles as they readied the trial. Then, as the Centurion gave the orders to stand by, then grip, then lift. To his relief, the huge log came off the ground, but it was obvious that the weight would overcome the men in short order. He immediately had the Centurion give the order to drop the log before it fell and crushed the life from any that would be in its way.

This setback he had planned for - indeed, the more he had looked at the massive log over the days, the more he was expecting his first attempts to fail. Now, he had longer poles inserted - long enough for two men on each side, for a total of forty-eight on the entire log. Now the ram came off the ground handily. It was obvious that the men were not going to run with their burden, but it was, at least, movable. Now, the order came, and the men stepped off in a slow march, both Marcus and the Centurion watching to measure the strength remaining in the haulers.

The second problem became apparent as the ram approached its sling structure. He realized that, with poles sticking out all up and down the log, there was no way to maneuver it into the loops of the ropes. Ordering it downed, he sent the men to their midday meal, then sat down with Maxentius and examined the problem.

"Could we tie the ropes around the log, then lift it, while men attach the upper ends?"

Marcus shook his head. "Nay, I do not see how." He pointed. "The men above would have to have a beam or platform to stand on, and it would mar the path of the ropes." Besides that reason, the ram tent was built as strong as possible, but light enough to be moved. They could not add any further weight and hope to get it from the far side of the hill to the gate in one night. He pointed to the camp. "Let us eat. A rest clears the mind, and ideas will come easier on a full belly."

At the table of the Adiutorae, the usual jests were forthcoming about the chariot of Marcus and the carrying chair of the noble Adiutor. The japes were not in mean in spirit - all liked the friendly aide of Brutus, but also, he seemed to have the favor of the King, and one such is not to be plagued. For himself, this day, he was totally oblivious to the bantering, letting Maxentius work with the play of words. He barely knew what he was eating, so deeply was he in thought.

Finally, a thought came, and a murky vision that would not quite... He rose to leave the tent with the endless chatter, walking slowly back toward the work camp. He could almost see, in his mind, the method of... Suddenly he set his feet to the camp of the quartermaster.

The overly rotund and red-faced officer of the supply corps was fully aware that the Adiutor had full sanction from the King, but still... "You wish to have ten perfectly good pilae beaten into... what?"

"I have no name for the item, but I will show the worker what is needed." As the man still looked at him with disbelief, Marcus hardened his voice. "Now, Quartermaster! I would not like the King to think that his battle is held up by slowness in your division."

The pilum was a short spear of Roman origin - at least, that is what Marcus had been told. Made to either wield or throw, it was far shorter than its Greek counterpart, and made in two pieces - a long and usually square rod of iron, beaten into a spearpoint at one end and flattened at the other to which an arm-long haft of wood could be pinned. The reason that he had chosen the weapon was that it was the only long piece of metal available, without sending - once again - to Rome.

It took the greater part of an hour for the ferrarius to heat his fire to the point that the iron shaft of the short spear could be heated to orange. Before the blacksmith started his work, the wooden haft of the pilum was removed, leaving only the rod of iron, about the length of a man's leg. The spear point was heated to softness, then cut off with a hammer and chisel-tool. Then, with the heating of the iron further along the shaft, he indicted that it be hammered into a circle and back onto itself, forming an eye.

Next, the other end of the rod was put in the coals, then beaten into a somewhat larger half circle. Had the Roman alphabet had the letter 'J,' it would have looked like that shape, but with a round circle attached to the top. The iron was dunked into a tub of water to cool, then Marcus hurried with it back to the work area, leaving word for the blacksmith to keep his fire hot.

At the ram tent, he had one of the rope slings cut - not at the bottom of the loop but further along - about head high. He then had two ropes, hanging from the overhead. One cut off at about chest level and the other almost touching the ground. The shorter was knotted, leaving a loop in the end just about large enough to put one's hand through. The other rope was fed through the eye of the hook that had just been made and knotted. Now he had the same rope sling as before, but one that could be broken, then pulled under the ram log, then with the large hook fed through the small rope knot, making the sling again.

He stood back and visualized the huge ram being trundled into the tent, the long rope with the iron hook brought under then attached to its shorter mate, then the log slowly lowered until the slings had taken the weight. Again and again, he thought through the steps, then hurried back to the blacksmith to order the other nine hooks to be made.

The next day, with the Centurion taken through the steps of the procedure, they began the practice, but with a long and narrow log, rather than the massive ram. Maxentius was standing by, watching and assisting when needed. The unit of forty would stand inside the tent, evenly spaced along the lifting poles, then entire structure would be raised on command. They would march forward for a few strides to represent the journey to the gate, then at command, set the wooden tent back onto the ground.

The forty would move aside, with their backs to the sloping walls on either side so as to free up the center of the structure for the next action. Now, the unit with the ram, that would total forty-eight on the night of the actual movement, would pick up the ram and follow the same path as the tent. In the case of this practice, a long, but narrow tree was used and with only twelve men, equally spaced along the log as if they were at the carrying poles. An attempt to use the full number of the unit on such a small burden would have a man tripping over the heels of his mate.

The ram, represented by the light tree trunk, would be walked into the end of the ram tent, the men stopping as they reached the front of the structure. The command given, ten designated men of the original forty, would step forward, take the iron hooks and bring them under and around the log, slipping the large hook into the hanging rope with the eye. The ram would be slowly lowered until the slings took up the weight and the men of the ram unit, would immediately exit the structure, running away from the putative wall just beyond the ram.

It worked. At least with the small pole that represented the massive ram log. Still, over and over he made them run the course during the day. It was important that they know intuitively what they were to do since the actual action would be at night with no more light than a few torches. The evening coming on, he had one last exercise...

"Ssssss. Marcus!" He turned to Maxentius, standing and pointing with his hand, shielded by his body. "The King!"

He looked across the field to see the horses of the King and staff approaching, and several men walking behind. Not the assistance that he was wanting at the moment. "Max." he said in a low voice. "You meet them and give the talk of what is happening if that is what they want."

Now the men suddenly noticed the approaching group and began to move, wondering where and how to make a formation. "Centurion!" Marcus barked. "Keep the men at work. It is not for them to receive the King. Again, start the assembly."

The King and his group - the Dux and Senator, and most, if not all of the Tribunes, and an assortment of men that he assumed to be the Senior Centurions of the millae - stopped half a hundred strides away, and the riders dismounted. He saw Maxentius bow and receive the officials, then he forgot the group, entirely.

Again, the commands and chants, with the ram cover moving forward, being placed, then the ram meeting with it and being slung in place. It was good. Now, he caused the ram tent to be moved back to its original position, with the massive ram about a hundred strides away and pointing toward its destination. Taking a deep breath, he ordered all of the men to their starting positions.

Up went the huge structure, it moved along to the putative gate - or about fifty strides, in this case, then settled to the ground, waiting for the ram. He knew that the gigantic log could be moved by the men assigned to it - for several days they had carried it back and forth, twice a day, to allow the men to get used to their burden and the motions needed to control it. What they had not tried, was placing it in the slings. If anything were to go wrong, it was likely that several men would be crushed under the massive log.

Another command and the massive burden was hoisted, then marched forward at a steady, but not full walking pace. As it approached its destination, Marcus suddenly realized that he was attempting this first test under the full gaze of the leaders of the army. If it failed, then... He dropped the thought. Too much was at stake to be dream weaving about things that might or might not happen.

At the cover, the march slowed, the men having to carefully step over the poles that formed the bottom of the wooden tent - the very poles that it had been carried by. From the view of the watchers, the log slowly disappeared under the triangular structure but did not appear out the other side. Inside, as it came to a stop, the ten rope men hurriedly went through their actions, with Marcus quickly examining the connections in a fast walk from back to front. Then with a word, the knees bent on the men at the carrying poles, and the huge weight settled into the slings.

Marcus looked up as the structure popped and groaned under the load, but held. The last order was given and the forty-eight ran from the structure and out of range of the putative archers on the equally imaginary wall, now supposedly trying to determine just what mischief was happening below.

Marcus told the forty men of the ram to stand easy and walked out into the open to see the King and his court - as Marcus thought of it - approaching. Straightening, he saluted and said, "Salve, Regis."

Tarquinius raised his baton in salute, then replied, "Salve, young Adiutor. That was an impressive drill. Might you give a tour of your impressive construct?"

"Aye, Regis." Marcus was feeling almost ebullient at the assembly of the completed engine, and the lack of any massive failures this first time. "But I would caution to stay near the walls, and away from the ram. Should the slings fail..." He needed say no more. Inside, he ordered the men along the wall that was approached by the King to exit out the front, to give room for the examination.

This was not a cursory inspection. The King was obviously absorbed in his examination of the structure. With his hand waving at this and that, he asked pointed questions on the build and the usage. Obviously satisfied that the young man had been capable of what he had claimed in the beginning, he finally exited to the fading daylight and walked around the ram to examine the outside. Finally, he turned to Marcus and asked, "So, Adiutor Marcus. When will it be ready for use?"

Marcus already had the answer, having calculated it nightly at rest. "Several tests remain to be made, Regis, but the dark of the moon is eight days hence. I would give that for the date."

"Then make it so."

Morning time showed that the ram was still sitting in the slings. At least, the entire structure had not collapsed during the night. It was time to test the use. As Centurion Rutilius counted the men onto the pushing poles, he walked around examining the entire engine one more time. Finally, he nodded, and the men set their feet and pushed the ram toward the rear of the tent. At the command, "Drop," the men quickly stooped to their knees as the huge log swung the other way on the release. It was at that point that he knew something was wrong. The entire structure was wobbling back and forth, opposite the direction as the ram was swinging. Telling the Centurion to stand down the men, he watched as the swings - and the movement of the tent - slowed, then stopped as it came to rest.

He gave the order to remove the massive log from the structure, then begin to run through the moving and setup exercises for more practice - but to not swing the ram, whatsoever. That done, he moved toward the area of the commissary, thinking furiously as he walked. Two large poles, dug into the dirt, and braced against the back of the structure? Nay. The work would have to be strong, and performed in the dark and under the eyes of the enemy. But...

Why was the tent so strong from top to bottom - so much as to hold, with ease, an entire tree trunk weighing... who knew how much? He knew the answer - it was the three-sided shape that gave the strength, up and down, and side to side. But, along the sides. He stopped and sketched into the dirt, a shape that was three sided in all dimensions. It looked familiar, then he realized that it resembled those Egyptian tombs that he had seen in drawings on the scrolls from the scribery inherited by Sabina and her mother. At any rate, it would not help him. It would take an entirely new structure, and would only have the position for one sling - totally inadequate for the ram that was needed.

At the commissary he made sure that enough hides were soaking in water to cover the entire outside of the ram tent, then strolled back to the work area, sitting down and just gazing at his creation. Nothing came to mind, and he could not risk making changes to the...

Informing the Centurion, he walked back to his tent and uncovered the little model that he had used for demonstration. He broke the little ram toy apart, breaking the glued sections carefully so as not to damage the materials. With the pile of sticks, he began to reassemble it with string for the bindings, rather than glue. He didn't bother with the construction of the entire model, but just a skeleton shape that mimicked the real thing.

Now he tested the strength in different directions. Just like the large one, this toy would now give if pushed on from front to back or in the reverse. But, with his fingers pushing down or inwards from side to side, the shape was immovable. That was expected, from his newfound knowledge of the strength of the three-sided shape. He needed to make the structure three sided from front to back but without... without being of a three-sided shape. That thought was ridiculous. He wiggled the model back and forth, holding this and that, trying...

"Ah, Marcus." He looked up to see Maxentius. "Your Centurion told me of your whereabouts. You are summoned to an assemblage at the tent of the King."

His friend escorted him to the knoll of the Royal enclosure but stopped outside. A guard lifted the flap to let him enter and he saw the officers of the Legion gathered around the table, with the King at the head. "Ah, Adiutor Marcus." Tarquinius waved him in. "Come. We are finalizing the assault and may have questions on the use of your engine."

Inside were not only the King and the Dux but their staffs and all the Tribunes. In addition, the generals, or whatever the ranks that the Latins were called, were in attendance also. The room was filled.

"...and the assault will begin at darkfall and the ram will be moved to the gate and assembled. The assembly will be timed to coincide with the rising of the sun. The Senior has a list of the Millae that will form for storming the gate when it falls, and the rest will form for an assault on the walls." That was interesting. He had given little thought to the battle that would take place if the ram succeeded in breaching the gate, but it made sense. Were they not to threaten the main walls, then as the gate fell, the men charged with entering the city might encounter the entire army of the foe.

After a while, Tarquinis looked at Marcus and asked, "Do you have anything to add, Adiutor?"

"Aye, Regis." He stepped forward to the table. "We will need to practice our moves during the nights so as to be able to work successfully in the dark. Therefore, I request that the men assigned to the ram be allowed to stand down and rest during the day so they can be trained in the darkness."

"Aye. And what force do you need?"

"The ram and structure are heavy and need to be carried by others than the working crew - at least until the gate is within arrow shot. I will need two units of forty-eight men each to move the ram, and two of forty each for the wooden tent, in addition to the two trained units that I now have. That will allow them to move half a stadium, then pass the load to the next unit, then rest. Just out of arrow range of the gate, my trained units will take over, unwearied by the move. I need no one stumbling from exhaustion in the dark."

"That is good. It is done."

"Pardon, Regis. I have one other request." A nod and he continued, "The Adiutor of Tribune Collatinus has been assisting during the construction of the ram and is familiar with the operation and the movement. I would ask that he be assigned to the unit for the assault. I need him to direct the movement of the ram, following the tent structure. And... he could assume the command in the case of my being struck down."

"It is agreed. Make it so."

The rest of the meeting concerned flags, signals, and instructions for the assault. Finally, the King concluded with, "I order that you make your men aware that this is not a mission to destroy Suessa Pometia as if we were barbarians seeking blood and glory. Nay. It is to bring that city under the hegemony of Rome and Latium and to return it to a productive community under the auspices of a Roman governor. We will kill all who oppose us, but there will be no wanton slaughter and burning." He looked at the Tribunes who would be responsible for the men. "Vultures and crows do not pay taxes and neither do they produce grain and meat for the markets of Rome and Latium."

Outside the Royal tent, he walked to Maxentius and said, "You have been assigned to me. Go and tell the men to return to their tents and rest. We will begin the practice in the night time." His friend nodded. "Then, go to Luci... the Tribune Brutus. He will give you enough men to make two units each for the ram and tent. They will make the initial moves to save the strength of our trained men. Begin their instruction on moving both. I will be in my tent."

There he pondered over the little model, pushing and pulling, but in the main, thinking. He tried to rest, but the thoughts would not stop to allow him to sleep. As the darkness fell, he was back at the work area. For the first night, the men went through their movement, but slowly, as Marcus attempted to determine the minimum amount of torchlight that would be needed. The practice was with the small log and went well - the men knowing exactly what each was to do by now and needing very little light to be successful. Not so, the units learning to move the big ram in the night. The trained group of men had no problem, but the other two units that would do the preliminary moves were clumsy, unfamiliar with their burden and the gait needed to move it. Twice the huge log fell as the men stumbled and tripped, crushing the life from three of the men, and leaving a handful of others with broken and mashed limbs.

Finally, with two hours to sunrise, Marcus called a halt until the next night. In the tent of Brutus, he collapsed on his mat, more from the effort of thought than of the need for sleep. He even dreamed of three sided shapes, and suddenly his house had miraculously changed into an Egyptian tomb. In fact, so did his bows, and they would not bend because of the shape was immovable. All on the street japed at him as he tried to demonstrate his new weapons, but could not find the strength to pull.

He woke in the light of day, trying to hold on to the dream that had been in progress. Desperately he seized the memory before it vanished like the morning dew, as the dream imaginings always did before the sleep left the eyes. As the men assembled in the work area after their morning break of the fast, he sent his carpenters into the woods to find trees of a certain length and width. Soon, the men were shaving the bark and planing the thicker end until they had four long and sturdy boards.   Following his direction, he ordered one to be fastened to the peak of the ram at one end, then the other to be nailed to the base at the other.   Then, another board was attached to the inside of the sloped wall, but slanting in the opposite direction. Finally, the same was done to the far wall with the remaining two long pieces of lumber.

After making sure the spikes were securely hammered, he ordered the ram itself to be laid in the slings.   Standing back, and visualizing the inside brace that could not be seen, he could see that, with the logs nailed to the opposite extremities of the sloping wall, they made the figure of a huge X, as the number for ten.   As such, they had produced on each wall, four of the three-sided shapes that resisted change by force.   The upper ridge pole, and the lower at the base, along with the two end poles were joined at the ends with the new lumber to make the almost magical shapes.

Now was the time for the test.   He ordered the huge log to be propelled in a moderate swing, then watched the structure as the ram swung back and forth.   Then again, with more rise, then yet another time with all the force that the men could give.   The swing of the massive log actually made the entire structure move back and forth over the dirt for a handspan or so, but there was no deforming of the wood itself. The idea had actually worked.

To Victory

Lucius and Collatinus were standing beside the massive ram structure with Marcus - all looking over the top of the low hill at the destination for the night. Behind them, in formations, were the units that would take turns in moving both of the pieces of the weapon down the road to the gate of the city. The sun had set, but the light had not departed as yet.

Lucius turned to his aide and took the young man's wrists in his hands. Saying nothing for a few heartbeats, he finally spoke. "I will take it extremely amiss if I am required to tell your beautiful Sabina that you have departed this life for a domicile on the slopes of Olympus. Your mission is to clear the path - not to stand with the Legionaries and hack at the foe. Do not disappoint me."

Marcus just smiled. "Aye, Sos. I would not put such a chore on your shoulders. And Sabina would be most wroth were I not to return to name our sons."

"May the gods go with you, Marcus," said Collatinus. Then, both nobles turned to return to their respective units. As the Mille of Lucius had been pilfered of men to form the moving units and the two sets of trained men who would both assemble and operate the ram, his now depleted unit was given the task of protection of the ram. Should the city folk realize the danger that was coming, it was possible that they might set a foray to destroy it beforehand. The unit would follow close behind, and wait. And, on the suggestion of Lucius to the King, the Tribune had the entire of the small contingent of bowmen of the army, ready to clear the walls above the ram of any who might wish to hinder its mission.

The day had been sunny, and the night would be clear and moonless. All movement would be under brilliant starlight. The ram structure was now reeking, with the green hides having been spiked to the sides, overlapping and the first being nailed to the bottom, then the next moving upwards, as the shingles of a building. Any liquids should flow freely to the ground without seeping into the inside. But... for further protection, the men were supplied with leather coverings that would protect their heads and upper bodies in the case of any fiery hot liquids dripping from above.

They had almost three stadia to march with their burdens, and with the exercises of the past month, he knew that the march to the wall would take about two hours. Thus, the action would begin in the last quarter of the night. For now, the men were in a ragged formation, but lying on the ground and encouraged to sleep while they could.   Marcus knew that it would be a waste of time for him to even try - besides, he had one further task before the marches began.

As the light began to fade, he waved the two soldiers to follow. Both were carrying leather bags that were bulky, but not heavy.   He began to walk rapidly down the road toward the gate that was their destination on the morning, all the while counting his steps.   At a certain count of strides, he would say, "Here."   A soldier would remove an item from the bag and set it in the road.   It was a flat board, about the size of a spread hand, split from some of the timber that had not been not used in the construction, and painted with a combination of lime and ground shells collected from the seashore, some thirty stadia distant.   Even under the feeble light from the stars, they were very visible as a white spot on the black ground.   At the count that indicated each half stadium, several would be placed in a row, across the road.   This would indicate where the men under the burdens would be relieved.   The last row, almost within arrow shot of the walls, was doubled.   Here, the selected men would take the toil and prepare for the assault.

Now, he - they, only needed for the night to pass away.

"Marcus.   Marcus!"   The young Adiutor opened his eyes, realizing that he had actually fallen asleep after reclining.   The person standing above him was just a dark shadow against the sky, but he knew it was Maxentius.   "It is time."

Standing to shake the sleep from his eyes, he looked to the heavens, seeing that the light of Jupiter was in the descendant.   Max was correct.   They had about three hours to daylight.   The men had already been roused, and shortly the Centurion, Rutilius, walked up and saluted in the dark.   "All is ready, Sos."

He made one quick inspection, making sure that the hides covering the walls were wet.   Indeed, they were soaking, and even now being watered by men on ladders leaning against the sloping surfaces. He gave an order and the men with buckets fell back, then the ladders were removed.

He checked his girding.   Helmet, armor, gladius and pugio. No scutum - a shield would be cumbersome for a man who was not expected to stand in the line of battle, and he needed no cumbering weight to slow his movements.   But, his bow was in the carry position over his chest, and a full quiver was on his shoulder.

The men would carry nothing but their shields, slung onto their backs.   With their massive burden, it was impossible for them to carry their weapons.   Instead, four men would follow the ram structure, their arms loaded with the spears of the forty who would be hefting the huge structure.

Maxentius would command the ram, with the Centurion calling the pace for the sling structure. In just a few moments the commands were called for the two burdens to be lifted, then the long journey began. Marcus walked in front, following the road. Under the starlight, the white boards at intervals were almost as torches, to show the way. As it was, in the clear night he could plainly see the lighter road piercing the darker fields, so the boards had been unnecessary, but he knew that over-preparedness was far to be desired over the opposite.

Behind him, he could hear the voice of the Centurion calling "Step... Step..." and barely, further back the voice of Maxentius doing the same. Usually, any commands from a sub-officer to the ranks was a bellow, but the man had remembered his instructions to soften his voice to just loud enough to be heard under the wood. At the first line of markers, the procession stopped, the burdens were set to the ground, and the men changed for fresh. Immediately, they were on the march again.

The timing was good. He watched the light of Jupiter descending in the western sky and knew that the pace was matching the plans. Finally, an hour before first light, they came to the double row of markers. In the distance, only a hundred paces or so, he could see the almost imperceptible shadow of the city wall. However, the night made no difference in his judging - on the wall at intervals, were torches - some bright, some almost extinguished. The distance was easy to gauge with such visible markers.

Now his two highly trained crews took their places - those of the ram and those of the sling structure. In a few heartbeats, they were marching over the last bit of distance. Marcus was waiting - and expecting - a shout and clamor from the walls, as someone noticed that some massive object was approaching the city, but as yet he heard nothing. In the closer distance, he could not even see men moving under their own torches on the top of the wall.

Now they were in the enclave made by the walls jutting out from the gate itself, and in total blackness. At a short word, the pace became as a snail, until his extended hand touched the thing that had been in his thoughts since the army had arrived in the field. Quietly, he called, "Slowly, Slowly," then ducking under the leading cross pole so as not to be crushed between his own creation and the gate, itself. Then it touched, and at a word, set to the ground.

The Centurion gave a command, flint and steel sparked, and a torch was set alight, then used to enflame three others. There was no chance of them being seen by men on the walls. In fact, only a man still on the road would be aligned properly to see the lights - such as the men still marching with the huge ram. The men backed up to the slanting walls to make room, then waited for the other half of their weapon to appear.

It was only a short while before a huge shadow appeared on the road, then resolved into a mass of men and a log, as they slowly walked it into the enclosure. As it stopped, a soft word was spoken, and the sling men quickly did their task. They started as the structure made its usual pops and groans as it accepted the weight - all thinking that the sounds could be heard as far as Rome and beyond, on such a quiet night. Still, it brought no cries of dismay from the city.

Now the ram carriers exited the cover, under orders to walk back slowly and out of step, unless they were seen and under engagement. Marcus did not want the steady tread of a march, or the pounding of feet in a run to alert his foe unnecessarily. To Rutilius, he ordered, "Send the signal."

The Centurion walked to the back and gave the command to the Signifier. In a few moments another torch was lit, and posted on a pole high under the tall roof. Through some magic known to the quartermaster, this one was red, having been sprinkled with some powder that made the usually yellow flame change to the color of war. In a few moments, the Centurion whispered, "Acknowledgment, Sos." Marcus could see the corresponding red dot of light far in the distance. Now, it was a matter of waiting for the sun. Already, the ground seen out the back of the structure was becoming more defined, as the first lights of dawn began to streak the sky. Now all eyes were on the red torch, far across the field.

Of course, now time crawled on leaden feet, but finally, behind him, he could hear a collective intake of breath as all saw the second red dot appear. At a word, their own second torch was ignited, signaling that the order had been received.

"Places!" he called. There was no need for stealth now. In a few moments, even the gods would know that the Romans were knocking at the gates. The order was unnecessary. The men had long since taken their stance at the pushing poles, their blood flowing hotly as they anticipated what was about to happen.

"All in the ready, Sos," called the Centurion. Marcus nodded. Now loudly, the sub-officer said, "Stance... And... Push."

With their pent-up excitement at the action they were now a part of, the huge ram moved farther in its backward swing than Marcus had ever seen. "Drop!" The men loosed their hands from the pushing poles and quickly moved aside. The log began its swing toward its target, reaching the low point of the arc, then impacted the wood of the gate.

All were expecting a loudness in the impact, but even so - the crash of the wood against wood was as the gong of the gods, closing out the world. What it sounded like in the city...

Unlike the training sessions, where the ram would reach the bottom of its arc then climb the other side of the swing then back and forth, now it stopped at its low point, allowing the men to immediately resume their stations, and begin the next blow. Being careful to remain a safe distance, he held a torch to see the results of the impact. There were none, other than an impression where the round log had hit, but he had no expectation that the gate would begin to yield at the first blows.

"Boom!" A pause. "Boom!" The impacts were deafening inside the enclosure, and probably also beyond the gate. Now, even with his ears ringing with the noise, he could hear babble beyond the gate and above. It was only a matter of time before the city defenders attempted something - anything to stop the monster that they could see below at the gate.

"Boom!" Now there was an indication of the power that was knocking on the wood. A round impression, three fingers deep, was now evident in the wood of the gate. Marcus hoped that the timbers of the portal were not overly weak, to let the ram punch a clean hole. That would gain the Romans no advantage, and give the city defenders time to buttress the gate before the ram could be disassembled and moved to gain a new impact point.

However, he had anticipated that problem. Should the massive blows of the ram begin to splinter only a small area at the site of impact, he had several massive planks made available that could be interspersed between the ram and the gate, to spread the blow to a much larger area than that covered by the end of the log.

Walking to the back, he could see the formations on both sides of the road, now assembling in a line to assault the walls when the signal was given. And, closer in, others were in a pretense to do the same, but he knew that those Millae were consigned to make the attack through the gate when the breach was made. But, assembled as they were, as in a formation to ladder the wall, they gave no indication to the foe that such an attack would be made.   It was a plan to hopefully prevent the city from massing a huge formation behind the gate.

"Boom!" Pause "Boom!" He had no expectation of the gate being shattered, or that the large pole that secured it for the night would be broken. Reports to him, by men who had been to the city, were that the pole that spanned the gate from side to side was massive. Not as the ram, but still a single log from a tree, plained to flatness, and no doubt seasoned to maximum strength. But... Hopefully, the weakness would be in the keepers that held the locking pole in place.

Suddenly, he heard a... sound. An impact, then a scrape... He realized that it was a large stone dropped from above and sliding down the face of the outside. Then more. Holding his torch high, he saw no change in the structure above. It was holding as planned.   Shortly, there was a veritable rain of impacts above, as the defenders desperately attempted to hole the ram enclosure so as to allow for hot oil or such to be poured on the men wielding the ram. Thus far, there was no sign of any such liquid rain, and he had expected none - at least not for a considerable time. Large quantities of liquid took time to reach any temperature that would be of use, even were the fires started at the first knock by the ram.

Uneasily, he looked at the gate, the impression growing deeper but with apparently with no weakening... He stopped, wondering at the light that was... When the ram cover was dropped, it was in virtual contact with the wood of the gate. Now, daylight was streaming through a gap at the front. Trying to understand, he walked forward and looked around the edge, first making sure that his head did not appear in the sights of an archer above.

Had the ram structure moved back a handspan? That was unlikely since there was no force from the impact transmitted to the frame. A quick look in the dirt showed that it was not the case. There were no marks of the structure sliding. That meant that the gate had to have moved.   But, how... He put his hand out to touch the wood, waiting for the next stroke. At the next deafening blow, he could feel the gate move inward but then spring back.   Possibly, the closure pole was breaking, or the holders were loosening.

He walked back to the rear of the structure. Now he could see what had to be the entire contingent of bowmen in the combined armies, standing in ranks, and shooting shafts up and over the ram. The support that the King had promised was now making the act of dropping stones or hot liquid onto the ram a perilous task. Even if the archers seldom connected with fleeting targets far above, the defenders would be hesitant to rise above the rampart into the storm of shafts.

As he walked back to his station at the front of the structure, he could tell that the gap had widened considerably. In fact, to almost a double handspan at eye level. But, what was moving under the continued blows? He stooped, then peered again around the front of the ram structure and along the gate. Then he noticed a discolored strip on the stone wall framing the gate, lighter in color than the darker exposed stone, starting from nothing at the bottom and widening at the top. In that instant of time, he realized what was happening. The entire gate structure - hinge poles, frame and all - was being toppled into the city. Now he examined the massive timbers that were the poles to which the gate hinges were attached. Made of logs larger than his arms could have encompassed, they extended from the ground - and under it for some unknown distance - to the arching stone overhead.

Now, almost knowing what he would see, he examined the bottom of the huge pole, where it entered the cobblestone base of the road entering the city. In the growing light, he could see slight bend of the wood where it left the ground. The gate was not the weak point of entry - it was the poles on which it hung. Unknown years of burial in the dirt, with water and wood-eating insects working at the wood, had taken their toll. The hinge poles were fracturing at the point where they entered the ground. Even as he watched, the angle increased and the discolored area that was slowly being exposed was growing wider.

Now he could see the result of the pounding in another way - by watching the swing of the ram. When they had started, the impact was at the bottom of the arc. Now, the huge log swung past the low point and began the rise to the other end of the swing before hitting the wood of the gate. As the gate leaned further inward, the impact of the ram no long met flat wood on flat wood, but rather, the lower edge of the log was all that struck, and the noise of the impact changed. Rather than the deep thunder of the strike, it was now higher pitched, as an ax hitting a tree. The intensity of the impact was no less - a monstrous ax and a tree from the land of the giants.

Walking to back to the Centurion, he spoke between blows of the ram. "The gate is giving way. It may collapse inward with any stroke."

Not taking his eyes off the men now taking a stance for the next blow, the man replied, "Aye, Sos." Then to the man still standing at the opening to the rear, he called, "Set the yellow, Signifier." Daybreak had made torches useless for long distance signaling, so the man unfurled and began to wave a large yellow flag on a long pole.

In only a few waves, the signaler called back, "Message acknowledged, Sos!"   Now the headquarters would know that the gate was indeed yielding.   Horse messengers would be galloping with orders for imminent battle to all units.

Looking around the corner again, the discolored area at the top of the masonry was as wide as a man is tall, and it took no study to see that the entire gate was leaning inward.   Now, he could even see the splintering of the hinge pole at the ground.   As the next stroke hit, he hurriedly ducked under the ram to look at the far side of the gate.   The view was identical with the other - both of the huge vertical poles were breaking at the base.

Up to this time, every stroke pushed the gate further inward, but would recover some of its loss as it rebounded.   Now, suddenly, every blow shoved the gate further over, with no visible recovery.   The blows came slower since the ram had further to go to reach the leaning gate, and rather than stop dead upon the impact, would swing back and forth for a considerable time before the men could corral it for the next attempt.

Now, he took the bow from its carry position - strung across his chest, wood at his back - and placed it between his knees and strung it.   There was more than an even chance that it would be needed if the assault troops were in any way tardy.

Then...

With the noise of fresh cane thrown in a fire - but with a loudness to equal the strike of the ram, but far longer lasting - the hinge poles gave up the fight, splintering at the bases.   The gigantic gate toppled inward to impact with the ground, raising a cloud of dust that almost looked solid.   The Centurion wasted no time.   "Stand down! Withdraw the poles! Signifier! Set the red!"   The handles that had been so useful in propelling the huge log in its work were now just obstacles preventing easy passage through the structure.   The four men, waiting against the walls, hurriedly handed out their load of spears.   As the men removed the shields from their backs and received their weapons, the officer continued with his orders.   "Stand clear! Cut the ropes!"

Multiple spearpoints began to saw against the thick ropes of the slings.   The rear of the ram fell first, then as more were cut, the remaining were too few to hold the massive weight.   They snapped like rotten string and the huge log fell with a crash that shattered the cross members of the structure.   Marcus had not visualized that to happen - this ram cover would not be moved again until much work was done on it.   But, that was the least of his concerns.

As the men began to arrange themselves, he jumped onto the log, now sitting on the ground, to gain a better view. It did him no good. The impenetrable cloud of dust was still just that - nothing could be seen through it. The dust did little to hamper sound, however. He could hear shouts, yells, screams - and close. It was obvious that the city folk had not decided to flee in panic from the men of Rome. Fortunately, they could see no more than Marcus.

The men began to line up in ranks, eight wide and six deep, spears and shields ready. Marcus looked back to see if the assault troops were coming, but the swirling dust had even reached inside the ram cover. It was not anywhere as thick as in the city, but it marred his view enough that the road could not be seen further than a hundred strides. And it was empty.

Marcus called to the Centurion. "Reach forward onto the wood of the gate, but do not move from under the arch of the stone." Their foe above would gladly drop stones on his men, even on the city side of the wall. By moving forward, they no longer had the huge ram splitting their columns.

Now, through the swirling dust, movement could be seen. Not a formation, but random movement in a run - in panic, he hoped, but certainly in affright at what had happened. The dust began to thin, and a few arrows were launched toward the line of spearmen standing on the shattered wood of the gate. Unaimed, they had little chance of claiming their mark with all soldiers behind their tall shields and only their eyes peering over the top.

Now, more could be seen with the dust thinning even as they looked. There! A purple-clad soldier with a full brush on his helm - an officer trying desperately to rally his men through the choking cloud. Marcus nocked an arrow, but before he could draw, the Centurion called to him. "Sos! The relief is here!"

Marcus looked around to see the front ranks of a column stretching into the distance up the curve of the road. They had almost reached the rear of the ram and were splitting to move around the huge log laying in the center of the structure. He made a chopping signal with his hand, then the Centurion turned and bellowed, "Ram unit! Withdraw!" At that, by prearrangement and much practice, the men split evenly down the center and moved to the side, against the bare stone of the gate entrance. The Roman and Latium soldiers poured through, under the ram cover, and into the city as a flood, shields held high and spears at the ready. Now the sounds of chaos became the sounds of battle, with the start of a general melee.

Marcus was as a man standing on a rock in the middle of a rushing river, men pouring past him on both sides. His men were standing on the banks of that same river, and there was little chance of either making their way back to their encampment until the flood had subsided. The soldiers entering the city split into three columns - not through any plan but just the instinct of a man in a battle. Once inside the gate, they either joined the men fighting down the main via of the city - straight ahead - or turned to either side to follow the streets that adjoined the walls. He wondered if the assault on the walls had succeeded this time, but had no way to determine such from his position both under the ram structure and inside the alcove made by the wing walls.

The dust of the gate had dissipated now replaced by that being raised by men in combat and kept him from seeing the ground of the columns where the fighting was taking place. The movement into the city had changed from a run to a very slow walk - it was obvious that the citizens of the city were fighting and not fleeing in panic. Still, as long as the mass of men trying to enter the city did not come to a halt, then the battle was progressing well and in their favor. Seeing a brief gap in the stream of soldiers, he jumped down from the log and threaded his way to his men standing against the stone of the gate opening. From there, he walked along the ram on the outside - there was ample room between it and the stone - looking up as he carefully passed from under the arch. He could see no evidence of enemy on the ramparts above, and there were no arrows or stones attempting to halt the flow of Romans into the city. Now, walking backward, so as to keep the top of the wall in sight, he moved far enough to see... Ah, it was Romans or Latins on the wall above.

Hurrying back to the front of the ram, he called to the Centurion on the far side of the marching columns. "Retire to the camp!" Then, motioning the men on his side to follow, he jogged past the ram and across the field to their encampment at the now abandoned work area.

Sub Hasta   (Under the lance are the spoils of war)

The men who had worked the engine that had broken the wall and ended the siege were now being called the "Forty of the Ram," although the actual number was a handful above that amount.   Many were the tales told by that group to their fellows in the adjacent Millae. Marcus smiled to himself as the accounts of his men expanded with every telling.   Some even had a modicum of truth, but all stories grew until the action with the ram was as intense as the mythic battle of Troy - wherever that foreign city was.

Still, Marcus was satisfied with both their efforts and his, and even more in that not a single man had been lost from the unit.   There had not even been an injury with all the stones, and logs and arrows flying hither and yon.   His men had no part in the battle in the city itself and had spent the last two days in relaxation among the shade of the trees.

Now that the battle and effort had come to an end, Marcus had time to reflect on his work.   He suddenly realized that he had enjoyed the building and use of the ram - to an extreme.   It was unfortunate that the project was for destruction, rather than building or constructive purpose, but the idea of examining a problem - insuperable by others - then following an idea and developing it into a successful result was...   exhilarating was not the word, but...   In any case, the satisfaction that he had gained - not even considering the knowledge - was great.

The battle was over, the city conquered, and even now the plunder being brought through the gate to the compound of the King. The casualties were fairly light, even among the city soldiers, who had decided to yield rather than fight to the death.   And with the prohibition of the King against slaughter and arson, the losses of the citizens were also minimal.   The leaders and nobles of the city were now in a guarded compound waiting their fate, but according to Centurion Rutilius, such a massive battle with so little spillage of blood was unheard of in his experience.

Of course, the stated purpose of the assault was to bring a productive city into the hegemony of Rome - not to gain laurels of blood and glory.   Marcus had no dispute with that.   He only hoped that this was the end of the King's forays and that they would shortly find themselves back in Rome.

The city of Suessa Pometia was both large and wealthy - the proof being the growing stacks of looted valuables growing in the guarded field next to the compound of the King.   It would still be large after the combined armies left, but the wealth would be gone. The men were in a joyful mood - all chanted to themselves and each other the shares that they would gain. As custom decreed, the Royal party gained half of the value, then the following quarter went to the noble officers. The quarter that was left would accrue to the common soldier, the amount depending on his rank. Split among the thousands of men, the individual shares might be insignificant when compared to their betters, but still would represent more value than they would hope to earn in a handful of years.

Finally, a half month after the fighting had stopped, a governor and bureaucracy had been installed, and a garrison told off, to keep the order. Now the Legion prepared to bend its steps for Rome, and their allies to return to their respective cities. But first, a formation in the large field that they had crossed, to give thanks to the gods of war and for the beneficence that been poured upon the armies of Rome and Latium. For whatever reason, the unit of Marcus that had built and operated the ram had not been folded back into the mille of Brutus, but kept separate. He hoped that it did not mean that another city was about to come under the assault and that another engine would be needed.

As it turned out, his worries were far off the mark.

Standing at attention with his unit, he passed the monotony of the occasion by dreaming of his home and family as the priests made this sacrifice and that inspection of goat livers - or something suchlike. The droning paeans to Jupiter and Mars and sundry other residents of Mount Olympus passed over him like the buzz of the crowd in the market square. Finally, Tarquinius stood to praise the cooperation of the combined armies in their successful attempt to prevent the pillage of Rome and the Latium cities by the machinations of their enemies. Marcus wondered if he expected the soldiers in the rank to believe that this war had been for the defense of their homes and families, rather than raw aggrandizement. And if they did.

Laurels and awards were given, to this unit and that man - any who had shown initiative and courage in the assault. Marcus greatly approved of the accolades given to Lucius, for his initiatives in the protection of the ram as it performed its task. Apparently, the King had decided that the Tribune was an actual supporter of the Throne. Surely, he would not be given such recognition had any suspicion still lingered about the deaths...

His internal dialog was halted in utter surprise by the Senior Centurion of the Legion stepping forward and shouting, "Adiutor Marcus and the Unit of the Ram! Stand forward!"

It took a moment for the shock to wear off, then he turned to his own Centurion and ordered, "March the unit forward." He strode to stand in front of the stand from which the King had been speaking, then saluted the Senior. Behind him, he could hear his forty or so men following and also stop on command.

Now, he shouted back. "Marcus, Adiutor to the Tribune Brutus, and unit reporting, Sos!"

The Senior stepped back, and the King raised his hands for quiet. "The Adiutor has shone unusual skill in his designs to reduce the defenses of our enemies. The men of the ram, for their efforts, will be awarded triple shares in deference to their skill and courage, and for being the spearhead that first entered the city of our enemy." He turned to motion to an officer, who stepped behind Marcus. "For the Adiutor himself, we have awarded this chain of valor." Marcus felt a heavy object being dropped over his head, to dangle down his chest but did not move his eyes from the forward attention to look at it.

The King paused, then spoke in a loud voice again. "Our officer, Marcus, is no longer to be an Adiutor. We have created the rank of Ingeniarius for him, to report only to the King or the Dux of the Legion. As such, he will be required to supply the Legion with any requirements for the reduction of defenses of our enemies. In this, he may not be hindered by any of the army." Another wave to an officer, who in turn ordered a soldier forward. Marcus could see that he was carrying a standard on a pole, that looked to be...

The soldier stopped in front of the King and planted the pole into the ground with a great heave, then disappeared from the vision of Marcus. "This is the standard for the unit of the ram, to be carried by the signifier at all formations." Now he looked at the young man. "The Ingeniarius and his men will follow my steed on our triumphal entry into the city."

Another pause - even a smile. "Finally. It has been brought to my attention that this young officer has never been honored with a proper cognomen." He waved his scepter at the young man. "We have decided that our Ingeniarius will be known henceforth as Marcus of the family of Callidus." Marcus could not believe what he was hearing. The idea had not even been in his imagination. Marcus the Clever? And not for the last time, was his thought that the ways of the Roman gods were... strange.

The formation over, he stood as Lucius and his fellow Tribunes pounded him on the back with such force to make him glad that he was still girded in his armor. His friend, especially, was profuse in his praise of the actions of his former Adiutor and his fertile intelligence.

With a grin, he turned to his fellow Tribunes, and said, "My Aide - or my Aide that was, to be exact, is a man for whom I myself and others - Collatinus and Publicola for certain - know as one who has an intense dislike of conflict and war of any kind. I would say that this was fortunate for the Volsci in their city. Can one imagine their fate were he a ravenous worshiper of Mars?" The roars of laughter and guffaws engulfed the group as they dispersed to prepare for the march on the morrow.

In their tent, Marcus removed the heavy chain, examining it with some amount of disbelief. As a decoration, it was decidedly plain, being only a chain without medallion, but... The links were as thick as his smallest finger and almost as long, and with one side of each cut to allow for the metal to be spread and removed from the chain. And made to be removed they were, being made of solid gold and with each link worth enough to feed a Plebeian family for their entire lives. Or to buy an occupation and kiosk outright. In fact, the worth of the entire chain would have easily have purchased the merchantry of Pythes and with much value left over. Still, it was not coin and gold that he wanted - rather a desire for this military adventure to end and allow himself to return to his life.

The march up the road was uneventful, and for the last night they stopped a handful of stadia from the city. Marcus wondered why they were extending their absence by encamping within easy walking distance of the walls of Rome. Lucius just shook his head at the lack of guile in his friend. "Once again, you have demonstrated the difference between the gens of Rome and your peoples, who apparently take life as a matter of reality. You have no need for self-aggrandizement, but I can assure you that a King does, and in massive quantity." He pointed toward the city. "If we enter in the evening, then the triumph will be cut short by nightfall, but by waiting for the morrow, the people will have the entire day to heap their adulation upon their hero. Including yourself, to a goodly extent."

"Myself? I agree that the King has given me a family name for my work, and a rank-title that I will have to ask Sabina to show the marks for, but I am still a waif from the mountains who has no roots in Rome. No one in the city beyond my neighbors knows of my existence, still less my name."

In any other man, Lucius would have known that the modesty was falsely spoken, but in the case of Marcus, he knew that the young man not only had no idea of his worth, but also had no need whatsoever for the acclaim of others. Again, he shook his head in admiration for such honesty. "Be that as it may, you will be receiving an education on the morn. By now, runners and the Criers of the city have spoken in fulsome praise of the Forty of the Ram and their young Commander who not only was the man who described the method for breaking the defense of the enemy, but who was also the tip of the spear that first entered the city. And, I have no doubt, the street bards are telling the tales of the man who slew twenty foemen with the dexter hand and twice that with the other before bursting through the gates of the Palace and lopping off the head of the King to end the battle for the glory of Rome."

Marcus looked at the Tribune with a wry expression. "Sos, you are talking like one of the street fablers yourself." He shrugged. "It will be goodsome to reenter our lives will it not?"

"Aye. In that you are correct. I yearn for my books and baths, and the chance to recline in the librarium with scholars, rather than standing in the dust looking at stone walls."

Morning time brought the marching formation again, but this time with the King and his officers, with laundered garb, and on their steeds, freshly groomed. Directly behind them was the unit of Marcus, with his forty men or so, and with their Signifier holding the standard in the front. The tall pole, carried by all units to give name to the host, was, in this case, in the shape of a two-sided tent with the carved likeness of the head of a he-goat extant between the sides, its massive and curved horns protruding to give a fierce expression to the animal.

Thus began a day that Marcus could not have distinguished from a dream after an evening meal of rich foods and too much wine. The main gates were adorned with festive ribbons and flowers, with citizens looking down from the ramparts - places which were usually forbidden to any not in the guard watch. Then along the main avenue, the Via Appia, the crowds were lined as deeply as the edges of the street would allow. More looked down from the roofs of the buildings. Marcus began to wonder if the noise of the shouts and acclaims were actually louder than the impact of the ram itself - certainly, his ears were bent with blows of sound as they marched along. Suddenly, he wondered at the violation of the law that prohibited armed soldiers within the confines of the city. Was it being breached, or did the rule not apply for triumphal celebrations after a victory?

The cries were great as the King and his entourage passed, of course, but when the crowds saw the standard with the symbol of the ram, they roared with approval. The chant of "Forty! Forty!" and

"Marcus of Callidus!" followed them along the via.   The chaos was worse than the clamor of battle.

Marcus felt that he was lost in a blizzard - not an uncommon occurrence by the villagers in the mountains - but in this case, the fall was not of snow, but the petals of flowers and the fronds of plants. And with his name being spewed out by the clamoring onlookers, he wished - again - for the gods to end this day and allow him to find his way to a world that was not only familiar but far more comfortable for a simple bow-smith.

The Appian Via ended at the Circus Maximus, and here the army assembled on the field, between the nobles in their stadium and the commoners on the far side, standing in the grass or on the wooden levels of the watching stands.   It was not the entire Legion, of course, as even the large grounds of the Circus would not have held so many. Rather, selected members of all the units represented the whole.

The King gave praise to the gods, and the people of Rome, and the skill of the army... at which point, Marcus ceased to listen, rather, thinking on other matters, only the half of an hour away by his legs. Then, finally, after an interminable time of babbling from the Royal stand, the men were dismissed, and the officers called to formation in front of the King.   Here they were given orders to report at the Nones of the next month, for further discussion on the suppression of threats in the peninsula of Latium.   That was far from the news that Marcus wanted to hear, but at least, it indicated that he would have a month and the good part of the next for his own use.

"I would ask you to my household for a cup to celebrate our successful return, Marcus, but..." Lucius grinned at him.   "...I fear that I would incur the terrible wrath of the lovely Sabina should I keep you from her for one more heartbeat of time."   He clapped his friend on the shoulder.   "The Domina will sorely miss your return, but we can alleviate that in the coming days.   Farewell, Marcus, until we meet again."

"A good day to you, Sos.   And my gratitude for... all that you have done."   The Tribune just waved in dismissal of the thankfulness and both began to wind their way around the milling officers - all trying to find the quickest way to their domiciles.

But for Marcus, the glorification of the day was not over.   As he reached the Forum of the Viminalis quarter, he realized that word had preceded him that the most famous citizen of that avenue had arrived.   Turning onto his street, the cobblestones were lined once again with cheering crowds, but this time made of people that he knew - or at least had seen before.   As he passed, they filled in behind him as an impromptu procession, moving up the street toward his home. Once again, the noise would have disturbed the gods in their faraway mountain. Speech and replies were impossible, as were greetings as all pressed close to take his hand or arm, or just to touch the young man who had been honored by the King as being the keystone of victory. With little or no practice in the art of receiving laurels, he could just smile and nod to this baker and that garb vendor as he passed. Until, he reached within the sight distance of his household...

There, ahead he could see the gate open and Sabina standing in wait. Behind her was Decima and Cleo - along with all in the household. Now the crowd seemed to realize that the young soldier would be as a ram of war against a gate of reeds should any stand in his way and all moved to give him a path. In a run, he flew up the remaining distance, with little notice of any who failed to move aside. In a moment, they were in an embrace that only just failed to squeeze the air from the breathing sacs of both.

There was little to say, and speech was almost impossible with the roaring crowd, watching the young husband and wife make their greeting. Looking around, he noticed Pythes and Valens standing in the courtyard, both smiling with gladness. He nodded to them, then raised a hand to acknowledge the crowd, then turned and walked into the house, still holding Sabina with an arm around her shoulders and both of hers around his waist.

Inside, with the door closed, the tumult quieted enough for speech to become possible. "Sabina, my wonderful wife. You are well? And our sons?"

Still gripping him, she smiled through tears and replied, "Still as hungry as always, my husband. They fill their little bellies at all hours of the day and night. And you? Need you a meal after your long sojourn in the wilds of the land?"

The question was unneeded. He could see the atrium table piled high with smoking hot viands - enough to feed half his unit of men. And, he realized, a meal by the house cocua would be a welcome change from the sameness of the commissary tables of the army. "Aye. I could eat a bite." Nodding to the mother. "And you, Decima? You are well?"

"Aye, Marcus. I have never felt better." She motioned to the kitchen maid to prepare the cups for the family and guests, then motioned all to recline at the table.

"Cleo. How is the household? And your good mother? And you, Ennis and Flavis - are the staves still seasoning well?" All replied in the affirmative and with deference to a man high in the status of the

King. It was somewhat disconcerting to have the working members of his household act as if a noble had entered their presence, but time would plane the roughness from that wood.

Marcus finally managed to unwind the arms of Sabina long enough to walk over to his old mentor. "Pythes. Valens. Our house is made gladsome by our guests."

They took each others wrists in the Roman manner, as his warden replied, "The pleasure is ours, Marcus. You have brought much honor upon your house, and mine. To receive a name, given by the King to a commoner, is a thing unheard of in my time, but I had little surprise when I heard that it was my young ward that was the recipient."

Valens stepped forward and placed a hand on the young man's shoulder. "Porcia, the baker, and Harom, Cassedes, and all on our street send their greetings and thanks to the gods for your safe return."

Pythes grinned. "Aye, and Porcia begs permission for the use of your name for a new baked goods that she is making. It is to be called the Bread of Callidus, in honor of your victory."

Marcus just shook his head with a wry smile, still disbelieving the happenstances of this day. He waved and all reclined to eat, although he had little to do but place the food in his mouth and chew. Sabina and the cocua filled his plate as fast as he emptied it. Decima and a maid left for a while, then returned with a bundle each. The young maid gave her burden to Sabina, and with her mother, displayed the sons to the father. He was astounded at the growth of the pair during his absence, but of course, the same astoundment was happening to many fathers in many households around the city even at this time.

Not wishing to attend a dinner without being fed, both began to complain about the lack of sustenance. As all here were family, or close to it, Sabina found it meet to feed them without retiring. With a light cloth, draped by Decima over her front for modesty, the two infants were soon at their own feast and quiet returned to the table.

It was long to darkfall, but all knew that only one thing was on the minds of the master and mistress of the house, and none knew it more than the men. After the youngsters had finished their liquid meal, Pythes spoke. "Marcus. It has been a long road for you, even as young as you are. I would suggest that you retire early and gain your rest for the morrow. I suspect that it will be busy."

Grateful for the suggestion of the old man that relieved him from giving rudeness by retiring with guests in the house, Marcus nodded. "Aye, Sos. I am indeed looking forward to the soft mat in our room, and without the clamor of men at all hours." He looked around. "I give thanks to all here, not only for their greeting of my return, but for the services done for my family and myself in my absence. Could I ask all to excuse me for the rest of the day, so as to begin my rest in my own home?"

All stood, the men bowing as they gave their encouragement for his rest. Then, with final farewells for the day, he and Sabina walked arm and arm up the stairs.

It must be said that little rest was taken by Marcus until the night was well along, and his body was indeed exhausted. But, by the next morning he was refreshed and bounded down the stairs to inspect his household, long missed in the preceding months. Sabina was long up, and in the atrium... and not alone.

Two men were standing with Sabina - and not the citizens of the street that were known to the household. These were not nobles, but were dressed as prosperous... whatever they were. Then, noticing the master of the house descending the stairs, both men turned and bowed deeply to the confused young man. Sabina spoke up. "My husband, this is Avitus, the Magistrate Rectoris of the Viminalis quarter and his second." Turning to the older man and extending a hand toward the stairs, she said, "This is my husband, Marcus of the family of Callidus, Ingeniarius to the army, appointed by the King of Rome."

Marcus could scarcely believe what his ears were hearing from his mate, but managed to maintain an expression of calm, rather than utter surprise at her effusiveness. The man bowed again and said, "My greetings, good Sos, and our wish to convey those of the people of the quarter. You have brought much honor and fame to our peoples, and they wish to return the benefit to your good self, although our attempts will pale in comparison with your feats." Now totally confused, Marcus just halted at the foot of the stairs and waited for some gleam of light through the darkness of the talk. "It is the feast of Lucria on the next Kalends, and the people of Viminalis would be gratified should you be our guest of honor on the pulpitum."

Marcus had no idea who or what was being celebrated, nor if Lucria was a god or goddess or a rite or... But, Sabina could fill that void in his knowledge later, but for now... Being displayed before the people of that section of the city was not a fate that he wished under any circumstances...

Looking at Sabina, beaming with the idea of even more honors being heaped upon her mate, he sighed within and answered, "Aye,

Sos. I will gladly accept this noble invitation, provided that it be extended to my wife, as well."

Now, with a huge smile, the magistrate replied with gusto, "Aye. Certainly, Sos. The wife of the Ingeniarius of Rome will be welcomed by all." There were a few more moments of flowery talk, then the two men took their leave.

He walked over to Sabina to embrace her, saying, "My work in the army was entirely pointed to return myself to you, and quickly, but it also appears that I may have been better served by returning at night, disguised as a peddler."

Behind him, he heard the voice of Cleo. "Master, the Factor of the Guild of Weavers is awaiting your pleasure." Turning he looked at his steward for a moment, then back at Sabina. He could see that she was suppressing a grin at his discomfiture. The young woman knew full well the indifference of her husband to accolades, but she had no intention of allowing him to refuse the honors that he richly deserved.

"While my husband was sleeping off his night's labors, many offers and invitations have arrived to celebrate your return and victory." Before he could reply, she continued, "You are no longer a waif of the mountains, as you call yourself. My husband is an honored and decorated officer of the Roman army and named by the King. As such, you have certain duties to the people of your quarter and one is to allow them to bask in your glory." That was as close to chiding her husband as the young woman would come for the nonce, but before being allowed to refuse his deserved rewards, he would have another battle to fight, and this one much closer to home.

He sighed. Finally home, after dreaming of the day for months, and he had not even had the chance to visit his workshop in the work yard. He slumped his shoulders in mock resignation, then turned and waited as Sabina said to Cleo, "Ask the honorable Factor to enter our atrium."

The morning went by quickly, with invitations and presents arriving in profusion, interspersed with requests delivered from Cleo to present himself at the gate to the street to receive further accolades by the lesser citizens who did not feel the worthiness to ask for entry into his home. One invitation in particular was gladsome - that delivered by a servant of the House of Brutus. And, after the noonday meal, both he and Sabina prepared to visit that noble household.

During his absence, both Sabina and her mother had replaced his inventory of clothing with new and exquisite garments such as a noble might wear. His normal tunics and such were placed in the basket that held his work clothes for use in the smithery. By now and since acquiring his new household, he had grown somewhat used to the need to display himself in something beyond a worn, but clean tunic, but he still had the feeling of being dressed for the acting boards as Decima looked him over for any slightest sign of a loose thread or marred seam.

His feelings against show and play-acting did not extend to his wife. He looked at Sabina, richly robed in her stola and with her coifed hair showing under her long shawl - the pella - now draped over her head and both arms. On this day, the colors of her garb were as from spun thread of gold - a departure from the usual stola of white cloth with stripes of color that were worn by well-to-do women.

"Pardon, Master and Mistress. The steward of the House of Brutus awaits." Cleo backed up, waiting to open the door to the courtyard.

Confused, Marcus looked at Sabina, then back to Cleo. "Nonus? Why would he arrive here?"

"As an escort to the House of Brutus, Sos."

This was making no sense. But, as it was time to depart, both followed their Steward into the courtyard. They had not yet reached the gate, when Marcus stopped in his tracks, then exclaimed, "Nay! I will not be displayed like a..."

Sabina knew well what would be his reaction upon seeing the lectica sitting at the gate. This carrying chair, from the household of the Tribune, was open and decorated - made for outings on a sunny day to festivities or other happy occasions. She gripped his arm with surprising strength and said quietly, but with force, "Husband! You must not give offense to your friend and sponsor, he who has sent the lectica to give you both honor and his friendship. Do not attaint your new name and household by refusing this gesture."

Realizing that he was defeated, he nodded and stepped forward as the steward, Nonus bowed low and said, "I bring greetings to Marcus of the House of Callidus from his friend, Lucius of the House of Brutus." Then waving with his hand, he invited the pair to enter and recline.

The slow journey down the street to the Forum of Viminalis was as another procession. There was not the cheering of the previous day, but all who saw the handsome young man and his beautiful wife in passing, bowed and waved, calling greetings and good fortune. It was obvious that all on the street considered the young couple to be a very goodsome addition to their neighborhood. Past the forum, and down the wide via to the Capitoline the accolades ceased, but any who saw the lectica pass knew that it contained a man and woman of substance.

Finally, at the door of the house of Lucius, the carrying chair was set to rest, and among many others. Apparently, more than he had been invited for this day. Nonus bowed as they exited, then motioned to the door servant to open the wooden portal, and they entered. Both were very familiar with the house and followed the Steward without need to look in awe at the riches lining the hallway. As they passed under the arch, Lucius immediately noticed his two guests and hurried over to bow to Sabina and take Marcus by the arms. "Welcome, my friend and his good wife. I am honored that you have accepted my hospitality for this day."

"My thanks to you, Tri... Sos, for the generous invitation for myself and my wife." Both were trying not to laugh at the formal give and take, made entirely for the audience that was watching.

Now, Lucius turned and faced the atrium and guests. "My friends. I am presenting the Master of the House of Callidus, and the new Ingeniarius to the army, and Sabina, his good wife. And more importantly, I greet my friend, Marcus, without whose good skills and courage, on more than one occasion, I would not be now among you."

Marcus could see that Collatinus and Publicola were present. And Tricipitinus. And several other Tribunes that he knew by acquaintance, but nothing about. Apparently, the gathering was only of young men of the rank of Tribunes and their wives. He noticed that there were no Senators or other nobles that might be expected at an assemblage at a house of such rank and wealth. Actually, that was not correct - many of the Tribunes were either Senators themselves or were the sons of fathers who were members of that ruling body.

For himself, he was sure that his face was bright red after the introduction, but if so, all pretended it not to be. Now the Domina walked to face the pair. "Good Marcus. And Sabina. You are welcome to our house at all times, and without invitation, but I give thanks this day that you have accepted our hospitality. And for keeping my son safe in the war."

Sabina bowed, and Marcus replied, "Our thanks to you, Domina. We are indeed honored by your invitation to us."

The wives, and the sister of Lucius, all came to take the hands of Sabina and marvel at her garments. Naturally, they retired as a group to the side of the atrium to speak of cloth, and stolae, and earrings. The men, however, gathered around Marcus, and just as naturally, spoke of the war just ended. Many were the questions asked of him, about the ram, and the construction. And, of course, they demanded a blow by blow account of the happenings as it touched the gate. The meal was served, but the conversation continued into the night.

Spurius Tricipitinus was the eldest of them all by far, being close to his fortieth year of life - fifteen years or more older than most of the younger men. High in the Senate was he, and close to the Throne, being called in consultation by the King on regular occasion. And this night, he had news of interest. "...and with the loot brought from the Volsci, he intends to rebuild the Temple of Jupiter Optimus Maximus. It is to be the greatest temple in the world, even to rival the stone structures on the Nilos river."

"Where is it to be?" asked a Tribune by the family name of Ennodius.

"On the summit of the Tarpeian Rock."

That was startling. "Where?" asked Collatinus. "There is little room for even a vendors stand among the existing temples, and certainly no flat place for such a structure."

Tricipitinus spread his hands. "The shrines of the Sabines are to be removed and the top of the summit leveled."

Lucius shook his head. "One would think that our King will soon be on a quest for more funds."

"Aye," replied Tricipitinus. "The temple is only the beginning. He intends to build the viewing stands at the Circus in stone, and far larger. And, to widen the Cloaca Maxima and cover it." That last was a mystery to Marcus. It was only later that Lucius informed him that it referred to the huge open sewers that ran through the environs of the city.

And, indeed, Tricipitinus was correct. Now there came a procession of stone and heavy timbers from any Via entering the city, to the construction sites all over the city. For the stonemasons and carpenters, the brick makers and marble polishers, the times became golden. All Rome was in agitation as the Criers announced this plan and that change.

But, even the plunder from the city of Suessa Pometia, and much did it provide, was far less than the grandeur plans of the Palace. Lucius had also been correct - the King was soon on a quest for more.

Dulce bellum inexpertis (War is sweet to the inexperienced)

Now the city that had garnered the unfortunate attention of Tarquinius was named Gabii - one of the few that had refused his offers at the Grove of Ferentina.   Once again, a single entity seemed to pose a major threat to all the Rome and the other cities of Latium, and must be reduced before they could bring harm to their peaceful neighbors.

The army was now enhanced with men coming from all corners of Latium, drawn by the tales of loot gathered in the conquest of Suessa Pometia.   By now, the stories moving along the trading routes had even the common soldiers living the lives of lesser nobles with their shares of the spoils.   And the fact that the victory was fairly bloodless gave every man the hope of an adventure of excitement to season their dull lives, followed by the purchase of a small farm, or taburna, or even a devorsoria to succor weary travelers for the night.

In this belief, that the experience of war would be exhilarating and covered with an aura of laurels and glory, they were no different than young men since the beginning of time.

The city of Gabii was only about a hundred or so stadia from Rome, itself, and therefore well within the reach of a half day's walk along the Via Gabina.   And, the lack of distance meant that there would be no surprise in this attack.   No doubt, before the Legion had even finished its assembly for the morning march, runners had already carried the word to the city.

Not long after the midday time, the front ranks of the army had reached their destination, a sloping hillside, across which could be seen their goal.   The bulk of the afternoon was spent in settling the units into an encampment.   And on the morrow, Marcus was standing in the huge field tent of the King, with the Tribunes and their senior Centurions.   He wondered just how many had ever seen the city that was the object of their mission, and if they realized just how difficult this conquest would be.

Tarquinius gave the usual opening statements and, again, the warnings that this city was to be taken intact and folded into the hegemony of Rome and not to be broken into a ruin for wolves and outlaws.   "...and your unit of horse, Tribune Lucilius, will scout the walls around the city and bring a report of the lands and possible approaches."   The officer nodded.   "Give your findings to the Ingeniarius for his perusal."   The King stopped as Marcus stepped forward and raised his hand.   "You have a comment?"

"Aye, Regis." Marcus turned and waved to the young man that was acting as one of his aides. Taking a very large roll of reed paper from the aide, he laid it on the long table. "I have information on the city, and a map - marked it on this scroll." The King nodded and, with the help of his aide, the stiff paper was rolled out and held down at the edges with small stones. All crowded around the table to look.

"With your permission, Regis, I will give my findings." A nod and Marcus began his spiel, rehearsed for the past month and more.

"...the city is built on the ground between two small rivers - actually, they do not deserve that title, being mainly wide streams fed from the mountains. The road to the city on the west is, of course, the Via Gabina that we traveled to arrive here. It exits on the far side and leads east to the minor community of Pedian. Both gates of the city are fronted by bridges over the streams - or were. You have noticed that the one on our side of the city has already been removed, and we can assume that the other has been, also - or will be."

Now he pointed here and there on the large map - made by Flavis and Sabina by gluing many sheets of smaller material together. "The lands around the city are low and marshy, but in the past months, the inhabitants of the Gabii have cast large stones into both streams above the city and caused the waters to flood out of their courses. Now the usual marsh is ankle deep in water, making the entire course around the city to be a leg-swallowing swamp. Any unit trying to cross will arrive without sandals, exhausted and still have to ford a shallow but swiftly running stream."

He looked up for questions, but all were still staring at the map. He waved a finger, pointing to the place where the road from Rome adjoined the wall. "The gates are in no way the equal of the massive structures we found at Suessa Pometia, being made of single planks of no thicker width than a man's hand. They are braced by a few diagonal cross members and the keeper pole is removable by only a few men." He looked up at the King. "In actual fact, the gate is so weak that we would be required to use a large and thick plank against the wood, else our ram would punch a hole at the first strike and be useless after." Another wave and pointing. "The gate on the west wall has two widened sections of wall adjoining to allow a few archers to oppose any below, but the eastern gate does not. Neither has an overhead to allow defenders to stand above the portal."

"Now, the wall from here... to here, is made of brick, backed by a few foot-lengths of rubble and faced with brick on the inside. Only this wall, from here... to here, guarding the approaches to the south is stone, but of lesser height than..." He stopped, suddenly realizing that all in the room had moved their gaze from the map to him. Confused, he ceased his lecture and said, "Pardon, Regis. Have I said aught to cause alarm?"

Only Brutus and Collatinus were looking at him with equanimity, knowing somewhat of where his stream of facts had come, but the rest were staring as if he were a specter come with news from the gods. Finally, the King exclaimed, "By the stinking piss of Jupiter, Ingeniarius! Do you run your own corps of spies, in addition to your carpenters and treemen?"

Holding back a grin, Marcus shook his head. "Nay, Regis. When the first intimations of the actions against Gabii were being spoken of, I desired information before the army set foot on the road. I arranged for my warden in Rome, a merchant of great respectability, to send a trading mission to the city, with myself dressed as a laborer in the caravan. While the majors were haggling in the city, I entertained myself by walking around and gazing upon the sights to be seen in a new place. The days were hot, and one of the men of the guards was not against accepting a cup from a stranger in return for questions. I had represented myself as a man disaffected by my employer and who would gladly change masters for one in the city, could I find work that was available." He spread his hands and shrugged. "But... the wine, supplied by my warden, to my request, was strong, and soon the man was willing to answer questions far beyond the realm of employment. In fact, he was proud of the measures that the city was taking, should the despicable Romans finally come for their tribute, and even gave much information without my prompting. Taking me to the guard post on the eastern wall, he showed me the diversion of the river to the outlands. And other measures of interest, being prepared."

"Alas, the wine of Terracina was stronger than the man, and by mid-afternoon I had to leave him to his slumbers and make my own way."

He stopped to let what he had said to be examined, then the King asked, "And what is your opinion of our direction of attack?"

"It will be difficult, Regis. The city cannot be approached in force across the marshes unless we make some massive effort to build an access. To attack from either road will require the rebuilding of one of the bridges - men can scramble across the stream, but not with a ram, even were it half the size of our last."

One of the Tribunes spoke. "The streams on either side, according to your map, make the bridges only about thirty strides from the gates. Were I in command, I would allow my enemy to complete nine parts in ten of the span, then rush out at night and fire it."

Marcus nodded. "Aye, Sos. You have taken my thoughts exactly. The road is narrow and the front of a unit would be the same, with little force to repel such a foray. And the city-side of the bridge would be well within arrow range of the walls, so men could not be permanently stationed to prevent such a sudden incursion."

The Royal Prince, Sextus, asked, "Even the builders of the bridge would be targeted easily, would they not?"

"Aye, Sos." Marcus put his finger on the paper, just at the point where the stream would be crossed. "I have thought of a way to alleviate that, by building a tall palisade on the far side. While it is being constructed, a unit of men with shields would be detailed to protect the workers, and after, the work over the stream would be in the shadow of our barrier, so to speak. It would also allow for defense against a sudden foray of bridge burners."

All thought of what had been said, then another Tribune said, "Then that should be our point of attack, obviously."

The King had been looking at Marcus, and now interjected with, "But, it appears that our cunning Ingeniarius does not think so..."

Marcus nodded. "Aye, Regis. It is certainly possible, but I have not yet given all that I found in the city. During my walk, I saw large piles of materials of no apparent use, and in the vicinity of both gates. My sodded companion gave me the reason." His finger jabbed at markings on the map here... and there... "This is a stack of huge stone blocks, and here, large timbers, cut from tall needle trees. At the first sign of our construction of a ram, the gates will be buttressed with the stone, stacked as another wall, but with the timber as an intermediate between it and the wood of the gate. His explanation was, and I agree, that the timbers, held in place between the gate and the blocks, will perform as a sponge, so to speak, absorbing the blows of the ram even before they can affect the stone, which in any case, would be a massive barrier even against a huge ram."

"So, Ingeniarius, you are describing a city can cannot be assaulted, even with a force such as we have, and with the cleverness of our weapons?" The King was not irate, merely sounding out his thoughts.

"No city is unassailable, Regis. Anything made by man can be destroyed. It only questions how much effort is required to be made." He tapped the paper at the length of the southern wall. "This wall is stone, but still, it could be reduced in the small part of a morning, if a ram touches it. Here, and here, the barrier is mere brick, and even a log manhandled by our men could knock holes in less time than it would take to prepare."

Another Tribune. "You said yourself, that the approaches would require the men to walk on water, did you not?"

"Aye. Men could approach, certainly, but not rapidly nor carrying any burdens beyond the ladders. With our men wallowing in the mud below the wall, I doubt that we would have any greater success in scaling than our last efforts."

"So, the fact that the walls are weak gives us little reason to rejoice." This was from Sextus again.

The King spoke and the murmurs died to quiet. "You have not spent your time in this study to tell us that the conquest is impossible, Ingeniarius. What is your recommendation for our problem?"

Marcus pointed to the southern part of the map. "We assault this wall, here and here, and with two, or possibly three rams. They need not be the size and heft of our last, as the mortared stone will collapse with any impact of magnitude."

Sextus spoke with some exasperation. "You have already said that the approach to that wall would swallow even the feet of the gods in mud! Do your plans for the new rams include wings?"

Marcus shook his head. "Nay, Sos. The stream... here ...is far enough from the wall to be out of any range of shafts, and any trying to destroy a bridge being built would face the same problems as an attacker. They would stumble through sucking mud from the western gate and arrive too weary and wet to strike their flint."

"But..."

"We build a road across the flats... from here ...made of logs laid crosswise and a walkway of planks on the top. Now, both builders and assaulting troops can run, dry shod, and without hinderance. And, such a roadway would not be conducive to burning - it would have to be attacked with hordes of men and disassembled with much effort. And, if our foe wishes to leave their walls to wade through mud to attack men standing dry and fresh - that would be goodsome."

Collatinus spoke. "Will such a wooden road stand against the flowing waters that might come."

Marcus shook his head. "You have hit the mark, Sos. We can begin to assemble our materials even now, but not to lay the roadway until the end of the wet season."

The talk went on, with this objection being taken, and that plan for its overcoming given. Finally, Marcus stood back to allow the King to give either credence or condemnation of his presentation.

It took only moments.   Tarquinius pursed his lips, then nodded. "Make it so."

Book 6

Intermissionis

Time passes...   (Tempus)

The years were good to Marcus.   His family and fortune waxed and grew with every passing year.   As his sons passed their second year and were now much more likely to survive until adulthood, they were named.   Unlike many double births, these were not as alike as peas in the pod.   Rather, while both had the same physique, they were as unalike as any ordinary brothers.   One became the Young Marcus, while the other honored the friend of their father, and gathered the name of Lucius.   And a pair of years after, they were joined by their sister, to become the Younger Sabina.   At least, that was her given name.   All knew, that in reality, the girl was the apple of her father's eye.   And later in her life, as she developed into a woman no less beautiful than her mother, woe unto the young man who cast his gaze in her direction without the sanction of the father.

The service of Marcus in the army did not end with the victory at the city of Suessa Pometia.   With his performance in the seemingly impossible reduction of the walls of Gabii, assumed by its defenders to be secure behind the soldier-swallowing swamps and water-lands, his opinion was deferred to in all future sieges.   His wood-roads across an impassible wetland were quickly built and soon allowed the massive Roman army to approach the walls of the city - walls that were quickly reduced to rubble and turned into gates for the Legionaries to enter the city.

His unit was the topic of many tales of admiration, in the taburna of cities, and around the fires of the encampments.   In jests - as in stories of heros of other lands - he was given the ability to wave his baton and part the waters before his men, or to call on the sprites of Neptune to have the swamps magically drain away.

Other towns and cities were discovered to be plotting invasions and war against the city of Rome, and naturally, the King had to meet the threats with defensive measures of violence.   No other walls of the magnitude of the first were encountered, but even a palisade made of wooden poles can be enough of a barrier to wreak havoc on the attacking forces.   Other rams were made, some with wheels to allow the structure to be rolled into action, and others to be carried if the ground to the assault were rough.

In addition to the engines' ability to reduce any gate to stovewood, he examined the possibility of assaulting a wall directly, but in a way in that the men on the ladders were not as marks in an archery tournament. The result was a tower, again on huge wooden rollers, that could be trundled to the wall and against it, allowing the soldiers to climb in safety, and engage the enemy from a platform at their level, and in sufficient numbers as to not be overwhelmed at the first contact.

And, with the success of his structures in the siege of Signia, his standing with the army and the King were risen to a stellar height. His unit of forty or so, had expanded to almost a thousand, and his word could cause a thousand trees to be felled, and wagons of iron to start on the road to his purpose. The quartermasters hastened to find his needs, rather than face the wrath of the King by failure to provide.

And with the rise of his reputation and rank, the wealth of his household followed. The mother of Sabina, Decima, had been no dull slattern-wife. She was intelligent and educated by her late husband. To Marcus, she gave advice that increased his fortune greatly. "Gold in a chest is of less use than old rags - those, at least, might be used for work by the maids. Coin is an attraction for thieves and robbers, and if known by the taxman, a target for their usury." So, with her assistance, he engaged a factor to invest his holdings of coin. And over the years, the value of his apartments and mortgages and loans came back many fold, to require even more effort to find a use for the increase.

In time, property was obtained across the street from the household and became the clothery of the House of Callidus. Sabina and Decima had a dozen weavers and loomers turning out fine clothes in linen and wool. Many were the noble women - and not a few of the Plebeians - who were sporting the garments of the house before their friends. And, with Decima passing judgment on every thread that left the premises, woe to the girl who gave work that was less than perfect.

In the course of the years, the enviable happened to the young apprentice, Ennis. A young maiden attracted his eye and he eventually asked for the permission of his master to wed. The young man had become an excellent bowsmith, in ways even surpassing his master - a given, since the time of Marcus was often taken by the army, to the detriment of his experimenting with wood and glue. Permission given, Marcus dowered the girl and loaned for the purchase of a house and kiosk for the couple. The smithery of Ennis and wife soon began to produce weapons greatly prized by the weapons merchants of the city. It took only a few years before the loans were returned in full and with interest.

Marcus knew that the same would happen to the even younger apprentice, Flavis. He had not yet the years for beginning an independent life, but he was already fishing the waters for his life mate. The nightly couplings between him and the young kitchen maid were not as discrete as the young couple thought. In fact, the pair of youngsters were the only persons who thought their unions to be secret - to all others in the household, it was an amusing dissimulation for casual talk when away from the ears of the young lovers.

But, now with his rank of Ingeniarius, he was privileged to have his own Adiutor, and he selected the young boy as his aide when Flavis had reached his growth. Of course, the youngster had no learning beyond what he had received on the street, or at the house of Marcus, but Sabina took him in hand, and for two hours a day, he learned the rudiments of numbering and scribing notes on wax. A scribe he would never be, but within the year, he could decipher and create written messages and even add and subtract to an extent. To a boy, formally a street urchin, whose normal life would have been to forever perform manual labor for a copper a day, the idea of being the aide to the famous officer of the army was overwhelming.

The household of Marcus and Sabina became the hub of the social life of the Viminalis quarter. No invitation was more eagerly sought by the citizens of their street than one to the atrium in the House of Callidus. And the societal interactions did not start and end on the street in the quarter. With the auspices of the House of Brutus, and the fact that he was an obvious favorite of the King, they became frequent visitors to other noble houses as well.

Marcus knew that his house would never become truly noble - even his ability and growing wealth was insufficient to break that Roman tradition from the ancient ages. But, his sons and daughter would be of the Patrician class, eventually, should his stature continue to grow in the city.

Young Marcus, and Young Lucius, as they approached the date of their manhood celebration, were as small images of their father in body, and would match it when grown, but each was as different in outlook as wine and water. And they were unlike that very young man that had once descended from the mountains in that they were as literate as a sage in the temple. Sabina had begun their learning of the written marks early, and had filled in her lack of knowledge with tutors - a novice-priest from the temple of Alon taught the numbers and a sage from the magistracy of records made them familiar with the history of their peoples.

As the two boys reached their size, Marcus engaged a Hastilarius to impart training with the short sword and the dagger - not in any wish to prepare them for war, but to allow them to stand tall against bullies and street ruffians. He still well remembered a young man without such ability, walking the streets of Rome at night, and the painful result of the lack of such knowledge.

Young Marcus learned the skills but had little interest in weaponry whereas Young Lucius was as a copy of his father and more. He reveled in his growing prowess with the blades and even the short throwing spear, the pilum. His bow skills were growing as well, and while not of a level with his pater as yet, there would be a day come when the age-declining proficiency of the father would be exceeded by the young eyes and aim of the son.

The friendship between the Patrician house of Brutus and his strengthened over the time. Brutus, also, had two sons closely approximating the ages of the twins of the house, and many were the times that one or both sons would visit and overnight at the house of the other. And included often, were the sons of Collatinus and other noble houses and prosperous merchants. Young Lucius mirrored his father in greatly enjoying the hunt, even without the need for vending his kills in the market. The groups of young men, led by him, would have been the envy of generals the world over, had they seen the weapons that were being used and the skill of their usage.

However, as time passed, Marcus noted the growing belief of the younger members of the house of Brutus - and others - to consider themselves as intrinsically worthy and somehow superior to others in the city, merely because of their fortunate accident of birth into a noble household. He remembered the story, given by the mater of Lucius, the Domina, that she had received the lesson that even a noble lady was not to consider herself above the work of a servant, should that become necessary. He had no desire that his children grow up as thinking of themselves to be the sons and daughter of a wealthy Plebeian family, and that menial tasks were below their stature.

Therefore, Marcus and Sabina taught both sons, and later the daughter, the meaning and value of work.

Young Sabina learned to sit and move the shuttle back and forth, just as if she were a loom girl. Naturally, she protested the menial labor as better suited for a servant than the daughter in a wealthy house, but her mother quickly and physically quelled her resistance.

For the two boys, he had them assist Cleo in procuring supplies for the house, and to wield the wood shaver to rough cut staves for Flavis. Or unload the stovewood from the cart of the vender and stack it in the kitchen. But, they were as unalike in desires as they were in looks. Young Lucius had an interest in bowsmithing and hunting as his father, and early on could build a decent weapon for the use. However, his brother, Young Marcus, had as little interest in woodwork and animal lore as Sabina, and his work gave good measure of that disinterest.

The house of Pythes was the answer for that problem. The old merchant was now reaching the years in which he could no longer travel the long roads up and down the coastal cities, and even Valens was feeling the passing of time in his bones. So... Young Marcus was apprenticed to the merchant, to learn the trade and use his ability at numbering.

An interesting bit of news was given to him one night, as he lay with Sabina. She spoke of the son of Collatinus and his apparent attraction to their daughter. They were seen together much more often than would be in the case of a casual acquaintance. But, only with propriety, she hastened to say - and always with others within view. Sabina had no wish for the natural protectiveness of a father to cause severe harm to a young suitor - especially with Marcus, whom she knew would trounce any young man who gave the slightest offense to his daughter - no matter the antecedents of the boy.

As the years passed, the city of Rome waxed in both size and power, as the King built and rebuilt temples, shrines, and civil structures. It was not a time of unbridled joy for the citizens, either Plebeian or noble. For the latter, the Throne and the advisers closely held, gave no credence to the desires of the Senate, preferring to rule by decree. Many Senators and magistrates who were seen to be obstacles in that path, were accused of treason for this act or another and executed, their family fortunes and properties seized.

The men of the upper houses were not weaklings - not all, at least, and more than one overbearing officer of the court failed to appear at his duties on occasion, never being seen again within the walls of Rome. The mood of the city had not risen to a point to be near rebellion, but it was an uneasy time.

For the lesser families - the far more numerous Plebeians - the overbearing had a different flavor. Rome was unique in the world as having few taxes on persons or their belongings. Rather, the continual flow of loot and seizings fed the construction of the city. It was the forced laboring on the projects that were the grit in the sandals of this carpenter, or that stone carver. Wharf hands and fishermen, bakers and drovers - all took a turn at loading and hauling and lifting. Required to assist upon demand, their hours were long and the pay was low and the work often would last for the month or two before they were allowed to return to their own occupations. Then, to be called again in the next year.

Marcus was not the only citizen whose fortunes waxed. His sponsor and friend, Lucius Junius Brutus had served the King well, and with distinction over the years, and also the people, with whom he had a reputation for honesty and fairness. It was the quadrumvirate of Brutus, along with Publicola, Collatinus and Tricipitinus who had finally removed the despicable Caeus from his position as Praefectus to the King. The cruel ravages among the people were finally his downfall, as the four Tribunes - now Senators, all - exposed his rapacious theft of money and property from all in the city - through false accusations of treason, adultery, or other crimes. With Tarquinius consumed by his lifelong ambition to make Rome the envy of all in the world, even he became filled with revulsion of the actions of his subordinate. Upon the advice of the quadrumvirate, he removed the man from office and created a new position - that of Tribunus Celerum, or Tribune of the Knights. As Brutus had the respect of the people, and had served the King without fail over the years, the position was bequeathed to him.

Only a few - Marcus, Collatinus, and the Domina - knew that Lucius had sworn vengeance for the murder of his Father and Brother by the King. And that it was still foremost in his thoughts.

During the years, the immense desire of the King to expand the reach of his Throne never ceased. The warfare seldom stopped, and even then only for the purpose of consolidation of the gains already made. Smaller cities knew their chances of resistance were nonexistent, and sent delegates to Rome to gain advantage in discussion. And, usually, upon payment of annual tribute and taxes, and the supply of a force of soldiers - sized to the population of the young men of that city - to assist the Roman army, they were left intact and with their leaders still in the ruling chairs.

Except for the Latin city of Ardea, the capitol of the people of Rutuli, now in revolt from the heavy hand of the Roman tax farmer...

Large and powerful themselves, and with massive walls fronting wetlands and waters that did not allow access by the engines of the Roman army, they sent the Roman demands for capitulation back with polite, but firm scrolls of refusal.

By now, the King had begun to believe in his own infallibility, and the refusal by Rutuli struck like salt in an open wound. Disregarding the advice of his Generals and Tribunes, he launched a war against the despicable peoples that had dared to refuse his demands.

Thus, Marcus and his well-trained unit of builders were once again set on the march to war...

Book 7

Chaos

March

The entire family was gathered in the atrium, including all the house servants and workers. Even Pythes had arrived in his chair - a necessity for his age, now. Marcus was giving his last orders and farewells, although all knew their duties and what was expected during his absence.

To young Lucius, he said, "Remember our reputation amongst the weapons merchants, and let no wood be vended that you would not be proud to own yourself."

And to his other son, young Marcus, he advised, "You also should heed our values, and give fair weights and measures to all your dealings." Looking up at his old warden, Pythes, he grinned and said, "I would not take it amiss should you have to beat your apprentice on occasion."

And to his daughter, now becoming a young mirror of her mother, he merely took her by the arms and kissed her forehead.

But it was to his wife that he gave his last words before parting. And she would be the one in his thoughts at leisure times. Sabina was now a mature and still beautiful woman, unlike most of the female mates on the street, who became rotund and heavy from both overwork and child bearing. The springtime beauty of that young girl from years ago had been replaced by a confident and assured woman, capable of running a large household and a clothing merchantry that was patronized by most of the well-to-do women of the city. And she was received as an equal in the houses of her noble friends, Lucretia, wife of Collatinus, and Iulliana, now the wife of the Tribune and Senator Amulius Tremerus. And others of her age.

Marcus also, was popular within the houses of the nobles, although he enjoyed such gatherings much less than Sabina, preferring to spend his hours in the work of wood, and bows, and, even engines of war. But, in the mate of Iulliana, the Tribune Tremerus, he found another with the love of hunting, and together they roamed the forests of the low mountains - each with the latest bows made by the younger Lucius or Ennis the bowsmith.

Now, with a final farewell, he motioned to his Adiutor - a young man by the name of Flavis - and they departed down the street toward the Forum, then across the city to the assembly area. Sending Flavis to secure a pair of mats in the senior officers barracks and to leave their equipment, he walked to the headquarters building. It was obvious that no meetings were in session, as the Tribunes and senior Centurions were standing in the shade of the veranda and conversing. He heard his name in a hail.

"Yo, Marcus!" Collatinus was waving, and he turned his steps to approach the group.

Collatinus was the senior Tribune for this campaign. His friend Brutus had not attended the army for the reason of a minor malady that kept him abed for a while, and the fact that as the officer of the Senate, he had much to do in the city of Rome of more importance than watching yet another siege. In the King's absence, he was the defacto ruler.

"What do you think, Marcus?" Collatinus vaguely waved toward the city, hundreds of stadia away along the southeastern via. "This looks to be another Satrium," he said, speaking of another city a few years in the past, built on much the same landscape as this one.

"Aye, Sos," he replied. "But in this case, they have no river to draw on, to flood our paths even deeper - just a stream feeding the canals. It will require only work - there is nothing new here to fill our days with planning." Marcus was well acquainted with the area around the city that was the target of their new campaign - he had taken a contingent of his officers on a journey to Ardea and spent several days surveying the land and marsh around it.

The Tribune nodded. "I would say that you use the ranks for any tasks not requiring skill. I want no repeat of the siege of Tarbol, with the idleness of the men causing more blood amongst themselves than had the enemy assailed by night."

Marcus nodded. They had learned long ago to keep the army busy, even if there was no battle in prospect - especially if there was no fighting to be done. An idle army was a toy that the gods of mischief made play with.

The city of Ardea was about twice a hundred stadia from Rome - a day's march - although it was only about twenty stadia from the coast, which would allow for shipborne supply of the army. The Via Ardeatina leading between the cities was broad and well maintained, so the route could be traveled at speed in all weather, save snow.

The move to the city was without event. The marching formation that the Romans would use for centuries was now beyond its early infancy and, while modified on occasion, became the standard.

Firstly, the light cavalry would invest the road many stadia ahead of the marching force, looking to the flanks for any foe in waiting. Behind them would be a century of Rorarii, young men lightly armored and equipped with short spears only and capable of rapid movement to any direction. They would engage any ambuscade with speed, giving the following army time to form for battle.

Next was the contingent of bowmen, usually no more than two or three centuries in number. At this point in time, Rome had not discovered the advantage of a mass of archers, standing on a high point, raining sheets of death over the heads of their own soldiers to fall unhindered into the bodies of their foe. Many of the bowmen were from far countries to the east, where the weapon commanded much more respect than in the great city.

The heavy cavalry preceded the King and his staff, ready to make a massive barrier between him and any who might pass the fighting to the front. These were the nobles of the city and the officers of the army - the only soldiers who could possibly have the coin for the purchase of their steeds and the equipment to accouter them. The worth of the equipage for a single mounted noble could exceed that of even a prosperous merchant in the city.

Following the body of the headquarters, with not only the mounts of the King and his staff, but those of innumerable aides and servants, were not a few useless hangers-on in the form of over-weight and over-aged Senators and sons of important personages of Rome - come to gather boasting rights upon their return to the city.

It was now that Marcus and his unit of constructors and workers would pass. Almost half a thousand in number, they had wagons of tools and supplies - everything required to build any engine required, save the actual wood from the trees. Behind him were the noncombatants that any army had to have to survive away from their home - the quartermasters, medicos, commissary units and suchlike.

Then, only after that huge preamble had passed - one that was larger than many armies of major cities in the world - did the power of the Roman army pass. Rank upon rank and file upon file of men, not uniformed with any consistency as would be done in the future, but in the main looking alike with their leather armor and helms and long spears. More light cavalry roamed the flanks looking for any interlopers that the preceding scouts had missed.

Then, even though any sane enemy would pause from attacking such a force, even spread out along the road, another century of Rorarii would bring up the rear, in protection from a very unlikely foray from the area that had been passed.

And this was only the army of Rome. Boosting their numbers by half would be the forces of the allied cities of Latium, also on the march by whatever road lead to their foe.

As was usual, the first days were sent in investing the city and erecting the encampment in the neat and regular grid layout that was fast becoming the signature of the Roman army in the field. Again, Marcus had voluminous notes about both the city and its environs and were the first items laid out for use as the tents went up. Unlike those early years of his career as a newly hatched Ingeniarius, with a single aide and Centurion for his unit, and responsible for all planning of his own, now...

His tent was filled with his officers, all gathered around the table and examining the maps, and the small wooden models that could be set in place to give a visual impression of what was being discussed. Long ago, he had discovered that an actual representation of a ram, or tower, or wall - anything - could give a much greater visual impact than mere words. On his staff was a model maker with apprentices who could build, in miniature, anything - and to any scale.

Behind the engineering officers, now being called Architecti after the sprites that assisted Ceres, the god of builders and maintainers, were the foremen that would guide the actual constructions - and those that would command the tree felling, stripping and dragging. The problems of the assault on this city were much as those of the siege of Gabii - large areas of marshlands and artificial canals crossing all of the other open areas made a direct attack almost impossible - at least, by the capabilities of the army in the early years of his career. Now, there was no hesitation - no wondering at what might be effective and what might fail. The men under the command of the Ingeniarius were experienced by years of battle-work and fortified by success - no city wall had ever failed to yield to their constructions if the foe was so unwise as to refuse to grant acquiescence upon the demand of the King. And the city of Ardea would be no different.

In a short time, the route of no less than three log vias across the swamps for attack were surveyed and the required spans to cross any canals were detailed. Towers and rams would follow, depending upon the necessity at the ends of the wooden roads over the marshes. Before the day was over, axes were ringing in the forest and oxen were dragging the trimmed logs to the work area.

Marcus, himself, was a Commander now, rather than a worker, to his regret. His days of actually wielding the hammers and measuring sticks were far behind him. He spent his days in examination of the city of the foe, and the measures that were being prepared against it - and in consultation with the King in his field tent. His senior Architectae were tried and tested, and Marcus had no qualms about their work. All knew that he accepted advice from even the most junior officer, to weigh and decide on its goodness - and would give credit to the man who made or discovered a new method or improvement.

During the periods of quiet, over the past years, his friend Lucius had given him lessons in equestry. Now, while he was no fell horseman, he could ride here and there with some competence. When his friend had proposed the learning, Marcus had protested his total disinterest in acquiring such a skill, but Lucius insisted, with the statement that a man who rode to his tasks could accomplish much more work than a man who had to walk the distance to his work. And that he would get there with much less fatigue in the legs.

Since then, he used his steed daily, to move here, and there, and on rare occasions, to visit Rome and spend the night in his own bed. Many times he requested from the Tribune Collatinus, the company of his aide, Maxentius. They had become close friends over the years, and the elevation of Marcus far above the rank of Adiutor made no change in that. They spoke as equals, unless in the formal ranks of superiors, and many were the nights that they sat and talked - about this and anything.

The days went by, and the three wooden roads began their inexorable march across the soft marsh. At their source, far enough back as not to interfere with the road-builders, and in plain sight of the city, the bases of the towers began to grow. These engines were far more formidable than the ones that Marcus had designed at the start of his career - those merely allowing for soldiers to climb to the height of an enemy wall in safety, and engage their foe at their level.

Now, with ever more improvements after the experience of each siege, they were as advanced over the early towers of those early years as a gladius over a flint knife. The tower moved on huge wooden wheels, solid and built to match exactly the runners on the wooden roads. Taller than the walls of the city they would face, the upper platform could hold a multitude of archers, protected by a low barrier of wood and able to shoot down at their foe, to clear the upper reaches of the wall to be assaulted. And, the Roman bowmen were using a new kind of weapon, one that had much more range and force than the usual stick and string. Both Lucius the Younger and Ennis, the bowsmith, were the suppliers to the selected archers of Marcus. Where the arrows of the defenders would loft, then descend in the hope of striking something, those of the tower archers would spring from the laminated wood with a speed that scarcely allowed the shaft to drop in flight, and usually only stopped when the fletching met flesh. And frequently, should the iron tip not encounter bone, might exit the unfortunate and strike his comrade behind him.

Under the archer platform was the one for the soldiers and with a huge plank, hinged like a horizontal door, that would be dropped to create a bridge for access to the top of the enemy wall. The tower, being covered in the front and sides by wet hides, the soldiers could climb to their required level in total safety from arrows and stones.

And, should the need be found, a ram could be slung at the lower level to pound wall or gate as the assault began.

The plan of attack was not complicated - indeed, it was much more straightforward than many in the past. Only, the distance to be spanned was greater than most, and the bulk of the spring and summer would be needed to prepare the way. And as it turned out, the worry of the Tribune Collatinus was off the mark - it was not the men who were tempted into folly by the length of the siege, but the Tribunes and officers, themselves.

Malignancy

The warm season was far along, and the water of the marsh had receded somewhat, greatly facilitating the building of the long wooden roads. Still, there was one part in three left before the vias would be complete, and the idleness of the army was only partially consumed by work. The work of tree felling and scarfing was moved between units so that all would have a turn in being active, but still, there was far too little need to keep an entire army busy.

The King took small contingents of his force to visit this city and that village to remind the inhabitants of the power that lay within the domain of Rome, but it was for the purpose of being active, rather than any need to suppress any latent rebellion.

For the officers, it was even worse. Of course, they had no hand in the manual labor, needing only to stand by in boredom and give this order or command - and seldom even that, as the men were effectively under the direction of the Centurions of the units. They spent the evenings, and into the nights, with their drinking and dicing - anything to alleviate the unending days.

Marcus was fortunate in that his days were filled with inspections and consultations about the roads and engines and such. By fall of night, he had little need nor desire to dally and carouse with the officers. Far more often, he would sit by the light of the oil lamps of his tent, looking at plans and proposals as Flavis wrote his directions for the morrow in wax tablets. On occasion, he could hear the bellows of laughter or moans of defeat from the adjoining shelters, as this jape was given, or that fellow lost the throw of bones. Even Collatinus, one of the most steady of the Tribunes, declared to Marcus on occasion that he and his fellows were as useless baggage thus far in the campaign. The night before, he admitted the same, again. "The Tribunes could well have stayed in Rome until your work is nearing completion, and your young man, Flavis, could have taken charge of the Legion, for any use that any of the officers have been."

Publicola was with him, both having come to the tent of Marcus for the evening meal. "Aye. The sages, with their stories of the glory and triumphs of war, were speaking with their scribblings, rather than with experiences." He emptied his cup and reached for the wine jug. "I have commanded my Mille in... how many cities have we assaulted? I have long lost count, but in every conflict, my only orders have been to move forward to the wall, then to watch from afar as the men disappear into a mass, not even discernible as a fighting unit. I doubt that the scribes of history will give effusive words to the mighty

Publicola, standing on the field of battle, heroically directing the victory from afar with his words and pointing fingers."

Collatinus glanced at Marcus, knowing that his noble friend was working himself into a black mood. "What we have been engaged in, my dear Publicola, is not war, but subjugation. Rome is like the bully of the street, given size by the gods over his fellows, and who makes himself master of the avenue by virtue of his bulk, rather than any intrinsic goodness or even worth. Should the cities of the south realize that they are doomed one by one, and band together as a single force, then we will not be cursed to sit in our tent and dice to pass the hours. Rather, we will bless the sunrise as we live for at least another day."

"I noticed that the caravan of Florus has set up by the King's compound." Marcus had little use for the corrupt Senator even though their paths had not crossed since those days, years ago when they were both students of the Hastilairius, Dursus, on the training field. His father having long since passed, Caius was now the Dominus of the house of Florus.

Publicola nodded with his cup. "Aye. The crows and wild dogs know when the battle is nigh, although I sully the names of those scavengers to compare them with that cowardly scum. Did I tell you that once, when we were in our classes at the Temple of Jupiter, he and I almost came to blows - until the priest laid into both with his rod? The settlement of honor was to be after the lesson, but as I arrived at the contest behind the kitchenry, he had hired two street toughs to hold his side." Another swallow, then, "But, fear not, when this battle is done, he will be first back to Rome with the lion's share of the plunder of the soldiers, and boasting of his prowess in battle." He looked at Marcus with bleary eyes. "It is a tribute to you, my illustrious Ingeniarius. For him to arrive now gives confidence in your task of reducing the walls - and soon."

"I envy you, Marcus. With your days filled with meaningful work." Publicola was far along in his cups, and tried to rise, but fell back, splashing the purple liquid on his legs.

Marcus looked up at Collatinus, who nodded, then knelt to grasp his friend under the arm, helping him to his feet. "I believe we have intruded upon the time of our friend enough, this day. We will wish you a good night, Marcus."

The next day, Marcus rode around the city to the far side, examining the gate and environs leading to the eastern wall of the city. It was more to give a difference to the day, than any need to gain information - he would have been informed immediately of any change to the defenses.   Upon his return, at midday, he was surprised to hear nothing coming from any of the tent Collatinus.   He asked a young Adiutor of the reason and got a surprise in answer.

"They have departed for Rome, Sos. On a wager of sorts."

"A wager?" That made no sense.

"Aye, Sos. I fear that they were in their cups, and... They were... ah..."

Marcus waved him into the tent. "We are alone, Adiutor. No one will hear of your words from me."

Inside, the aide continued. "Well, Sos. They were wagering on the virtue of each of their wives, and which was the noblest and most dedicated matron of their houses. Thus, a secretive and surprise visit to examine each.   Even the Dux, Sextus, went along with the group."

Marcus shook his head, disbelieving. "That is ridiculous. What do they think to find upon arrival?"

"In fact, Sos, I would not be surprised to find them lost and stumbling on the road by morning. Each was far along in wine."

"Aye. I can believe it.   And they will be lucky should that happen.   The happiness of a household will not be enhanced by a group of drunken men being shown into the atrium, with questions on the fidelity of the wife springing from their lips." It was unbelievable that a group of high-born and intelligent men - not to mention a portion of the officer corps of the Roman army - would act like Cupid-struck youngsters. He wondered what the King would say, should it be brought to his attention that his son and senior Officers had departed on such a mission...

The next day brought an inspection of the first completed tower, and a test roll along the wooden road.   Unlike that first ram, built in secret so as to surprise the defenders, these engines were being constructed in plain sight of the city walls - the hope being that the foe would realize that their doom was certain and only the time until the breach was unknown.   The day was satisfactory, and he had Flavis note only a few changes to be made.

That afternoon, the Tribunes and the Dux returned from Rome, not at all looking either noble or regal. Far too much wine and too little sleep from the night before were obvious in their countenances.   Walking over to the tent of Collatinus, he waited for the Tribune to dismount, then asked, "And which of you won the wager, Sos?"

The noble threw the reins to his horseman and shook his head to Marcus. "You heard, then?" At the nod, he continued, "Wine will

be the ruination of us, should not some action come about - and soon."
He pointed to his tent and they entered, to sit on cushions and rest.
"Our mission to inspect our mates, and without their notice, foundered
on our empty wineskins. I fear to think what my Lucretia thought of
the spectacle of five men entering, and well in their cups, to ask about
her virtue. Or Papiria, wife of Tribune Anthony, who actually ordered
us out of the house. And... others, of which my memory is defective,
but which I doubt were impressed by the visitors."

He just sat for a time, apparently communing with himself on
the subject of self-loathing, then said, "This, I vow, and to touch the jar
only for mealtimes - and well watered - until this cursed siege is
finished." He gave a wry smile. "But, to answer your question, my
Lucretia was gracious and ennobled, even to the sotted boors who
entered her presence. All agreed with that, even if not conceding the
wager. But I make no claim to it - rather I would consign it to a
forgotten thought."

Marcus said nothing, but was glad that the Tribune was
attempting to alleviate his intake of wine. Such imbibing as the
officers had been engaging for the last months would eventually cause
them to develop the belly-swelling wine disease that struck all who
consumed an access of the undiluted drink over time. For Marcus
himself, he had no great taste for wine, and would have preferred to
refresh himself with the clear water that flowed out of the springs of
his boyhood mountain. Alas, water in the lowlands was less than
palatable, and in fact, could cause the disabling flux - or worse - if not
mixed with a portion of wine. It had long been known - if not the
reason - that the mixture was far more healthy than just water alone.

The next morning, a runner came to the tent during the
morning meeting with news of the progress of the road to intersect the
wall in the western sector. "Centurion Balbus sends greetings, Sos."
Marcus nodded and the officers waited for the message. "You are
informed that the via has entered the range of the walls, Sos. A soldier
has collected a shaft in the leg. A fortunate mark out of many, the
Centurion says, but..."

Marcus waved him to silence. "My greetings to the Centurion
and tell him to withdraw the workers out of range. Quiricus..." This
to one of the officers standing at the table. "Send the palisade forward
to position for the via of Balbus. Lucan and Rufrius..." Two other
officers of his staff. "Inspect the progress of the other roads and
determine when the barriers will be needed there also." All three
officers and the runner saluted and departed through the tent flap.

Any work within range of the wall - of any city under assault - would draw arrows as honey draws flies. This he knew from his first engagement. Thus, when work was required in such proximity, such as the extending of the roads to the walls, a movable barrier - the palisade - was used to shield the men on the construction. This device could be moved forward - on skids - as the need required and it was as equally effective on dry land as flooded marsh. And with a pair of archers on duty behind each palisade, watching and waiting, the defenders would soon learn to view the encroaching Romans with caution.

Marcus and his staff rode out to examine the progress. He was satisfied that there was still little chance of a sudden foray from the city to destroy, or delay the buildings of the wooden paths. From the gate to either of the vias in range, and even with the dry weather these past months, the marsh was still wet, if not deep in water. To give battle, an attacking force would have the same problem that faced the Romans, had they tried a direct assault on the city. That is, to slog along the outside of the wall from the gate, through foot-sucking mud to reach their dry shod opponents, and those having much time to enjoy the exhausted slathering of their opponents as they approached.

The third via was aimed in the middle of the southern wall, many stadia from either gate and fairly immune to attack from either direction. Unless, ladders were lowered and a surprise attack was to be launched over the wall. He doubted it, but sentries were on duty at all work points to guard against such at night.

The towers had long been finished, and were waiting at the far end of the roads. Since they spanned the width of the roadway, it was not possible for them to be positioned on the wood until it was finished. Such a placement would be a barrier against the workers as a cork in a jug of wine. Still, the movement would be only part of a day, and would be moved at daybreak of the assault, and reach the wall long before midday.

Now, at least, the officers could see an end in sight to the summer of boredom. With the overwhelming forces at their disposal, even a city of the size of Ardea could only hold out for a few days at the most, after the assault began.

But, as a rock rolling down the hill can be deflected to a new course by a mere pebble in its path, so may the plans of the many shift on the actions of a single man.

"...Sos! Sos! Wake up!" He opened his eyes to see a man standing over the mat, with Flavius holding a torch beside him. It took a moment, but he recognized him as a young aide for one of the equally young Tribunes. His natural reaction was that the soldiers of Ardea had made a night foray into the camp - as unlikely as that might seem - but the lack of any furor outside the tent made that idea remote. Nonetheless, he jumped to his feet, grabbing his belt and gladius as he rose.

"What..."

"The tent of Collatinus. With haste."   He followed the aide as they hurried through the flap and down the path. The night was moonless and the man could barely be made out as a darker patch on the blackness ahead. He could tell that the camp was totally quiet and this summons was not a call to arms.

Finally getting his belt latched, Marcus closed up to the aide and asked in a low voice as they walked. "What is happening?"

There was no answer for a moment, then, "I can only say that the Tribunes are as a hive being robbed. Ask me no more."

Did one or more of the bored Tribunes, in their cups, finally take an argument to the point of iron? Or... Or... He could not think of anything to cause a furor in the middle of the night. Unless, one of them had expired from natural causes.

A torch - not an oil lamp - was flaring in the tent of Collatinus. Marcus stepped through the flap and immediately was surprised to see Brutus standing with the group of Tribunes. His greeting of pleasure was immediately throttled at the sight of the expression of his friend. Rather, the Tribune walked to him and took his arm, guiding him back out of the tent.

Walking to the open area by the now dead campfire, Brutus stopped and released his arm. Then... "This is a night to speak of tragedy, Marcus. And utter evil. Lucretia has succumbed to a dagger by her own hand."

Stunned, Marcus looked back at the tent - or rather, the thin line of light escaping through the flap. He hadn't noticed Collatinus during the few moments that he had been in the tent, but with it full of Tribunes and aides, he could have missed the man. Or, he could have been well on his way back to Rome, by now, after receiving such news of his wife. Still, that line of thought brought no answers. He just began, "What..."

"She was taken, forcibly, by Sextus. The tale is long, but she gave it to me, and it is a case of pure assault and lust, and not on her part."

Had not the words been coming from Lucius, Marcus would have given such a tale a very short shrift. Sextus was indeed a man with ravenous needs for lust - that was well known and had been for

years, but... The idea that the Prince of - the son of the King...
Engaged in the rapine of the wife of a Senator of Rome... That was
barely believable, even coming from a trusted friend.

Marcus suddenly exclaimed, "The Tribune. He will take his
vengeance even as we..."

"Nay! He is already bound for the city, in escort with
Publicola and Paulinus. They will guard against such sudden choler
until the time is right."

Marcus nodded, unseen in the darkness. "Then what can
we..."

He stopped as a hand was placed on his shoulder. "I have not
finished with my tale on this night of woe." A hesitation, then Marcus
felt his entire body grow cold, suddenly and without known reason.
"I... At the evening..." Another pause. "Sabina was in attendance
with Iulliana, no doubt all of them doing womanly things with gowns
and hair and bows. My sister had left, but... your mate tarried to
assist Lucretia with... with..." There was a loud intake of air from his
friend. "The man of Sextus, the one known as Petronius, had traveled
as escort to the city with the Prince, and he apparently accosted
Sabina, even as his master was committing his wicked deed." Marcus
said nothing, just standing, frozen as a stone statue of some forgotten
ancestor. "Your good wife did not acquiesce with favor. By the tale
of the housemaid, she fought as the Furies, until the man overpowered
her with his strength. But, in the struggle she assaulted his
pouchstones with her leg and his grip was broken enough to allow her
to rise and began to flee, but to no avail." Another pause. "The cursed
spawn of Hades gave into his fury and thrust his pugio into her."

Brutus took Marcus by both arms. "I would make any pact
with the gods not to be the one to bring you the news, but... Your
good Sabina has passed on to the slopes of Olympus. And without
shame and any ruination by a man. She is a tribute to the fierce tribe
from which she was named."

Marcus just stood, as time stopped for him. The words of
his friend were not even yet accepted by his being. Instead, he was
standing as a dead man, his thoughts not even moving through his
being.

Malignity

Even though the Tribunes had attempted to keep the sordid tale of the night close to themselves until a formal agreement on the action to be taken was formulated, it spread like wildfire through the camp. And, the King, through a series of missteps, threw more kindling onto the blaze.

At first light, as the court nobles brought word of the actions of his son, he stood in disbelief until the Prince had been summoned to his quarters. Then, listening to the tale of the accused - he giving a sordid story of a noble woman lying with a slave and being marked for death to prevent scandal on her house - assumed that it was truthful and laid the blame onto the shoulders of a wanton woman. His words, overheard by the contingent of Tribunes that had gathered in the headquarters tent, stunned all who heard, and even those who had received the tale on the second or third speaking. The defense of the Prince, by denigrating a woman whom all present knew to be a most gentle and dignified matron of Rome, infuriated the Tribunes almost to mutiny.

Still, the greater surprise of the officers was for the reaction of the common soldier - at least for those of Roman birth. It was true that many Legionaries were hoping for gain from the war, and others were here from a desire for adventure, or to leave a destitute and tiresome life, but all had a sense of pride in their serving of the city. But... The news that a helpless woman was set upon - and in her home - by not only a soldier from their encampment, but by the man on whom the crown of King would descend... Then, as the word spread that the perpetrator was to be cloaked in innocence, giving all blame for the woman, the wildfire spread beyond containment. Torches flared all over the encampment as the entire army awakened to the news. Despite the attempts of the Centurions and Optios and Decanuae to gain order, the men refused to renter their tents - all milling in their own groups trading this news for that gossip.

Marcus, among the officers, was almost the only one without surprise at the reaction. He could have told his fellows that even a common man looked upon his women with no less affection than those of the gilded classes. If a woman from a household of the highest class could be a victim of rapine and pillage by an officer of the King - without penalty - then what chance did an attractive girl in the lower quarters have?

Brutus had stayed by Marcus until the morning, for support and any assistance, but mostly to assure that his friend did not storm into the tent of the King with gladius in hand. It wasn't the skin of the Prince that he was worried about, but that of his friend. He well remembered how the same favor from his young Adiutor saved his own life, years ago, when the same royal family caused harm and rage to the house of Junius.

Before first light, Marcus and Brutus, along with several Tribunes and their aides, set their mounts on the road to Rome, leaving behind an encampment still boiling as an ant heap, kicked by a boot. In respect to the man with the loss, the men let him ride alone and tempered their conversation to a level that would not intrude. For himself, his mind was blank, refusing to let in the knowledge of what he was told. Anytime his thoughts began to examine the idea of... what had happened, he savagely jerked his attention back to the road, seeing only the stone distance posts that they passed.

Passing through the gate, they could tell that the city was... disturbed. Not as in a hive of bees that are being robbed, but more as a smoldering mountain that was indicating that the forge of Vulcan was about to erupt. As he turned his horse up the street leading across the city to the quarter of Viminalis, Brutus called, "Nay, Marcus. Sabina is still at the house of Collatinus." Marcus just nodded, and turned his mount to follow his friend.

At the house in the Capitoline, they gave over the beasts to the handler, and entered by the front door. Inside, immediately they were met by the Senator Tricipitinus, the father of Lucretia. The older man bowed and said, "I cannot bring the words to give alievement to this day of sorrow for both you and my son." Marcus also bowed and nodded as the Senator continued, "Know that your wife is laid in repose in our atrium with her friend, my daughter, and it is our honor to do so." The Senator looked at Brutus, then continued. "You may wish to mourn your loss in your own home, and I will well understand, but know that we would consider it our duty to give the Funeris Laudiae to Sabina in companion with that of my... Lucretia."

Marcus was barely listening but nodded in acquiescence. "My gratitude to you, good Sos, and my sorrow for your loss and that of the Tribune. If the members of my household may also give respects within your hospitality, then..."

"Of course. Of course. Even the lowliest servant of your house will be greeted as royalty in their mourning. But, your family is within, even now."

Marcus had little practical use for the deities of Rome - or anywhere else - other than a vague belief in their existence, and no interest whatsoever in some nebulous afterlife. He certainly did not believe that a person, in death, cared where or how they were mourned. It was the here and now that concerned him, and the fact that his lovely partner would never again accompany him on his journey through life.

The Senator and Brutus stood aside as he walked down the wide foyer to the atrium. There, on a bier, was Sabina, laid out beside... Suddenly, he saw the master of the house, Collatinus, come to visit the shade of his own loss, standing beside the other bier. Wordlessly, both looked at each other with full understanding of the other's forfeit. For Marcus, the fury toward the man who caused the harm to Sabina would come - and soon - but not yet, as he was still consumed by his loss and sorrow.

But... For Collatinus, the self-loathing was white hot, as he knew the cause of the evil and the person who had unleashed it. To the end of his days, he would curse the drunken boasts of that night, when the bored officers stood into Rome in their quest to examine the virtues of their wives, and only on the basis of a stupid and meaningless wager. But for that foolish bit of pride, the women would still be sitting and weaving their female desires, waiting for their men to return from the war.

Never again was he seen to drink from a cup of undiluted wine.

Beside Sabina was her mother, Decima, who looked up at her son-in-law with water filled eyes. And beside her was his... her two sons and daughter. Away, and standing against the ceiling pillar, was Cleo and Ennis. All just looked at Marcus, and with no words, as he walked to the bier and looked at his wife.

As all knelt in quiet sorrow, the house was continually visited by Senators, magistrates and nobles from all quarters. Brutus and Tricipitinus, both, quietly told them to meet in the Hall of Assembly in the Forum, that being the only building in the city capable of holding so many. In a while, both left, leaving a steward at the door to direct any further enquiries to follow - and to make sure that the mourners in the atrium were not disturbed.

Eventually, Collatinus stood and walked across the room, wordlessly putting a hand on the shoulder of his fellow mourner. With a slight motion of his eyes and head, he indicated for Marcus to follow him to an alcove off the atrium, overlooking the garden. There, both sat on a bench, waving away a servant carrying cups.

Eventually, Collatinus spoke. "My friend. I have no words to express my sorrow for the loss that you have sustained in my home. A lifetime will not be sufficient to repair the harm." Marcus just shook his head, but before he could reply, the Tribune continued, "I will not ask for your forgiveness, but know that I would give my own life if I could reverse the injury done to you and your family."

Marcus just looked into the garden, unseeing for a moment, then... "There is much blame to these acts, and it will be addressed, but none of it is of your making, Sos.   Already, you have shown much honor to my... family.   It is the act that I do not gather.   For what reason would Sextus and his men leave the camp to journey to Rome for such a heinous deed?   It is not that there is a lack of camp followers for their use."

Collatinus just stared into the distance for a while, then... "There is a reason, and it is despicable - even in the eyes of those gods for whom whimsey is a game, but I pray you do not ask me this day."

Marcus looked at the Senator and Tribune for a moment, wondering...   Finally, he said, "Aye, but what is done is done, and no explanation will temper our losses, but this I vow - that the man Petronius will regret the day that his father lay with his mother in that cursed coupling that spawned his being.   I will leave the Prince for your retribution and will not rob you of his atonement."

Collatinus laid his hand on the shoulder of his friend.   "Aye, my friend.   But... Do not initiate an action without thought.   Both men have no doubt of their peril, and will be well guarded against any sudden foray on our part.   Do not through your life away to the blades of his men."   Looking back over his shoulder, he continued,   "Let us not dwell on the facts that cannot be altered."   "Rather, we can use our losses for the common good.   Come, Brutus has asked us to attend after our grieving this day."

Puzzled, Marcus followed the Senator into the street and along the Capitoline Via to the Forum.   The huge square was filled with milling throngs, all of whom knew that the day was as disturbed as dark thunderclouds on the horizon, but most had only tales of the reason - and many of those.   Inside the Hall of Assembly, the nobles were also engaged in loud converse, all giving and hearing tales of the dastardly act that had been performed in their city and by one charged with the sheltering of the citizens.

Suddenly, the pair were noticed as they walked through the entrance and men began to call for silence.   The buzz of talk suddenly quieted as all gave their quiet sorrow to the two men.   Brutus and Tricipitinus, along with Publicola and several of the Senators were standing on the platform overlooking the crowd.   The crowd parted to allow the two men to approach the podium, then to mount the steps and receive the silent and sorrowful greetings of several of their friends.

Then, quietly, Brutus said to them, "This day we will begin the avengment of our families, and the gods willing, turn out the evil usurper of Rome." He turned to the watching crowd and called, "Close the doors and let no man enter or leave until our decisions are made!"

Brutus stood silently for a while, waiting for the building to be secured and marshaling his thoughts. Then, "As Tribunus Celerum, appointed by the King, I call you to order as the ruling members of Rome. With me are Lucius Tarquinius Collatinus and Marcus Callidus - two good men who, like myself, have suffered the ultimate losses at the hands of the King. I will not enumerate the families and citizens of Rome, both Patrician and Plebeian, who have been devastated - nay, even exterminated - by the overbearing greed of Tarquinius."

He paused, then continued, "All of the crimes against our families could, perhaps, be considered by the gods to be in the interests of the glory and growth of Rome. At least to those for whom the losses have not brought heartbreak and sorrow. But now... Now, the family of Tarquinius has committed a crime, not for Rome, but only from lust and hunger of one that belonged to another. Even this might be excused by the gods, as being from the overwhelming needs of some men and the lack of process to contain it. But, the son of the King has not only defiled a noble woman of Rome but has not the manly fortitude to admit his weakness. Instead, he casts the blame on the beautiful and gracious wife of the Senator Collatinus." He glanced at Marcus. "In addition, his weakness is that even his man was not afraid to commit the same offense against the mate of my friend and our celebrated Ingeniarius. Any Plebeian committing such a crime against a woman would be nailed to a crosstree before the sun had set. And a noble would be cast from the Tarpeian Rock with the curses of the crowds below."

"Even though we have much of importance to accomplish, I cannot allow the rumors and tales to continue about both women. I will give the facts as I found them and they will be passed to the cryers of the city to proclaim the innocence of the women." He gestured to Marcus. "The wife of my friend, of the family of Callidus, was as a daughter of Venus, not noble, but with all the aspects of any such, and she was welcomed in the houses of the city, both for her manner and her skills as a clothier. Her name was Sabina, and she was well named. By the sworn testimony of the servants, this fiery matron did not submit to the scum of Sextus without protest. Instead, she fought as if descended from that fierce tribe for which she was named and only succumbed to the iron of the cowardly wretch, after feeling the pain that she inflicted on his man-parts." Another glance at his friend, standing iron-faced before the crowd. "I would not care to be the man known as Petronius when my friend accosts him for his crime."

The crowd was quiet, in respect for the loss just described and for the memory of the woman of Rome, who had passed with honor, even in the throes of despicable perpetration. Now, Brutus gestured to Collatinus. "The wife of the Senator Collatinus was named Lucretia - a gentlewoman who brought honor and grace to his house. She was woman who had never a sour word to any, no matter the quality of that worth, be they Patrician or Plebeian. Lucretia was also a Domina of great beauty, but such description never came from her own lips, but only from those who beheld her."

"You have heard the tale of Sextus, that this... this noblewoman was found in juxtaposition with a slave, engaged in coitus in defiance of both her husband and the mores of civilized society. And that he slew her for the honor of both." He stepped forward and waved with both arms, emphasizing his coming words. "In fact, and on the words of trusted and loyal servants, his tale is shown to be as false as the stories of the god Mendacium. And, indeed, the claim of his slaying of the offending woman is known to be utterly false by myself and her father..." He gestured to Tricipitinus, standing beside him. "...and not from any tellings of the household."

"Now hear the sordid tale from her vantage." The assembly was dead quiet as the men waited for the words from the Tribunus Celerum. "On the night of the deed, as the Senator and I were relaxations at his household, the door burst open and the maid of the good Lucretia entered our presence and cast herself at the feet of the Dominus. The girl brought forth a tale that we could scarcely believe that our ears were hearing, and, in fact, were certain that it was the result of insalubrious drink or food that must have been consumed in that house. In haste, we hurried to the house of Collatinus and there found both the bloody deed that had been cast upon the wife of Marcus Callidus and the crime that had been forced upon the innocent Domina. We were given the story of the violation and butchery by the servants and then by the despairing woman herself." He paused to give the assembly a moment to reflect on something that even now, sounded like a tale of the bards.

"I have to admit to all, that my fury was such that I had trouble formulating the questions that needed to be asked, and I am sure that the thoughts of the father were even more in the extreme. Still, the deed had to be understood so that proper action could be taken. Messengers were sent to summon men, to act as witnesses, so as to have impartial listeners unattached to the family of Collatinus. The Senators Publicola and Tremerus arrived, and were as horrified by the senseless acts of the night as we."

"Now, Lucretia gave her tale to us. The son of the King, she said, had suddenly appeared that night, without notice and without asking for entry. The wife of Callidus was in residence, and the women were doing... women's work with garments and pretties, as is normal for any household. At a word, Sabina and the two female servants were removed from the room, leaving only Sextus and the Domina in the sleeping room of the household, in violation of all the proper forms of our society. There, she said, he demanded that she give herself to him, else the tale would be told that she had been discovered laying with a slave, to the dishonor of the house of Collatinus. Knowing that such a story, even if unbelieved, would crush her beloved before his fellows, she acquiesced. Then, upon his leaving, she discovered the horror that had occurred upon her friend."

He bowed his head for a moment. "Now I will speak of the substance that gives the lie to the claims of the Prince. As we discussed the matter - and most furiously I will say - to decide what action must be taken, the good Lucretia stood and addressed us. She asked for her husband to hear the tale from our mouths and not those of rumormongers and gossip casters. And to ask for his forgiveness for her shame and the disgrace brought upon the house of Collatinus." He walked to the husband of the violated woman and put his hands on the shoulders. "There was much shame and disgrace brought about by the act of the night, but all is reserved for the spawn of Hades, Sextus, and his men. Certainly none can be cast in any amount upon a woman whom all knew to be gentle and gracious, and dedicated to her mate and household."

Turning to the assembly again, he raised his voice. "She suddenly, and without notice, drew a small dagger from her night garment and plunged it into her own heart. We - all of us standing, were caught amiss by the sudden move and before our eyes could deliver the deed to our understanding, the good Lucretia had gone to her place on Olympus."

Quest

The gates of the city were closed and barred, guarded by the veterans of the army who, for reasons of age or infirmity, had not traveled to the war. Any citizens or traders who left or entered the walls had to do so by means of the small sally ports in the wooden gates. These allowed for individuals, and even pack animals to enter and leave, but not wagons or carts. Trade was restricted because of the limited access, but the city could not be stormed through the small entrances.

With the actual army, and most of the young men away with the King, there was little chance that the walls could be held against such force as Tarquinius had in the encampment at Ardea, but such men as had had military training in the past - and sometimes in the far past - were engaged as defenders on the walls. But then...

By the next morning, a happening began that gave hope that the newfound city of Rome might last longer than the time of the next new moon.

Soldiers began to appear on the Via Tibura - the road leading from the city of Ardea. It was soon apparent to all that the Legionaries had made their choice between the King, and their families and friends. Marcus was gratified to see that his entire unit of officers and men had deserted the King in mass, and actually marched back to the city as a disciplined group. And his aide, Flavis was with them.

All day and the next, men flowed into the city and by nightfall of the second day, the chances of Tarquinius taking the city by force was almost nil. The King still had the forces of the Latium cities, but there was no way of knowing - as yet - if those men would stand loyal to a foreign leader whose own men had deserted. Inside the city, the newly arrived men were sorted into defensive units and stood to the walls, waiting.

In the city, the newly formed government hurried to sort out the needs to replace the monarchy - the only form of government that the city had known since its founding centuries ago. By the third day, the agreed structure would be that the monarchy would be replaced by two men, elected by the Senate, and given the rank of Consuls - and only for one year. No action could be taken unless both agreed, and any decrees had to be formally voted on in the Senate. This would, it was hoped, put sufficient obstacles in front of any man who wished to aggrandize his power over the city. Finally and formally, the title and position of Monarch were outlawed for all time.

On the morning following the gathering of nobles in the Hall of Assembly, Brutus and the Senators called a meeting of the leading Plebeians in the Circus. There, he gave the story, truthfully and without histrionics, but with skill, of the happenings in the house of Collatinus. By the end of his speaking, the people were as infuriated by the actions of the Prince as had been the noble classes. And, upon the statement that the Monarchy was now to be removed, to be replaced by a form of government where reasoned discourse would take the place of decrees, the crowd roared as an assembly of madmen. All the day, the crier platforms across the city were thronged with citizens listening to the news, over and again.

By unanimous vote of the Senate, Brutus and Collatinus became the first Consuls of Rome.

Marcus had little to do with either the army or the new government. For a defense, inside the walls of the city, his skills with engines would not be needed, and there was little for the men of his construction unit to do. Besides, he had the task of the Funeris of Sabina before him - not a task that gave him pleasure, but one that he would never assign to another. All came to help - Flavis, Ennis, Pythes, and Valens. And many more were to come by to ask if their assistance could be used. The body of Sabina was now reposing in her own beloved atrium, waiting out the proper number of days until the rites could be completed.

With the army now within the city, the gates had been opened, but well guarded with at least a Century available for each, in case of need, to hold the position until the bulk of the citizen-army could be alerted. Now, the funeral procession could take place in the normal manner, and all in the Viminalis quarter and many from others were there to give honor to the wife of Marcus. He was gratified at the actions of the city toward his wife, but the day went slowly for him. The usual Roman rituals were just as meaningless, and even more, since they were for a person who - to his mind - was long gone away from her physical body. That night, he just sat in the atrium, on the bench that he and she had used for many wonderful sessions of talk, planning this and that and discussing all and anything. The members of the household tiptoed around, not wishing to make the slightest sound to disturb the master. Cleo, especially, threatened any with brutal punishment who vexed the head of the house.

Then for the days after, he wandered the house, feeling the emptiness without his life partner. He watched as young Lucius and his apprentices shaved and polished and laminated, but it was without interest on his part. At other times he would sit in the atrium, and let his mind stop for the while.   On occasion, he walked to the house of Pythes to visit his old warden and young Marcus.   Or, across the street to watch the fine cloth and clothes being made under the eye of Decima, now well into her sunset years but still able to function as an active person, if somewhat more slowly with every year.

And, he sent his aide, Flavis, on this task and that.   No one in the household knew why the young man was gone for days at a time, and none took it upon themselves to ask.   He spent much time in mindless practicing with this bow and that, testing many that his son had produced over the years.   To keep his skill with the weapon as polished as the wood he was using, he would walk to the training field outside the walls and practice his art at a bundle of old leathers and at long range, and taking along a young boy from the streets to retrieve his shafts for a small coin.   It was just a way to pass the time with some enjoyment - he had not been into the forests on a hunt in...   far too long, he realized.

He had little interest as yet with the news of the reformation of the city into something that might, in time, be of great importance, but still, often he would walk to the platform of the Cryer and listen to the daily news.   It was here that he heard that the King had waxed exceedingly wroth with his son, Sextus, who fled to the city of Gabii in fear of his life, hoping that the peoples that he had abused during his stint as governor would give him succor.   Then, also, that Tullia, the wife of the King, had fled the city between dark and dawn, fearing for her life in the retribution of Brutus and the Senators.   And, it must be said, that not a few of the Senators, along with certain nobles and magistrates who had been overly supportive of the Monarchy and had profited by the reign of the usurping King, had also decided that distant climes would be of greater health to them and their families.

But, even in his current state of unconcern, Marcus was gratified that Brutus and Collatinus had taken no actions against the friends of the King.   Even those Senators whose actions might be suspect were not removed from office.   Both men, like himself, had had family members brutally taken from them by the Regency.   The common people would have understood - aye, even applauded any such action against those guilty of the crimes.

Still, the city was waiting as if for some expected, but unheard storm to descend suddenly.   All knew that Tarquinius was not a man to just meekly withdraw from the position of Monarch over the most powerful realm in this part of the world.   Eventually, they would hear of his response to his dethronement.

Marcus woke to voices, wondering why such would be coming from the balcony at this time of night. "...Nay! The master sleeps badly enough without being disturbed at this hour." He could tell from the loud whisper that it was Cleo. "The morning time is sufficient for whatever news you bring!"

"I am following his instructions, and that is to report the instant that I return! Now move aside, else I..." He stopped as the door opened and Marcus walked out, almost nude except for a slight loincloth.

"Your pardon, Sos. But I..."

Marcus waved Cleo to silence, then asked of his aide. "You have news?"

"Aye, Sos. It is true that..." He stopped as a hand waved him to silence.

Marcus looked his aide up and down, then asked, "Were you pursued? I have seen men fleeing for their lives that were issuing less skin water than you."

Flavis shook his head. "Nay, Sos, but my mount went lame, and I was required to travel the stadia from the distance post at the Low Water Bridge on foot."

Turning to Cleo, he gave a series of orders. "Roust the kitchen and have a light repast prepared for my aide. And hot water so that he may refresh himself. We will speak in the atrium when he is ready." To Flavis, he said, "Go and clean yourself and put on dry clothes." Both men disappeared down the stairs, and he turned to don a night tunic before following them.

Telling Cleo to go to his rest, and to order any others in the household that might have been roused to do the same, he and his aide talked for a considerable time in the privacy of the atrium. Then, satisfied, he retired and fell asleep instantly and without the usual hesitation.

"I am sorry, Sos, but the master has been gone this quarter moon."

Brutus was standing in the atrium of the house on the street of the Poet and both young Lucius and Cleo were standing frozen in the august presence of the co-leader of Rome. The rest of the house was in silent hiding, not knowing the reason for such a man to visit a Plebeian house without call. "Gone? And where?"

Lucius shook his head. "Again, Sos. I do not know. He just vanished one night without leave. I saw him to his bed that night, but the next morning the room was empty, and he has not been seen since."

"And he made no notice of his leaving. No indication of the reason?"

"Nay, Sos. But his aide, Flavis had arrived from some task, two... maybe three nights before and with considerable exertion showing on his countenance, as was told to me by Cleo, here. They conversed together for a long while, then the following night both were gone without a word to any." He paused then, "Neither did my brother or sister receive any notice of his departure."

"Did they take their kits? Perhaps to join a unit at the assembly field." Brutus shook his head, then answered himself. "Nay, that would make no sense. He would have reported to me before assuming the service again. And besides, he would certainly have told his sons of his departure."

"And, Sos, neither took their equipment. I have even checked the room of Flavis... his aide. Their leathers and helms are still here. And most of the other equipment that travels with them to war. Only their blades are missing."

Brutus nodded. "Aye. No sane man would leave his own house in this day without arms, even if just to the fruit merchant." He thought for a moment, then suddenly was struck with an idea. "Your father would never consider traveling without his bow. Is it missing?"

Lucius shook his head. "I cannot say, Sos. He had... has several in his quarters, that he would test, or use for practice, and they change from time to time as new ones are made. One could be gone or not. I do not know."

There was little more to gather here, so Brutus took his leave with, "If... when he returns, tell him that his presence is needed at headquarters. It would appear that Tarquinius will not give up his Throne without effort. And I do not wish to go to war without the advice and company of my old friend."

Retribution

The road to Gabii was filled with the normal amount of traffic, with traders and farmers taking their wares this way or that. Still, there was an aura of anticipation, as if a long and black cloud far in the distance might be an approaching storm. Men and their animals hurried, and few stopped to tarry at the numerous kiosks along the way, preferring to take their cups inside the safety of a wall at the end of their travels. Few people in the lands of Latium had any idea of the actual meaning of the turmoil taking place in the upper strata of Roman society, but all knew that some form of upheaval was taking place. And troubles in that ruling city could easily spill over into the lives of people far away.

On the road, also, was an itinerate trader, with his single ass loaded with bundles, and guided by a young man who was probably his son. The man was of indeterminate age - neither young nor old - and was apparently from that great city by the Tiber, as he was clean shaven and carried a short sword - albeit a decrepit and scabbardless blade - in the manner of the men of Rome. But, no matter their antecedents, the pair was unremarked by the patrols and guards along the road as being no different than innumerable like travelers the world over. Certainly, they posed no threat to the tranquility of the land, even in this time of uncertainty after some massive and still not well-understood revolt in that massive city on the Tiber.

The distance from Rome to the city of Gabii was an easy walk in a part of a day for an unencumbered traveler, but for the pair leading an ambling beast of burden, the pace was slowed enough that they arrived only shortly before sundown, but, fortunately, before the gates had been closed for the night. The city was a large one, and taburnae and inns were plentiful, even for such disreputable travelers as they. Of course, they had to show their coppers first, before being pointed to a small cubicle in the rear, with hay for sleeping and their beast, but they settled in comfortably and were soon served a plain, but hot meal by the kitchen.

In the evening, they paid a servant to watch their pack-ass and bundles, then walked into the night among the torches illuminating the main via of the city. The trader had no worries about their putative trade goods being plundered, but it would have been unusual to not give the appearance of concern. Now, both men carried with them the only items of any real worth from their bundles - their blades, exchanged for the two rusted and pitted mockeries that they had displayed in their travel, and a bag containing other garments. And, the older man had a strange looking bow in the carry position across his body.

The appearance of the two was still of being only itinerant traders, clothed in their ragged clothes and re-knotted sandals and with their sharp and oiled blades disguised within stained and ripped scabbards.   Even the bow was encased in a worn sheath to hide the polish and quality of the weapon.

At a wineshop, both entered and found their way to a center table in a room of such tables, illuminated by flaring torches around the walls.   Showing a few pieces of copper, they ordered two bowls of wine and relaxed, listening to the talk around them.   They waited long, and past the time of the evening cups, until the room was almost empty of patrons.   As the taburna keeper came to check on his long sitting guests, the older man asked, "Sit and have a cup at our expense, good Caupo, and tell us what the tale that seems to have your patrons in their excitation."

The taburna keeper was glad to remove his excess weight from his feet after the long day, especially at the expense of another. Sitting, he asked with some wonder, "You are ignorant of the forcible removal of the King of Rome?   You must have wintered in the mountains or other such far lands to have no knowledge of such happenings."

The trader laughed.   "Nay, Caupo.   We are well aware of the usurpation of the city by the Senators, but as our trade does not allow for any long sojourn in any one spot, and we have only bits and parts of the tales of the day.   But, I was referring to some local disturbance, rather than that far story of Kings and Senators.   About some past ruler come again...?"

"Ah.   The son of the King.   Aye, but the stories are intermixed and have cause with each other."   He took a gulp of his overly filled bowl, then continued.   "Sextus, his name is, and he once was the governor of Gabii after a siege by the Romans.   That was before we became into the Roman realm, I am sure you know.   There are tales, and more, of his violation of the women of the city, and the execution of any husband or male member who dared protest."   He looked around, although only two other men were within the room and they far in their cups and beyond caring about other conversation.   "There was - and is - much choler in the city toward the man who ruled us."

The trader just nodded, as if thinking over what he had heard. "But, why has he returned?   To gather support for the deposed King, perhaps."

The taburna keeper shook his head. "As I understand it, his actions of late, whatever they may have been, have required him to quit the city of Rome so as to allow him to keep a whole hide. It maybe so. I know not, but little support will be forthcoming from the people - that I can say. The Patricians and their sons that survived the evil reign of Sextus have vowed vengeance, so the tales go. And I have heard of them enough to believe that there is more than a little truth in the stories of the pledges."

"Where is the man now?" asked the trader.

"I have heard that he is ensconced in the governor's mansion, but in truth, I have never laid eyes on the man." Yawning, the caupo rose from the bench and said, "My gratitude for your custom, Sos, but it has been a full day, and the morrow will come sooner than my legs will desire. I wish you a good night."

Back in the street, the trader said to his younger fellow, "It is just as you said, apparently. Possibly there is an undercurrent that might be diverted to our cause."

The young man looked around to make sure that the dark, under the waning torches, was empty of ears. "Will you contact the nobles of the city, Sos? A small push might bring action."

"Nay. If any should discover that an officer - and his Adiutor - of the Roman army was skulking around the streets, their imaginings would conjure up any number of plots by Rome to further oppress the city. We will bide our time and find an opening."

Both settled onto their blankets, made soft by the hay of the stall, but sleep did not come immediately. Rather, thoughts and musings ran one after another until, "Flavis?"

"Aye, Sos."

"What is the destination for your life? Surely not to be an Adiutor to myself, or another, until you are a doddering graybeard, although you certainly have excelled in the task for me. And you are certainly a competent apprentice to a bowsmith, and in time could become one yourself, except that I know that you are not drawn to the lamination tables as are Ennis and young Lucius."

There was a pause in the dark, then, "Well, Sos... As to what I would have been, had you not taken me under your wing when a dirty street urchin... I can only say that my rank now is almost as King, in comparison." Another pause. "But, truly. I have enjoyment in the army, and would continue it if I may. The work with staves and glue and shafts in your household is... fulfilling, but... I would learn more about the building of structures and engines of war, even to try to approach in some small way, your knowledge of their construction."

Marcus had known for a considerable time the interest of his aide in the work of the Architectae on the field of battle. Many times, during the sieges, he had left Flavis in charge of this minor construction or that, as he was called elsewhere for a time. And, always, the young man competently performed the task of foreman, even ordering changes at times when another method or procedure would enhance the structure being built. Finally, he replied, "I have confidence that, with the help of the Consuls, a position as a Mechanicus can be obtained. I will inquire upon our return." A chuckle in the dark. "Assuming that we do return. But... I see no reason why you might not even ascend to the rank of sub-Ingeniarius in time. Perhaps, even to take my position eventually."

Now there was complete silence in the dark. Marcus knew that his young aide was turning over the conversation in his thoughts, probably even awestruck by the notions that had just been given by his superior. He let the silence stay for a while, then said, "But first, we have our mission ahead of us. And this is what is engaging my thoughts. You will remember my first tasks for yourself when you were barely head-high to my chest..."

This taburna was a hovel, even compared to the ramshackle structures on the north side of the city. The wine was sour and the tables nothing more than rough-hewn stumps of trees. The benches were little better, being logs flattened somewhat on the upper surface to at least serve as seats until the wine numbed the buttocks of the patrons. Marcus had the table in the far corner, next to an opening leading to the little room for storage of amphorae and barrels. Since the door to the storeroom was little more than a ragged cloth hanging from the overhead, he could easily hear any conversation within. With a large coin of silver to the caupo, Marcus had secured the table for several days, and the use of the room behind it for both meetings and sleep. The ragged garb of the two men did not match their purses, but the inn-keeper gladly took their coin and made no notice.

He could hear Flavis, on the other side of the cloth, speaking quietly to a double handful of youngsters, none older than ten or eleven seasons and some considerably less. All were copies of that urchin that he himself had hired for reasons long ago in Rome - dirty, hungry and intelligent with the knowledge of how to exist in the back alleys of the lower quarter of a large city. His aide had had no trouble rounding up as many as needed - not with a purse full of coppers that were plainly heard by the dirty orphans. And, his experience with once being one of the unwashed street urchins, meant that he knew the proper form for gaining their trust.

For three days, the youngsters came and went. During that time, Marcus just prowled the city, looking and listening. Gabii had no forums with Crier's stands to give the news of the day. Rather, in the late afternoon, a gong would sound, indicating the time to gather in front of the Governor's podium, should any citizens wish to hear any news and decrees of the day. A single note of the gong would indicate a day of news. Two would give the notice that something of importance was to be given. If three...

The platform at the gate of the Palace was once the stage on which the King of the city would meet the citizens - either to praise or punish or decree - but with the conquest of the city, and the Royal family banished years ago, the Palace had become the governor's mansion - with the head official appointed by the King in Rome.

And, during his daily walks, he would wander among the houses across the wide street, looking at this and that, apparently interested in the construction of the buildings, from the roofs to the ground.

From the taburna gossip, Marcus knew that the son of the King and his men were ensconced within the mansion for protection from the wrath of his father. Why Sextus had thoughts that the city of Gabii would be a sanctuary for himself was completely beyond understanding. His governorship of the city had been more like the reign of a particularly cruel monarch, and his appetite for the young women of the city - willing or no - had not endeared him to the citizens. As the two years progressed, during which he was the ruler of the city, fewer and fewer young - and not so young women - were seen on the streets and in the market places. All knew that even an escorted and married female could become the instant plaything of the rough-hewn men around Sextus. But, before the wrath of the citizenry boiled over in revolution, Sextus had gone to the wars with his father, and a new governor, of a much milder temper, was installed in his place. But, the memories remained and were still raw - that much Marcus could easily gather from the gossip in the taburnae.

And in fact, even now those memories were being rubbed in the way of a new pair of sandals might irritate a leg still raw from a previous injury. As the urchins of Flavis fanned out across the city to spread their gossip, the citizenry had no difficulty in believing the stories. Indeed, as the tales were told from this mouth to that ear, they grew in the normal way of such stories - and since they were about a man already hated and despised, they were easily expanded out of all proportion to the original telling.

And in fact, the stories of the urchins were partially truthful - being just that the despised Sextus was returned and desired to claim his old rulership over the city. The breathless news that he had already begun his old custom of taking women by force was added as the tale moved from taburna to wineshop. Even the sudden claim that he had already had a man seized on a fraudulent writ, so as to take the beautiful wife for sport, was easily believed by all. Of course, none could name either the husband nor the woman, but that did not delay the spread of the inflaming gossip.

On the forth day, the urchins were overheard talking of the latest offense of the guest of the Governor - some tale involving a young woman being groomed for her wedding day, and suddenly being seized for service to the man despised by all. Like a fire in a field of ripe grain, driven by the strong winds, the fury suddenly kindled across the city. By mid-afternoon it had spread to all corners within the walls and merchantries, and kiosks and homes, all - and even temples - were emptied as the citizens swept down the street toward the Governor's mansion.

The city guard was caught by surprise, and could do nothing but stand arm to arm in front of the Palace gate, spears leveled, as the crowds grew in both size and loudness. The sun was within a handspan of the top of the wall when a stentor-voiced soldier mounted the guard post at the gate and shouted for silence. Then, he gave the word that the Governor himself would address the crowd at the podium platform. Then all heard the gong sound its note, thrice.

Both Marcus and Flavis were watching the crowd move from the gate to the podium, then they disappeared among the narrow alleys of the houses. He had long measured and investigated various vantage points in the city, at places that might give vantage for an onlooker. In this case, they came to a low shed behind a moderately prosperous house, then looking around for any eyes that might be watching, Flavis boosted his master to the low roof, then was pulled up in turn. Quietly, they moved across the roofs of the houses, avoiding those with thatch for cover and remaining on those with wood construction. They moved stealthily, even though it was unlikely that any occupants would be inside with such commotion happening only a street away.

Finally, they came to a point where the podium could be seen, across the main via and over the heads of the growing crowd - a mass of people both restless and still growing. The platform was merely a flat area, just outside and adjoining the Palace compound, made of stone and high - taller than a man, and obviously made so as to give a measure of safety to the King of the past - and now the Governor - from any sudden rush of unhappy citizens. It was even more secure in that there were no external steps to the platform from the street - only an access through the gate that allowed entry from the compound. Even so, the platform remained empty until a double row of soldiers were assembled at the base of the podium, spears and shields at the ready. These soldiers were not Romans - although their officers were from that city - but volunteers from the ranks of the old army of the city.

Both men, in their vantage point, knelt down behind a facade, and watched the activity. In a while, Flavis said, quietly, "Your skill in fomenting the citizens of a strange city is beyond my understanding, Sos. Would not such be a valid method to take any city under siege?"

Marcus was looking over the facade, only his eyes above the wood. Without looking at his aide, he shook his head. "Nay. I am no acolyte of Laverna, no trickster to cozen a mob. But these good citizens are as a boulder on the side of a hill - only a slight push is needed to send the stone rolling down the slope. Such trickery as we made with your boy-soldiers would never deceive a man in the normal way, but with the hatred felt by all to the accursed Sextus, only the minor push was needed. Hatred feeds on itself with little need for outside stimulus."

Now he looked at the young aide. "And, we know not if it will accomplish our desire. Sextus may decide that discretion is the more worthy deed of the moment. Were I he, even now my horse would be at a gallop away from this city." At a sudden clamor from the crowd, both raised their eyes to the spectacle below. An individual robed in the Roman manner appeared on the platform, flanked by several others and even more guards. Marcus knew that this was the governor - and by coincidence, named Marcus, but with the family name of Serranus. He was of a Patrician family, high in the ranks of the nobles and known to be of a mild and retiring nature - probably the reason that he was given the rule of this city, after the rage-inducing reign of the Prince.

But, there was no sign of Sextus. Possibly he was in agreement with Marcus, that distance might be a preferred attribute for this night. That, of course, was the hope. There was no chance of vengeance while the Prince was ensconced within the governor's mansion, guarded well by a troop of soldiers. But, should he take flight to a lesser city...

The Governor raised both hands for silence, and gradually the babbling of the crowd receded enough for him to speak. In a surprisingly loud voice, he began, "Citizens of Gabii! I am distressed that you have been inundated by tales that have no substance, and indeed, not even the least foundation on which to be told. I will not attempt to address the stories that I have heard, as they are altered with every telling and have no genesis in truth. I will say that the governance of this city has not changed, and will not change without direction from Rome. It will certainly not be overturned by the mere arrival of one individual, no matter how august he may be." That seemed to mollify the crowd somewhat - Marcus could see men nodding to each other at the words. "We are all aware of the events happening in the city of Rome and at this time there is some uncertainty of how it will effect Gabii, but by all accounts, there is no change in the status of the affiliated cities. Citizens should go about their lives, and merchantry should continue in the knowledge that our city is at peace and prosperous with trade."

Suddenly, a question was shouted from his audience, followed by a general shaking of heads in agreement with the query. "Why is the dross of the King come to the city, if not to assume his pursuit of our women?" Now the roar of the crowd rose again, causing the Governor to raise his hands for silence again.

"It is true that the son of Tarquinius has come to the city, but for the purpose of avoiding strife in his home city - and not with any writ to assume a position in the city. I vow this to be true. I have neither orders nor authority to allow his inclusion in the governing in any way, and without such and will not do so." He paused to allow his words to be examined in their entirety. Finally, he began again. "Now... Sextus Tarquinius is a free man, and a noble, and a member of the regency. We... I do not know the outcome of the upheaval in Rome and which agency will be the primary that assumes the mantle of rule over the lands. But, remember that the King is still King, and, by all reports, has a considerable army at his disposal. It would not be in our interest to give violence to his son. Any father among you would be wroth at such offense to his own, and to do such to a man with such power would be mad."

He gestured to a guard Captain behind him, then turned back to the crowd. "I will present the son of the King, Sextus himself, and allow him to assure all of his benign intentions toward the city. You may see that he is invested with no trappings of authority in Gabii."

Marcus watched through narrowed eyes as the hated man walked to the front of the platform, accompanied by several aides, or associates - all armed, but not garbed in any noticeable fashion that they were in an official capacity. This was a boon of the gods, completely unexpected but utterly welcome for that. Flavis watched also, with eyes wide open in apprehension, then whispered unnecessarily, "There he is, Sos."

Marcus made no comment and only an automatic nod. For him, time had stopped as the face of the vile and despicable criminal that had taken his reason for being, appeared in his vision. He heard nothing of the speech of Sextus, as the man attempted to dull the hatred of the crowd for a man that had caused much harm to their city. He saw little but the man standing on the platform, as if he were staring down a long tunnel at across stadia of emptiness. Had his thoughts been of a normal nature, even he would have been surprised at the calmness of his demeanor at this long sought meeting.

Without any conscious volition, he rose to his feet and nocked the arrow on the string - the single shaft that he had selected from the hundreds in his workshop. It was perfect, with a straightness and balance that even Apollo would have claimed as his own, and tipped with a broadhead point that could shave the fine hair from a woman's delicate skin. In the setting sun, mostly behind his back, it was unlikely that anyone would see the sudden threat on the roof across the way, even had any been looking in that direction. And he had little care if they did.

He slowly pulled the tension in the bow, taking no notice of anything but the man. Only the man, the violator of his Sabina, the murderer of the mother of his children, the woman with whom he had planned a life of wonderment...

At full draw, he saw only the chest of the man - the sinister half, under which the red and beating heart lay. It seemed that he stood there for hours by the water-clock, holding the man's life in his two fingers, although in reality, his was a normal draw, taking only the small part of a moment to center his aim. The man wore no armor, but it would have made no difference - the weapon was the best that the House of Callidus could make. At that distance, and with such power, the shaft would have almost no drop and lose little speed from string to quarry.

And so it did. In fact, the arrow was sent in such swiftness that it was unseen by all in the dimming light, and passed completely through the body of the man, stopping only at the stone wall further behind the officials. To the assembled mass, the man just seemingly fell to the podium for no reason.

Marcus just stood, his emotions blank until Flavis frantically managed to pull him back to his knees and behind the facade. "Sos! Sos! We have to flee before the source of the arrow is determined!"

Marcus allowed his aide to tow him across the roofs and back down to the street. The bow was left on the roof, by previous thought, although Flavis had to take it from the hand of his superior, and drop it himself. It would have been most unwise to appear on the streets with such a weapon as was used to execute a man in the presence of the Governor. The assembly might have had no immediate account for the sudden collapse of a person beside them, but it would only be moments before the spreading blood from the front and back of the unfortunate, and the spent shaft made the reason plain.

But, by that time, the pair were on a minor street, a half stadium away and moving quickly back to their disreputable taburna - just two destitute and shabbily dressed traders as could be seen any day in any city in Latium.

Mourning

"The Ingeniarius of the Army, Consul." The guard Captain stepped aside as the man that he had announced stepped into the room.

In surprise, several of the men sitting at the long table rose to step toward the man in the doorway. "Marcus! By the gods. We had been reduced to hoping that you would at least send a farewell message before you boarded the ferry over the river, Styx." Brutus had a broad grin on his face, as did Collatinus and several others. As they took each others arms, he continued in a more serious tone. "I told you that mourning ceases at last. I had to learn it, as will Collatinus - and as you will, if it has not ended yet."

"Greetings, Sos. The hole left by the departure of Sabina will never be filled, but, aye, I am no longer filled with my own remorse. I received your summons upon the return to my home, and... here I am." He nodded at Collatinus - the man with whom his sympathy was in tandem. The noble wasn't laughing, but he, also, seemed to have come to terms with his loss.

In actuality, he and Flavis quit the city of Gabii - over the wall - at the first darkness. It was an easy walk back to Rome and unhurried since they knew that the gates would be closed until morning. They paused at an empty farm stable for the rest of the night, their meal being some dry rashers that had been purchased days before just for this event. The break of day found them on the street of the Poet and shortly thereafter in his household, enjoying a proper meal and a bath. Afterwards, Marcus walked to the old Palace, now the headquarters for the Consuls and the army.

Brutus turned to the table. "All here should know our illustrious Ingeniarius." There were nods all around, and indeed, Marcus knew all in the room, although several just as names and faces. Brutus pointed to the benches. "Sit down. We are searching our options for the response to Tarquinius."

Marcus was surprised - he had heard nothing of an assault by the deposed King. "Has he given indication of a march on Rome?"

Brutus shook his head. "Nay, but he is not one to steal off into the night. He will attempt to gain his Throne again - that I can vow."

Another Senator spoke - one Lucius Tiburs, by his memory. "Aye. It is known that he is petitioning the cities of Tarquinii and Veii, at the least, for their armies, promising them equal shares in the rulership of the lands."

"Were I the rulers of those cities," said another, "I would take good notice of the past emptiness of the promises of this King."

More comments came, then Marcus spoke up. "You will have little need of my skills in wooding, as I assume that there is no plan to assault further domains."

"Aye. That phase of our history is over," commented Collatinus. "Rome will have no need in the future to forcibly acquire other peoples." That statement would be ridiculed by future generations of Romans - and others in conquered lands - but for the present it was true. The city mostly desired a span of peace and quiet to allow for the new Republic to stabilize and grow from within.

"Still," added Brutus. "You are a skilled and experienced campaigner and one who does not allow hope to interfere with his observations. We would be fools indeed, to allow you to depart from service."

Marcus thought of that for a moment. He had no desire to campaign as an officer of men, and little actual battle experience to claim, although he had watched many military endeavors that were successful and more that were not. "Then, Sos, may I offer this - to take charge of the units of archers. At least, with that weapon I can claim some skill and knowledge of use." A pause, then he added, "And I believe that those units have been... underused in the past."

Another Senator spoke up. "And what if the skills of the builder until are needed - possibly for bridges or roads. Will that not take you away from your units, and maybe at a critical time, leaving them leaderless."

Marcus shook his head. "Nay. I have thought of that and have a candidate to take my place in the construction units. Flavis, my aide, is a skilled and thoughtful man, who has followed me in the campaigns of the years."

Brutus looked in askance, with a doubtful expression. "Flavis? Is he still not young for such an important command?"

Marcus smiled. "And what was I, Sos, in that tent in front of Suessa Pometia, when we needed to gain entrance to the city without the approval of its citizens?" He looked around the table. "Besides, there will be little need for complicated towers and rams in the defense of Rome, and I will still be with the Army, should such complications arise and experienced consultation needed."

Brutus looked around the table, and as there was no objection, said, "Very well, then make it so." He turned to the large map laid on the table and began to discuss the possible moves and countermoves that could be taken, should... or when the deposed King made his move. As he spoke, another soldier entered with a scroll which was taken by Collatinus.

"...and if he gains the support of Tarquinii, and even Veii, his numbers will be less than ours unless the entire of Latium closes with him. Even then, our..."

The Senator who was speaking suddenly stopped, looking at Collatinus. Then, all followed his eyes to the Consul who was reading the scroll with a look of utter surprise on his countenance.

"Lucius?" asked Brutus. "What is the missive?"

Collatinus looked up, his mouth still open in astonishment, maybe even shock. "This is from the Governor at Gabii. Sextus had fled to that city after the wrath of his pater threatened his being..."

"Aye, we knew that," said a man at the table.

"But, on the evening last, the citizenry of the city rose and stormed the old Palace, taking the Prince and his men in force. They were seized by the mob and stoned to death in front of the... podium?" There were exclamations around the table by all - not in regret at the demise of an individual they hated to a man, but at the surprise of the sudden news. "Hold a moment; there is more. Archers in the mob targeted others on the platform, narrowly missing the Governor. By the time the soldiers regained control, most of the party of the Prince was dead, and even their bodies unrecoverable."

"Was the Governor harmed?" asked Tricipitinus. "If so, then we will have to respond or look impotent to all other cities in our confederation."

Collatinus shook his head. "Nay. This missive was penned by him. The crowd did not give offense to the magistracy, other than some soldiers who were injured in the melee." He passed the scroll to others, but there was no more information to be gleaned from it.

Brutus looked at Marcus, who was calmly gazing at Collatinus. Marcus bent forward and quietly said, "I am sorrowful that your vengeance against the evil perpetrator has been taken from you. It is your blade that should have entered his heart."

Sadly, Collatinus just shook his head. "Nay, there was little chance of that by myself, and if the fates have decreed the mission to another, then I can only rejoice. But, the act by anyone will not bring back Lucretia - nor Sabina."

For the next few days, Marcus called an assembly of the bowmen in the army. In all, there were only about two centuries in the count, and most were not citizens of Rome, but men who were serving in the army in return for receiving the citizenship when their service was ended. Except for the elite unit that had been detailed to protect the workers on the various engines, most used their own normal straight bows. Those in the special detail - about twenty in all

- were equipped with the laminated weapons from the houses of Callidus or Ennis.

Marcus had seen the archers in action, during the years, but they always acted as individuals, spread here and there among the spearmen. As such they certainly made their mark on the enemy, but he wondered at the effect should they be used as a mass. It was an idea for which he wished to test the effectiveness. Of course, the problem with a separate unit of bowmen was that they would be as stalks of grain against the scythe, should they be suddenly and surprisedly assaulted by a rank of men with blades. That was a problem that he would have to work out, later. For now, he needed to see if a century - or two - of archers could be controlled as if they were spearmen.

As he stood on a platform for observation, his aide sent this order and that to each Centurion of the two units. His new Adiutor, a young man from a house in the Viminalis quarter, was filled with boyish enthusiasm with being a soldier - a common failing for almost all of his age. Marcus grinned to himself as he watched his son, Lucius, attempting to look imperious before men who had seen the throes of battle.

Although they used the training compound outside the Mon Oppius gate, the men were allowed to return to their homes if they were citizens, or anywhere they found lodging. Many of the foreign-born slept in the barracks, having no other place of residence. Marcus, of course, spent the nights either at his house, or at the much closer residence of Pythes.

For the first few weeks, he just maneuvered the men in this formation or that, testing the fastest method for assembling in mass, then moving this way and that to approach or retreat from a perceived threat. In the far corner of the compound, he had rows of posts set in the ground and with large dried gourds on the top, representing ranks of putative spearmen - a whole century in count and more. Many were the japes of the other officers passing through the area at the threat of empty-headed foes standing against fearsome archers.

The jests began to fade away as Marcus refined his formations and actions.

"If our grainlands were as fertile as your mind, my family could supply the world with bread from just the fields beside the Via Nomentana."

Marcus turned to see Brutus looking up at the raised platform that was used to observe the maneuvers. "Greetings, Sos." He swung down and dropped lightly to the ground. "And what brings the august Leader of the city to the hot and dusty confines of the training field?"

"An escape from chattering Senators, it must be said," came the reply with a grin. "When I think of those days when we were loose and free, moving across the trails on our own accord... ah... to be young and a Tribune-elect again. That would be a gift from the gods."

"Aye," replied Marcus. "We have traveled some strange roads in our time." He paused, then asked, "But again, you did not walk this far for reliving memories." Marcus could see no sign of a lectica, so the Consul had indeed walked on his own legs - a very unusual decision for a man of his stature. Most nobles would almost require a chair to visit the latrine - but, most were rotund with good living and better food and their legs complained at any amount of work.

Brutus looked at the young Adiutor, then said to Marcus. "I would have a word with you..."

Marcus immediately turned to the young man. "Lucius. Send the men to the mess tents for a rest and a cup. We will end this day and enjoy an early evening."

Watching the aide run off, Brutus finally said, "A delegation from Tarquinius has arrived." The eyes of Marcus widened in question. "Their task is to negotiate the return of the private property of his family. That is their story, at least."

"But you think that the mission is to accomplish... something else." It wasn't a question.

"Nay. I have no actual reason to accuse Tarquinius of treachery, but..." Marcus just tilted his head, waiting. Brutus chuckled. "I used to be astounded... Nay, I still am, by your ability to detect the scent of a man - or the individual condiments of a stew - for many stadia in distance. And I can barely tell what is in the meal if I am standing in the kitchen door." Another chuckle, then a serious look. "But, a city-man has his own senses, and mine are sensitive to currents that may not be evident to one from the wilds. And I can detect the undercurrent of..." He stopped and shook his head.

"But, you are naturally wondering what my fears have to do with you." Marcus just waited. "You have your own network of spies in the city." Now Marcus opened his mouth to speak, but Brutus continued. "Nay, I do not accuse you of malfeasance, but I have long known that you prefer your news of the city to come from underneath, rather than through the crier's platforms, and that Flavis is the gatherer of it."

Marcus nodded. "Aye, Sos, but that has not been true of late, as I have no need for such information now."

"But, I do. And so does the Senate. Possibly your network could find the truth of the visit of the delegation. And I am sure that it does not come for the clothes and doodles of Tarquinius."

"Very well, Sos. I will speak to Flavis this night and find if his street skills have atrophied or nay."

Brutus nodded. "Aye, and you have my thanks once again for the help." He paused, then looked sideways at his friend. "I have received an interesting report from the Guard Captain of Gabii. He reports that, on the night of the uprising, a single arrow came out of the mob, and unerringly found the heart of the aide of Sextus, one Petronius by name." Marcus just looked back with a blank expression, as if the news was ordinary. "By coincidence, the same misbegot that so violated your family. Interesting is it not? And even welcome by all who value justice."

Marcus kept his voice level, and replied, "The men of Sextus, no doubt, had as many enemies as himself. It is not surprising that some man took the opportunity to cast vengeance upon the violator of his family. I certainly would have done so, had I the chance and he come to Rome."

Brutus just nodded. "Aye. In any case, both he and his master will not be missed by honest men of this world. We can hope that their shades are held to their crimes in Hades. But... I would have you come for the evening meal, soon. With my mater gone to her reward and my sons away on their duties, I have no one to speak with during the long evenings on which Consul matters do not intrude."

"Aye, Sos. And I thank you for the invitation. I will certainly plan an evening for such."

Book 8

Finis

Perfidy

Flavis still resided in the household of Callidus. There had been no reason for his leaving, even though he was now independent of Marcus with his own rank in the Legion. Even more, his selection of the housemaid, Lydia, as his future partner was the greatest reason for his wishing to stay. And, of course, his gratitude to, and even friendship with, the master of the house was also a bond unbreakable.

He was in charge of a small organization of the best constructors taken from the old unit of Marcus, the rest being discharged to return to their lives. These men were volunteers and proud of their skills. For the present, as no engines, or bridges, or roads were needed, they practiced their craft in the training compound outside of the Pricius gate, mainly because it was the closest compound to a forest with trees of any size. The men assembled their practice constructs three days in seven, the rest of the time given to their own lives.

For Flavis, the skills of his youth were brought forth again, having recently been exercised for a certain purpose in the city of Gabii. Coppers were placed into grubby hands, and the owners disappeared into the alleys and back streets of Rome.

Marcus attended the meetings at headquarters on occasion, but to date, nothing more had been heard from the far reaches of the lands about Tarquinius and his plans.

The highlight of that time was the visit by Consul Collatinus one evening, unannounced and with no fanfare. In fact, when Cleo entered the atrium with the announcement of the arrival of the noble, Marcus immediately assumed that important news had come of the deposed King - and suddenly, as he had spoken with the Consul only that afternoon.

"Marcus, my friend. I give my apologies for this interruption in your own home."

"Nay. No visit of a friend can be considered as anything but gladsome, but I admit to some surprise at the suddenness. I hope that your coming does not indicate that my men need to don their battle gear."

Collatinus smiled. "Nay, it is not so dire as that, but rather, to preserve my sanity from the constant implorments of my son, Manius." The eyes of Marcus widened as he realized the significance of the statement. "Aye, he has directed me to ask for your permission to make the nuptials between himself and your daughter."

Marcus just stood for a moment, the words still sinking into his consciousness, then he waved to the Consul. "Come. Let us take a cup and... and... Cleo!" he shouted. "Two cups in the atrium - and the best."

As they sat, Marcus said, "This is indeed an honor for my young Sabina to be sought by a young man of such stature."

Collatinus waved one hand in dismissal, as he accepted a cup of wine with the other. "Nonsense. A woman with the grace and beauty of your daughter could find a much better mate than my clumsy offspring. He has little interest in the world beyond his scrolls and learning. In a lesser family, he would be a scribe, and no doubt." He paused, then continued, "But... I will have to say, when... and if he becomes a Senator, at least he will have some knowledge of the world - something that I cannot say for many of my colleagues."

Marcus smiled. "The pater of my Sabina was a scribe of such - actually in the office of the Quaestor, then later on his own as a Rhetor. And his family was of grace and deportment." He waved to Cleo, waiting in the kitchen hallway, to attend. "But, I must say this - that I promised Sabina that her daughter would not be forcibly married to a man without considering her desires." As the Steward stopped beside them, he said, "Ask Sabina and her grandmother to wait on us. I assume that they are in the clothery."

Collatinus watched until the man had disappeared. "Marcus, I envy you your rebound from the loss of... of..." He stopped for a moment. "You seemed to have put it behind you and are back in the stream of your life. I have had no such fortune." He raised his hand to stop the comment as it was being formed. "With my Lucretia taken, I have had little reason, nor desire, for anything, much less pretending that I have an interest in my existence. Nay. Nay. Let me finish." He gestured vaguely toward the mountains, far to the east. "I have a farm and a villa up the country. The area is sparsely populated and very pleasant, with clear waters and clean air. I was thinking about moving there and reclining with my scrolls and tablets. Maybe the cool air sweeping down from the mountains will allow me to clear my mind of its black thoughts that plague me at night."

"You will give up your Consulship?"

Collatinus nodded. "Aye. I have no interest in, nor ability for the position. And least of all, do I wish to embark on a war with Tarquinius, as necessary as it may become." He took a sip of the wine, then more as he seemed to enjoy it. "My son will become the Dominus of the House of Collatinus and take his place at the head of the family in Rome. If they make the match, then young Sabina will be propelled to the upper reaches of Roman society." He smiled wryly. "Aye, I know that you yourself would have little interest if given the crown of all Latium, but for a young woman of her character..."

Young Sabina appeared, with Cleo assisting her grandmother, Decima, across the room. The old woman was well into her years and with her full reason, and even still ambulatory, if not spry. She had lost none of her peppery seasoning, even with the tragic loss of her daughter. Indeed, she had transferred her matronly duties to the younger girl, making certain that the forms were obeyed by a proper maiden of the city. Marcus wondered just how the son of Collatinus had breached the citadel of the old woman to be able to even speak to Sabina. Both stood, waiting for the old woman to be assisted into a chair beside the eating table - it being too difficult to lay on an elbow in the Roman manner. Or rather, to regain her feet without assistance if in recline.

Marcus nodded to his mother-in-law, and said, "Consul Collatinus comes with surprising news, this night. It would appear that his son, Manius, wishes to become affianced to Sabina." It was immediately apparent that the surprise of the night was to himself, only. The eyes of Sabina lit up with the news that the request was finally being made, and he could tell that the grandmother was not without knowledge of the possibility, also. "What say you, daughter?"

"I would beg that you agree, Father," was all she replied, but with obvious joy on her countenance.

He turned to the older woman. "Decima? I would have your opinion, also."

She smiled. "He is a good boy, Marcus. And like you in many ways when you first met her mother. He has treated with Sabina many times, but has never taken liberties or made undue familiarity in his visits." She looked at the Consul. "I have expected this for some time, but cautioned her that a noble family might look in askance at a son taking a wife from a Plebeian family. It appears that my misgivings were in error."

Collatinus smiled in return. "These are turbulent times, good Decima, and the forms are changing. The house of Callidus is noble in all but ancestry. The surprise should be not that my family has tendered the offer, but that the girl has not been spoken for long ago."

Decima shook her head. "The speaking has been long and constant, in fact. Many tenders of the nuptial joining have been asked of her, but she has held out for your son."

This was news to Marcus. "Offers of marriage have come before now? Without my knowing?"

Decima gave a wry smile. "Nay, Marcus. Your familial responsibility has not been impugned. I speak of young men asking Sabina for themselves - while you were away at the wars - to get her agreement before making the request of the father to approach you. I gave that you had far more to your tasks on the field of battle than being required to mediate the desires of children and that your return would be soon enough. But, Sabina has eyes only for the son of Collatinus."

Certainly, Marcus had no qualms. He had known Lucius Collatinus these many years and as an honorable man from a highly respected family. And Manius, a quiet but proper lad, who had visited his house to gambol with his own sons innumerable times. Mild mannered, and even shy - unlikely to become a forceful leader of the city in the future, but probably destined for happiness because of that lack. If Sabina wished it, then...

"Very well, I give my blessing for this joining, and hope that you are as happy in it as your mother and I when we were together." No more words needed to be spoken, as Sabina dropped all decorum before a guest and threw her arms around the neck of her father, and sobbing with joy until he finally unwound her so as to be able to escort the Consul to the door.

The flowers of spring came and went, and turned into the heat of summer. Flavis had received much information from his street rats, but only about the normal happenings in a large city. Marcus smiled at the putative idea of himself being a Magistrate, with knowledge of the information that was being collected. He could become fabulously wealth with the snippets from the urchins. The Factor of Senator Antinus was selling grain stolen from the wharfs at Ostia and the merchants on the street of the Wolf had conspired by moving their wares from one merchantry to another ahead of the taxman. Even more damning, was the city clay foundry in selling four bricks and delivering three to the constructions around the city. Bribes, thievery, watered wine and sour beer - he suspected that it was the same the world over. He knew that Senator Florus was behind much of it, but the street toughs in his control were in such number that none would dare to protest.

Marcus continued his training with the bowmen - now in a count of three Centuries - almost two hundred men. They had made the transition from individual archers to acting in a mass upon command and were able to maneuver quickly to this way and that - from a fast travel march to a long line facing the enemy, or a solid block that issued sheets of shafts, row by row.

By now, Marcus had found and promoted many men who became the sub-officers of the units. And, overall was the Centurion of the old mille of Brutus, Rutilius, met at that first siege of Suessa Pometia, years ago. Marcus had full confidence in the professional soldier - though the man was not a bowman himself, he quickly grasped the full potential of the weapon, and could be relied upon to command even should his superior be absent - or killed.

Marcus delved into the experimentation with archers with the same intensity as he had learned the art of siege engines, but in this instance, it was to keep his mind busy so as not to dwell upon his still green and heartsore loss. It was the hope of himself that his men would attain superb proficiency in their art of war, and never be required to use it.

He had always been a light sleeper, but now even the scurrying of a rodent would waken him, so this night, he heard the familiar steps of Cleo on the stairs long before the quiet knock on the door. He wondered at the hour, but with the overcast sky, he had no view of the stars through the gauzed windows.

"Pardon, Sos, but Master Manius has come with urgency."

Manilus? Why would that youngster be out in the night, and more to the point - what could be the need... Marcus hurried to his feet, throwing on his ragged night tunic as he followed Cleo down the stairs. This could not be good news, whatever it was.

In the atrium, he saw the son of Collatinus by the dim oil lamp, fully dressed and even armed with a blade. Now Marcus was becoming alarmed, but he nodded to Cleo and waited until the Steward had disappeared into the dark.

"I fear the reason for your coming, young Manilus, but we are alone here, and there are no ears to hear..."

The young man bowed slightly. "Aye, Sos. It is news of some worry, but I was at a loss about how to reveal it. I was afraid my father would be marked, should I confide in him, and he is... well, not in his..."

Marcus waved for the boy to sit on the bench. "Aye, I know of his heartsickness and have full compassion for it. To lose a loved mate is... difficult for a man at any age. And you - you lost a mother by the same act." He looked around, not expecting to see anyone, but just as a reflex before he continued in a low voice. "What blackness have you to report."

Manius weighed his thoughts for a moment. "You know of course, the delegation of the Kin... Tarquinius, to retrieve his family property and familial possessions? Of course, you do - you are high in the ranks of the Army." Marcus waved a hand impatiently. "I fear that the... mission of the delegation is not what it seems."

Now the young man also looked around to the shadows before he continued. "I was approached by Titus with a... strange proposal - nay, it was formed as a conjecture as to my being a Senator ahead of my time, should events of some strangeness come about."

"Titus? The son of Brutus?"

"Aye. We were taking a cup in the magisterial library, watching a troupe of performers in their actions from the window. He mentioned that there was some concern among certain leaders of the city as to the wisdom of fighting Tarquinius, an experienced warrior, and only for the reason that... You will forgive me, Sos, but the words were, 'Because of the actions of a few wanton wives, lonely in their beds.'"

At that, the jaw of Marcus tightened up as his sinews of the mouth clenched. Such words, and from Titius, the son of a respected Senator... nay, a close friend almost from himself coming to the city... He took a deep breath, and said, "Continue."

"It was a strange proposal, and I gave no further thought to it until I had occasion to visit the scroll chamber of Aridolis of Corinth. You may have heard of him - his father was Greek and the family came to Rome after the city was invested by the Carthaginians."

Marcus had only a scattered knowledge of the history of Rome, and only because of the teachings of Sabina, and none at all about the far lands of Greece, although he knew that Carthage was a large and prosperous city far away across the Central Sea. "Nay, but let that not bother you. Continue."

"His collection of Greek scrolls is second to none, and after the help of my father, years ago, over some matter concerning taxes and a rapacious sub-magistrate, I have been welcome in his reading room when I wish." Marcus could not see any possible connection between dusty scrolls of a foreigner and Tarquinius, but he just nodded for the boy to proceed. "As it happens, the window of the room overlooks the

Via Mycelium, and directly across is the scrivener post of the Senate. You probably know that it is the building where the decrees and rescripts of that ruling body are read to the scribes as they put the words to ink and scroll."

"I did not, but continue."

"It has been largely unused for years, in fact, since long before my time, as the proclamations are - were - issued from the Palace during the reign of Tarquinius." Apparently, suddenly remembering that he was lecturing to a man whom he had woken in the middle of the night, Manius attempted to lean his talk. "Again, I can clearly see the building from my chair in the scroll room of Aridolis. And several times, now, I have seen the men of the delegation from Tarquinius meeting for considerable times with members of the Senate, and others, including both of the sons of Brutus. I would have thought nothing of it until I was approached by Titus with the odd reference to a possible change in Senators. And..." He paused, thinking.

At a nod to proceed, he finished with, "As I reflect back in my remembering, they do not leave as an assembly that has completed its discussion, but in singles and pairs over time, as if not to draw attention to the gathering." A pause, then, "And none use chairs, which is unusual for many of them, and is another reason to believe that they do not wish to be noticed on that street."

Marcus just sat for a moment, having trouble believing the direction that young Manius was pointing. That the delegation of Tarquinius, and even some of the older Senators, might be conspiring against the new Republic he could readily believe, but that the sons of Brutus were involved - Nay, just the fact of their presence must indicate something far less conspiratorial than... Still, the fact that they were meeting in the far reaches of Rome, rather than at the old Palace was indicative that someone wished the trysts to be concealed - that in itself was troubling.

"You have done well, bringing your doubts to me. We will hope that the meetings are innocent, and if so, our conversation will go no farther than us. But do not tell your father. He is still mourning the loss of your mother, and needs no further problems until those raw wounds are healed." A thought came to him. "And you. Do not attempt to espy on those men. I do not wish to help my friend bury his son, also, in the event that your worries are correct. I have... ways to find out the truth."

As the sun rose, Marcus accosted Flavis as he came from his room, prepared to travel to his construction unit for the day. Taking him to the far end of the atrium, he gave the story of the night and certain instructions.   Shortly, Flavis was hurrying from the house, but not toward the compound outside of the Pricius gate.   Marcus knew that the street urchins would soon be infesting the Via Mycelium, invisible as the rats and mice of the quarter.   Where a lurking man, attempting to gain information from those who had reason to hide such would be easily noticed, a dirty youngster might be cursed or kicked, but never suspected of anything but stealing a bite of bread.

This day, he walked to the smithery of Ennis to get information on certain contract that he had let.   Of course, as he walked through the door, he was greeted effusively and made to sit for wine and sweetmeats with his past-apprentice - now a respected bowsmith of growing wealth.   Then, conversation brought each other the news of the happenings with the families in the last month, and finally, to business.

"I can show you, rather than trying to enumerate."   Ennis waved him to follow around the house to a shed attached to the back of the smithery.   In it were bundles of arrows - sheaf upon sheaf, stacked almost to the ceiling.   Ennis had not made the projectiles - rather he had contracted the work to innumerable workers - anyone who could whittle a straight shaft from a limb of wood, at the rate of a copper for a sheaf.   Then, the shafts, cut to length were delivered to yet other workers, who would glue the fletchings and the simple iron points to complete the arrow.   Absolute perfection was not needed for these, as they would not be used for hunting, or marking down a specific target. They only needed to be of a quality to be launched and travel the distance with some accuracy.   "All I need from you is a wagon to haul them away."

Marcus nodded, impressed. "You have done well in such a short time. I will send for them this afternoon, but... He thought a minute. I will need another quantity of equal number."

The eyes of Ennis widened somewhat, but he nodded. "Aye, it will be done, but... Are you in fear of a horde of barbarians descending upon us?" It was a jest, but only partly.

Marcus just smiled. "Nay. But, should it happen, then I fear that my men will be engaged in other activities rather than the whittling of shafts."

Treachery

Marcus was reclined at the mensa in the atrium, his thoughts as black as the night outside. Young Lucius and Flavis sat cross-legged across the table, sipping at their wine, but holding their speech. The household was as silent as a mountain slope in winter, all within padding around on silent feet so as to not raise the wrath of the master. Cleo had become the target of that choler earlier when he had entered to offer service for the cups or pastries. The bark of Marcus to depart was the answer he received.

The Steward knew that his master would offer his apologies on the morrow, but it was obvious that his vexation was immense this night. And that it boded ill for... someone. Cleo gave strict orders for silence in the household and for none to approach the atrium for any reason, as he waited in the shadows of the kitchen in case of a summons.

Realizing that he had reached for the wine even again in the same thought, Marcus whipped the cup toward a planter, the residual liquid splattering in the leaves. Clear thoughts were needed now, not wine-sotted musings. Finally, in a low voice, he said - more to himself than the two young men, "The house of Brutus has been our friend since my coming to the city. I would be a carver with a storefront kiosk and making stick-bows for coppers were it not for the Domina and her son. How can I confront my friend with this?"

Both young men knew that an answer was not being requested, and maintained their silence until he spoke again. "Still... We cannot ignore the reality of the matter. It could even affect ourselves and anyone associated with the new government."

A few hours before, Flavis had appeared at the household and accompanied by a much younger man - more than a stripling and older than most of the street rats in the pay of the officer, although he had not gained his full size yet. This was the Adiutor to Flavis - a designation that was a jape between the two older men, but not one of derision. Indeed, the Tribunes of Rome would wish that their aides had the intelligence and diligence of this street-trained youngster.

His name was Cursor - the ancient word for runner. And indeed it was true - between the blink of an eye and the next, a loaf of bread could move from the warming tray to the clutches of the youngster and be out of sight before the baker could call his curse down upon the thief.

Flavius had tested him intensively, emphasizing that nothing was wanted that was hearsay, or gossip - only the absolute facts, seen by his eyes or heard by his ears - or that of his associates - and that any caught bloating their news would be cast back into the starving dirt of the streets. And Cursor ran his troupe of rats as if he were a Centurion of the Legion, taking commands from his Dux, Flavis. Any that did not measure up were cast out and replaced by the innumerable urchins wishing to join the ranks.

The eyes and ears of the dirty youngsters were fairly useless in the Capitoline quarter, where they would stand out like an ass in an atrium, but in the Plebeian areas of the city, little could escape their attention anywhere they be ordered to investigate. And, again, they were seen as little threat to any but unwatched food, and mostly unnoticed by the citizenry. The sight of an unwashed boy squatting next to a wall was so common as to be as unseen as the cobblestones of the street.

Of course, the boys had no ability to write, nor any concept of the meaning of the conversations that might be overheard, but they could certainly repeat what had been said, even if it made no real sense to themselves. Two of the urchins earned a few small coppers as piss-pot boys, sitting at the door that led to the latrine of the old scribe building, and emptying the bowls upon use. They were ignored by the men assembled, and frequently, one or the other of the youngsters would rise to amble from the area on some unnoticed task outside.

Down the street, in a small hut rented by Flavis for the occasion, he and Cursor waited for the boys as they left the meeting periodically. There, the youngster would repeat what he had heard to Flavis, then would amble back to sit beside his comrade. As the urchins had little understanding of what they were hearing, their reports were sometimes ludicrously corrupt, but enough was delivered to indicate the villainy that was being concocted down the street. Much of the dialog was the men bargaining among themselves for gain, should the old King return. And, in his long view down the street, Flavis could see that only a few would meet at any one time, but by his count on just this one day, at least a handful of Senators were involved. And if one took into account the previous three or four meetings, it was a significant number of traitors.

By the end of the day, the extent of the treason by some men of the city was without doubt. Now, as Marcus and the two young men sat in his atrium, the question was what to do with what they knew. Now he looked at Flavis and asked, "Do we know the status of the men who have come from the King in the delegation?"

"I have no idea of the men from Tarquinius, either their names or ranks, but I have seen Duilius, Verginius, Atilius... and... Lucianus and his son, at least. Ah, and Florus. All Senators." He thought for a moment. "Nay, there was also the Aedile of the Corn market, Hilarius. And two or three more that I have seen, but do not know their names."

"Florus." Marcus just repeated the name, obviously deep in thought.

Now Young Lucius spoke. "The Senator that controls the wharfage in Ostia?"

Flavis shook his head. "I do not know. The pedigree of nobles of such rank is not a topic that I have concerned myself with."

Still in thought, Marcus, nodded idly. "Aye. He owns most of the leases on the docks, I believe." He looked up at his son. "Why?"

Lucius shook his head. "No reason. The name is familiar. Brother Marcus said that he and Valens had a trading mission assailed by a paid mob in the port city. Supposedly, because of the unhappiness of the Senator that his services were not used."

The elder Marcus nodded. "He is a brute, and that is true. And tender of his own skin. When he ventured to gain the plunder of the city of Alatri, after it had fallen, he traveled in the midst of a troupe of toughs almost sufficient to take the city themselves." He looked at Flavis. "Did he attend the meeting with guards?"

"Aye, but only two, as I remember."

Again silence as Marcus looked at the situation from all sides. Then, "Lucius. At first light, call out Centurion Rutilius, and have him tell off... say, ten men. Good men and from the defenders." The defender unit was a strategy by Marcus to protect his massed archers from a charge of spear wielding foes. He had culled the soldiers from his unit that had some familiarity with blades, as well as bows, to stand in the front rank - ready to change wood for iron should the conflict become close. "No spears or bows, just blades. Have them garb as ordinary citizens, not soldiers. Bring them by ones and twos to the hut on the Via Mycelium. Then have a half Century unit gathered, then move them around the walls to the Mycelium gate. Give to the guards, there, that you are in a training march, and demonstrating how to approach a gated wall. Then, wait for word for me."

"Flavis. Have Cursor tell off his rats to watch the house of Florus. I wish to know when he leaves, and where his feet take him."

Finally, "Now. Get to your mats and rest. The morrow will come early and not without risk." His tentative plan was entirely illegal, looked at from any aspect - especially from a mere Plebeian, no matter how well ranked in the army.

Before the first light of day, Marcus was in the small hut on the Via Mycelium. The street was wide and filled on both sides with houses, from huts to comfortable homes, and with merchantries of all types - ragged awnings under which sat an old woman or man selling her few eggs and fowl, and porch fronted establishments of some prosperity. This was fortunate, since the gathering of a group of men in an old hut would be unlikely to be commented on, or even noticed, by the crowds of locals.

Not long after, Flavis arrived with the ten men, who settled to the floor in the back, waiting for... what, they did not know, but it was a change from the constant drilling on the training field. In a short time, most were asleep. From the little spies of Cursor, he knew that another meeting was planned for the day - the men still sparring with each other as to who would reap which spoils should certain events come about. Now it was just a matter of waiting for the men to arrive - and one in particular.

Marcus sat at the small windows and watched the flow of the day's commerce, then said, more to pass the time, than speaking of anything of importance. "It is interesting that the men meet so openly. One would think that for a plot of such magnitude, they would have their tryst in the dark of the forest."

Flavis, sitting beside him, replied with some jocularity. "Ah... That musing gives the indication that you have not had the benefit of education by growing up on the streets of Rome as a destitute waif. I learned long ago, that when fleeing with a fruit, or loaf, and ahead of the wrath of the vendor, a crowded street is safety. One cannot hide if he is the only body in a deserted alley. There is a saying among the street thieves, 'Conceal a rock among rocks, a man among men.'" He pointed down the street. "The merchants might wonder at the coming and goings of so many high-born, but not so that they would make something of it, and their assumption would be that the scribery is being used again."

Marcus nodded. Of course, the young man was right. Slinking along to a meeting place, in an attempt to hide the action, would be a sure way to garner attention. But, openly walking the streets to a common building, and as one who had business there would gather no suspicions even from a noble of the city - in the unlikely event that one of that class would be on this merchant street of a Plebeian quarter. Besides the plotters, he corrected himself.

It was halfway to midday before Flavis, sitting at the window, spoke. "Sos, there is one. I have seen him here before, but do not know his name."

Following the pointing finger, Marcus said, "Placus. The Ratiocinator of the Treasury." He nodded. "Aye, the accountant of the finances would be a good ally to have on your side, should you decide to change the aspect of government."

They waited. Both watched from the shadows, as Flavis pointed this man and that - unnecessarily "Ah, there is Atilius... And Hilarius, with... hmmm, his companion is a new face..." Verginius, Cannius, Tullius... the naming went on and on. Many were the faces of several other high placed families.

Suddenly, Cursor appeared, breathless. "The man Florus has left his abode. His steps are this way."

"How many guards?" Marcus asked.

The boy held up four fingers. "And..." He counted on his fingers, then held up the count of six. "This many slaves for his lectica."

That was a surprise. "He is in a chair?"

"Aye. He leaves it at the Cryer's circle, then walks the way."

Marcus nodded, then turned and barked to Flavis. "Wake the men." In mere heartbeats the ten were on their feet as and being given their orders. Four men left the hut, splitting into pairs, then moved into the street, but within a few paces of the doorway. They relaxed, talking with each other, just men with leisure between tasks and passing the time.

Time passed. A few other men were seen to enter the door of the old Scribery, then finally, the obese shape of the Senator was seen up the street, flanked by his four toughs, walking the center of the cobblestones. It was obvious that Florus was trying to maintain a low profile - usually his escort reveled in pushing merchants and citizens aside, scattering their wares and holdings, so that the august person could pass without the polluting touch of a commoner. But today, his guards were uncharacteristically gentle, and the man himself was dressed in far less than his usual flamboyant robes.

As he approached the hut, Marcus nodded to Flavis. The young man hurried into the street and stopped in the path of the march. The toughs raised their hands to the hilts of their blades at the sudden appearance, but as no weapon was evident on the young man, they did not seem to be threatened. And, Flavis had his hands open and within view.

Before the fat Senator could speak, Flavis looked around, feigning concern, then said in a low and urgent voice. "Sos! I come from Tertius Verginius. He begs you to attend him in yon hut. And warns, do not go to the scribery!"

Now the Senator looked around, then asked, "What is the cause? Why does he hide in a hut?"

Flavis shook his head. "Nay, Sos. I am just the messenger, but you are in danger here. Come!" He turned and walked quickly to the door of the indicated structure, followed by a now frightened Senator walking so quickly as to move in front of his guards.

Moving from the sunlit street to the dark inside of the single windowed shack, he could only see shadows within, as neither could his men. Still, it took only a heartbeat before the treachery was known, and the instant reactions of two of the toughs doomed them. As they reflexively drew their weapons, they were cut down with multiple blades, already drawn and waiting. The other two, blessed with slower responses, stayed their hands before drawing iron. Now, the four men who had stood outside, blocked the entrance from both inquisitive intruders and to prevent any sudden bolting from the hut.

It had taken a considerable time before the Senator realized that he was not going to be cut down, to begin his protest. "What means this? If you are after my purse, then take it and be gone."

Marcus ignored him, motioning to Flavis. The young man instantly disappeared out the door and up the street. Outside the hut, the commerce continued - the sudden action seemed not to have been noticed by any, or, more likely, self-preservation dictated that one not intrude into an unknown affair. The two remaining guards were thrown to the ground and their hands bound behind them. The Senator himself, was pointed one of the two chairs at the crude table in the center of the room. Now, Marcus stood at the doorway again, motioning to a boy lounging against a wall across the street. In moments, Cursor was standing before him.

"Now, take the message, then return to me for more orders." The boy instantly took to his feet in a run down the street toward the walls. Now Marcus turned to treat with the Senator, still standing at the table. "Sit down, Senator Florus. We have much to discuss."

The man was getting some of his courage back. Since he was still alive, then this had not been an assassination attempt. "I recognize you. You are Marcus of Callidus. The Ingeniarius of the army." No response. "You have committed a grave offense. I am a Senator of Rome and may not be hindered in my movements." He looked around at the soldiers on all sides of the little room. "All of you are marked for death for such a heinous crime as accosting a member of the Senate." Still no reply was spoken. "I will intercede for you before the magistrates, since it is obvious that you are just following orders - illegal though they may be. Now, I have urgent business and will be on my way." His imperiousness was less than it might have been, with his eyes jumping from Marcus to the dead men that had been dragged to the back of the hut.

Marcus would have been amused, had the situation not been so dire. Of the ten men in the detail, no more than two were of Rome. The rest were foreign born, come to serve in the army in return for citizenship in the future. Most spoke little Latium, other than what they had learned from the orders and curses of their officers, and most had no understanding of one in five of the highborn words issued by their captive.

"Nay, you will not, Senator. Rather, you will speak with some friends that will be here shortly."

"Friends? What friends? Let me say again, you will release me this moment, or I will see you nailed to the crossposts in the Circus before the sun leaves the sky!" Marcus gestured to the two soldiers on the other side of the rough table. Immediately, they pushed the man onto the short bench and held him there with their hands on his shoulders.

"If he speaks again, do not cut his throat - we need him to be able to talk." Marcus paused theatrically. "Cut an ear off, and if he continues, the other one. Then a finger... and another." The Senator opened his mouth, but immediately closed it when he looked into the face of his captor - it was obvious that the threat was real.

Marcus sat back at the window, seeing at least two other nobles walking the street. Since it was very unlikely for any such to be on this Plebeian via without their steward, they were, no doubt, destined to the scribery, also.

He heard the midday gong, far away in the Cryer's circle, then finally, Flavis hurrying up the street in the lead of several men. He could see not only Brutus and Collatinus, but also Publicola and Tricipitinus and another... Ah, it was the son of Publicola.

Flavis had been told to request the presence of the Consuls and not to give the reason. And it was obvious that he had not, given the surprise on the faces as they entered the hut, now fairly crowded with soldiers and Senators. Immediately, the fat Senator attempted to rise, but was held down by the two guards standing behind him. That did not stop him from shouting, "Consul Brutus. I demand punishment for this man, and immediately. He has had my attendants murdered, without reason, and even took it upon himself to cause outrage to my person. He will be taken to the Mamertine immediately, and held for this outrage."

The room was now crowded to a considerable degree, with soldiers and Patricians and the guards of the Senator taking considerable room, also - both the two still alive and those looking back upon their bodies from the far side of the river Styx.

Marcus ordered Flavis to send the men to wait outside, except for the pair waiting at the side of Florus and the man standing guard over the bound men. Only then did he turn his attention to the nobles, all now attempting to ask the same questions.

Marcus held up his hand, then said to Brutus. "Consul. You requested that I send my... agents into the street to confirm or deny certain worries that you were having about the city."

Brutus was still staring at the captive sitting on the bench of the table. "Aye. But I did not..."

"...and I may say that your concerns were valid. Hold your wonderments for awhile. The Senator, here, has much to answer for."

Florus was becoming his imperious self, now being in the protective company of his equals. "I have to answer to nobody. Consul, I repeat my demand that this man..."

Marcus nodded to one of the guards standing behind the man. The sweating Senator looked to his side to see a pugio pulled from a belt and felt a rough hand pull an ear away from his head. The demand was immediately lost in an involuntary cry as he felt the blade touch his skin. It did not continue the slice, but no doubt the resting blade could be felt by the Senator.

"You were not brought here to talk, but to listen. I will tell a story, but you may interrupt to give any repairs to my tale if I should be inaccurate in any way." Marcus looked at the stunned Patricians, still attempting to understand what they had walked into, then lowered himself onto the other bench, across from Florus.

"In the last month, about the time of the Nones, a delegation from Tarquinius came to Rome. It was an innocent mission, to negotiate for the return of the family possessions left behind when his family vacated the city." Marcus could have been reciting a lesson on bow making - his voice normal and calm. "The new leaders of Rome are honorable men, and would have no objections to such a request, and in fact, ordered that any and all of the desired articles be packed for transit."

The man across from him just looked back, with little expression except for the voluminous amounts of skin water flowing down his face. "But that was only part of their charge, was it not? Other meetings were arranged, some at your household, and some at the homes of other Senators. It was a give and take, carefully testing each other for signs of understanding."

A pause, but only with dead quiet within the hut. "Some of the other Senators were discontented with their stature under the new Republic. The reign of the King had given them far more opportunity for... actions of a lucrative nature, now forbidden by law and the requirement for approval by the magistrates. The taxation of the Ostia port, now to be managed by the appointed men, rather than yourself, put a great restraint on a highly remunerative income, did it not? Nay, I am talking. You will be given your place on the acting platform in time."

"And the illegal taxation of merchandise still unsold was a welcome addition to the coffers of Cannius... and others. It was not welcomed by the merchants of the street, but few would do more than grumble after seeing several of their fellows set upon and beaten for protest. Or worse. Of course, Tullius with his imaginary brickworks and equally fanciful deliveries is facing ruin now that the city requires an accounting of both product and invoice."

"How much more convenient would it be to have the old King back, especially as he would, no doubt, be exceedingly grateful to those who returned the crown to his brow." There was still no expression on the face of the man, but there was no doubt that his attention had been gathered. "Of course, your plans would have little effect without force to give them reach, but with the army stood down and only the magistrate patrols and the guards of the wall..."

He paused for a moment, but none of the men interrupted. "Your bands of street toughs and alley scum would have an easy task of overpowering the guards during the night, and opening the gate to allow the forces of Tarquinius to enter and overpower the city." Now the man showed his alarm and was vigorously shaking his head, still mute and with the feeling of the blade of the dagger resting on his ear. "By morning, the bloodbath would be over, with the leaders of the Republic slaughtered in the night, along with anyone else who might be considered a menace to the return of the King. And, we all know of the wide net that is cast by the reign of Tarquinius to find men who are less than supportive."

Marcus nodded to the guard with the pugio and tossed his head slightly. The blade was withdrawn and the hold on the ear released. Leaning over the table, he said, "Have I misrepresented you or your cohorts in any way?"

The shake of the head now issued a rain of water droplets to both ends of the table. "Nay! Nay! You have given a false issuance of the truth." The Senator spread his hands on the table, palms up, in his plea. "I have had no assemblage for any such reason..."

He stopped as Marcus held up a hand. To the guard standing over the bound prisoners, he ordered, "Cut that one loose and stand him before us." In moments, the street tough was dragged to his feet and pushed to the end of the table. Marcus stood also and looked straight at the man. "I will give you one chance for your life. Should you not wish it, then you may expect to be nailed to the cross beams in the Circus this day. Speak truthfully and I will give you escort to the city gate and freedom." The man just stood, frozen. It was unlikely beyond all bounds that such scum would be privy to the plans of the traitors, but he almost certainly would know certain gatherings of men of his ilk.

The five nobles had not said a word, all surprised - nay, almost stupefied by the act being played out before them. Confusion, disbelief, incredulity - every possible emotion crossed their countenances. Suddenly, Marcus barked at the standing tough, "Where is the band of men being assembled for the rush on the gates?"

There was no immediate answer, even though the mouth opened to speak. For a moment, the words seemed to hang in his throat, then, "Sos... Sos... I know of no design about a gate, but men have been told to hold themselves at the ready for a command to push the will of... of..." He pointed. "...the master, Florus, at some night foray."

The fat Senator again offered his hands in supplication. "My man knows nothing of my affairs. Do you consult with your servants for your day's work?"

Marcus knew that this man was the master of subterfuge and that his entire life and being were based on dissimulation and misdirection in every aspect of the day. Given the opportunity and enough time, he could convince the standing Patricians that he was as pure of thought and deed as the springtime breeze. For Marcus to match wits against such a master would end in his being tied in his own ropes of thought. A distraction was needed - a sudden interruption to disrupt the webs being woven in the mind of the fat conspirator.

Suddenly, and without preamble, Marcus pulled the pugio from his belt and in a high and lighting-swift swing, plunged the blade into the rough sawn top of the table. The thick wood gave enough resistance to end the movement when the blade had sunk to the length of three fingers. The open palm of the Senator gave little opposition, however, as the iron blade passed cleanly through on the way to the wood.

It took a long instant of time before the realization of pain traveled from the hand to the consciousness, but the eyes of the man opened wide in disbelief, then the mouth in a long scream of pain.   He instinctively grabbed the hilt of the dagger with his free hand in an attempt to withdraw the blade, but his sinews were trained for a life of luxury, not work, and the act was futile.

Now as the pain-racked man stared at his pinned hand with massive eyes in an agonized face, Marcus began the assault.   "You and the other men, Verginius, Lucianus, Duilius and others were conspiring to deliver the city to Tarquinius so that you might gain your past positions and income!   Do not deny it!   I have been a party to the assembly and your thoughts through many eyes and ears.   A full accounting has been written down and will be delivered to the Senate." This last was untrue and probably without worth.   That ruling body would give little credence to words heard and repeated by the dirty urchins of the streets - especially against a powerful Senator.

The man was flowing water from his skin in what seemed to be ladles from the well.   Florus spoke through gritted teeth.   "Nay! Nay! I was not a party to the intrigue.   I was as appalled at the prospect of treachery as you, but I could not just condemn it and leave.   They would have slain me on the moment."   That denial was not given in a smooth protest, but between gritted teeth and grimaces, all the while as a hand still futilely attempted to free the other.   "I was... was attempting to halt the despicable plans before they came to fruition. Failing that, I would certainly have warned the Senate of their danger!"

Turning, he gestured to Flavis to approach.   "Lend me the use of your pugio for a moment."   Taking the short blade from the young man, he turned back to the sweating man and forcibly took the free hand from its futile attempts to withdraw the blade from its mate. With some effort, Marcus turned the hand palm up on the table and raised the borrowed pugio.

The fat Senator was looking at the raised hand and blade with even wider eyes, if that was possible, as Marcus said, "Your story does not match my beliefs in your motives."   Turning to the tough still standing at the end of the table - with the point of a sword in his back - he demanded,   "Speak of the men who were given orders to assemble at the old corn granary."

While standing there, the man had obviously weighed the difference between entering the evil auspices of a man who would have him killed for a copper coin, should that bring profit, and the pugio of another, less noble in stature, but of a far more immediate threat.   "The granary was our assembly point when the bidding to gather was sent."

"How many were under the orders?"

"Sos... I have no skill for counting. But... Maybe... a double line from here to the fowl merchant... there." He pointed out the door.

Now to the trembling man pinned to the table, he asked in a tone that indicated that the pugio would descend at any dissatisfaction of the answer. "And your reason for assembling your private army in the dark of night?"

By now the voice of the man was hoarse - almost gone - as he answered through clinched teeth. "Nay, Sos. It was only for my own protection against the conspirators. And to assist in protecting the city against any attempt by the... anyone who..."

"So... You admit that the group of men are attempting the overthrow of the Republic, and the removal of the current men of the Senate, barring those who are in on the plot."

It wasn't a question, but as the fat Senator hesitated, he saw the hand of Marcus clinch its grip on the pugio of Flavis, and step forward. "Aye! Aye! All there intend to give the city back to King Tarquinius! And remove any who might be unwilling to accept the reversion."

"Give the names of all who are involved."

Now Marcus just stood as Florus reeled off name after name of titled men. Men of old and respected families - some with ancestors from the days before Romulus had founded the city. As he waited, watching the names trigger disbelief in the assembled nobles, he was dreading the sound of two names - the sons of Brutus. But...

"That is all I have knowledge of. Of course, it may be that some have garnered support on their own, but I will have no way of knowing that."

Marcus was astounded - and relieved - that the man had left off the names of the two sons. Was he forgetful, or even now making a plan to enter the good graces of Brutus?

As the naming came to a halt by the Senator, his inquisitor stood and faced the frozen men, standing as if they had been escorted into the full gaze of the Gorgon. Through the doorway, he could see Cursor standing, and at a gesture from Marcus, nodded vigorously.

"Now, Consuls... Senators. Shall we attend the assembly of the dissatisfied men and ask them of their intentions?"

It took a moment for the attentions of the men to refocus on Marcus, rather than the man pinned to the table, but then Brutus said, "That would be most unwise. It would be as entering the lair of the ursa unarmed." Turning to Publicola, he said hurriedly, "Gather the Senior Centurion, and if he is still at the field camp, the Palace guard and all the men..."

Marcus was waving both hands. "Nay, Sos. It is unnecessary. The conspirators will be waiting and with no capability of plunging their blades into our hearts."

Tricipitinus was of a mind with Brutus. "I doubt that men who suddenly find that their lives are forfeit for treason would be so forgiving. We will march into the hornets nest with much armor to see this act to the end."

Collatinus held up his hand. "Wait. I have learned long ago that our friend does not speak merely to hear his own words. Let him finish."

Marcus nodded to the Consul. "Aye, Sos. I had my son, Lucius waiting at the Mycelium gate with half a Century. After you had arrived, I sent word for him to conclude our plan. By now, he has invested the scribal building and has all there waiting for us."

Forfeit

Marcus stood, gazing over the panorama of the city from his vantage point, many man lengths above the Forum of the Capitoline. He remembered that time, years in the past, when a young man, newly come to the city, walked across the vast area below and was startled by the sight of men being thrown to their deaths from this very spot. That young man would have been utterly disbelieving had the gods granted him the view of his future, now standing as the officer of the Century detailed to give security for this action of the Senate.

All of Rome seemed to have gathered below, packing the Forum even beyond its usual crowds, all looking up at the top of the cliff known as the Tarpeian Rock. Of course, never had such a spectacle been promised in the entire known history of the city. Now, almost a hundred men were condemned to death on this hill for their part in the conspiracy with the deposed King. And more - those of less than Patrician status - were even now closing out their lives in the circumference of the Circus, nailed by hands and feet to posts and beams erected hastily for that purpose.

Marcus was less than comforted at the haste at which the Senate called down the punishment onto the heads of the conspirators. It seemed that immediacy was more important than the assurance of the guilt of the accused, some of whom no doubt were swept up in the plot with little understanding of its meaning. But, Brutus gave short shrift to his mention of the worry, saying in effect, "When one is attacked by a pack of wild dogs, one cannot pause to determine the fierceness of each animal."

Only two men had escaped punishment, and that only partly. The fat Senator, Florus, was spared, with his assistance in identifying and testifying against the plotters, although his wealth and accumulations were seized, leaving him only his house and life. And, the street tough - the guard of Florus - that had spoken that day in the hut, and had been promised life in return, was personally escorted to the gate by Marcus and watched as he disappeared safely in the distance.

That day, about a half of a month in the past had been turbulent. Marcus had detailed four men to guard the hut and the prisoners within, and upon leaving, pulled the dagger from the table, freeing the hand of Florus. That man almost collapsed with the pain, but that was of little concern to either Marcus or the nobles.

He had led the little party of nobles and the other six soldiers down the via toward the old scribal house, but now the indifference of the street had been replaced by a chattering clamor. The people knew that something of significance was in progress, and there was a general movement up the street and away from... whatever was happening. As the rumors grew that soldiers in mass had been seen, most citizens had decided to wait for the news elsewhere, rather than attempt to gather it themselves.

Long before they approached the entrance to the building, the street had almost emptied itself, and they could see men in arms standing in the street - not threatening and in battle stance, but alert and waiting. Then, Marcus saw Rutilius, the Centurion of his archer units, standing at the door. As they approached, he stiffened and saluted, "Salve, Sos. We have the building invested, and the Commander Lucius awaits within."

Marcus just nodded and passed through the doorway into the scribery. Inside was a sight that he had anticipated, but not one that the Patricians following him were expecting. The large room was ringed with soldiers - some with swords at the ready and others with arrows nocked on the string. And, in the center, and against the two walls that had no openings, were an assortment of men - about thirty and mostly nobles - and in various states of disarray. Three men on the floor had obviously already crossed the river Styx, and several others that had been attendants and guards for the Patricians were in various degrees of impairment.

He had given his son orders not to harm the Senators and any of their ilk if possible, but to allow none to leave the building under pain of death. Obviously, several of the menials had been either ordered or made to try to protect their principals - a foolish attempt against a half Century of armed soldiers.

Now, with Brutus and Collatinus and the other Patricians standing and looking from behind the row of soldiers - still in some disbelief - the crowd in the building of the scribes knew they were undone. Most were older men - Senators who had been comfortable with the reign of the King and were pining for the return to the stability of his Throne. Marcus assumed that such was true the world over - young men craved change and excitement, and their elders wished only for peaceful smoothness in their ages.

Tricipitinus stood forward and called, "Atilius! You and I were boyhood friends together. Your pater and mine were as brothers. How can you come to such an affront to your people?"

The man made no answered, and Tricipitinus looked at another. "Tetras! The men of Tarquinius butchered your pater on the

Senate steps with King Tullius. By what grounds do you call for the support and return of the tyrant?"

The man was no coward, even knowing that his life was forfeit in all probability, and answered with his head high. "You are still high in your stature, Spurious Tricipitinus. You have not seen your family fortunes crumble with the new laws and rulings, and such decrees that change with the phases of the moon. I wish only for the stability of law. All men are ruled by kings - why think you that any civilization can be governed with co-hosts and that the gods would give exception to Rome?"

Marcus suddenly noticed Brutus. His face was as the vision of Hades itself. Following the sight of the noble, he saw the two sons standing in the crowd of conspirators. With a sinking heart, he realized that his hope that the two young men would not be in residence today was not to be fulfilled. He had planned to accost them - to seize both if necessary and have a unit of soldiers spirit them away to a villa or other place of hiding until he could concoct a tale of their heroism in infiltrating the dastardly plot and assistance in its destruction. Possibly, he still might accomplish that, if...

Now, Brutus shifted his vision to the center of the room. Then, turning, he gave an order in a brutal voice. "Commander. Your men will take these traitors to the Mamertine without fail. Inform the Captain of the prison to see that none escape, on penalty of his own head!"

Young Lucius was not actually a Commander - he was an Adiutor - an aide - given the position of unit leader by his father for this one action, but Marcus proudly watched as the youngster saluted the Consul in a firm voice, then turned and barked orders to his men.

"And Commander..." Lucius turned and saluted again. "Kill any who attempt to flee!"

By evening, the entire city was in an uproar - Patricians and Plebeians alike. The meeting of the Senate went far into the night and starting at the sun on the morrow after a brief rest, continued until it was gone from the sky - and not only on those two days. Marcus had no desire to attend such turbulent and frenetic meetings, and had no right to as a Plebeian and non-member of that body, but Brutus overrode the law that none but Senators might speak on the marble floor and demanded his presence. Knowing of the unhappiness and fury of the Consul - and the reason for it - none had any desire to contest the noble in any way.

Marcus gave a straightforward and quiet accounting of the events that led to the discovery of the conspiracy and answered a few questions from this Senator and that. His tale was taken as truth - all present knowing of his character and the absence of any motive for him to dissimulate. He found it interesting that many of the men - maybe a third part of the whole - had indicated a disposition of mercy toward the accused, despite the knowledge that their own lives would have probably been ended had the plot gone forward. The rest of the assembly, led by Brutus, was having no talk of such. Their only concern was to ferret out the rest of the plotters wherever they might be.

To that end, the inquisitors at the Mamertine were busy with questioning, and under the furious goad of Brutus, were not gentle in their interrogations. Every day, more men were led to cells under guard until the count became in the hundreds.

Now the rift between Collatinus and Brutus came into the open. Brutus had known of the disinterest of his friend in being co-Consul, or in any of the matters of government - or even his own affairs. And, he well knew the reason why and indulged Collatinus in his extended period of mourning for Lucretia. But, now, with the discovery that his own sons would be traitors to both Rome and their family, Brutus had little patience with weakness. The tension finally boiled over during a session in which Collatinus was vacillating over the proposals of the Senators for the resolution of the difficulty. Suddenly, and against all propriety of the rank of the co-Consul - or the fellowship of a lifetime, Brutus jumped to his feet and shouted over the words of his friend. "I will hear no further irresoluteness on this matter! We are not gathered to discuss the guilt or innocence of the accused - that has been established beyond all bounds!" He pointed a finger at Collatinus. "You, Consul, have given your opinion that this office is beyond your desire and capability. So be it, then. I call for your resignation of your position, or failing that, the decree of the Senate for your removal."

The marble chamber was dead silent, both for the sudden interruption of a ranking Consul by another and by the knowledge of the breakage of a friendship in view of the entire Senate. With his head bowed, Collatinus raised his hands for quiet, and the uproar faded away. He stood for a moment, then looked at the assembly before speaking. Then, "The co-Consul is correct in both his thinking and his speaking. I am unfit for the position, especially now in these turbulent times. One must be of active blood to lead Rome into the unknown future, and I must say that my being is not of that worth - not now, and maybe never more."

Again the pause before continuing. "I will resign my Consulship at this moment, and allow the Senate to cull out a replacement from among the honorable men assembled herein. To my good and venerable friend, Lucius Brutus, co-Consul, I hope indeed, that the pain brought to your life, through no imperfection of your own, will subside in time and that you might find a future, however remote, that gives peace to your being. To all here, I will wish the grace of the gods for your future deeds, and leave you to your august tasks."

Collatinus turned and strode from the building.

That evening, Marcus and young Sabina arrived at the house of Collatinus and were received with gladness by the noble, and his son in attendance, Manius. As the cups were poured, the master of the house raised his hand before his guest could give his sorrow at the happenings of the day. "Nay, good Marcus. Have no sadness on my account. I am as one who has been relieved of a great burden, and now can retire to allow my being to rest and refresh itself." He gestured to Manius. "My son will assume the Dominacy of the house, with all rights and reasons within, as of this day."

Marcus nodded behind his cup. "Then, Sos, will you make to the farm and villa that you spoke of earlier in the season?"

"Aye. My servants have already left with the essentials for my use." He looked across at the young girl with a smile. "But, fear not. On the date of the nuptials I will certainly return to see the progression of our families into the future." Looking aside at his son, he said, "Perhaps you and Sabina would prefer your own company rather than listening to men speaking of matters of disinterest." To his steward, he said, "Make the garden ready for the two young people, with Turullia as attendant."

Quickly, the two youngsters took their leave, gladsome beyond their hopes, and retired to a bench in the garden to speak of those things of interest only to such young people. And of course, always with the maid in full view to maintain the proprieties of an unmated couple.

The night went on, both men speaking only of old times, and favors - leaving the uncertain future from the conversations, with only the exception of the marriage of their son and daughter. Then, late, suddenly...

The steward entered and said, "Your pardon, Sos. The Consul Brutus sends his greetings and requests your pardon for the intrusion." Both men rose in some surprise as their old friend entered the Atrium.

Brutus spoke first. "I would have greatly regretted the loss, Lucius, should you have left Rome before my chance to alleviate the words that came from my mouth this day." He raised his hand to stop the reply. "Nay, my speaking was for the interest of Rome and I do not withdraw the meaning, but my choice of words was an offense to our long friendship, and I greatly regret my outburst."

"There is no friendship, however strong," returned Collatinus," that does not endure a small storm on occasion. The test of the strength of the bond is the refusal to allow such weather to capsize the vessel." He stepped forward to take the wrists of the Consul. "I took, and have taken, no offense at your words. Indeed, I will admit before the gods that they were spoken in all truth and regret only that I put my friend in such a position to have to utter such. I should have vacated the post and allowed for another to take the responsibilities long ago." He shook his head with a wry smile. "Nay, I should have refused the post at the beginning."

Marcus was overjoyed at the reunion of the two old friends and gestured to the low table. "Come. We were discussing the past and all the paths we have walked together, and with no speaking on the unknown future. We would be gladdened by the addition of your memory to ours."

Now, Collatinus was gone to his farm in the hills, his son assuming the position of Dominus over the household. It must be said that much of his time was spent in visits to the household in which the young Sabina resided - but not, it must be said, for the purpose of speaking to the master of the house. Marcus was amused, thinking of the similarities to another young man, years ago, that used any excuse to visit a certain household on the street of the Poet - and for the same reason.

Those happy thoughts were not in his mind today, standing in the front of his detail of men - the security for the happenings on the top of the summit of judgment. Publicola was the Judge of the Ceremonies this day - an appellation that Marcus thought odd given the circumstances. Funerary Director would seem to be a better name for the position.

Standing on the small platform at the edge of the cliff, Publicola was reading the proclamations of the Senate in a normal voice, but repeated in a shout to the people below by a leather-lunged magistrate from the Hall of Records. The tale of the plot was given, and the list of perpetrators that had been discovered, to the extent of many hundreds of names. Finally, the decree of punishment was read, and Publicola turned to the assembled Senators, standing on the leveled top of the small mountain. To Tricipitinus, the newly elected co-Consul, replacing his son-in law, he asked, "Does the count of the members of the Senate confirm the charges against the afore listed men?" At the reply of "Aye," he asked, "Does the Senate, in its majority, confirm the punishment for the elaborated crimes?" Again, another answer in the affirmative. Now, he faced the people below and said, "Both the guild and the punishment have been confirmed by the Senate of Rome." Turning to a group of men, garbed in the uniform of the civil Vigiles - the policemen of the city - he said, "Carry out the will of the Senate."

An elderly man, unknown to Marcus except for the knowledge that he was the head of a minor house, was brought forth, walking between two of the vigiles to stand on the square rock at the edge of the cliff. Each escort had a grip on an arm, to prevent the man from hurling himself onto the rocks below. It was important that none of the accused be allowed to offer their own punishment, but rather to have it placed upon them by the law.

The crowd below eerily silent - Marcus had never heard such quiet on the streets of Rome since he had come to the city. Now, the pair of vigiles suddenly flung the man over the edge of the cliff. From his stance, he could not see the unfortunate in his journey, but it took only the time between one breath and the next for the man to impact, broken, on the rocks below. Such was the punishment for traitors.

Now the crowd roared in... in... for what reason, he did not know. The removal of the threat from the city was a necessity, but he saw no reason for it to become a venue for entertainment in the Forum. But, his opinion was obviously in the minority - the citizens approved for whatever reason - desire for security, or pleasure in the misfortune of another, or just to bring excitement to their lives. Indeed, young Sabina had asked to be allowed to accompany her finance to the execution - a request that had been denied with no little heat and considerable emphasis. And, in fact, he had warned Cleo, and with no uncertain meaning, that she was not allowed out of the household for the day.

The next man was brought and flung to the rocks below. And the next, in an endless parade. Even the crowd began to gain their surfeit of the gruesome sights, and their roars of approval began to subside. Many even set their feet away from the Forum, for home or taburna, no doubt to engage in discussion of the events throughout the day and evening.

Then, Titus, the son of Brutus, was led forward to the execution stone. Moving his eyes, but not his head, Marcus watched the Consul for his reaction. There was none. Brutus just stood there watching as if the man were a stranger.

The sun was only a handspan above the western walls when the last was flung to his death, and the parties on the Tarpeian Rock began to disperse. Below, the crowd was only a skeleton of itself, most of the populace having long since tired of the spectacle. Marcus dismissed his men and set his feet for his own household. There, with a quick meal, he retired for the night and collapsed on his mat.

The activities of Marcus in experimenting with the unit of archers was a blessing. The days were full of strenuous exercise, and his mind was kept busy along with his sinews. Night brought weariness and immediate sleep without the long hours of wakefulness that were always filled with images and memories of Sabina.

Young Lucius was made his Optio - the second in command of the unit, now numbering almost three hundred men. Ennis and his contracted shaft carvers were kept busy supplying wagon loads of practice arrows to replace those that had been made ragged and splintered from being nocked and launched too many times.

He had many talks with veterans, trying to determine the optimum use for archers under different scenarios and terrains. As a result of the experiences, given over cups at this taburna and that, he had decided that the greatest threat would be mounted troops. A unit of Cavalry that managed to surprise a mass of bowmen, or planned their assault within thick foliage unsuited for arrows, would ride his archers down like ripe grain under a scythe. Against a unit of horse, his line of blade-wielding archers would be insufficient. Much thought and even more cups of wine with old soldiers went into the problem.

Then the problem became more than mere thought-play.

Marcus stood as the soldier was shown into the Atrium. The man came to attention, saluted, then said, "A missive from the Senior Centurion to the Commander Callidus, Sos!"

He dismissed the man, then read the small slip of reed-paper. Then, "Cleo! I will be away for the while. Find Lucius and have him come to me. Now."

The Headquarters building, adjacent to the old Palace, was filling with officers. The news had already gone around the room - that Tarquinius was marching - or about to - with a body of men from both the cities of Veii and Tarquinii. The numbers would rival those that could be put into the field by Rome.

Brutus was standing at a table, scanning this tablet and that scroll, and with aides coming and going from all sides. As Marcus approached, the Consul looked up and nodded, saying, "Commander. You may yet receive the chance to test your ideas on the field of battle."

"So, it is true.   Tarquinius is on the move."

"Aye. And with great force. Your men will need to be called to formation after this assembly."

Marcus nodded. "Lucius is already at the barracks and with orders to garb for march and battle."   He hesitated, then continued with, "Might I request that the unit of Flavis be assigned to myself for the nonce?   This campaign will have little need for rams, but I may have a use for his skills."

"Aye. I have no objection. But, now, let us attend to this meeting."

Trial

This would not be an adventure for aggrandizement and pillage, as those that had come before. Now, the future of Rome as a self-governing entity was in the balance. There was no doubt in the minds of all, that should Tarquinius claim victory, the lives of most of any position in the city would be both short and unpleasant.

In the household of Marcus, the entire family and all that lived within were gathered in the Atrium to say their farewells. In addition, Pythes had arrived in a chair, with young Marcus and a servant with burdens. Young Lucius was present, of course, as was Flavis and Manius, now a newly fledged Tribune. Marcus had had the new officer assigned to himself, so as to be able to watch over both the son of a friend and a potential son-in-law.

A final meal was taken, too early for the midday eating, but far too late to be considered the break of the fast. Still, it would be the last repast of any quality for a considerable period. From this time on, the food would be marching rations. Young Sabina had hired another cook for the occasion and made the meal a banquet for her men.

Now, young Marcus stood and motioned for his servant to enter with a large and heavy bundle. He looked at the four men about to leave to the wars, and said, "My brother can attest that my knowledge of blades and iron is probably no greater than that of my sister - and maybe less, but..." He motioned for the bundle to be set down. "...I have engaged your old friend and comrade, the Hastilairius, Dursus, for advice. He sends his greetings, but also his regrets that the number of seasons behind him prevents his attending your leaving."

Marcus had not seen the - now - old man for ages, it seemed. "How is my old sword teacher?"

"His wit is sharp, but, alas, his body has not stayed the course of years. He is confined to the soldier home with his comrades, mostly telling tales of old battles over cups, it seems. But, he gave advice about my purchases, and, fortunately, they have moved the distance from the far land of their creation to here in time for use."

He pulled a long object from the bag - a sword, in scabbard. Handing it to his father, he retrieved another and gave it to his brother. Then one each to Flavis and Manius. The men automatically pulled the metal from the leather holders, looking with professional eyes at the weapons. No products of a Roman forge, these - they bore the names of the weapons-makers and the telltale marks - nu, tau, and phi - that indicated testing with ten full strokes against wood, a shield, and stone - each. These were the fabulous blades of Sparta, which far off Greek civilization that had been dedicated to war since its founding in the mists of time. But, unlike the iron carried by the men of those lands, whose propensity was for length, these were short gladiae, about arms length, in the Roman style.

"I will take it greatly amiss if any of you fail to return from your duties. These may assist in that endeavor. I doubt that these have greater quality than your faithful old blade, Father, but the Roman edges carried by Lucius and Flavis and Manius should be consigned to the cocua for skinning of meat, not defending against strokes from an unfriendly arm."

With widened eyes, the younger men looked at the shining blades, gleaming silver and with a sheen of oil in the light from the opened roof-window above. Sabina laughed. "My brother and his friends have seen their new loves."

Marcus looked to his like-named son and asked, "How did you procure such in the month from our call-up?"

Now Pythes spoke with a chuckle. "Nay, Marcus. Unless he has much favor with the god, Mercury, and the mount of Pegasus as his steed, no trades could make the distance in ten times that month. Rather, he has placed his order at the time when the King was deposed." He nodded to the young man. "He has the gift of far-seeing, that one."

"Our thanks to you, my son." This was echoed by the others, but the younger Marcus just waved a hand in dismissal. "I am thinking of merchantry, Father. Profit is more steadily made in peaceful times and the sooner those have arrived..."

The farewells were made, Sabina and the women giving the proper sobs of anxiety for the men, and the four made their way to the encampment outside the walls of the city. To the younger Marcus, the Father gave a last bidding to maintain a watch over his sister, and her household until the return of the soldiers.

Once again, the Roman army was on the march, leaving only the older veterans for the defense of the city. The usual marching formation was taken, and soon the tramp of feet could be heard even over the walls. Marcus and his unit of three full Centuries were far back in the procession, and followed by Flavis with his unit of mechanici and architecti - they leading a caravan of oxen-pulled wagons with the implements of their work - and also, certain products of possible use.

One hour before sundown, a traveling encampment was hurriedly laid out, and the men called to mess. In the tent of Brutus, the unit officers met for news and instructions. Tricipitinus was pointing to a hastily drawn map, scribed on the tabletop itself with a charcoal stick. "Tarquinius is reported to be east of Veii, encamped about... here. Between the forest and the hills."

A Tribune pointed to the area and replied, "A strange destination for an army of size. That is all woodland and uneven terrain, unsuited for horse or marchers. The roads are few and narrow."

Marcus agreed with the statement. He had never been in that area, but it would be the same as the foothills of his youth, and the Tribune's statements would match the actual reality. Of all the men at the table, he was the only Plebeian, and only real grounds for his being present were his friendship with the Consul Brutus - now the Dux of the army - and his previous prowess at battle. Even young Manius, a Tribune by virtue of his noble blood, was more entitled to a spot at the table than he - even though the youngster knew little more of war than the loom girls of Sabina.

He knew that his opinion was not desired in a campaign not needing the reduction of walls or gates. But, to himself, the question of Tarquinius and his combined armies was not the fact that they were encamped in the foothills, but why. The open plains along the seacoast were the natural battlefields and had been since time began. Armies could see each other, and maneuver freely, each trying to gain ascendence on the other. But in the uplands, the last man in even an eight-man Contubernium could barely see his Commander in the front through the brush and trees. Other than one-on-one skirmishes, formal battle was almost impossible. Tarquinius might be a tyrant, but he was no fool. That he had a good reason for his unlikely camping spot, Marcus had absolutely no doubt.

The meeting ended with little more news of use, and Marcus followed the men into the gathering dark. Suddenly, as he set foot for his encampment area, he stopped, seeing a familiar face under the red brush of a Centurion.

"Maxentius! By the gods, it has been... how long?" They met and took each others wrists in greeting. "The last I heard, you were the given assign to the Governor's officer in... where was it? Narii?"

"Aye. Until the word came about the revolt." A pause, then, "And the cause." Maxentius lowered his voice. "I was saddened by the evil news of the passing of your Sabina."

Marcus just nodded, and his friend knew that nothing more was expected. Then he asked, with a grin, "I knew you had earned the red brush, but my source didn't know the unit."

"Ah. Collatinus got me the leadership of the seventh Century before he... decided to rest for the while. My Tribune is Darnus - a good man, if somewhat of a gambler." He punched his friend in the shoulder. "And you have certainly not been deficient in your rise through the ranks."

Marcus looked around in the fading light. "My tent is at the road with the wagons of the Architecti. Come to our mess tonight and we will speak of old times."

The evening was pleasurable, and with his fellow Adiutor-of-old sitting beside him before an unneeded fire, they spoke of their long friendship, starting at that training barracks years ago. Manius and Flavis also sat and listened, and finally the conversation came around to the current situation. "...and why would Tarquinius decide on this spot rather than another? He must take some advantage in position by selecting these lands as his choice. Why not just march toward Rome and take battle when we collide?"

Maxentius shook his head and replied, "I can only give you what I have overheard in the Tribune tents." He raised himself on his knees and smoothed the patch of earth before him. First a big circle was drawn with a stick. "This is the provence of Silvanus - don't ask me what that means, but it is not all forest, as seems to be the belief among us. One of the men in our Century was a lad in this area, and hunted with the father of his father - a furrier in trade." A line was drawn in the dirt. "The foothills come down the mountains to here, and..." Another line. "...the forest ends here. It is called the Silva Arsia, but again, do not ask me the meaning. Our soldier says that between it and the hills is a long grassy flatland, and from his memory might be as wide as the men of four centuries holding hands. The area was used in the past as a sacred assembling ground by forgotten peoples and at the time of the man's youth, had a crumbling temple in the middle of the flats."

Marius spoke up. "But why come to the mountains for a battle, when the lowlands have vast plains for all the armies in history?"

"Ah. You touch it with a needle. According to my Tribune, speaking from talk at the command tents, it is because of this year, and in particular, the rains that we have received."

Marcus nodded. It had been an exceedingly wet month, since the heat of summer had subsided, and had caused problems with not only travel, but with the fishermen on the Tiber and the farmers in the grain fields. This he had heard in many complaints from his son, young Marcus, and about the losses that all merchants were sustaining from the unusual downpours.

Maxentius continued, poking his stick here and there for emphasis. "Tarquinius has considerable cavalry, and of good quality it is said, and he obviously wishes to use it to effect in battle. Thus, hard and dry land is needed that can only be found in the uplands at the present."

"And our horse?" asked Flavis. "It is of a worth to battle the foe?"

Now Maxentius looked around, here and there, before answering in a lowered voice. "I have to repeat what a stabler told me. That most of our riders would be overtaxed in riding an ass to market. They are all men from noble families, and with shining equipment and weapons, but most have little experience beyond galloping their mounts in the Circus to the applause of women. What they will do when faced with a thundering onslaught of real horse..." He left the sentence unfinished.

The morning time brought news that, indeed, Tarquinius and his army were encamped on the edge of the forest that was named Silva Arsia, and just... waiting. A long days march would bring them to the area, and after a meeting of Commanders, it began.

The light was fading when they reached their destination, and the establishment of the camp had to be accomplished in partial darkness. Marcus hoped that extended posts were set out, as the mass of their foe was just on the horizon, it was said. For his unit, he gathered the sub-officers and ordered that word be given for the men to sleep with their weapons close - not strung, but capable of being so in the time of two or three breaths. Any with long blades should keep them at hand. He knew that battles had rarely ever taken place in the darkness - in fact, during the early years of his trying to learn the art of war, Sabina had not found any history where anything other than a skirmish had happened in the darkness - but he and his Tribune had learned, years ago, in foothills not unlike these, of the penalty that could be given for unwatchfulness.

It was the leader of the Roman Legion that was the uppermost in the concern of Marcus - Brutus. Since the discovery of the treason by his sons, the man - now the Dux of the army - had changed. The amiable side of his being had fallen away, its place taken by an ever deeper hatred of the man that had caused offense against his family since the day of the succession by force. The murders of his father and brother long ago, the degradation of the family name for sport, offenses by the royal family against friends - and now, the taking of the gens of Brutus by treason. All fed on each other in his mind, now, to the exclusion of all else that had been a good friend.

The worry of Marcus, was that the desire for vengeance would override any ability to lead in war. Far more was needed for the outcome of this battle, than just the death of Tarquinius. No doubt, there were other generals within the host of the foe who would gladly step forward to take the place of their leader, and continue the attempt in the subjugation of Rome.

The first rays of the sun were barely streaking the sky over the mountains to the east, when both Marcus and the Centurion, Rutilius, were riding toward the low foothills toward the sun. Neither had any great skill on horseback - and certainly not to the extent of engaging in battle from the backs of the animals - but they could certainly use the beasts for transport, and a mounted man arrived at his task much faster than one on foot.

On a low hill, they stopped and waited for the increasing light to reveal the extent of the landscape. Soon, it was apparent that the soldier in the ranks had spoken truly - between the hills and the start of the forest of Arsia was a long plain, not as flat as a grain field, certainly, but certainly open enough for armies to clash. Far in the distance, they could see the smoke from the morning fires of their foe, and of course, much closer, the Roman encampment.

"I would say that the distance to the trees is about three stadia," commented Marcus.

"Aye, Sos. At least that," replied the Centurion. He pointed down the field, along the side of hill. "That is a ravine, it would seem, so I would take that the cavalry will take the field on the other side."

Marcus did not care about the plains themselves. Wherever his archers would make their stand, it would not be in the open of the grassland - that would be foolish. Rather, he turned his gaze upon the hills and valleys on the sun-side of the field. No barriers for men, these, or horses, but no units could maintain any formation in movement here. And in one way, at least, that was gladsome.

Now, he turned and led his sub-officer in a canter back toward the encampment, passing the outposts of the Romans without pause. By the time the sun had appeared, they were on the opposite side of the field and at the edge of the forest. It was far thicker than those of his youth - and more like the low brush lands of the coastal plain, except that the trees here were of the needle type and much taller. Bowmen would be useless in this mass of wood, but, it could give cover for any deployments.

"I have seen enough. Let us return to our morning meal and the staff meetings."

As the men fed, then began to enter their formations, the Commanders gathered in front of the tent of the Dux. The general command structure had not changed from that set before leaving Rome. Brutus was the Dux of the Legion, but would take command of the Roman horse, but not from the back of an animal, Marcus assumed. The co-Consul, Triciptinius, was in charge of the infantry, with Publicola taking command of the Velites - light auxiliaries composed of men with javelins and slings, and even some archers of indeterminate skill.

Brutus gave a swift series of formation orders, ordering this unit here and that one to there. A discussion of tactics followed, then the questions tailed of as the officers waited for the order to return to the units.

Marcus realized that the briefing was about to end without any discussion of his orders. "Sos. If I may ask about my unit of bowmen? My suggestion is that we can best mass our strength at the end of the line." Marcus had no words for military argot - the terms 'flank' and 'inflade' and 'defense in depth' were not in his vocabulary, but his practical mind could see the concepts all the same.

Brutus looked at him for a moment, obviously with his mind on the coming battle rather than the placement of a few units of men with little use - to his mind - in this battle. Finally, he said, "Nay. Your men would be as insects under the hooves of their horse in such openness. Set your formation behind the center of Triciptinius. You may engage any that might appear to be gaining an opening." With that, he strode to his waiting horse, mounted and galloped off with his staff in trail.

To Marcus, the orders were totally unsatisfactory. To stay in the rear of the huge mass of infantry would make them blind. And, shooting over the heads of their own men in the chaos of a battle would take the chance of marking down a friend. Obviously, the Dux thought as most Commanders - that a bowman was useful for a siege, or harrying the enemy outposts, but of no use for standing in a line of battle.

Still, the orders were sufficiently vague that one might bend them here and there.

Resolution

Marcus had seen many a siege, but never a pitched battle between almost equally numbered armies. And this day, he was not to add to his experience with any haste. Lucius had his men in marching formation to the eastern side of the encampment, but with orders to let the men rest in their own manner, rather than standing interminably waiting for commands that might not come. Once again, both he and Rutilius were on horseback and standing on a low hill overlooking the long field. Both armies were lined up in formation, standing and, at least, ten stadia apart. Far enough that neither could tell one individual from another.

The formations were simple - soldiers were lined shoulder to shoulder across the centerline of the field, spears raised like a field of martial grain, and in ranks many men deep. At the far side from where Marcus and his Centurion were watching were the milling throngs of the horse cavalry, then the bulk of the Roman army, the heavy infantry, and closest to their vantage point, the much less orderly lines of Velites.

And, in the center behind the heavy infantry, were the three centuries of archers. To anyone with the leisure to glance around the field, as Marcus and his Centurion were doing now, they might be puzzled by another group of men - about a Century or so - behind the mass of bowmen. But, these men were not in formation and were clustered around a double handful of small wagons.

Moving back and forth behind the formations were two small groupings of horsemen, and even from this distance could be seen to be well accoutered. These were both infantry Commanders, Triciptinius and Publicola and their staffs. In the usual fashion, they would lead from the rear, sending commands by runner to here and there, although in actual fact, once the field of battle was joined, few commands would be acted upon, or even heard, by men attempting to stay alive in a forest of spears and blades.

Looking down the field, even that distance he could see that the forces of Tarquinius were arraigned in much the same manner. A small group of horse could be seen to move back and forth along the front of the foe. Marcus assumed that it was the deposed King giving the obligatory martial words to his men before battle.

And in the same manner, a group of men stood in front of the Roman forces - Brutus and his staff. And several priests of Mars. On a small wooden altar, they were examining the entrails of some unfortunate animal, attempting to ascertain the will of the gods on this day. Or maybe, entreating that deity to lend his sword arm to the Romans. Marcus doubted that livers and intestines had any ability to see into the future, but it was the Roman way, and the lack of such ritual would be seen by the soldiers as an evil omen.

"Tell me, Rutilius. Do the men just march toward each other and begin the fray? No maneuvers or other tactics?"

The Centurion was gazing across the field at the army of Tarquinius, far to the north. "Aye, Sos. So it has been in my experience. I know of no other way that it could be done."

To Marcus, it was... unsatisfactory. He had no experience in battle beyond the assault of a city, but in all of history, certainly some general must have formulated a different strategy than just walking forward to hack and slay. Maybe to send a formation to harry the enemy from behind, or to at least give the impression of doing so, and draw the attention of the enemy to another quarter. He nodded to himself. Aye, if the mass of Roman cavalry were to hit the enemy from the side, they might drive through the infantry of the foe like an arrow through a butt of hay. Or...

"The rites are over, Sos." The priests and their acolytes were retreating with alacrity through the formation. Now, Marcus expected the battle to begin in earnest, but the Commanders seemed to have no sense of haste. Considerable time passed before any movement could be seen, then finally, the lines began to march forward. Far down the field, a ripple of movement could be seen - the lines of Tarquinius were also in movement.

Now, Marcus motioned to follow, and he walked his horse along the hilly ground so as to keep abreast with the marching line of Romans. The Commander of the bowmen, his son, Lucius, had been ordered to withhold any action until his return - unless the situation admitted of no delay. Marking down individual soldiers was not in the training of his men, nor in his plans for their use. And the marksmanship needed for such accuracy on a field of battle would be difficult for any archer standing elbow to elbow in a mass of his own comrades.

The time passed, and the men marched at the pace of a walking steed until the two armies were separated by about a stadium of distance - about two hundred long strides. There, both stopped and began to demonstrate to each other. Marcus wondered if it was initiated by officers, or just from the impulse of men who were standing with hot blood racing in anticipation of what was coming. From the hill of their observation, and at the very eastern end of the

Roman line, the shouts and curses were merged into a general clamor with little discernment.

Suddenly, the mass of cavalry of the foe lunged forward in full gallop toward their opposite mounted foe, on the far side of the field. Marcus assumed that the engagement had started, but in only a few heartbeats the thundering horses were pulled to a stop, then turned to retreat to their line of start. Then, unbelievingly to Marcus, the same maneuver was made by the Roman cavalry. This was like the sparring of two young boys, circling one another and waving clinched fists, but not actually closing to strike in the fear of the possible consequences that might come from such conflict.

Marcus knew nothing of cavalry, and even less of its use in war beyond the casual discussions with his noble friends. Still, he knew that the main weapon of the mounted rider was the hooves of his steed, and in mass could ride a formation of infantry into the ground. Secondary to the fearsome capability of trampling a foe underfoot were the small sheaths of spears - pila - that were carried in two leather pouches - one on each side of the mount. These would be thrown in passing or into the massed formations from a position away from the foe. Using a spear in the usual manner, or swinging a sword at a man standing with his feet firmly on the ground, was an excellent method to become unhorsed. With only a rosined blanket and a firm grip with legs preventing the rider from being ejected from the back of the horse, any violent thrusts or movements were to be avoided. Indeed, in a rapid charge even the use of the throwing pilum was not to be attempted, as even the arms of the riders were needed around the neck of the horse if the man was not to find himself rolling and stunned on the ground.

On and on it went, the infantry of both formations shaking their spears, or blades, and throwing curses or japes at their foe. And again the horse of both armies made their mock charges that resulted in no battle.

Marcus shook his head, then bit off a scathing remark about such boys and their mock courage as he remembered that his Centurion was a blooded veteran of the army and might take such japing as offense. Rather, he asked, "Is this a preamble to battle that is the normal course?"

The Centurion nodded. "Aye, Sos. The men demonstrate as a way to gather their spirits for the fray. It will not last much longer."

He was correct. A few arrows lofted from the ranks of the Tarquinian army, falling far short of the Roman line, but it was as if a sudden agreement had been reached between the foes. Now the infantry of both began the march toward each other, the spears of each suddenly falling from the high carry position to the horizontal. It would only be another few...

"Look, Sos. The Dux is at the lead, now!"

Marcus could see the mount of Brutus with the red blanket, and at the lead of the charging Roman cavalry. That was the act of a madman or one who cared little for the continuance of his life. The Consul was not a young man and was in a battle where youth counted for much. Also, the leader of the Roman horse would be the desired mark of all who saw him.

The Centurion could not believe what he was seeing. The general of the Army - any army - did not lead the point of his force. "He has lost his reason..." The sub-officer stopped, realizing that he was not only criticizing an officer in front of another, but the Dux of the entire Legion. "I mean, Sos. It is most unwise for..."

Marcus shook his head. "Nay, Centurion. You may say your mind. It runs the same course as mine. The gods have taken his sanity this day." Unlike Rutilius, he had known of the bending of the mind of his friend since the day that his sons had been exposed as traitors. Like Collatinus, after that worthy's loss of Lucretia, his desire for the continuance of the thread of his being had evaporated, although Marcus had not suspected that Brutus might descend to the depths of self-immolation. He realized in sorrow that his friend would end his life this day.

And, indeed, this sortie by the horse of each army did not end in mock retreat. Rather, they met like two stones rolling together at speed. Even at this distance, the clash was loud with the meeting of both metal and flesh. As he watched the distances between the infantries closed until suddenly, the battle was general. Lines of men, stadia in length, all thrusting and dying together.

The clash of the infantry continued unabated, but the two units of cavalry untwined and retreated a distance, then returned together with speed. Now both men and horses littered the field, some motionless - others attempting to limp or crawl away, and those, many times, trampled into the ground by the next charge.

The light units of Publicola, being closest to the hill from which Marcus and Rutilius were observing, could be seen more clearly than others. And they were not fairing well. The neat formations from which they had started had fallen apart and the men were fighting in a huge amorphous mass. Or attempting to. Some men were finding the extent of their courage did not reach far and were already moving back through the ranks. Indeed, a few were in full flight across the grass toward the Roman encampment. Marcus had anticipated that, being warned by his Centurion beforehand that the steadiness of light troops was weak, at best. These were the soldiers from the lowest classes of the city, poorly equipped and armored and certainly untrained in battle. In a way, this was the method with which the Army culled its recruits. Those that stood steady would eventually graduate to the regular ranks of the veterans while those that ran would face shame - and punishment.

Of course, if Rome were not victorious, then the cowards would have little to fear from their leaders.

Across the field, the battle of the horsemen was taking its toll of both sides. Rome had the greater number, but it was fairly obvious that Tarquinius had the more experienced riders. Still, one weakness countered the other, and the masses of both human and animal flesh now littering the far side of the battlefield did not seem to favor either side.

Suddenly, Marcus saw the center of the Roman line, steady until now, began a steady backward movement. This would be the ultimate disaster if the core of the Army was giving way. Instantly, he thought of his options, and if his mass of archers could slow the push of the enemy by shooting over the friendly formation. Turning to Rutilius, he said "Quickly, we will ride to our unit and give our force to the center. Mayhap we can stall the withdrawal."

The Centurion waved his hands emphatically. "Nay, Sos! It is not as it seems... Pardon, Sos... but..." He stopped, uncertain as to his ground.

"Speak your thoughts, Centurion! I do not wish military correctness over the truth and especially not this day."

The man nodded, the pointed. "Consul Tricipitinus is no fell tactician, but he is a steady hand at war. I was there, many seasons ago, when he was a young Tribune, and I just a man with a spear. In the fight against the Etruscans at Coheni, he steadied the line even as his superiors were smitten with panic." Another point of his hand. "Here, he has ordered the line to step backward a few handfuls of paces and for reason. By that movement our men will still be on firm ground, but their foe will be stumbling over the bodies and broken equipment of both sides. See now, the rearward move has already ceased."

And it was true. What had seemed to be the beginning of a disaster was, instead, a proper military move. But... To counter that was the obvious ineptness of Publicola. The general was galloping back and forth along his crumbling line, apparently giving this order and that, but not waiting to see it carried out. Were it not for the steadiness of the officers and a number of his men, the units would have dissolved into vapor. But, slowly, that entire wing of the Romans was being bent back like a hinged door.

Again, Marcus tried to think of a counter for the weakness. To mass his unit behind the troops of Publicola would just get them trampled and routed if the line gave way completely. But, even three hundred archers could not possibly step out and face a double thousand or more without a thick line of spears for protection during their work. Not at close range, at least. Fortunately, Tricipitinus had seen the problem - or had been told of it - and rode over with his staff to alleviate the situation. Marcus and the Centurion saw his staff members ride to various parts of the line. In a few moments, the rear of Publicola was shifting, drawing inward to make a shorter line, but with thicker ranks. It took a while to see the effect, but the rearward movement ceased. Then again, the main body was ordered to step backward and for the same reason as before, but to also allow the realignment of the formations with those of Publicola.

The movement now froze on the field. Neither army winning nor losing, but with the front ranks of both fighting until the men were either dead or exhausted - falling or stepping back and being replaced by fresh ranks from behind. Marcus was appalled by the slaughter taking place. In comparison to the far less bloody sieges of his city-breaking, this was a scene from Hades. There would be many a household - both high and low - with missing sons and husbands and fathers at the end of this day.

On the far side, the horsemen of both armies had finally ceased their charges. More than half were laying on the field as casualties, and a good part of those left mounted were sorely wounded and being led to the rear by their horse-handlers. Neither had gained the victory over the other, but it was obvious that the inexperienced noble youth of the Romans had received the worst of it. The riders of Tarquinius - exhausted men sitting on blown horses and sorely depleted in numbers - were at least still gathered as a unit, whereas the Roman mounts and men were scattered hither and yon across the field behind the infantry.

Marcus suddenly realized that the time had come. If the remaining riders of Tarquinius gathered their wind, they could ride around the left and hit Triciptinius in the side. Even if done by tired men with little power, it might be enough to disrupt the line that, thus far, had held steady. He kicked his horse into a gallop down the slope and along the line behind the infantry. Lucius and his officers were waiting in a group at the front of their men as he vaulted from his horse and began to issue orders.

Now the months of maneuver on the training fields came back with much profit. The orders were understood without question, and the sub-officers scattered to their units to begin the move. Marcus boosted back onto his mount and waited - his duties done for the nonce. Now the man from Apulia, or Campania, or Saminum, or any of the many provinces of the world that were represented in his units, would make the tale. He would far rather be standing in the ranks with a bow, but a Commander did not have the satisfaction of striking the personal blow against an enemy.

Or, at least, one who was proper fulfilling his command duty did not. He briefly thought of Brutus, and the chances of his being alive, even now. And he was certain, without actually knowing, that the Dux - his lifelong friend - almost assuredly was not.

At least from horseback, he could gain a much farther perspective than a man on the ground. The clash of combat from the infantry units was still paramount, with neither side gaining - or losing. Toward the other direction, he could see the men of Flavis trotting along with their burdens - four and five to a man. And in front, the loping column of archers snaking along behind the fighting.

Now was the time of danger to his plan. If his men were hit by a force before they assembled and made ready, then they were doomed. Looking over the mass of struggling men, he was comforted that the calvary of Tarquinius was still standing in their place, beyond and aside of the fighting. The line of men came to the gap between the forest and the end of the infantry, previously used as a corridor for the calvary to advance and retreat, but now empty except for the bodies of both men and mounts.

Quickly, his men formed three long ranks, a Century long, each, and one behind the other, and placed diagonally to the line of fighting, with the far end at the trees being forward many paces. Bows were hurriedly strung and arrows nocked, but, the formation was not yet complete. In the front of the three lines was another, shorter and also composed of bowmen, but these were men who had some measure of experience in war. These also carried the long Greek spear that, grounded, would give protection against charging horses. But, even they were not the front rank of defense.

Now the men of Flavis arrived and ran along the front of the formation, about ten paces forward of the lines of men, each man tossing his burdens to the ground, here and there, as if he were sowing some evil kind of seed. Shortly, the line of archers was fronted by a field of strange, but sinister looking devices, and their bearers hurried out of the line of combat for the relative safety of the wagons many strides behind the bowmen.

These were the results of the many trials by both Marcus and Flavis to the problem of protecting archers from frontal attack by foot soldiers and, mainly, calvary charges. Simply made of two arm-length rods of iron, sharpened on the ends and forged together at the center point of both, then bent to form a device that could be tossed to the ground without worry about which side was given the rest. Tricipitinius, upon seeing one displayed by Marcus months ago, gave it the name of Calcitrapa - a foot-trap. And he commented on the clever tetrahedron shape that allowed it to be dropped in any position and to give the same menacing aspect to anyone who approached. But, to Marcus, without the assistance of his beloved Sabina, the words meant nothing. Instead, he used the name given the device by his men - Spinepig, after that strange animal of the forest that protected itself from all directions with a covering of sharp needles.

The ground in front of the archers was now as an evil cabbage patch, belonging to some particularly cruel demon of war. With their position, diagonal to and hinged at the line of Roman infantry, the archers could cover the entire approach in a fan, from the tree line to the mass of milling men, fighting to the death.

And for now, it was this last that was their point of aim. The front ranks of the foe, in close engagement with the Romans, could not be marked - else many arrows would find lodgment in the bodies of friends, but the following ranks, both those that were fresh and unbloodied, and the withdrawing wounded and exhausted, were fair game. It was important that the power be brought to bear before the foe could realize the coming of the bowmen.

Now, Lucius, standing in the forefront of his unit, gave a command to his flagman, who then raised a yellow flag. The mass of archers, taking both their aim and slant from the long and brightly colored pole, raised, drew and released. From behind the hinge point of the formation, Marcus and Rutilius could hear the mass of shafts - almost a third part of a thousand - as they left the bows and arced over the battlefield. It was like a loud wind through the needle trees, presaging the start of a fierce mountain storm. It was doubtful that any within hearing - and with the leisure to wonder - had ever heard such noise made by the hand of man. But, the result was noticed by all who viewed the point of descent of the arrows.

Coming from the side, the shafts avoided the shields, held to the front in anticipation of joining the carnage on the front line. In the densely packed formation of the Tarquinian infantry, more than one in two entered a man in some part of his body - arms, torso, legs, neck, or head. No matter if the wood made a kill - any man with an arm-long shaft suddenly protruding through an appendage was no longer a foe that had to be faced by the sweating and cursing Roman infantry.

But the power of the massed archers was only beginning to be displayed. The first shafts had barely impacted when the roar of the wind was heard again, and more death rained from the sky. Then again and again, until the ranks of the foe, on their side of the field, began to disintegrate. Most did not know why, being immersed in a mass of their own comrades who shielded the far off archers from view.

A red flag was raised, to indicate a change of aim. Now the pole indicated the same direction, but with an increased slant. The farther point of aim had the effect of spreading the placement of the impacts, but that made little difference. And the new victims of the rain of wood had even less understanding of where their deaths were coming, being on the far side of several hundred men.

Only the western ranks of the enemy could be targeted, since, even with the skill of the Roman archers, the far end of the line was out of range of even one of the magical bows from the workshop of the House of Callidus. And, only a few of the men had been equipped with such wood.

"I have a count of five and twenty, Sos." Marcus nodded. The Centurion had been tasked with numerating the number of expended shafts so as to allow for replenishment to arrive should it be needed. As all men were carrying a double quiver, thus far they had only used one in four of their wood. He looked behind and toward the Roman encampment. There was Flavis and his wagons, piled high with more shafts, should they be needed, and only waiting for a white cloth to be waved by Marcus, to cause his men to run forward with armloads to refill the quivers.

Now, the action of the unit was being noticed and understood by the officers far across the field. Messengers could be seen hurrying back and forth, no doubt with orders to shift forces to confront this new threat. Then came the action that Marcus was anticipating with some concern. The remaining cavalry began to form and move forward.

Marcus watched his son, and with no little pride, as the young man commanded his men as if he were a decades old veteran. Standing beside the young Commander was Manius, his future son-in-law, who was charged with the observation of the entire field of conflict, and to warn should some threat appear that was not noticed by men concentrating on their immediate foe.   Collatinus would be proud of his normally quiet and retiring son, also.   The Manius was exhibiting the excitement and anxiety of any young man new to battle, but he stood steady at his post, watching to here and there.

Not knowing if Lucius, in his concentration on the Tarquinian infantry, had noticed the assembling of the new threat, he was about to send the Centurion to give the alert, but suddenly the red flag appeared and the archers shifted aim.   There was no release, as the horsemen were still out of range, but their new foe was being measured for destruction.

Marcus knew - not from experience, but from many queries to experienced horsemen - that the animals recovered from exertions much more slowly than a man.   And as the mounts of both armies had been run to almost staggering collapse, he did not expect a thundering charge.   Rather, the force would approach closely, then expend the remaining strength of their steeds in the final distance.   It should make no difference, he hoped.   If the men stood steady in the face of an approach that would be terrifying to the usual foot soldier, it was unlikely that horse or man would endure the rain of wood from the sky.

Still, there were more horsemen than archers, and if only a few entered the ranks of the bowmen, the results would be devastating.   Once again, unbidden, came the old thought, "An archer on a hill is a king.   In close combat he is a dead man."   Hopefully, the scattered and numerous spinepigs to the fore, and the rank of long spears ready to be raised and grounded, would give at least some of the protections of a hill.

The horsemen grew larger as they trotted forward, entering the maximum range of the bows, but Lucius held his command.   The first volleys needed to be both a surprise and effective since at a gallop the cavalry could cover the distance in less time than the men could nock and draw a handful of times.

Now, he heard the stentorian voice of an aide call the ready.   The flag with its pointing and ranging was not needed.   The archers could well see their targets approaching in the open field.   Now, Marcus raised his prayers to some god, somewhere.   The foe was in a tight and grouped formation - normal for calvary as it gave the maximum thrust at the point of impact.   But, in their weariness - or maybe ignorance - they failed to consider that their objective was not a like body of enemy horse, to be hit and hopefully scattered, but a long line of men with little depth.   The Commander should have realized that a stretched out and widely scattered formation would make his men vastly less vulnerable to a rain of wood.

Then, with a shout, echoed up and down the line by sub-officers, that deluge began. The arrows, coming from a century wide and triple line of archers, naturally converged on the tight grouping of riders as water gathers in a funnel. The riders at the front of the pack went down as if the club of Hercules had been wielded against the leaders. The men and their mounts died almost to a man, transfixed by arrows too numerous to count. And now the storm began in earnest.

The forward riders, rearing, falling, and bolting, were an obstacle to the following horsemen. Marcus had seen the Commander - a man with a white brushed helmet - fall with almost a quiver of arrows in both he and his mount. But, before his second, wherever he might be, could call his men to order the whistling roar descended again. And again. Any rally by the foe was undone before it could be called. Even their attempt to withdraw out of the deadly rain was a confused mass of screaming horses and frantic men - many sporting new appendages sticking out of some part of their body.

Then, it was over. The remnants galloping - or moving as fast as blown horses could stumble - to the rear. Lucius gave no time for rejoicing. The pole with the yellow flag was raised again, and the storm of wood once again descended on the near infantry of the foe.

Marcus just sat, his heart beating as if a drum calling men to battle. The engagement that he had prepared for - had examined day after day in his mind, and talked with in innumerable conversations with this horseman or that... It had been the most trivial part of the battle for his men. The spinepigs had not been needed - indeed, no rider had even approached one close enough for his eyes to wonder its purpose. The galloping charge that had been expected had not begun, having been destroyed in gestation.

Still, his men had been shooting at riders who had already rendered their all in battle, and whose mounts had even less remaining to give. Had the skirmish been against the full unit of horse, unwearied by previous battle, and at full strength, then the outcome could well have been different. He doubted that three hundred archers, no matter how skilled and stouthearted, could have stopped a full charge of a unit of a thousand horse before they closed the distance over the range of an arrow. Still, the day was about results, not examinations over what might have happened.

The near infantry of Tarquinius had almost dissolved from the arrows, allowing for the Tricipitinus to move men fronting that area to buttress the center of the line. Now that formation, with the additional men, became narrower and much deeper. And that depth began to tell. There was a steady drift of men out of the ranks of Tarquinius, and toward the rear. Not cowards - they were not fleeing - just men who had given all they had to give, and had no more render this day. Marcus was debating whether to allow his men to advance, so as to target the line of infantry beyond arrow range from their position, but the gods began to intervene - or rather, to his mind, the soldiers themselves had decided that this day was in need of an end. Gradually, then with greater haste, the lines began to separate, the men stepping backwards, weapons still leveled and unsheathed, but no longer in action.

As he watched the foe began a general withdrawal, leaving the Roman line standing in a field of Hades. From the standpoint of position, the Consuls had won the day - the field of battle was theirs. The men of the two armies could not be discerned from each other by either equipment nor garments, but by the position of the dead and wounded on the field, it appeared that both had suffered alike. Certainly, Rome had possession of the field, but to call this a victory was to bend the substance of the word out of all meaning. Any more such triumphs would reduce Rome to a starving backwater of widows and orphans.

Scattered across the field were hundreds - nay, thousands of men. At the line where the battle had been joined, the bodies were in such proximity as to allow one to walk the length from the hills and almost to the trees and not let one's feet touch the ground. Then, in both directions, leading away from the battle were the men, not immediately deprived of life, that had managed to stagger or crawl some distance before expiring. Further on were the lifeless bodies of soldiers who had made a considerable distance, staggering along, before the lifeblood drained to the point that they fell to their end.

And, he knew that the tents of the medicos - of both armies - would be surrounded by others, still alive but with grievous wounds, missing limbs, and horrible gashes, showing both sinews and bone. Many of these would not see another sunrise.

He stopped his musing as Tricipitinus and his staff rode up and saluted. "Salve, Marcus. Again you have astounded the world with your inventions. Were it not for your timely destruction of the King's flank, the day might have gone differently."

Marcus saluted, then replied. "Nay, Sos. I sat on this steed and watched the battle unfold. My son, Lucius, stood at the forefront of his men and called down the destruction this day."

The Consul looked across the bowmen, now filling their quivers from piles of arrows brought forth by the men of Flavis. "He will be honored, and rewarded for his actions this day. As will you and your men." Then in a quieter voice, he asked, "Brutus has been taken, I am told."

"Aye, Sos," replied Marcus. "I did not see it, but I had no doubt when I saw him lead his men across the field."

The Consul nodded. "He was seeking death, to my mind. In effect, I believe he was searching for the deposed King on the battlefield, to take vengeance for a lifetime of harm. Or so he dreamed, and without much hope, I am sure." He shook his head. "I doubt that he expected the Commander of the army to lead the ranks of men on the battlefield - and certainly not a graybeard such as Tarquinius. His old bones are creaking, as are mine, after a day on the back of a horse."

Coda

The air was as he remembered it in his youth, long ago - clean, pure and cool, with the scent of the needle trees and mosses giving a tang to the smell.   He had been used to the humid and, ofttimes, fetid smell of the city for so long that he had forgotten the liveliness that was induced by the purity of the mountains.   The day was so clear, almost crystal in its transparency, that he could see all the way to the sea - a thin blue ribbon just on the horizon.   The city of Rome could not be seen, of course, being a very considerable distance to the south, but the smoke from several villages far down the slopes of the mountains rose straight up on the windless day.

Years ago - half a lifetime, in fact - he had trod these paths as a very young man, just into his size and without concept of the world beyond the needle trees and the mountains.   That youngster, with his simple stick bow and crude pugio would not have recognized himself today.   Then, he moved as the cat through the trees, or as the doe slowly winding through the tall grass, in fear of older men that might take it upon themselves to corral a boy for labor to their needs.   Now, his older self walked with confidence, a bow strung across his body that would have seemed a weapon of the gods by his younger self, and in place of the iron pugio was a gladius of a worth that would have purchased food and garments for his village over the entire lifespan of the oldest graybeard.

A half year had passed since the battle of Silva Arsia, and much had happened since.   The defeat of Tarquinius had not dampened his resolve to regain his Throne by any means.   In fact, word had come that another army was being assembled in the Etruscan city of Clusium.   No doubt, another great battle would be fought in the near future, but, Rome had validated itself as an independent entity, and the citizenry gained great pride from the fact.

With the greenness of the memory of Sabina beginning to fade, Marcus no longer needed to keep his hands and mind busy to prevent unwanted thoughts from intruding, both day and night.   Suddenly, the craving to revisit the land of his youth became paramount.

His lovely daughter Sabina was now the wife of the noble son of Collatinus, Manius, and was now Domina to that great house.   Her respected grandmother had passed on to her reward in the green fields of Olympus, leaving an emptiness in a house with no matron to keep order.

Young Lucius was on the staff of Tricipitinus and was the Commander of the unit of bowmen, now greatly expanded and given much respect after the impressive demonstration of their strength in support of a battle line. As the production of the house of Callidus and that of the bowsmith, Ennis, allowed, the unit was gradually being equipped with weapons of superior range and power. Marcus suspected that, should Tarquinius attempt a siege of Rome, he might be unpleasantly surprised when his men came within range of the walls.

And, it must be said that the young Commander was now engaged in many skirmishes not of a military nature, as he fended off the invites of matrons all over the city - fêtes and feasts and festivals, all intended to parade this daughter or that to a man now considered to be a prime catch for a girl.

Flavis, too, had risen and had become the ranking Ingeniarius of the army, and both youngsters were seen together at every opportunity.

Young Marcus was building an impressive empire of trading wealth, and was now the official and registered heir to Pythes. With the corrupt and vicious domination of the seaport of Ostia by the Senate-gelded Florus now ended, he was expanding his trade through ships to far lands - even to Alexandria and beyond. He too, was seen as a potential son-in-law, but as to date, he was in love with his figures and tablets to an extent that his interaction with women was limited to a tryst with a maid on occasion. But, Marcus knew that eventually, a girl would appear to cause the normal confusion and uncertainty that was the lot of young men at least once in their lives. And, as Valens was approaching that age when a man prefers to sit in the sun and dwell on times of old, young Marcus had taken a smart young lad as an apprentice. Cursor was the youngster's name.

Marcus had little hope of finding the old spot of his village, nor the boy's cave in the high mountains. His memory had only the vaguest idea of the general direction of both, and indeed, could have been on the side of more than a double handful of mountains in the general area of his remembrances. It did not matter. The village lands, by now, would be nothing more than forest and his small hide-a-way just a hole in the rock. Still, his encampments on the slopes of the mountains, the hunt for meat for his meals, and the complete lack of city-clamor was a balm for his being.

It was the beginning of the hot season in the lands below, but the days here were cool and the nights, even cold. He would descend the mountains long before winter came - of that he was sure. This sojourn was pleasant, indeed, but he was no longer a man of the wilderness, to be satisfied with an existence composed entirely of hunting during the day and rest during the night. The city was now a part of his makeup, and there would come a day when he would have a surfeit of loneliness, and began to crave the bustle and clamor of the city.

His tentative plan was to work his way northward, and with no haste, but to eventually reach the remote farm of Collatinus, to finally accept the long-standing invitation from that old friend. His only regret, and one that could now be examined without pain was that he had been unable to escort his Sabina through the lands of his youth.

He had come far from that orphaned boy who had considered riches to be an iron blade in his belt and a roll of furs on his back. His was a respected family, spinning off children who would begin their own Patrician gens and not a single scapegrace in the three. His belief in the gods was still ambivalent, but some Fortuna, somewhere, had guided his feet from that mountain village long ago.

He still had half a lifetime to live, the fates permitting, and should it have the worth of even a small iota of the past, there was much yet to be enjoyed and discovered.

25692914R00242

Printed in Poland
by Amazon Fulfillment
Poland Sp. z o.o., Wrocław